PRAISE FOR C. L. WILSON'S EPIC DEBUT!

"An absolutely wonderful new voice for romance with all the bells and whistles for pure escapism! It exceeded all my expectations."

—Kay Meriam, RWA Steffie Walker
Bookseller of the Year 2003

"I LOVE this book! A thrilling, captivating story that stays with you after you put it down. The best book I've read in years."

—Christine Feehan,
#1 New York Times bestselling author

"Lush and evocative. A powerful epic fantasy to savor."

—Gena Showalter,
New York Times bestselling author

"Brilliant and breathtaking! *Lord of the Fading Lands* debuts a fascinatingly unique world populated with characters I fell in love with—and can't wait to read about again."

—Alyssa Day, *USA Today* bestselling
author of *Atlantis Rising*

"This debut will draw you into a magical weave of spirit and air that won't release you until the last word is read."

—Jessica Stachowski, bookseller,
The World's Biggest Bookstore

A TRUEMATE'S DESTINY

"It may take more to rouse the tairen in you, *shei'tani,* but never doubt it lives in your soul, and it is fierce indeed."

Pride and approval radiated from him, wrapping her in warmth and soothing away her fierce reaction to the Eye's rough treatment of him. But even his approval could not soothe the choking tightness in her chest. The fates of both the tairen and the Fey rested on her shoulders, and he expected her to somehow miraculously save them.

"You do not stand in this alone, Ellysetta," Rain said, clearly sensing the emotions swirling about her like a fearful cloud. "This task belongs to both of us. All I ask is that you help me find a way to save my people."

She looked up into his beloved face, so beautiful, so sincere. All her life she'd dreamed of him, all her life she'd wept for the sorrows he'd endured and prayed that the gods would give his soul peace. And now here he was, standing before her, asking for her help.

How could she possibly deny him?

Other *Leisure* books by C. L. Wilson:

LORD OF THE FADING LANDS

C. L. WILSON

LADY OF LIGHT AND SHADOWS

TAIREN SOUL

LEISURE BOOKS 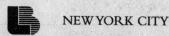 NEW YORK CITY

A LEISURE BOOK®

November 2007

Published by

Dorchester Publishing Co., Inc.
200 Madison Avenue
New York, NY 10016

ISBN 10: 0-8439-5978-9
ISBN 13: 978-0-8439-5978-9

Printed in the United States of America.

10 9 8 7 6 5 4 3 2 1

Visit us on the web at www.dorchesterpub.com.

For Christine Feehan, an amazing talent and an even more amazing soul. Your friendship is one of my greatest treasures.

And for Diana Peterfreund. Because you believed so strongly, because you wouldn't let me quit, and because when I got "The Call," the only person on the planet more excited than me was you.

And for Lisa Richter, my sister Lisette, just because. You know all the reasons.

Acknowledgements

A special thanks to all the terrific folks at Dorchester Publishing, especially Alicia Condon, Renee Yewdaev, Erin Galloway, Brooke Borneman, Tim DeYoung, and Diane Stacy. All of your enthusiasm, encouragement and support these last months has meant the world to me.

As always, thanks to my friends and critique partners, my wonderful parents, and especially to my husband Kevin and our children Ileah, Rhiannon, and Aidan for being so understanding of all the long hours I've spent sequestered in my office.

A special thanks to bookseller Rosemary of Rosemary's Romance Books in Brisbane, Australia for all the wonderful e-mails and support. Rosemary, you are great!

Thanks to the richly talented artist, Judy York, who so perfectly captured my vision of Rain, Ellysetta, and the tairen with her gorgeous covers—and for letting me use them on my Web site!

And once again, thanks to the wonderful men and women of Tampa Area Romance Authors (TARA) who've been my writing family for the last five years. TARA Rocks!

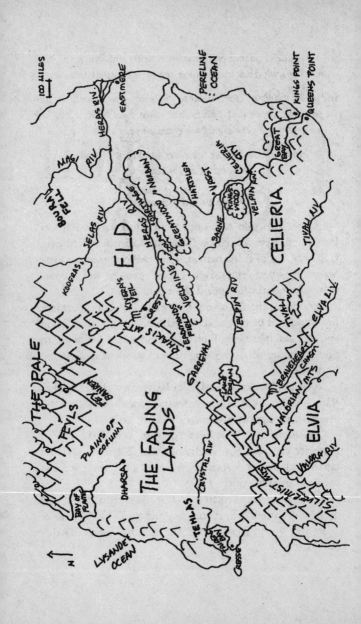

LADY OF LIGHT AND SHADOWS

CHAPTER ONE

*I dream of wing and fang and pride, I dream of
   venom swift and sure.*
*I dream of song and cloud and sky, I dream of
   flame that scorches pure.*
*I dream of dancing crystal winds, as high aloft I
   soar.*
*I dream of enemies and prey that flee my fiery
   roar.*
     —Tairen Dreams, by Jion vel Baris, Tairen Soul

Ellysetta Baristani stood in the dark, fire-lit cavern of Fey'Bahren, the
fabled nesting lair of the tairen. Nearby, six leathery eggs lay incubat-
ing in a thick, cushioning layer of hot black sand. A massive,
cinnamon-furred tail curled protectively around the eggs, its black tip
rising and falling rhythmically, raising clouds of fine dark dust as it
thumped the sand. The dust swirled about Ellie like shadowy mist,
darkening her skirts with a fine layer of sooty ash. Unshed tears
clogged the back of her throat and stung her eyes.

The tairen were dying.

Ellie couldn't explain how she knew it. The knowledge was just
there in her mind, and it felt familiar, as if it had been there for a long,
long time.

Calah, the last fertile female of the tairen pride, was growing feebler
with each passing day, her life's essence draining as she struggled to
maintain the viability of her six unhatched kitlings. The last hope of a
future for the tairen rested with those tiny, unborn lives—three of them
female—their life force weakening even as their small bodies matured
in the egg.

The mother tairen's cinnamon fur was dull and shedding. Her proud
feline head—larger than Ellysetta's body—rested wearily on her
forepaws, and her piercing golden eyes were closed. Breath heaved in and

out of her enormous body in great windy gusts. She had not eaten in two weeks. Her mate, Merdrahl, was frantic with worry. He paced restlessly by the entrance to the nesting grounds, brown wings rustling, massive paws padding not so silently back and forth across the sands, low growls emanating from his powerful chest and rumbling through the cavern like thunder. His dark brown tail curled and uncurled, flicking in agitation. His fur was ruffled, his ears laid back, and his fangs dripped deadly tairen venom. Every so often, he would pause, dig his claws into the rock, and heave an angry jet of flame.

If Merdrahl could have slain something to bring peace to his mate and protect their offspring, he would have. And Ellysetta would have helped him.

A growl sounded overhead. She looked up into the gleaming green eyes of Sybharukai, the wise one, oldest of all female tairen and makai—leader—of the Fey'Bahren pride. She crouched on the ledge above, her unsheathed front claws curling into the rock of her perch. Her dark, silver-tipped gray fur gleamed like thunderclouds and smoke in the flickering light of the cavern. The rounded tips of her ears flicked continuously. Her dark gray tail swished restlessly in the air, and the lethal bony spikes hidden in its furred tip stabbed at the rocks around her. Her wings unfolded and stretched high above her back, flapping twice. The sharp claw at the mid-span joint on each wing gleamed like a curved mei'cha blade in the flickering light.

«I will find a way, Sybharukai.» A deep, masculine voice sang the vow in the rich, vivid tones of tairen song.

Heat curled in Ellysetta's belly, drawing inner muscles tight in a series of small, rippling shudders of remembered pleasure. She turned and found Rain standing beside her.

Rainier vel'En Daris, the Tairen Soul, the legendary Fey shapeshifter who had once scorched the world in a wild, grief-stricken Rage over the death of his beloved mate, Sariel.

Rain Tairen Soul, King of the Fey, who had stepped from the sky to claim Ellysetta as his shei'tani, his truemate, the only woman ever born with whom he could form a soul bond even stronger than the love bond he'd held with Sariel.

His long black hair hung down his back, straight and fine, framing a face of breathtaking masculine beauty. Black Fey leathers hugged broad shoulders, slim hips, and long, lean legs. His deadly swords and the scores of throwing knives tucked into the bands crisscrossing his chest gleamed golden in the flickering firelight. His lavender eyes were glowing, his beautiful mouth grim.

"I will find a way," he said again, aloud this time but still addressing the majestic gray tairen. "I will not fail you."

Turning, he strode off the nesting sands towards a wide opening at the end of the cavern. Ellie hurried after him and together they jogged up a long, winding passage through the mountain and emerged on a wide, sunlit ledge high above the Fading Lands. Ellie raised a hand to shield her eyes, blinking at the brightness of the Great Sun.

When her eyes adjusted, she gave a gasp of awe-filled wonder. They were standing near the top of the steep, dark mountainside of Fey'Bahren, the tallest volcano in the majestic Feyls range that formed the northern border of the Fading Lands. Below, the rippling golden grasses of the Plains of Corunn spread out for miles. Ellie drank in the breathtaking scenery, which seemed at once familiar yet new, like a forgotten memory, freshly renewed.

"Oh, Rain," she breathed. "It's so beautiful."

Beside her, magic gathered as Rain summoned the Change. Ellysetta's body tingled as the surge of energy swept around and through her. A fine gray mist billowed about him, about them both, and she threw back her head on a swell of pleasure so intense it bordered on pain. Though it was Rain, not she, who was the shapeshifter, she felt his body dissolve and expand as if it were her own, felt the echo of awareness as his Fey senses grew even more acute. Fur sprouted, wings spread, claws speared the rock.

Moments later the mist cleared, and a magnificent death-black tairen with huge lavender eyes crouched on the ledge where Rain Tairen Soul, the Fey King and Ellysetta's betrothed, had stood. The tairen spread his enormous ebony wings, gathered strength in his haunches, and sprang into the air with an echoing roar.

Behind him, standing alone on the ledge, still trapped in her human form, Ellysetta cried out, "Rain, come back! Don't leave me!"

Ellysetta woke with her heart thumping and tears cooling on her cheeks. The emotions of the dream still held her heart clutched tight, making her want to weep in despair for the dying tairen and the terrible, grieving emptiness that had struck when Rain took to the air and abandoned her on that ledge.

«Another nightmare, shei'tani?» The familiar sound of Rain's Spirit voice, low and husky with sleep, sounded in her mind. An arm tightened around her waist. There was a warm, heavy weight pressed against her in her narrow bed—and it was most definitely *not* her twin sisters, Lillis and Lorelle, cuddling up with her as they sometimes did.

She turned her head slowly, and her breath stalled in her lungs.

For the first time in the last five days, there was no little courtship gift beside her when she woke. There was, instead, a great big one. All black leather, white skin, and inky hair, Rain lay beside her on her narrow bed, his long limbs draped over her.

Thinking she must still be dreaming, she closed her eyes, inhaled, opened them again.

He was still there, solid and warm, his face pressed to her neck.

She should leap up and get dressed before her mother came in and found her like this, but she couldn't seem to move. Instead, she lay there, staring at him in dazed wonder. Through her bedroom window the first pale rays of the rising Great Sun shone down upon them. Dawn was breaking, and Rain Tairen Soul was in her bed.

His eyes opened, and her breath caught again. The brilliant lavender irises were glowing, surrounded by thick dark lashes and centered by slightly elongated black pupils that were growing more catlike by the moment. The limbs draped over her body hardened and drew her more closely to the hard wall of his chest and the harnessed strength of his leather-clad legs.

«Shei'tani?» he prompted. *«Were you having another nightmare?»*

"No," she croaked. When Rain looked at her with such intensity, she had no desire to speak of the horrifying visions that had haunted her sleep all her life. She cleared her throat and whispered. "It was just a dream."

«You were weeping.» He touched the dampness on her cheek. "It was a sad dream."

His hand slid down the curve of her jaw. His thumb smoothed over her lips, tracing their outline. His gaze followed, so focused she could feel it brush across her face like a slow caress. The gaze lingered on her full lower lip and glowed a little brighter. The tingle of Spirit magic whispered over her skin. An invisible mouth tracked kisses in its wake. *«Tell me.»*

Breathless from the magic his hands and weave were working upon her, she stammered out a quick summary of the dream. His Spirit kisses slowed when she told him about Fey'Bahren and the tairen dying, and about him singing a vow to the great gray tairen Sybharukai, then stopped completely when she told him how he'd flown off and abandoned her on the mountainside.

He rose up on one elbow, his gaze fixed upon her face. His face was solemn, expressionless except for the warm glow of his eyes. *«You wept because you dreamed I left you.»*

"No, I . . ." A blush suffused her cheeks when his brows lifted at her poor attempt at a lie. The dying tairen had torn at her heart, but that was not why she'd woken with tears streaming down her face. "I begged you not to go, but you just kept flying."

He pressed a gentle finger to her lips, silencing her. "I would never leave you, *shei'tani*. Not for any reason. My place is at your side, and has been since the moment you called me from the sky." His hand brushed through the tangled spirals of her bright, flame-red hair.

"I—it was just a dream."

"You should not doubt me even in your dreams."

In hypnotized fascination, she watched him bend his head over hers. Long black hair draped around her, enclosing her in a shadowy veil within which only she and Rain existed.

"Ver reisa ku'chae. Kem surah, shei'tani. Your soul calls out. Mine answers, beloved." He whispered the vow of *shei'tanitsa* claiming, first in Feyan, then in Celierian, his voice low and stirring. "Trust in that, Ellysetta. Trust in me."

Slowly his head dipped down and he claimed her lips. Illusion spun away. Reality took its place, so much better than the weave.

Mercy. Her eyes rolled back and her eyelids fluttered down. Good, sweet Lord of Light, was it possible to die of pleasure from a single kiss? It must be, because she had no doubt that she had just died and gone to the Haven of Light.

Flows of warmth wrapped around her, enclosing her in a snug embrace even as his arms did the same. His mouth trailed a burning path from her lips to the line of her jaw and below to the sensitive skin of her neck. She arched her back, baring her throat to his kisses, gasping for breath as sensation threatened to steal all reason. "Stop. You must stop. My parents . . ." But her hands clutched him far more fiercely than her words tried to drive him away.

She sensed the power gathering strength within him, knew that the tairen—the fierce predator that lived inside him—was preparing to spring, but before she could even think to be afraid, he released her and twisted in one smooth motion to sit on the side of her bed.

With a groan, he hunched his back and buried his face in his hands. She sat up, staring at the long curve of his spine, the broad strength of powerful shoulders, lean muscle, hard bone, sinew, all trembling.

"Rain?" She reached out a hand, but her fingertips scarcely brushed against his back before he sprang to his feet, scooping up the pile of leather and steel by her bed.

"*Sieks'ta*. You are right, this is not the time, no matter how much I wish it. Though in my defense, you make me lose all sense of reason. Dangerous woman." He shook his head, his expression torn between admiration and dismay as he pulled on his leather tunic and tightened the laces. "I had not meant to fall asleep." He glanced out the window at the lightening sky. "Nor stay past dawn."

"What are you doing here in the first place?"

The hands knotting his laces went still. He turned to face her, his eyes narrowed. "You do not remember?"

Ellysetta gulped down a knot of fear because for a moment her mind was a complete blank. Then the floodgates opened, and the memories rushed back. "Of course I remember." She laughed to hide her relief. "It's not every day a woodcarver's daughter dines with the king and queen and the heads of every noble House in Celieria." Last night had been her first official function as the future Queen of the Fading Lands.

"I meant after dinner," Rain prompted. "Your nightmare, do you remember that?"

Her pulse sped up. She recalled the hazy images of a nightmare more disturbing and horrific than any she'd ever had—and that was no small feat. Ellie saw things in her dreams that would have made battle-scarred veterans quake in their boots.

"It was a bad one." She looked at him for confirmation. She had a wavering vision of blood, bodies, her room shredded into a shambles. She glanced around. Her room looked as it always had, small but tidy, not a thing out of place. But of course, the Fey would have repaired the damage.

"You were attacked in your sleep," Rain clarified, "by someone using your dreams as a conduit to your unconscious mind. Someone most likely wielding Azrahn." Azrahn, the soul magic, forbidden to the Fey but widely used and mastered by their greatest enemies.

"You believe it was a Mage."

"*Aiyah*, I do. That seems the most logical answer. Dreams are the place where Azrahn and *Mena*—Spirit—meet, and night is when the dark powers of Azrahn grow strongest." He reached for the leather belts filled with dozens of Fey'cha throwing daggers and slipped them on one by one, crisscrossing the straps over his chest.

"I told you about my seizures," she murmured, "and my childhood exorcism. I've never told anyone about that before."

"You did, and you can put your fears of demon possession to rest. I believe someone has been hunting you all your life—the Shadow Man, you called him—and that your nightmares and seizures are the result of his attempts to access your mind."

"Those afflictions began long before I called you from the

sky," she pointed out. "When I was just a woodcarver's daughter. No one worth a Mage's notice."

He pinned her with a hard look. "Ellysetta, I am the Tairen Soul, the most powerful Fey alive, and you are my truemate, my equal in every way. Even though you have spent a lifetime denying it, your magic is beyond powerful. It always has been. Some part of that power must have attracted the Mages' attention even though they obviously didn't know who you were or how to find you." He picked up his wide leather sword belt and strapped it around his waist.

She watched him fasten the belt buckle and adjust the two curved *mei'cha* scimitars hanging in their sheaths at his hips. A curl of pleasure tightened low in her belly. There was something incredibly intimate about watching Rain dress and don his weapons. The sight roused fresh memories: watching Rain through a dreamy, sensual haze, the feel of his arms around her, the dizzying whirl of stars, a burning, endless emptiness. Other sensations followed the first: Rain's bare skin beneath her hand; the rich scent of cinnabar oil, magic, and Rain washing over her; the slow, relentless burn of his body filling hers, completing her, immersing her in exquisite sensations like nothing she'd ever known before.

"Rain," she said in a low, choked voice, "did you . . . did I . . ." Her face flamed. "Did you . . . *mate* with me last night?"

He went still. His head lifted, his gaze locking on hers. Then he took a step towards her and cupped her face in his hands. His thumbs brushed slowly across her lips, outlining the shape of her mouth. "*Aiyah, shei'tani,* I did indeed." Her womb clenched in melting response to the purring satisfaction in his voice and the light, stroking caress of his thumb. "And if I thanked the gods every chime for the next ten thousand years, it would not be enough to honor such a wondrous gift." Then he frowned. "Though perhaps our mating was a greater gift to me than you, if you do not remember it."

"I remember." Her voice came out as a strangled whisper. Everything was coming back to her now. Especially that. "Vividly." The sudden blaze in his eyes sent fresh waves of heat rolling up and down her body. She scooted back out of range of his enthralling hands.

"Our bodies joined in Spirit only, *shei'tani*. I did not break my oath to your father. And, believe me, keeping my honor intact has never been so difficult."

Her brows drew together in consternation as she realized she couldn't recall the end of last night's dinner or how she'd gotten home. The memories were clear up to a point, then grew disturbingly hazy, as if parts of the night were wrapped in a fog. She remembered sweet blue wine that packed a surprising punch and being warm, so very, very warm. Oh, gods, what had she done? What sort of fool had she made of herself?

She swallowed. "How did I get home?"

His gaze fell away from hers. He stepped back to retrieve the two *seyani* longswords propped against the window and slid his arms into the harness straps. "I carried you."

"Because I was ill?" Please let her dim memories be wrong.

"You were not ill." He settled the two swords in place on his back and bent his head to focus with suspicious concentration on the task of buckling the straps.

"If I wasn't ill, then why did you carry me?" she persisted. He was Fey, and though he could and would dance around truth and evade questions with far more skill than he was displaying now, the Fey did not lie. When pressed for an answer, he would give her the truth.

He sighed and met her gaze. "You had too much pinalle."

"I was drunk." Her stomach lurched at the thought. *Now* she felt ill. Oh, gods, what sort of fool had she made of herself before the nobles whose support Rain was so desperate to win?

"Not exactly."

"What does that mean? What did I do?"

"You'd had too much pinalle."

"You already said that!"

He gave her a look that made her bite her lip and subside into unhappy silence. "You'd had too much pinalle," he repeated in a deliberate tone, "and then you had a cup of keflee."

He stopped, a wry look entering his eyes. "Let me just suggest that you *not* combine the two in the future."

Ellie covered her hot cheeks with her hands. "What did I do?" He didn't answer immediately, and she could see him weighing what to tell her. "Just give me the truth, whatever it is. If you don't, I'll drive myself mad conjuring up all manner of awful possibilities."

"The pinalle lowered your inhibitions," he admitted, "and the keflee—were you aware that keflee can act as an aphrodisiac on some people?" He didn't wait for her to answer. "You're one of them, apparently, though in most the reaction is considerably less intense. Of course, it wasn't until after the fact that your quintet revealed they knew about your . . . unusually strong . . . response to keflee. Not that it would have mattered. Who could have guessed you would weave Spirit that way?"

"What way?" she whispered. But she already knew.

"What were you thinking just before I carried you out?"

"Oh, gods." She buried her face in her drawn-up knees and draped her arms over her head. Blood heating like fire. Desire heightening to unbearable need. A yearning so strong the ache became torment.

"The effects of the weave didn't wear off until the small bells of the morning. Around three, to be exact. Seven bells of incredibly acute, inescapably relentless sexual desire, Ellysetta. That is what you wove. On *everyone* at the dinner last night."

Her stomach took a sickening lurch. "I'm going to be sick." Best just to die now and get it over with, because surely she would die of mortification the next time she had to face anyone else who'd been in the banquet hall the night before. She'd woven lust on the highest-ranking nobles in Celieria— worse, on the king and queen!

Rain muttered a soft curse and came to her side. His thumbs slid over her cheeks, caressing gently. Regret and shame whispered against her senses from the point where his skin touched hers. "*Sieks'ta*. I am tired and behaving badly. I should have found a way to give you the truth without causing you such distress. You are not to blame for last night's weave. You did

not understand what you were doing. Even I did not understand it at first." He tilted her chin up and waited for her to
meet his eyes. "One thing, however, is inescapably clear. There
is great magic in you. Of that, there can be no doubt."

She nodded miserably. She could no longer deny the truth.
Somehow, by some wicked trick of the gods, Ellysetta Baristani
possessed magic. And it seemed determined to get out.

"You must be trained. Great power such as yours can be
dangerous in untutored hands."

"All right," she whispered. If training would keep her from
doing something as mortifying as what she'd done last night,
she would be a devoted student. "When we reach the Fading
Lands, I'll take whatever training you think I need. I'm sorry I
made such a mess of things."

He finished dressing and stood regarding her for a moment.
"Hold out your hand, Ellysetta." Hesitant, she did, and he
placed a small velvet bag in her palm. "This is your courtship
gift for today. Open it."

She loosened the silk cords and tilted the bag. Three large,
perfect pearls, one white, one pink, one deep blue-gray, rolled
out into her palm.

"Beautiful, are they not?"

"Did you make them?"

"*Nei*. Except when magic is part of the symbol being offered, the Fey do not use magic to make their gifts." His mouth
curved. "It can be an inconvenient custom. I dragged an unsuspecting glassblower from his bed to make the globe for the
small weave I gave you last week." His small smile grew rueful.
"And while your weave was still spinning last night, a cold
swim in the ocean seemed a prudent idea." He plucked the
dark pearl from her hand. "Do you know how a pearl comes to
be?"

"Oysters make them, from a bit of sand."

"*Aiyah*. From a bit of sand." He rolled the pearl between his
fingers. "All pearls begin as something unpleasant that the oysters
cannot expel from themselves, even though they may want to. So
they embrace these things that will not leave them, shaping them

and smoothing away the sharp edges, until over time, they make of these unwanted things great treasures."

"What are you saying? That in time the heads of Celieria's noble houses will be *happy* that I wove seven bells of lust on them? Or that, after a few centuries, it will turn out to be a *good* thing that I singlehandedly destroyed the Fey-Celierian alliance?"

Strengthening that alliance had been the real purpose behind last night's dinner. For a thousand years, Celieria and the Fading Lands had been the staunchest of allies, but recently, anti-Fey sentiment had exploded throughout large portions of Celieria. *Dahl'reisen*—terrifing former Fey warriors who'd slipped down the Dark Path and been banished from the Fading Lands—had been accused of murdering Celierian villagers in the north. Many powerful Celierian nobles were promoting a new, more welcoming relationship with the Eld—the Fading Lands' oldest and most bitter enemy—as a way to counteract centuries of Fey influence over Celieria.

Last night had been Rain's chance to win the confidence and support of Celieria's lords before they voted whether or not to reopen their borders to the Eld . . . and what had she done? She'd woven *lust* on them! They would never forgive such humiliation.

Ellie groaned in misery and spun away, covering her face with her hands.

"Las, shei'tani." Rain closed a hand over her shoulder and pulled her gently back to him. "If this is the turn the gods decided our path should take, we will follow it together."

"But, Rain—"

"Ssh." He pressed a kiss to her lips to silence her objection, then smiled with tender reassurance. "Listen to me, Ellysetta. The purpose of the gods is not always obvious, but believe me when I say that even from the most unpleasant beginning can come a treasure beyond price." He returned the pearl to her palm and closed her fingers over it. "I thought my heart would always belong to Sariel. My will was to live only until my duty to the Fey was done and I could join her in death. And then you entered my soul. I did not want the connection, I admit. But in these few short days, you have wrought unexpected changes upon me. You've brought back to me the laughter I lost a thousand years ago, you've made me remember what hope is." He ran a finger down her cheek. "I would not change you, Ellysetta. To me, you are already a pearl beyond price."

"But the alliance . . . I know how important it is, and since the day we met, I only keep making things worse."

Rain sighed. "If the Fey-Celierian alliance does not survive last night's excitement, then it was not long for this world in any event. Would I change that if I could? Of course. As you reminded me yesterday, the Fey need Celieria. For millennia, your country has guarded the gates to our lands. But the Fey need *you*, also. *I* need you . . . more than any alliance. All I ask is that you try to find a way to live in comfort with those gifts you are afraid to face. I do not know all there is to know about *shei'tanitsa* bonding, but I do know both parties must accept what lies within themselves before they can open their souls to the other, as they must to complete the bond."

Ellie bit her lip and glanced down at the pearls in her hand. "I'll try, Rain."

"*Beylah vo.* I must return to the palace briefly, *shei'tani*, but I will return as quickly as I can so you do not have to face the tradesfolk alone."

Ellysetta knew what he left unsaid. He needed to return to the palace to begin repairing the damage she'd wrought with her weave. "I'll be fine on my own. I'm sure there are much more important matters requiring your attention this morning."

"Are you certain?"

That he didn't deny it proved she was right. He was worried about how the nobles would react to what she'd done to them. And she would not compound the trouble she'd already caused him by acting like some clinging ninnywit. "Go. I'll be fine."

"*Beylah vo, shei'tani*." He brushed a kiss across her lips. "Do not punish yourself for what happened at the dinner last night. Your weave may have embarrassed some, but ultimately it was harmless. Your countrymen will realize this. Besides," he added, "only those who wield magic themselves could know it was you who spun the weave."

"Lucky me," she said glumly.

He smiled and kissed her again, longer this time, his lips coaxing hers to open, his arms holding her until she melted against him. When passion warmed between them, he gave a regretful sigh and pulled back.

"I will return at midday to take you flying." He slipped through the window and leapt into the sky. His body dissolved in a cloud of sparkling magic and mist, only to re-form as an enormous, sleek black tairen winging across the early morning sky.

When he was gone, she donned a blue muslin dress—one of her own gowns, not any of the fancy silk and taffeta confections Lady Marissya had ordered for her—and slipped quietly downstairs to start breakfast. She'd have to change before the tradesmasters arrived, but for another bell or two at least she could still be plain Ellie Baristani, woodcarver's daughter.

Four tall, deadly-looking warriors stood in the corners of the small home's main room. Their black leathers merged with the early morning shadows, and the faint glow of their luminescent skin gleamed off the myriad swords and daggers each of them wore strapped to his body. A fifth warrior crouched near the door to the kitchen, his back to her, his long black hair hanging free about his shoulders.

Ravel vel Arras, the leader of the secondary quintet who guarded her whenever Belliard vel Jelani and his men were otherwise occupied, turned to face her. A look Ellie could only describe as embarrassment flitted across his face before he marshaled his features into the typical mask of Fey stoniness.

Ravel gestured with a graceful sweep of his hand back towards the icebox in the kitchen. "The little cat is not happy with the stronger weaves we put around the house," he murmured. "She's been hiding beneath that small chest all night and refuses to come out. Kieran will not be pleased. He and Bel warned us to take care with our magic around her."

Ellie smothered a smile. There was something very endearing about lethal warriors living in fear of ruffling a tiny kitten's fur. "Let me take a look." Ellie stepped into the kitchen and crouched down to look under the icebox. Beneath it, huddled against the back wall, was a tiny ball of white fur dominated by a pair of big, gleaming blue eyes. The kitten opened her mouth to hiss and display needle-sharp fangs.

"Poor little Love," Ellie crooned. "I'll bet last night was even more frightening for you than me." As the Fey had discovered last week, Lillis and Lorelle's kitten could sense magic woven nearby—and to say she hated it was an understatement.

"Come here, sweetling. Come here, kit, kit, kit." Ellie reached under the icebox, hoping to scoop the little kitten out, but when her fingers were close enough to brush against soft white fur, Love gave a loud hiss and swatted out with razor-sharp claws. Ellie yelped and yanked back her bleeding hand.

Like a bolt of furry white lightning, Love shot out from under the icebox, raced across the main room, and leapt up the stairs towards the relative safety of Lillis and Lorelle's bedroom.

Ravel stepped towards Ellysetta, green Earth and lavender Spirit already spinning out from his fingertips to stop the bleeding and steal away the sting of the deep furrows scored across the back of her hand. "Shall I summon Marissya to heal it?"

Ellie gave a small laugh of disbelief. "For a cat scratch? No, I'm sure I'll be fine."

Ravel frowned at her, black brows drawing close over remarkable violet eyes. "I will inform the Feyreisen," he insisted. "He will make certain Marissya's schedule permits her to attend you."

Ellie caught herself before rolling her eyes. She'd been wounded under Ravel's care, and both his masculine Fey instinct and his strong warrior's code of honor compelled him to see her healed. He couldn't do it himself. Though masters of extraordinary magic, Fey warriors could not heal wounds as their women could. They could only staunch the flow of blood and temporarily seal rent flesh.

"Thank you, Ser Ravel," she said, "but please, make sure they know it's only a scratch. Poor Love. I shouldn't have reached for her, I suppose, but usually even when she's frightened she lets us hold her."

"Perhaps she has reason to be more frightened than usual," a grim voice announced.

Ellysetta gave a start of surprise and turned to find her adoptive mother standing in the kitchen doorway. "Good morning, Mama. I didn't hear you come down."

Lauriana Baristani was already fully dressed, her mink-brown hair tamed in a bun at the back of her neck, her body covered from ankle to neck in a practical burgundy dress. She raked Ellie from head to toe with a penetrating gaze, hazel eyes sharp and probing. "How are you feeling this morning, Ellysetta?"

Ellie's heart sank. She knew that intense, scrutinizing look. Mama was looking for some remnant of last night's terrible nightmare, some visible sign of the dread affliction that had no doubt prompted Ellysetta's natural parents—whoever they were—to abandon her in the forests of Norban when she was but a babe.

An old, familiar tension coiled inside Ellie. "I'm fine, Mama."

"Are you?" Her mother's eyes had always seen too much, too clearly. It was one reason Ellie had grown up such a scrupulously obedient daughter. "Last night you were nowhere near fine. You haven't had such a terrible . . . event . . . since Hartslea."

Silence fell between them. They never mentioned Hartslea, the northern city where they'd lived years ago, the city they'd fled after Ellie's childhood exorcism. Ellie had only been eight at the time, but she still remembered the smell of sago flowers and incense, the malevolent gleam of long needles in the flickering candlelight, the deep scarlet of the exorcists' robes and the dark fervency in their eyes.

"I'm fine, Mama," she insisted, shoving those old terrors to the back of her mind. She would not think of those awful days.

"Ellysetta . . ." Her mother reached out to take her arm, then stopped as Ellysetta drew back. A hurt look crossed Lauriana's face but she suppressed it quickly. "I'm concerned, Ellysetta, and you know why. You also know I'd do anything in my power to help you." Her voice softened. "I love you, kitling. I only want what's best for you."

Guilt stung Ellysetta. Her rigid shoulders slumped. "I know you do, Mama, and I love you too. But, please, don't worry. If there's any way to stop my nightmares, Rain has sworn he and the Fey will find it."

"That's all well and good, Ellie, but what if he can't? Magic is more likely the root of your troubles, not the solution."

Ellie bit back a sharp remark. Mama was as fierce in her loathing of magic as Rain was in his loathing of the Eld. There was no talking to either of them when those subjects came up.

Before Ellie could think of a response, her father's voice called out, "Good morning, Ellie-girl. I hope you're cooking a feast. I've a belly so empty, I could eat a dragon." Entering the kitchen, Sol Baristani greeted his daughter with a warm, broad smile and a casual joviality that didn't extend to his bespectacled brown eyes.

"Good morning, Papa." Grateful for his timely interruption, Ellie wound her arms around his neck and kissed his cheek.

He smelled of soap and freshly laundered clothes rather than the scents of wood shavings and pipe smoke she loved so well, but the unfettered welcome of his embrace made her heart brim with love as it always did. He didn't ask her about last night, and she loved him even more for that. She would go to him as she always had when she was ready to talk, and he was patient enough to wait. Besides, unlike Mama, he actually liked the Fey. Despite their strange and magical ways, he'd welcomed them into his home because he knew Rain Tairen Soul was the man Ellie had dreamed of all her life.

"I was just about to get breakfast started," Ellie said. "Will three eggs be enough to fill a dragon-sized hole, do you think?"

"Hmm, make it four—and fry up some sausages and a dozen

of those corncakes of yours while you're at it. I'm going to be working late again today." Sol bent to curl an arm around his wife's waist and kiss her until the tight clench of her jaw relaxed.

"Papa! Papa!" Heralded by the sound of clattering feet, Lillis and Lorelle tumbled downstairs, raced across the small home's main room, and leapt into their father's arms. Mink-brown curls hung in unbrushed tangles down the backs of the twins' matching white cotton nightgowns.

Sol hugged them both and bussed their soft cheeks. "Good morning, my sweet kitlings. Aren't you both the prettiest sight a papa could ever wake up to?" He set the twins back on their feet and smiled down at them. "Go put on your frocks, and have Mama brush your hair, then you two can help me set the table while Ellie cooks."

"Yes, Papa," the girls chorused.

Ellysetta gave her father a grateful smile when Mama herded the twins back upstairs, thankful for the reprieve even though she knew this wasn't the end of her mother's interrogation.

Whatever had happened last night—whether a Mage had attacked her as Rain suspected, or a demon had possessed her as Mama feared—one thing she knew for certain: The Shadow Man, who'd haunted her dreams all her life, stalking her, calling her night after night as she slept, had finally found her. Who he was and what he wanted with her, she didn't know, but she couldn't shake the fear that the real danger was only just beginning and that things were about to get much, much worse.

A thousand miles to the north, hidden deep beneath the dark forested surface of Eld in the subterranean fortress of Boura Fell, the High Mage Vadim Maur, leader of the secretly reconstituted Mage Council, walked down a long, wide, sconce-lighted corridor.

Here, the raw, dark earth was richly veined with *sel'dor*, the black metal of Eld, one of the few elements capable of disrupting Fey magic. That earth had been carved to smoothness, the floors, walls, and ceilings of the corridors covered with *sel'dor* plating seven inches thick, then finished with mosaic tiles set in continuous, intricate patterns of power.

This was one of three levels in Boura Fell designed to house Vadim's most dangerous and magically gifted guests.

He stopped before one of the many *sel'dor*-clad doors, inserted a heavy black key into the lock, and whispered a Feraz witchspell. Magic rippled across the door. He turned the key in the lock and waited as the series of tumblers inside the door clicked open, retracting a dozen heavy *sel'dor* bars that penetrated two full handspans into the surrounding rock wall.

The door swung inward, and Vadim stepped into an impenetrable magical prison disguised as a noblewoman's luxurious bedroom. Furniture, delicate and beautiful, was arranged in comfortable groupings—a library filled with books in one corner, cushioned divans in another, and in the far corner of the room, a wide bed draped with swaths of brightly colored silk that hid the *sel'dor* manacles he rarely used anymore except when cruelty suited his mood. Beneath the outward beauty of the furnishings, every inch of wood, metal, paper, and cloth in the room was threaded with *sel'dor*.

A woman lay on the bed. She sat up as Vadim entered. Long, spiraling coils of flame-red hair tumbled down over slender shoulders and across the thin silk covering her breasts. Large, heavily lashed golden eyes, the elongated pupils lengthening to catlike slits, regarded him without expression.

Despite the *sel'dor* infused in every item in the room, despite the ten *sel'dor* rings piercing her ears and the barbed manacles piercing her ankles and upper arms, even despite his own vast powers, Vadim could feel the draw of her magic tugging at him. She was enchantingly beautiful. Just the sight of her unveiled face could send kings to their knees, begging to do her bidding—and that even before she wove the first hint of her formidable magic.

He took a step towards her. She flinched and inched back before she caught herself.

As if to make up for that brief show of fear, her chin lifted. "You had a bad night, Mage?" Her eyes flicked contemptuously over the seared skin on the side of his face. Ellysetta Baristani's magic had proved so powerful last night that the burst of Fire she'd woven in her dreams had actually scorched him in the physical world.

"On the contrary, my dear, it was a very good night. Though I doubt you would agree." Vadim smiled. Coldly. The temperature in the room dove towards freezing. He took a step towards the woman, and his smile widened as her spurt of mocking defiance faded and her already pale face lost all color.

"Elfeya, my pet, you've been keeping secrets."

CHAPTER TWO

At the guard barracks adjoining Celieria's royal palace, Rain found Belliard vel Jelani and the other warriors of Ellysetta's primary quintet still sleeping off the excesses of the previous night. They had not escaped Ellysetta's weave either, and the last Rain had seen of them, they'd been running for the brothel district.

Rain rousted them with a few well-aimed kicks.

"Tairen's scorching blood," Bel muttered. The leader of Ellysetta's primary quintet and Rain's oldest friend rolled to a sitting position and rubbed the heels of his palms against his eyes. Rumpled black hair slid over his face and shoulders in tangles. Bleary cobalt-blue eyes blinked, then squinted against the light. "Be gentle, Rain. There's neither a bone nor a muscle in my entire body that doesn't ache."

"I had to face worse," Rain informed him, "so don't look to me for sympathy."

"Lord of Light love her," Rowan vel Arquinas, holder of Fire in Ellysetta's quintet, groaned from his rack and flung an arm over his face. "I'm sorry I didn't warn you about the keflee. I'll never hold something like that back again."

"The next time you think to play a joke on me, vel Arquinas," Rain warned, "remember this."

"I will. I will." Rowan had admitted last night that he'd talked Bel and the others into keeping Ellysetta's extremely sensual appreciation of keflee a secret in the hopes of using that knowledge to play a joke on Rain. Of course, as tame and well-behaved as Rowan had been last week, Rain should have known he was plotting something. The Fey was deadly fierce in battle, yet unrepentantly wicked outside of it. Only his brother Adrial and his sister Sareika—both of whom he utterly adored—were safe from his jokes.

Kiel vel Tomar, the Water master of Ellysetta's quintet, attempted to rise up on his elbow, only to go pale and flop back down. "Can a Fey die from too much sex?" he asked.

"Yes," Bel replied bluntly. "Another bell and we would all have proven it."

"What's wrong with Adrial?" Rain glanced at Rowan's brother, who was still unconscious in his rack, his black hair spilling down off the pillows in tangled waves.

Rowan shrugged and rubbed the back of his neck. "He seems to have gotten the worst of it."

"By far," Kieran vel Solande agreed, plucking more than a dozen rumpled pink cards from the waistband of his breeches, each printed with the name of a Celierian pleasure girl who'd invited him to visit again when next he came to the city. At a mere four hundred years old, the son of the truemates Marissya and Dax v'En Solande was the youngest Fey in the quintet—the only Fey child born since the Mage Wars, in fact—but he was so powerful and so skilled with his blades, Rain had not hesitated to appoint him the Earth master of Ellysetta's quintet. "The weave drove us all, but nowhere near as badly as it drove Adrial."

Rain looked at them, the five who represented the best of all Fey warriors, and shook his head. A child with a wooden sword could defeat them at this particular moment. "You reek of spirits. Were you drinking as well as mating?"

"It seemed like a good idea at the time," Rowan muttered.

"We were hoping to dull the effects of the weave." Kiel was looking decidedly green around the gills. Giving a rattling moan, he lurched to his feet and stumbled rapidly towards the bathing rooms down the hall.

Rain smothered a laugh. "Well, I would suggest you seek out Marissya for a healing, but I think you all deserve to suffer a while longer."

After trading a few more insults, he sobered. "Give Adrial another bell or two, then wake him up," he said. "Ravel's quintet guards Ellysetta, and she's protected by a twenty-five-fold weave, but I want you there as soon as you're fit. Something attacked her last night."

"What?" Bel shot to his feet. To their credit, Rowan and Kieran—and even Kiel, who had just stumbled back from the bathing rooms—also flashed to stone-cold lethalness in an instant, their hands instinctively reaching for weapons. "Why did you not tell us immediately?"

"She is unharmed," Rain assured them. "And there was nothing you could have done even if you had been there. The attack came through her dreams."

"Mages?" Kieran asked.

Rain nodded. "Most likely. The shields did not protect her, and neither Ravel nor any of his men sensed anything until she woke screaming."

"We will wake Adrial and go to her immediately." Bel's face was an expressionless mask.

If Fey men sensed emotion the way empathic Fey women did, Rain knew he would be feeling Bel's shame and self-reproach washing over him in waves. The warrior was Elly-setta's bloodsworn champion—willingly bound by *lute'asheiva* to defend her against all harm—yet he'd not been at her side when she'd been attacked.

"*Nei*, let Adrial sleep, and do not torment yourself." Rain reached out and clasped his friend's shoulder. "There is nothing you could have done, my friend."

"I should have been there."

"As should I," Rain replied. "But I was miles away on a

beach at Great Bay, fighting her weave and trying desperately to keep my distance lest I dishonor myself entirely."

Bel's eyes narrowed. "I know you are not taking this as lightly as it seems. Your mate was attacked. Where is your rage?"

Flags of color warmed Rain's cheeks. A Fey warrior should be deathly furious over an attack on his mate, yet Rain's calm would not wane.

"She would not let me keep it." His hands spread before him, palms open in a gesture of surrender. The blood of millions lay upon those hands, and yet at this moment he could scarcely see the stain. "Last night, my song sang to her, and she spun the first thread between us." While trying to soothe the terrors of her nightmare, he'd sung tairen song to Ellysetta. The music had resonated in her soul, as a tairen's song resonated in its mate's, and in one perfect moment of communion, Ellysetta had forged the first shimmering filament of oneness between them.

Even now, the memory of that joy brought tears to his eyes.

Bel stared. "Tears," he murmured. "From eyes that have not wept in a thousand years." His cobalt gaze moved over Rain's face, searching for every tiny difference. "The bond truly does begin."

"*Aiyah*," Rain admitted softly.

Rowan, Kieran, and Kiel crowded closer. Their usual Fey-stoic masks fell away to reveal a mix of awe and envy. No warrior had truemated in a thousand years, not since before the devastation of the Mage Wars, and there was nothing a Fey warrior longed for more. But the gift of *shei'tanitsa* bonding was so rare, the usual lot of a warrior was to live and die without ever finding the woman born to complete his soul. It was the reason Fey warriors strived for centuries to master the intricacies of magic and swordsmanship, the reason they vied to be the best, the bravest, the most honorable of all warriors—hoping, always, to prove themselves worthy of the gods' greatest gift.

"What does it feel like?" Rowan asked.

Rain rolled his shoulders, searching for words. These were his friends, his blade brothers and the warriors sworn to defend Ellysetta with their lives. Although Rain's feelings were very personal and intimate, the wonder of the *shei'tanitsa* journey was a treasure that courting Fey had always shared with their unmated blade brothers.

"Peace," he said at last. "Like waking in a field of soft grass on a warm spring day and knowing for the first time exactly who you are and what your purpose is in the world. And humbleness, as if you were standing before the Bright Lord with all the dark ugliness of your soul laid out before you, and despite everything, he showers you with light until every last stain fades away." A smile spread slowly across his face. "Flame, too—especially under the effects of her weave—but I'll say no more about that. Some things should remain private between a Fey and his mate."

The warriors, who had been nodding in silent awe and trying not to show their envy, now grinned and laughed.

Bel put a hand on Rain's shoulder. "May the gods light your way, Rain, and your journey end in joy."

"*Beylah vo*, my friend." Rain exchanged a warrior's arm-clasp with Bel and pulled him close for a brief, tight embrace. Of all the Fey, there was none he loved so much as Bel. A week ago Rain had feared for his friend. The darkness that eventually consumed all untruemated Fey warriors had been so close to claiming him. But Ellysetta—miraculous, unexpected Ellysetta—had wiped centuries of death from Bel's soul with one effortless touch of healing warmth, and now Bel had joy once more.

One after another, Kieran, Kiel, and Rowan followed Bel's suit, exchanging arm-clasps and embraces, thanking Rain for sharing his felicity and offering their own well wishes in return.

By the time he left them, they were moving with brisk purpose, shaking off the weariness and excesses of last night. Only Adrial was still sleeping, but Rain doubted the others would let him do so much longer. Ellysetta had been attacked, and fierce Fey honor would demand that the warriors of her primary quintet take their place at her side, protecting her from all harm.

Kolis Manza, apprentice to the High Mage of Eld, groaned as he came back to consciousness. His head was splitting. His mouth tasted as though he had swilled raw sewage. He hawked and spat a foul-tasting glob of spittle on the floor.

Bright Lord's lice-infested balls. That little witch's Spirit weave had been beyond powerful.

He rose up on his elbows and grimaced in distaste as a limp hand slithered down his chest into his lap. Numerous limbs were draped over him, plump, naked, female limbs. They belonged to the four plump, naked, female bodies that lay scattered like so many dead leaves across the bed, eyes open and sightless, chests gaping from deep, slashing wounds that some other man might find astonishing for the lack of blood surrounding them. The index finger from the right hand of each woman was missing.

Kolis shoved the bodies aside and stood. His dagger lay on the floor beside the bed next to a small, bloodstained leather pouch. He bent to retrieve both and inspected the black jewel on the weapon's pommel. The dark gem sparkled with rich, satisfied ruby lights. At least he had not wasted last night's bed sport. Four new souls were trapped in the stone, awaiting his judicious use of them. And with so many Fey infesting Celieria City at the moment, they would come in handy. His first use would be to open a path through the Well of Souls so he could travel to Eld to bring the High Mage his news.

Despite the pounding in his head, Kolis's lips curled in a satisfied smile. At last he had the proof his master Vadim Maur had tasked him to find: the Tairen Soul's red-haired truemate possessed magic—and far more than just a small hint of it.

Though only the heads of Celieria's noble Houses had been invited to last night's dinner, Kolis had attended in the body of Jiarine Montevero, the lovely Celierian noblewoman who'd granted Kolis access to her soul in return for wealth and increased power. Jiarine had enough hearth witch in her that through her eyes he'd been able to see the flows of magic emanating from Ellysetta Baristani.

Those flows had been astonishingly powerful. Even inhabiting another's body, Kolis hadn't escaped the effects of Ellysetta Baristani's irresistible Spirit weave. After leaving Jiarine to her mindless rutting, he'd stumbled his way to this small, filthy house in the brothel district, summoned the madam and all three of her girls, and mated them time and time again until the small bells of the morning, when he had taken their blood and their souls in a last frenzied burst of passion before falling deep into a well of unconsciousness.

No, Ellysetta Baristani was no simple hearth witch like Jiarine, no Celierian child altered by remnant magic left over from the Mage Wars. Her weave had been too pure for that, too strong. Without a doubt, she was the one who had been lost so many years ago, the one the High Mage had been seeking for so long. Without a doubt, Vadim Maur's great experiment had borne powerful fruit.

Kolis called Fire to dispose of the bodies of the four dead whores, then used the basin and ewer on the table beside the bed to cleanse himself and tidy his appearance. He wasn't worried about visitors; everyone knew the girls would still be abed at this hour. He wasn't worried about servants either. This wasn't one of the wealthier pleasure houses in the city. The women had cared for themselves.

Taking his time, Kolis donned the blue coat of his Sorrelian merchantship captain's disguise, re-inked the blue tattoo of crossed swords high on his cheek, and finger-combed the long oiled black curls threaded with gold rings. Few people would question—much less remember—a sailor wandering the pleasure-trails at break of dawn.

When he was dressed, the Elden Mage scooped his black dagger and the bulging, blood-spattered leather pouch off the table and slipped out the brothel's back door into the dark, unpleasant rankness of the alleyway.

***

After leaving the barracks, Rain headed into the palace to locate Marissya and Dax. The *shei'dalin* and her mate had made it back to their own chambers last night, but were still abed when he reached their rooms.

By the time they dressed and met him in the king's private dining room for breakfast, Rain had already finished his food and was savoring his second cup of keflee, rolling the flavors around on his tongue and trying to imagine why the drink had such a profound effect on his *shei'tani*. It was a tasty brew, to be sure, but nothing that made him want to sit up and purr. Still, if Ellysetta liked it that much, he'd keep his palace stocked with the stuff. Well . . . only *after* she was sharing his bed. Smiling wryly, he set the cup in its saucer.

"Why are you smiling?" Dax growled. He glanced at his *shei'tani*, who was in the process of lifting the heavy veil off her face, and repeated crankily, "Why is he smiling?"

Rain felt a whisper-soft probe, an intrusion that made him scowl, but Marissya only smiled in the face of his irritation. "He has decided keflee might have its benefits," she revealed to Dax. "His courtship is progressing. The first thread of the bond has been forged." She took Rain's face in her hands and rose up on her toes to kiss him on both cheeks. "*Miora felah, kem'feyreisen.*"

Dax turned to Rain, his grouchiness melting into genuine pleasure, a broad smile spreading across his face. "*Mioralas*, Rain. Good news indeed." Like Bel and the others, Dax offered a hand-clasp and well wishes for a joyous outcome.

"*Beylah vos.* Thank you both." Rain sipped his keflee and arched a brow at the *shei'dalin*. "You know it's rude to probe a Fey's mind without permission." He tried to scowl again, just to prod her, but Dax's grin and his own burgeoning happiness made it impossible.

"*Aiyah.* Almost as rude as waking us after such an eventful night." Marissya poured herself a cup of keflee, then took a seat next to Rain, touching him lightly with her hand. "You are tired. You are expending too much effort to maintain your control. Permit me to assist you." Cool, relaxing power lapped over him, smoothing the edges of his fatigue, fortifying him with strength and calm. "That is all I can do for now," she told him, removing her hand. "It should be enough to see you through this afternoon with your *shei'tani*."

Rain nodded his thanks. This was not the first time Marissya had lent her strength to help him keep a grip on his own. It would not be the last, either. The courtship was far from over.

Dax groaned a little as he lowered himself into the chair beside his truemate.

"You have not seen to your mate?" Rain asked Marissya, surprised.

"Oh, she saw to me, all right," Dax answered with a tired but wicked grin. "Again and again and again. That's the problem. I think I may be too old for such . . . vigorous . . . activity."

"Rain was referring," Marissya sniffed, "to healing. As you are well aware."

"Ah. My mind must still be on last night." Dax drank half his keflee in a single gulp and gave Rain a wide-eyed look. "Do you have any idea what this woman can do with a—"

"Dax!"

Despite the agony he'd endured for seven bells last night while Ellysetta's weave had driven him so relentlessly, Rain decided it was almost worth it to see the cool, imperturbable Marissya turn such an interesting shade of scarlet. The Fey were modest about some things, but relations between matepairs was not one of them. Which meant things must have been far more than merely interesting in a certain suite of palace rooms last night if Marissya was still blushing this morning.

"My mind boggles at the possibilities." Rain shook his head and laughed.

Embarrassment forgotten, Marissya turned to Rain with a look of wonder in her eyes. "That's the first time I've heard you laugh in a thousand years. I had never thought to hear the sound of it again." Tears shimmered in her lashes. She blinked and they spilled over, silvery trails tracking down her cheeks. "Joy to the Feyreisa indeed if she can bring laughter back to my dear friend Rain."

Marissya's tears touched Rain's heart, and for the first time he realized how difficult the past centuries must have been on her. All the ancients who had survived the Wars had surrendered their own lives to create the Faering Mists. They'd left Marissya, the strongest remaining *shei'dalin*, to lead the Fading

Lands while Rain struggled through centuries of madness. She'd borne it all without complaint and without casting the slightest blame upon him.

He took a deep breath and released it slowly. "Though I did not welcome it at first," he said quietly, "and though it may still end badly, I am grateful for this blessing the gods saw fit to bestow upon me. It has been too long since I remembered why life is worth living. Ellysetta has reminded me."

"Then I, too, say joy to the Feyreisa," Dax said. "Though, gods love her, may she never again weave Spirit the way she did last night."

"At least not so the weave lasts *seven bells*," Marissya amended.

"Witnessed," Rain seconded with a wry laugh. A moment later, he rose to refill his cup and weave privacy wards around the room. "That's twice now that I've seen her weave such strong Spirit. She is more than just a master of it. And the Air weave she spun the other day was no third or fourth level skill either. With such strong command of two magics, there must be considerable Fey blood in her ancestry, but I don't understand why no hint of it shows. She looks pure mortal, but her magic seems pure, powerful Fey."

"Rain, how can she be Fey?" Marissya countered. "Can you honestly believe truemates have lived here, undetected, in Celieria since the Mage Wars? What possible reason would they have to exile themselves from the Fading Lands? Even if there was such a pair, once they realized their unborn child was female, they would surely have returned to us rather than endanger her in the unprotected world."

"I must agree with Marissya," Dax said. "No Fey lord worthy of his steel would put his women in such peril. More likely, it is as her mother said, remnant magic from the Mage Wars—"

Rain shook his head. "No remnant magic can account for the way she called a tairen from the sky, or the way she healed Bel's soul and wove Spirit last night with such mastery."

"Then perhaps her birth parents weren't pure mortal," Marissya suggested. "Perhaps they carried within them the gifts of some ancient magical ancestor—Fey, or Elves, or Danae—and perhaps that is what the remnant magic of the north awakened."

"Have Sian and Torel found anything in Norban to help solve this mystery?" Dax asked.

"*Nei*," Rain said. "They mentioned a lead they were going to follow up yesterday evening, but no one was in any shape to receive their report last night."

The two warriors had traveled north to investigate Ellysetta's origins. A young woman who could truemate a Tairen Soul hadn't just sprung up from the ground like a cabbage sprout. And despite Dax and Marissya's doubts, Rain was convinced Ellysetta came from pure, powerful magical stock. Who her parents were and why they'd not brought her to the Fading Lands after her birth was a mystery Rain intended to solve.

"Whatever she is," Marissya said, "she must discover and embrace her true identity before the bond can be complete."

"I know it. And at least she has finally accepted that she *does* possess magic and had agreed to be trained in its use." He fell silent for a moment, then said quietly, "She shared my dreams this morning. I was dreaming I was back in Fey'Bahren. I didn't realize it, but she was there with me. She saw Calah and the kits, heard the vow I made to Sybharukai. She saw everything just as it happened in my dream."

"Sharing dreams has happened to us a time or two," Dax said. "You should be happy, not concerned. It's a sign of a strong bond."

Marissya watched Rain's face closely. As always, she saw far more than he would have liked. "You haven't told her about the tairen."

Rain stared at his keflee cup and ran a thumb over the glazed handle.

"Rain . . ." Marissya only said his name, but her tone alone was sufficient admonishment.

"What good would it do? She's uncertain enough as it is. Shall I cement the destruction of our bond by piling the fate of two races on her shoulders?"

"The Eye of Truth sent you here to find her, Rain, because

the fates of those races rest on her shoulders whether she knows it or not. You must at least let her know what's at stake. There can be no secrecy between truemates. Besides, if you tell her the truth, she may surprise you. There is courage in her, even if it isn't readily apparent."

"When the time is right," Rain said, "I will tell her everything. At the moment, we have a more immediate crisis to deal with."

Marissya stared at him for an irritated chime. "There are challenges enough in the completion of a truemate bond without your adding to them, Rain," she warned. "Trust her, as a *shei'tan* should trust his mate."

His jaw tightened and he met her reproachful look without flinching. Her lips compressed, then she huffed and let him change the subject. "Ellysetta's weave was localized within the banquet hall," she said. "Only those of us inside were affected. Once we realized what was happening, Dax wove redirection and privacy around the Hall. Those caught up in the weave will remember, but no others will have seen or heard them. And we did what we could to send most of them to the privacy of their own rooms."

"Quick thinking," Rain approved. "More than I was capable of at the time."

"Rumors may still spread," Marissya cautioned.

"We'll deal with that if it happens. At least you granted us a little time to prepare." He leaned back in his chair. "What did you learn last night?"

Dax ran through the list of Celierian lords he and Marissya had talked with before and during dinner. Of the two hundred members of the Council of Lords, only thirty still declared themselves undecided as to how they would vote on the upcoming treaty with the Eld, and the Fey, unfortunately, would need almost every one of those votes to keep the Eld out of Celieria.

Too many of Celieria's nobles had grown openly antagonistic towards the Fey. Some had even gone so far as to suggest that Rain's return to Celieria after a thousand years of self-imposed exile in the Fading Lands was proof the *dahl'reisen* and Fey were working in concert to destabilize Celieria. And though Rain would never say so to Ellysetta, her weave could well have ruined their hopes of winning the upcoming vote.

"What happened last night could have changed everything," Dax added. "Obviously, Marissya and I haven't yet had a chance to gauge the aftereffects of Ellysetta's weave."

Marissya blushed again and sipped her keflee, lifting her eyes to inspect the elegant gilded plaster moldings on the ceiling.

Rain looked at Dax and raised an admiring brow, but took mercy on Marissya and let her blush pass without comment. "So, basically, there are thirty lords who hold Celieria's fate in their hands," he summated.

"Assuming more do not change their votes this morning," Dax agreed. "Of those still undecided, Great Lords Orly and Verakis are the most powerful. If we can gain their support, we may have a chance. Each of them will likely pull another dozen votes from the lesser lords."

"I'm still surprised Dorian won Morvel to our side. He bears no love for our kind. He made that abundantly clear last night."

"He's got five unwed daughters and no takers for them," Dax said. "If you saw them, you'd understand why. His income has suffered thanks to poor harvests these last few years, and he can't offer large enough dowries to sweeten the pot. I know he told you he wants to provide for his bastard son, but in truth, he's seeking gold enough to get those daughters off his hands."

"Dorian also promised him two prestigious estates in the south," Marissya said. "He'd be the second-largest landholder in Celieria. That's quite an incentive for a man like Lord Morvel."

"Well, I hope greed still holds the power to lure him after last night." Rain grimaced as he considered the possible fallout from Ellysetta's weave. "The last I saw him, he was hustling his wife away from the table, and she was shedding clothes as she went. Ah, gods." He rubbed his face. "I pray they made it to their rooms before . . ."

Marissya nodded. "He would not be one to forgive a public humiliation."

Grimly the three of them looked at one another in silence. It wouldn't take the nobles long to realize that magic, not simply an overindulgence in pinalle and keflee, had compelled their actions. While the Fey might shrug off a night of uninhibited, weave-driven mating with laughs, groans, and a few blushes, most Celierians were much more tightly laced about such matters. Worse, unintentionally woven though it had been, Ellysetta's magic had overridden the wills and inhibitions of Celieria's most powerful nobles, individuals who reigned as kings on their own estates. Last night, those kings had danced like puppets on strings beneath the unyielding dictates of her weave.

"We must assess the damage and mend what bridges we can," Rain said. "I don't want blame to fall on Ellysetta. If you are questioned, imply the weave was mine. Who's to say it wasn't my own need that drove her in any case?"

"I'll speak to Dorian," Marissya promised. "If he didn't realize the weave was Ellysetta's, there's a good chance none of the other lords will have either."

Rain's jaw tightened at the mention of King Dorian's name, and he gave a curt nod. He knew he should approach Dorian personally, king to king, but Marissya was far more levelheaded when dealing with her nephew than Rain could ever be.

The man could have ended this entire political struggle by invoking *primus*—King's First Right—to keep the borders closed to the Eld. It was what a strong king would have done. But Dorian had surrendered too much of his power to Celieria's noble Houses. He sought consensus when he should have provided leadership; and despite Rain's warning about the growing darkness in the north, without hard proof of a reconstituted Mage presence, Dorian refused to override the will of the Council of Lords.

"Teleos pledged his support," Rain said, "though I doubt any lords who distrust us will change their votes because of him." Teleos had too much Fey blood in his ancestry for the comfort of most pure mortals, and it showed in his Fey eyes and faintly luminescent skin. "Lord Barrial is—at least, was—in our corner, and he seems to be well liked by most of the other lords. If last night's weave didn't turn him against us, he may be a very useful ally. Did you see the *sorreisu kiyr* he was wearing last night?"

"*Aiyah*," Dax said. "We were wondering about that ourselves. He's not a regular at court, and that's the first time Marissya or I have seen him with the crystal."

"I'll ask for a meeting with him and see what I can learn." Rain leaned back in his seat and sipped the warm keflee. "For now, let's focus on finding a way to convince these other lords that the Eld still pose a threat—or at the very least make an alliance with the Fey seem more lucrative than one with the Eld."

Sunlight filtering through her closed eyelids filled Queen Annoura's gaze with a wash of red, like a sea of watery blood. She peeled one eye open, then groaned against the stabbing light and dragged a pillow over her face. Gods' mercy, she ached all over. From the tip of her toes to the crown of her head, every muscle, every sinew, every inch of skin felt sore and raw.

A rumbling snore sounded in her ear, and she turned her head just enough to find her husband Dorian sprawled out beside her, naked, one arm and leg flung possessively across her.

She glanced down and found her own body spread-eagled with vulgar abandon atop the tangled bedsheets. Had the servants come in and seen her like this? Celieria's queen, naked and flung open like a starfish, bared to any gawking fool? Grabbing one edge of the silk sheet, she pulled it over herself and hissed as even that slight pressure irritated raw, whisker-burned skin.

Good gods, what a night.

How had something as tediously banal as a palace dinner gone so wrong? Her hands clenched in fists around the bedsheets as the memories flooded back, clear and sharp as glass. The palace dinner. Dorian's unexpected and very unwelcome coup in convincing Great Lords Barrial and Morvel to offer marriage ties between one of their sons and Ellysetta Baristani's young sisters. Rain Tairen Soul squiring his common-born mate around the palace as if she were the Queen of Queens.

The affront had been too much. Annoura's simmering resentment had bubbled over, and her desire to put the wood-carver's daughter in her place had turned to bitter deter-mination. A whispered word in a trusted ear ensured that a never-ending flow of heady blue wine poured into the girl's glass and a special brew of intensely potent keflee found its way into her cup.

Get the girl drunk, ply her with the overwhelming aphro-disiacal effects of the keflee, and watch her make an unmiti-gated fool of herself before the heads of every noble House in Celieria: that had been Annoura's plan.

Only it hadn't worked out the way she'd intended.

Rather than Ellysetta Baristani humiliating herself before the court, every other person in the banquet hall had done so in her stead. Celieria's most powerful nobles had fallen upon each other like ravening wolves. Lords and ladies, Great Lords, even she and Dorian—all helpless to resist the driving sexual hunger.

"Spirit weave," Dorian had gasped into her ear as their hands had reached helplessly for each other. It was only thanks to Dorian's Fey blood that he'd been able to withstand the call of the magic long enough to get them to the privacy of his bedchamber—but even so, he hadn't been able to counter the weave or reduce its power. He, like she, had been a puppet dancing to the magic's capricious command. They'd made love with fevered intensity for more than seven bells. Orgasm after orgasm, each one more shattering than the last. Every climax followed by an even deeper, more insistent burn.

Annoura's throat closed up tight at the memory of it, and her heart pounded like a mallet in a chest that felt as if heavy stones were squeezing all the air from her lungs. As a princess of the Capellan royal House, she'd been sternly reared to assume command of any situation and never relinquish it. Yet last night, with a single weave of magic, the Fey had robbed her of every last illusion of control. She'd been powerless. Enslaved. Dominated and controlled by the magical will of another.

She sat up and drew her knees to her chest. Helplessness was not a feeling she understood, nor one she knew how to deal with.

Behind her, Dorian stirred. She felt the mattress shift as he moved, felt his hand touch her hip, his fingers curl possessively around her waist.

"Annoura?" His voice was raspy, thick with sleep. "Come back to bed, *kem'san.*"

She flinched at the Fey endearment and cast a glance over her shoulder. "Come back to bed?" she echoed in disbelief. "Surely you cannot want more mating after last night?"

He chuckled wryly and peeled open an eye. "Doubt I could summon the energy even if I did, my love. I just like the feel of you in my arms. It's been too long since we woke together." His hand stroked her waist, his thumb tracing a line up her spine.

Despite her aching soreness, she felt the nascent tingle of desire bloom in the wake of his hand. She'd never been able to deny him. Not from the first moment they'd met. Her eyes had locked with his, and from that moment on, she'd wanted him—his kiss, his love, his hands upon her, the joy of his smile making her feel as if she could fly.

Now, for the first time in her life, an ugly thought crept in. *Had Dorian been working Fey magic on her all these years?*

The possibility couldn't be ignored. Powerful Fey blood ran in his veins. Ten generations ago, his ancestor Dorian the First had wed Marikah vol Serranis, sister of the *shei'dalin* Marissya and twin of Gaelen vel Serranis, the murderous *dahl'reisen* known as the Dark Lord. That marriage had introduced powerful Fey magic into the royal Celierian bloodline. Even now, diluted by ten generations, Dorian's Fey heritage ensured he would live a life three times that of a normal Celierian. He was exceedingly healthy—common mortal ailments had never afflicted him—and he could weave Air and Spirit, though according to him he possessed less than a tenth the mastery of his magical kin.

Until now, she'd always believed him, always thought her devotion and desire were just natural byproducts of her love for him. But after last night, she had to wonder which feelings were her own and which were the result of Fey influence. Dear gods, could she have been enslaved by Dorian's magic and never even known it?

"Come back, *kem'sharra*, let me hold you a while longer."

She flinched away from his hand and rose from the bed. The long platinum mass of her hair tumbled down her back to just above her buttocks.

"Annoura?"

"The day is already half gone. The court will be wondering why we have not yet put in an appearance." She stepped over the haphazard pile of discarded clothes she and Dorian had ripped from each other's bodies last night and reached for the silk dressing robe her maid left out for her each evening. Annoura slid her arms into the sleeves. The thin silk helped make her feel less naked, less vulnerable. More herself.

She tugged the belt into a knot at her waist and turned to face her husband. He was propped up on one elbow, frowning at her.

"You need to think about what you're going to do now, Dorian," she said, pleased to hear the familiar sound of command back in her voice. "You cannot let this pass unpunished."

He sat up, his frown deepening. "What are you talking about?"

"The Tairen Soul's weave last night. He broke the terms of the Fey-Celierian alliance. He manipulated our minds and our bodies with his magic. You must make an example of him."

"Rain didn't spin that weave," he said. "It was the girl, Ellysetta Baristani."

Annoura stared in shock. "But she's Celierian!"

"So am I, my dear. So is Teleos. That doesn't mean we can't weave magic."

She caught herself before asking him if he'd ever woven magic on her. "Then you must make an example of her. She is still your subject, after all."

"What purpose would that serve save to anger the Fey? The terms of the alliance don't prohibit one Celierian from spinning a weave on another." He threw his legs over the side of the bed and stood up. "Besides, I'm quite sure the girl didn't know what she was doing. She's a complete innocent. You have only to look at her to see it shining from her. I will not mortify that poor child by holding her up to the retribution and ridicule of the court for something she did after we got her drunk on too much wine."

Annoura went stiff. "*We* got her drunk?" Had Dorian overheard her quiet command to her steward? Worse, did he know about the frightfully potent keflee?

"We were the hosts last evening, Annoura. The condition of the guests dining at our table is our responsibility."

He didn't know. Relief at his ignorance warred with outrage over his indifference. She glared. "That's it? You're just going to let this pass?"

He looked surprised. "Why would I not? What harm, really, was done to anyone?" His mouth curved in a slow smile. "You can't tell me you didn't enjoy at least some of last night. And I can promise you there were at least half a dozen older lords who'd probably pay the girl a king's ransom to . . . er . . . invigorate them that way again." His smile became a roguish grin, but the expression faded quickly when she didn't respond in kind. "Come now, my dear, you're being entirely too tight-laced about this. It was an accident."

"It was dangerous, Dorian! If she can do that, what else might she do?"

His face hardened. "The answer is no, Annoura. You will not attempt to punish the girl. If I know the Fey, they will find a way to accept responsibility for what happened so that any blame falls on them, rather than her." He stalked around the bed to the crumpled pile of last night's clothes and yanked on his wrinkled breeches. "And that, my dear, should made you very happy, considering your numerous attempts to discredit them."

"Dorian!" She gaped at him in disbelief. How had he turned this around and made *her* out to be the villain? No matter what she'd done to foment last night's weave, she was a victim of it! Her will had been usurped. Her pride and dignity trampled. The queen of Celieria had been enslaved by magic—and her husband the king would do nothing to avenge her! He saw it all as some humorous joke, some titillating farce.

Dorian tugged his full white silk tunic over his head, leaving the neckline gaping open to show faintly bronzed skin and the dark hairs sprinkled across his chest. He left the rest of his clothes where they lay. "Last night was a pleasure beyond words—at least for me. I regret you don't share the sentiment. I will take my leave of you." He bowed with perfect, studied grace. It felt like a slap across her face.

"Dorian." Despite herself, she took a step towards him, one hand extended in supplication, but he was already walking out.

When the door shut behind him, her hand curled into a shaking fist. The Fey. Always, when he was asked to choose between the Fey and his own wife, he chose them. Never her.

The betrayal bit deep. She'd turned her back on her own family for him. She'd been raised for the sole purpose of wedding a royal husband and directing the strength of his kingdom to further the power of Capellas. Only she hadn't done that. She'd loved Dorian too much to see him become a pawn of her parents. She'd established her seat of power in his court, to be sure, but she'd used every ounce of her will to make Celieria strong enough never to need or fall prey to Capellan might. Thanks to her, Celieria now led the world instead of Capellas—and her parents had never forgiven her.

All she'd ever wanted in return was for Dorian to extend the same loyalty and devotion to her, but now she finally realized he never would. For Dorian, the Fey would always come first.

With that realization, the love she'd always felt for him died a little, and a cold, stony seed of resentment took root in her heart. Fear and betrayal hardened to anger and new determination. Dorian might cling to the old ways and hug close his childish trust in the Fey, but she would not. Annoura of Celieria, born a princess of Capellas, now the most powerful queen in all the world, would not allow the Fey and their cursed magic to lead Celieria about on a leash.

The Eld had offered an alternative—economic and military supremacy that did not include the Fey. More importantly, they possessed magic strong enough to thwart even Fey weaves should Dorian's immortal kin object to Celieria's independence.

While Dorian would do everything he could to see the Eld trade agreement defeated, Annoura was going to make sure that it passed.

CHAPTER THREE

Ellysetta's morning passed with excruciating slowness. Each time one of the queen's craftsmasters arrived she waited for the tittering whispers and sly, knowing glances that would indicate he'd heard about the weave at last night's dinner—or, worse, heard she was to blame. To her surprise, the dreaded mockery never came. The craftsmasters went about their business with the same veiled arrogance and brisk dispatch as before. Either they had no idea what had happened, or they were taking great care not to show it.

Worse than the shame of last night's weave, though, were the horrifying memories of the nightmare that had followed.

The pit of darkness. The rats, swarming around her, crawling over her, shredding her flesh from her bones with their sharp teeth and claws while the Shadow Man taunted, "Show yourself, girl." The vast battlefield thick with the corpses of everyone she knew and thousands more she didn't. The immense army, so huge it stretched beyond the limits of her vision, covering the world like an ocean of foul darkness. The chilling, sibilant voice hissing, *"You'll kill them all. It's what you were born for."*

Horror after horror, the Shadow Man had shown her. Bel

and her quintet, slaughtered, Mama, Papa and the twins, slain—
their bodies a gruesome feast to be fought over by crows.

Worst of all had been Rain. Dead at her feet. The glow of
Fey life extinguished forever, his beloved eyes gone milky in
death. Even the memory of it made her shudder and cry out.

Just as she'd done last night.

That one, anguished scream of denial had been her undoing.
A lifetime of hiding shattered in an instant, and she'd revealed
herself—and her magic—to the Shadow Man.

Vividly she remembered the icy clutch of his hand clamped
around her throat. His chilling triumph, as he crowed, "I see
you . . . Ellysetta," and threw back his black cowl to reveal his
face.

That face was her own.

She was the general of the Shadow Man's armies, the instru-
ment through which he rained destruction on the World.

«Feyreisa.»

She was the evil creature who'd led the armies of darkness
to slaughter her friends and family.

«Kem'falla.»

He'd claimed he was showing her the future. And even now, in
the bright light of day, she was terrified he'd been telling the
truth.

«Ellysetta!»

"Ellie?"

The sound of two voices calling her name in sharp unison
snapped her back to the present. She shook off the specters
from her nightmare and glanced up to find Mama and Ravel
standing beside her, watching her with deep concern.

She suddenly realized the room seemed stiflingly hot, and
the seamstresses surrounding her were fanning their flushed
faces and wiping beads of perspiration from their brows.

«You are weaving Fire, Feyreisa.» Ravel watched her with an
unblinking violet gaze, and she could see the subtle tension
gathered in him.

That was when she felt the tingle of magic simmering inside
her skin and realized the Air and Fire masters from Ravel's

quintet were actively weaving to dissipate the room's quickly rising temperature. Ellie gave a quiet gasp, and the hum of magic within her fell instantly silent.

"Ellie," Mama said again, "are you all right?"

Ellysetta glanced at her mother and forced a smile. "I'm fine. I'm sorry. I was just lost in thought." She flicked a glance at Ravel and repeated, «*Sieks'ta. I didn't realize what I was doing.*»

Mama didn't look convinced, but didn't pursue the subject, and for the rest of the morning, Ellie worked hard to keep her thoughts from wandering. She was mentally exhausted by the time Ravel and his quintet escorted her and her mother to the Grand Cathedral of Light for the second of the six devotions required before Ellysetta could receive the sacrament of the Bride's Blessing and marry Rain.

Outside the Baristani house, there was no sign of the protestors who'd gathered there in anger at the Fey presence. They'd been dispersed by the Fey and kept away by a redirection weave erected this morning in a four-block radius around the house. Beyond those barriers, however, the crowds had grown much larger and visibly more agitated. The Fey crowded close and raised dense, glowing shields around Ellysetta and her mother.

"Must they do that?" Lauriana muttered, glowering at the visible threads of the weave.

"It's for our protection, Mama," Ellysetta replied. "Rain did warn us that he wouldn't be taking any more chances with our safety."

"Though I commend the sentiment," her mother huffed, "I don't approve of the methods. Magic causes more problems than it solves." Her jaw clenched. "And if these Fey think they're going to follow me around everywhere I go, surrounding me in some great, shining sorcerous bubble, they can think again." She scowled at the warrior closest to her. He merely gazed back without expression.

A few chimes later, they reached the golden bridges that connected Celieria City to the holy Isle of Grace, the small island in the middle of the Velpin River upon which the magnificent Grand Cathedral of Light was built. All white marble

nd gleaming gold-leafed roofs, the cathedral rose like a palace
of sunbeams and clouds from the isle's exquisitely manicured
awns and gardens.

Selianne Pyerson, Ellysetta's best friend, who had agreed to
erve as her Honoria during the Bride's Blessing, was already
vaiting when they arrived.

Ellie hurried up the thirteen marble steps to greet her friend
with a hug, a smile, and a searching look. "How are you, Sel?"

Fortunately, Selianne seemed happier today than she had at
yesterday's devotions. The darkest shadows of worry in her
deep blue eyes had faded, and the smile she gave Ellie when
hey embraced was warm and genuine. "I'm fine, Ellie. Well,"
she amended with a grimace and a flick of a glance at the
sword-bristling warriors swarming over the isle, "as fine as can
be expected under the circumstances." Her eyes narrowed on
Ravel and his quintet, and the hand clutching Ellie's tightened.
"Those aren't the same Fey that were with you yesterday."

"Don't worry," Ellie rushed to reassure her. "They've sworn
he same oath not to read your thoughts or eavesdrop on our
conversations. You can trust them," she added when Selianne
continued to look skittish. "Fey don't lie, and they won't betray
a sworn oath."

"If you say so, Ellie," Selianne muttered, but she didn't look
very reassured.

Her fear was understandable. Sel was terrified the Fey—or,
worse, Rain—would discover that Sel's mother was Eld rather
than Sorrelian as everyone believed. Considering Rain's especially vehement loathing of his ancient enemies, even Ellie
feared what he might do if he ever discovered the secret.

Before Ellie could say anything else, a mocking voice announced from behind her, "Well, well. Ellie Baristani. Fancy
seeing you here."

Selianne grimaced and bent close to whisper, "Sorry . . . I
meant to warn you."

With a sinking feeling in her stomach, Ellie turned to find
her childhood nemesis, Kelissande Minset, standing just inside
the cathedral entrance. She was staring straight at Ellie, her

summer-blue eyes positively glacial while her lips curved in a
cloyingly sweet, mocking smile. A handsome young nobleman
stood at Kelissande's side, looking haughty and rather brittle.

"Kelissande," Ellie greeted.

Daughter of one of the wealthiest bankers in the city, Kelissande was dressed as finely as a noblewoman. Her gown was an
elegant confection of blue watered silk, sapphires and diamonds dripped at her throat and ears, and on her left hand she
wore a huge new diamond ring circled by several rows of small
sapphires in varying shades of blue. Kelissande's gaze swept
over Ellie's equally elegant saffron silk gown, and her smile
tightened. "I see the Fey have been improving your wardrobe."

Ellie returned a smooth smile, knowing Kelissande Minset
could find no fault with Ellie's appearance. "Actually, it was the
queen who was kind enough to ask her dressmakers to attend
me." She saw Kelissande's fingers clench and changed the subject. "I didn't realize you attended services here."

"Kelissande just got betrothed," Selianne said. "She and her
intended, Ser Challen Sonneval, were meeting with Greatfather
Tivrest to plan their own wedding. Ser Sonneval, may I introduce my friend Ellysetta Baristani, who was herself recently
betrothed to the Tairen Soul."

"Ah." The young nobleman finally spoke. His voice was a
bored drawl, thick with affected court accents. "I had heard
talk about the Tairen Soul and a woodcarver's daughter." Cold
brown eyes swept over Ellie from head to toe. "Interesting."

Ellie blinked at his chilling rudeness, and beside her, Ravel
took a threatening step forward that made Ser Sonneval's eyes
widen.

"*Nei*, Ser Ravel, it's all right." Ellysetta lifted a hand to fore-
stall any trouble.

Around her waist she wore the black Fey'cha dagger that Bel
had given her when he'd bloodsworn himself to her service. Her
fingers closed around the silk-wrapped hilt, and the feel of Bel's
bloodsworn blade in her hand filled her with reassuring confidence.

"It is happy indeed that we live in such enlightened times," she continued, "that a woodcarver's daughter can wed a king and a banker's daughter can wed a Ser."

Ser Sonneval paled, then flushed as the blades in her remark struck home. Beside him, Kelissande's eyes blazed with scarcely contained fury.

Keeping her expression composed and polite, Ellie finished coolly, "On behalf of my family, I offer you our felicitations, Kelissande. May you find all the happiness you deserve in your marriage."

Ravel stepped forward, his face carved from stone. "Mistress Minset, Ser Sonneval, I must ask you both to leave. The Feyreisa's devotions begin soon, and the Fey will be warding the isle."

As he spoke, two dozen warriors spread out along the perimeters of the isle to spin protective weaves that would keep anyone from entering or leaving the isle as long as Ellysetta was there. Since canon law forbade anyone to enter the Grand Cathedral bearing weapons, the Fey had insisted on erecting their barricades of magic to protect Ellysetta each time she was there, and though he spluttered in outrage and threatened to tell the king, not even the Archbishop himself had been able to stop them.

"She truly hates me," Ellie murmured as Kelissande and her betrothed took their leave.

"She's never liked anyone to best her," Selianne said. "The way she was crowing before you got here, you'd think she was wedding a lord, rather than a mere Ser. He's as poor as a *dorn*, of course—the seventh son of a small southern lord—but he's of noble blood. He liked the size of her brideprice, and her father liked the blueness of his blood. Personally, I think she couldn't stand the idea of your wedding the Fey king, and this was the best she could do to trump you." Selianne rolled her eyes. "It's a shame you'll miss her wedding. It's sure to be a grand event."

"I'd have missed it anyway," Ellie replied dryly. "I sincerely doubt Kelissande Minset would invite me."

"Ah, but you're the Tairen Soul's bride now. Of course she'd invite you."

"Then I'm even sorrier to miss the spectacle of Kelissande Minset currying my favor." They both laughed at the preposterous idea.

The sound of Selianne's laughter and the familiar sight of her bright smile and dancing eyes sent a wave of love rushing over Ellie. She'd missed this so much these last few days: giggling with her very best friend in the world. They'd spent so many years growing up together, sharing confidences and laughter, hopes and fears. Outside of her own family, there was no one in the world she loved more.

Selianne's smile faded as tears glistened in Ellysetta's eyes. "What is it? What's wrong?"

Ellie shook her head and blinked back the tears before they could fall. "Nothing bad, Sel. I was just thinking how much I love you. I know how difficult this has been for you—I know you'd rather have seen me wed Den Brodson than Rain—but I'm so very glad you're here with me, standing as my Honoria."

"Oh, Ell." Selianne flung her arms around Ellie's waist and hugged her tightly. "You're my sister in every way that counts. Where else would I be but at your side?" They both cried a little, then stepped back to laugh and wipe at their tears. "Come on," Selianne said, linking her arm through Ellysetta's, "we'd best get inside. Greatfather Tivrest looks ready to pop a vessel."

As the women stepped across the cathedral threshold, Den Brodson, Ellysetta's former betrothed, stalked down the cobbled streets of the West End, his jaw clenched in brutish determination.

Enough was enough!

The urchin he'd paid last night had brought him word that Batay, the Sorrelian merchant ship captain, had returned to the Inn of the Blue Pony, and now it was time Den and the good captain had a little heart-to-heart talk. The bare-fisted kind of talk, if necessary. Den's knuckles popped with a series of satisfying cracks as his thick fingers curled tight.

Almost a week had passed since the Sorrelian captain had

approached Den, promising to help him take back his bride. Thus far, however, the Sorrelian's promises had amounted to nothing but hot air. Though Den had spent most of last week gamely playing errand boy on behalf of Batay and his mysterious master, he was no closer to reclaiming Ellie Baristani than he had been the day King Dorian had declared Den's betrothal null and void.

"Light save you," Den's friend Garlie Tavitts had exclaimed last night over a pint of ale, "your pa's rich as a king now. Go find another girl. Why'd you need to tangle with the Fey?"

Garlie didn't understand. No one did. The Fey gold paid to break the betrothal belonged to Den's pa, not to him. And Den was tired of being his father's lackey. Ellie and the money he planned to earn with her magic were Den's chance for a personal fortune all his own.

But this wasn't even about the money anymore. Now it was about pride and respect and victory. Rainier vel'En Daris had stolen something that belonged to Den. Every sewer rat in the West End knew if he dared steal so much as a crust of bread from Den Brodson, Den would chase the thief down and stomp his jaffing liver out. And that went for honey-tongued Sorrelian sea captains, too. Den Brodson was no pinchpocket's mark.

It was time for some action.

Den shoved open the doors of the Inn of the Blue Pony and stalked inside. After a curt consultation with the innkeeper, he made his way to one of the private dining rooms down the back hallway and rapped twice on the door before opening it. The now-familiar face of Captain Batay smiled from across a scarred wooden table. A partially eaten meal sat before him. He was drinking from a glass filled with bloodred wine.

"Ah, Goodman Brodson, please come in." Captain Batay set his wineglass on the table and waved Den in.

Den hesitated. One look from the Sorrelian captain, and every ounce of Den's righteous fury evaporated as ice ran down his spine. He stood there, shocked and confused, trying to banish the fear that suddenly clung to the back of his neck.

What the flaming Hells was wrong with him? Batay's smile held nothing but welcome. His vivid blue-green eyes contained craftiness, to be sure, but if the captain were not a crafty man, he would be little help to Den in his efforts to reclaim his wayward bride. Still, Den couldn't quite stop himself from glancing over his shoulder as he stepped into the inn's private dining room and closed the door.

"The innkeeper said you'd come by last night looking for me and that you'd received the note I left for you," Batay said as Den drew near. "Did you bring what I asked for?"

Despite every one of his earlier intentions to set the tone of this meeting and claim a position of power, Den found himself approaching the dining table like a supplicant and meekly pulling the small wooden music box from his pocket. The box had two paste jewels embedded in its carved top and played a tinny rendition of the overture from the symphony *Rainier's Song*. Den had thought the tune ironically appropriate.

"Excellent," the captain said. "That will do nicely." He held out a hand, and Den gave him the music box.

"What makes you think she's even going to open the gift?" Den asked.

"She will, I assure you. She will feel compelled to open it." The Sorrelian reached into his coat pocket and withdrew an empty glass vial.

"If it even reaches her to begin with," Den said. "It's not like those Fey are going to let me give her anything."

Captain Batay placed the vial on the table and reached underneath his coat. "When the gift is ready, I will make arrangements for it to be delivered."

Den shrank back as the Sorrelian drew a long, wicked-looking black dagger from the sheath at his side. The double-edged blade was narrow and wavy, the long hilt tightly wrapped with black and red silk cords. A large black jewel clutched in golden prongs glittered in the pommel.

"What's that for?" Den asked in a voice that cracked.

"Relax, Goodman Brodson. I just need a little of your blood."

"Why?"

"So many questions. You weren't so curious when I first offered my help."

"You weren't asking for my blood then."

"But now I am." Captain Batay smiled. "Just a drop or two."

"And if I say no?"

"Then I'm afraid our association is at an end. The door is there." He pointed. "Close it behind you on your way out." He set the knife down on the table and returned the empty vial to his pocket. The captain raised his glass, drank deep of the ruby wine, and raised his brows when Den remained where he was. "If you want to free your bride from the Tairen Soul, Goodman, you may stay. But the price for staying is your blood."

Den thought of Ellysetta's abilities, of the riches that would be his. Of the wealth, the power. Of the satisfaction that would come from beating the arrogant Tairen Soul at his own game. The demon-souled Fey sorcerer had stolen Den's prize. Den was going to steal her back.

"Just a drop or two?"

"That's all I require."

Den held out his hand.

❧

The second of Ellysetta's six devotions passed with surprising calm, and though Ellysetta wouldn't exactly say the cathedral was overflowing with happiness, there was at least a certain level of acceptance instead of the dread and disapproval that had hung over yesterday's initial service. Greatfather Tivrest conducted the devotions in a sober, sonorous voice. When they were done, Mama and Selianne left together—without Fey escort—to visit Madame Binchi's shop on Queen's Street for their dress fittings, while the Fey escorted Ellysetta back home.

Bel and the rest of Ellysetta's primary quintet were there waiting, looking worse than she'd ever seen them, and the brief lightening of her spirits she'd enjoyed after sharing Selianne's company faded in an instant.

"I'm so sorry," she told Bel miserably when Ravel's quintet had departed. She felt near tears at the sight of the five warriors who'd become such dear friends. They looked so weary and wan, and she'd done that to them. She and her weave. "I swear I didn't mean to do it."

Bel only shook his head and smiled gently. "*Las, kem'falla*, we know that." Far more forgiveness than she deserved shone from his cobalt eyes. "Your magic is awakening, and that is never a tidy process."

"Bel is right, Feyreisa," Kieran said, smiling as he glanced down at the tiny white kitten perched on his shoulder. Love had decided that Kieran's shoulder was a much more comforting place than her hideout under the icebox. She stuck out her chin for a scratch and regarded the Fey Earth master with a look of pure feline adoration. Her stubby tail flicked his ear, her tiny claws curled into his leathers to secure her place, and despite the powerful magic shields still in place around the house, she was purring so loudly, Ellie could hear her all the way across the room. "You are not to blame in any way."

"*Aiyah*," Kiel agreed. "Besides, no one was hurt, and no real harm was done."

"I'll wager there's many a man who'd pay for such . . . invigoration," Rowan pitched in helpfully, "if you catch my meaning." He grinned. Rowan had a sense of humor that Ellysetta was coming to realize was pure mischief. He was the kind who would poke monsters with a stick and laugh when they roared. "In fact," he added, "our lads Kieran and Adrial started a few new Fey legends in the brothel district last night."

"Kieran Blue Eyes, they called him," Kiel said, sidling up to Kieran's side and giving him a simpering, syrupy look of adoration. "One look had them swooning."

Kieran flashed his charming smile, fluttered his now-famous blue eyes, and caught Kiel when he pretended to faint. Love, unamused, swatted at the blond Fey.

"And baby brother was Adrial the Unstoppable," Rowan added proudly. "He had them swooning, too, but for a different reason." The Fey waggled his brows and grinned again with wicked, roguish humor.

Ellysetta covered her blazing cheeks with her hands and sank weakly on the arm of a settee. "This is not helping." She couldn't believe they were laughing about what she'd done. She didn't find anything funny about it at all.

Adrial apparently didn't either. Instead of laughing with the other Fey, he had retreated to the other side of the room and stood there, staring into space and trembling as if some great emotion gripped him.

"Adrial?" Concerned, she went to him. His Fey-pale skin was even whiter than the others', his brown eyes dilated and unfocused. She reached up and pressed a hand to his forehead. His skin felt clammy, and she gasped as blinding despair battered her senses. Adrial lurched away from her, and the emotion faded.

"Don't touch me." His voice was weak, thready.

Ellie was aware of the sudden alertness of the other Fey warriors in the room, but she ignored them, focusing her attention on Adrial. "You're ill," she said. "You should be in bed."

"*Nei.*" He rubbed his face with trembling hands. "I'm all right. I'll be fine."

"Adrial. Little brother." Rowan approached. His laughter was gone, replaced by worry. "Listen to the Feyreisa." He reached out to grasp his brother's arms, but Adrial threw him off.

"*Nei.*" White sparks flashed in Adrial's eyes. "Don't touch me, Rowan. I said I'm fine."

Love the kitten hissed furiously, jumped off Kieran's shoulder and went racing for the kitchen. A globe of light sprang up around Ellysetta as Bel, Kiel, Kieran, and the five warriors of her secondary quintet leapt forward to surround her.

"Then why are you summoning Air?" Kieran asked.

Adrial frowned. "I . . ." The sparks in his eyes faded. "Was I?" He pressed the heels of his palms to his temples and squeezed his eyes shut. "Perhaps I should lie down." He allowed Rowan to lead him to the couch.

"Talk to me, Adrial," Rowan urged. "You've blocked me out. I can't reach you with Spirit. You must talk to me." He spared a brief, fierce look at Bel. "We need Marissya."

Bel nodded, and his eyes lost focus as he reached across distance with a weave of Spirit. He was calling Marissya. "She comes," he said a moment later.

«*Shei'tani.*» Rain's voice sounded in Ellie's mind, strong and clear, but with an underlying tone of concern. «*We are on our way. Stay away from Adrial.*»

Stay away? She looked at Adrial and bit her lip. But he was in such pain. Her every instinct demanded that she help him. She stepped towards Adrial, only to find her way blocked by Belliard.

"*Nei*, Ellysetta. You must not defy the Feyreisen on this. Until we know what ails Adrial, you must not go near him."

"But—"

«*Ellysetta, obey me!*» There was no hint of the kind, courting suitor now. Only pure, autocratic king, accustomed to obedience, demanding it without question.

She flinched and glared at Bel, mostly because Rain wasn't there to be glared at, but also because she knew Bel had told on her. "I only want to help."

"You can help most by doing as your *shei'tan* tells you." Bel glanced at Rowan and Adrial, then added silently, «*Ellysetta, listen to me. You saw Adrial summoning Air without realizing it. He wields Earth, too, and some Fire. He could hurt you, badly. The shei'-dalin in you wants to help him. But you are also the Feyreisa. You cannot put yourself at risk.*»

With every muscle in her body protesting, Ellie backed away from Adrial. She hated the Fey's rigid belief that the Feyreisa must be protected from all harm, hated watching Adrial's pain and being refused even the chance to try to help him. The one thing she'd always been good at was easing the wounds and emotions of those she loved.

"Talk to me, Adrial," Rowan urged again.

"I can't think." Adrial pressed his hands over his eyes. "It's so flaming hard to think. My mind is going in a thousand different directions." He leaned his head back against the couch and gave a soft, despairing groan. "Last night it was as if there was someone else in my mind, and now it's as if part of me, part of my soul, is missing. I keep searching but I can't find it. I'm lost. Gods, I'm so lost." His eyes opened. Hollow, devastated eyes. He grabbed his brother's tunic. "Help me, Rowan."

Rowan was weeping. "I will, Adrial. I'll help you. On my soul, I swear it."

Ellie was weeping too. She had done this to him. Whatever now tortured Adrial, it had entered his soul because of her, because she in her ignorance and drunken daydreams had spun a weave that left him vulnerable.

It was too much. She couldn't just stand by and do nothing. Adrial's pain was ripping at her, tearing her heart. She stared hard at him, took a deep breath, and for the first time in her life, deliberately tried to use her magic. She thought about the shining threads she'd seen Marissya weave. Imagined glowing ribbons of light and power, weaving together in a net of healing magic. Imagined the net settling over Adrial. She concentrated, trying to turn the images into reality.

Nothing happened.

She tried to remember what she'd done last night, emboldened by pinalle and keflee, but it was all still so hazy. She hadn't intentionally woven magic, she'd just let her mind wander. Ellie cleared her thoughts and tried letting her mind wander now. She took deep, calming breaths and thought soothing things, calming thoughts, trying to project them onto Adrial.

Again, nothing happened.

What good was magic if she couldn't use it on demand? Frustration and empathetic pain beat at her. Adrial's Fey-beautiful face was carved with lines of anguish, his warrior's body shaking as he clung to his brother and wept, pleading for someone, anyone, to help him.

Biting her lip, desperate to repair the harm she'd somehow done him, Ellysetta closed her eyes and prayed. "Gods, please, help him. Make it stop. Take away the pain."

CHAPTER FOUR

"You took away his memories, Ellysetta."

"I said I was sorry!" Ellie met Rain's angry look without flinching. Well, with only a little flinch. Still, it was easier to face Rain's anger than the sad disappointment in Bel's face. Anger let her get angry back. Bel's disappointment made her feel like a belly-crawling *porgil,* as if she'd somehow betrayed him. "You told me not to go near him, and I didn't." She glared at Bel. She hadn't betrayed anyone. "I didn't! You never said I couldn't try to heal him."

When Marissya, Rain, and Dax had arrived, they'd found Adrial resting quietly, with no memories of the previous night or the emptiness that had haunted him this morning. The last eighteen bells were a blank slate in his mind, wiped completely clean. And when Marissya had made that announcement, a dozen pairs of accusing eyes had turned on Ellie, who had only been able to bite her lip and say, hopefully, "I'm sorry?"

It was, of course, the wrong thing to say. It started off a firestorm of recriminations from Rain, an angry tirade that was still going full steam even now, a full quarter bell later. Adrial had already returned to the palace, accompanied by Marissya, Dax, and Rowan. Teris and Cyr, two warriors from

Ravel's quintet, had returned to replace Adrial and Rowan. And Rain was still lecturing Ellie furiously.

She was starting to get angry. All this time, they'd been telling her, "Use your magic. Embrace your magic." She didn't think it was exactly fair of Rain to blame her for following his advice. She had taken away Adrial's pain, after all. Maybe not the way he would have liked, but the pain was gone and other than a few missing memories, Adrial was perfectly fine. She'd even healed him of all remnants of last night's excesses. Lady Marissya herself had said the healing had been masterfully done. You'd think *someone* would be at least a little grateful for that!

"I didn't mean to take his memories. I only meant to help him."

"You should not have touched him," Rain said for what must have been the twentieth time. "Not in *any* way!"

"You didn't specify. Weren't you the one who told me, 'When you wager with tairen, take care with your words'?"

His rush of anger was so hot, so fierce, Ellie half expected to see flames shooting out of his head. "That was a game! This could have cost your life. You knew what I meant when I said to stay away from him."

"I *knew*? Am I supposed to be able to read your mind now?"

"You could," he snarled. "If you would accept the bond between us, you would know every thought in my mind as if it were your own."

Angry that she was being yelled at for trying to help a friend, angrier still that she hadn't even been able to do *that* right, Ellie shouted at Rain, "Then maybe I don't want to accept this stupid bond! Maybe I don't want your thoughts in my brain. Maybe I prefer to keep my mind my own! *Maybe you should just go back to the Fading Lands and leave me alone!*"

The echoes of her shout rang in the dead silence that ensued. Every member of her quintet found a reason to inspect the ceiling, the floor, the bare walls.

Rain said softly, "You don't mean that, Ellysetta."

"Don't I?" she snapped, but already her flash of anger was

fading away. His voice had trembled ever so slightly when he'd said her name just then, and even if their bond hadn't allowed her to feel the uncertainty rising in him, that faint tremble would have given it away. She'd struck him deeply, in a spot vulnerable to no one but her, and she knew it.

Ellie closed her eyes, rubbing her temples. She was tired. Her head hurt. Her heart ached. She'd made a mess of things last night, and that mess had somehow resulted in Adrial's pain. Then she'd tried to heal Adrial, only to make a mess of that too. And now, with angry words that she didn't really mean, she'd hurt Rain as well. His pain was like a burning hollowness inside her, as real to her as if it were her own.

"I'm sorry," she said. "Of course I don't mean it. I'm not myself this morning." Then she laughed at the absurdity of that remark. "This morning? I haven't been myself since the day you came out of the sky and frightened me half to death." She crossed her arms over her chest and forced herself to meet his gaze. "Perhaps it's best if we don't go out today. We're both tired and angry. I don't think there's any point in being alone with each other."

"You are afraid." He sounded uncertain, as if he were groping to understand her mood. "I've been short-tempered with you, over things you didn't mean to do. It's only because of the danger to you that you don't yet even understand. Ellysetta, don't fear our bond. I know I'm not the easiest of men to accept. I know my own soul, and there are vast wells of darkness in it, but believe me when I say I want only your happiness and your well-being."

It was the first time Ellie had ever seen Rain's self-assurance rattled, and she didn't like it. He was her hero, the magic prince she'd dreamed of all her life, a legend larger than life. She was just a twenty-four-year-old woodcarver's daughter, a nobody. She should not have the power to make a legend tremble, and yet she did. She didn't want that power. She could not bear to see Rain humbled, especially not by her hand.

"Last night I didn't know what I was doing," she said. "This morning, I did. I tried to help Adrial, even knowing you didn't want me to." She met his eyes and shrugged. "The ironic thing is, when I tried to help him, nothing happened. It was only when I wasn't trying that I succeeded. What good is that to anyone?"

She grimaced and heaved a sigh. "In any case, it's I who owe the apology, not you. I shouldn't have tried to use powers I don't even understand. I shouldn't have done something you'd told me not to do—even if you weren't specific. And I shouldn't have said I wanted you to go away and leave me alone. I don't want that." She looked at her feet and scuffed the toe of one shoe against the wooden floor. "If you believed me, and you left, I'd regret it all my life."

She didn't hear him move. She only briefly saw the dark shadow of his boots step close to her own slippered feet before she felt his hands cupping her cheeks, long fingers sliding deep into her hair as he gently raised her face to his.

"I know this has all happened so fast," he said. "I know the demands we have placed on you are many and it is hard to become comfortable with so many changes in so short a time. And I am . . . short-tempered, even on my best days." His voice lowered to a husky whisper, and his thumbs stroked her cheekbones in a gentle caress. "I did not mean to shout at you nor wound your feelings. *Sieks'ta*, I have shamed myself. If it pleases you, *shei'tani*, I would begin this day anew. All harsh words forgotten."

"I would like that."

"*Doreh shabeila de*. So shall it be." He raised her hand to his lips and kissed it, a tender gesture that made her heart melt. "Come. Let us dance the skies together."

They flew for more than a bell, heading west and north, past Kingswood to the rolling farmlands of central Celieria, landing in a wooded glade near the tranquil, clear waters of the Sarne River.

Majestic fireoaks cast their cool shadows over the glade, and the long, flowing branches of water-loving Naidja's locks dangled in the gentle current like the water spirit's tresses for which they were named. Pink button daisies grew abundantly by the riverside, their slender white petals surrounding bright pink centers that filled the air with a delicate scent. Rain plucked a bouquet of the wildflowers for Ellysetta, and as she dabbled her toes in the cool water, he surprised her by braiding a dozen of the flowers into a daisy crown and placing it on her head.

"My queen," he declared.

She hunched her shoulders. "Not a very good one, I'm afraid."

"A warrior is not made in a day. Give yourself time, *shei'tani*. You will grow into your new role."

"Maybe. In twenty or thirty years." She toed a smooth river rock. "Assuming, of course, that I haven't single-handedly destroyed every Fey alliance in existence before then. And caused gods only know what harm to all my friends." She flopped back on the grassy bank and stared up at the brilliant blue Celierian sky above.

"Whatever ails Adrial is not your fault, Ellysetta. None of the rest of us suffered any ill effects from your weave save weariness and, for some, a little embarrassment. And the alliance isn't destroyed. King Dorian holds no grudge."

"That's what—one?—out of two hundred?" She flung an arm over her eyes and groaned. "I knew I shouldn't have gone to the palace last night. Even without that stupid weave, I knew the nobles would be offended by my presence among them. And they were. They resented having me there—and resented you for bringing me. They are peers of the realm, and no matter what you say, no matter what title you grant me, no matter even if you draped me from head to toe in Tairen's Eye crystals, I'm not their equal, nor ever shall be."

He sat up straight, flinging long swaths of midnight hair over his shoulder. "You are right. You are not their equal. You are my *shei'tani*. My truemate. And I am the Tairen Soul. By the customs of Celieria, the only man in that room last night who was my social equal was Dorian. The only person who was my true equal was you."

"How can you say that? I'm a nobody. I'm just a plain, simple woodcarver's daughter."

Rain laughed wryly. "*Ajiana*, you are far, far from simple."

"You know what I mean."

"I do. And you are wrong." He leaned over her and brushed a lock of hair from her face. "Ellysetta, the *shei'tanitsa* bond does not form between uneven halves. It only forms where there are two evenly matched parts of the same whole."

She sat up, drawing her legs in and wrapping her arms around them. "Well, that just proves my point. We're as far from being evenly matched as . . . as"—he searched for a suitably ridiculous comparison—"a tairen and Love the kitten!"

Rain's lips curved in a faint smile. His lavender eyes, which could at times seem so cold, glowed with warmth. His fingers brushed the smooth skin of her cheek in a soft caress. "You've only just begun to discover your many gifts. Would you berate a child for failing to read when first you set a book before her? Or for failing to walk when first you set her on her feet?"

"I'm not a child."

"In this you are. No one travels a new path without making an occasional misstep."

"A *misstep*? Missteps are little things. Like sewing a poor seam or burning dinner. Last night was a catastrophe. And then I compounded it by what I did to Adrial."

Rain's eyes grew shadowed and his smile faded. The hand by her cheek dropped away. "Ellysetta, I once scorched the world. Millions died by my hand—including thousands who were my friends and allies. *That* was a catastrophe. What happened last night was merely an embarrassment."

She felt the swell of horror and self-revulsion within him, and for just a moment she heard the echoes of the screams that haunted him before he clamped his barriers tight. Every day of his life, he suffered unimaginable guilt for what he'd done in a few irreversible bells of madness. And she had unwittingly compared one humiliating evening to that.

Tears burned in her eyes. Why did everything she said and did lately seem to come out wrong? "I'm sorry. I didn't mean it like that." She stared at her tightly clasped hands as they grew blurry and wavered. She could not bear to disappoint him or diminish herself in his eyes, yet at every turn she seemed to do exactly that. "You must think I'm a complete idiot." Her throat closed up, making her voice crack.

"*Nei, shei'tani.* I could never think that."

His voice was so soft, tender, and full of regret. The barriers she'd maintained all day to keep her emotions in check came crashing down. Tears poured from her eyes in a graceless flood. She covered her face and sobbed helplessly. Rain uttered a small, protesting sound and drew her into his arms, but that only made her tears fall faster.

"*Las, shei'tani. Nei avi.* Don't cry. *Ve khoda kem'san.*" Rain rocked Ellysetta gently and stroked the wild tangle of her hair. Her feelings of inadequacy and despair stabbed him like a thousand digger-thorns, the kind that burrowed deep in a man's flesh and released a painful, toxic venom.

Guilt assailed him. From the moment he'd claimed her, he had torn Ellysetta from the familiar comfort of her previous life, and thrust her—with far too little preparation—into the dangerous, unfriendly currents of his. Worse, he hadn't even told her why.

She'd done her best to hide her fears. She'd put on a brave face while she let strangers mold her into whatever queenly form they thought appropriate. As if she were not already queen enough to outshine them all.

He bent his head, resting his forehead against hers, and closed his eyes. All at once he knew Marissya was right. There could be no love or trust between Ellysetta and him until first there was truth.

He waited for her tears to stop, then from somewhere dredged up his own courage. "There is something I must tell you." He turned his head to kiss her palm, then rose to his feet, putting distance between them.

She rose too and started to follow him, then stopped when he turned to face her. He knew his expression had turned to stone. He could not say what he had to say without hiding behind the mask of Fey stoicism, but her uncertainty, the hesitation that dimmed her brightness, made his control falter.

"Ellysetta . . ."

She swallowed, holding his gaze even though he could see that her hands shook and her pulse beat rapidly beneath the delicate skin of her throat. "What is it, Rain?"

"Do you remember when I told you that the Eye of Truth sent me to find you?"

"Because I am your truemate."

Rain nodded. "*Aiyah*, I'm certain that was part of it, but in truth our matebond was an unexpected boon. I had consulted the Eye on another matter, and asked it to show me the solution to my problem. It showed me Celieria . . . and you."

Ellie took a half step backwards before stopping herself. "What problem did the Eye say I would solve, Rain?" There it was again, that quiet courage. She wanted to flee. He could feel the urge fluttering within her like a trapped bird. Yet she stood where she was.

There was no easy way to tell her, no segue to lessen the blow. So he gave her the truth bluntly. "That dream you told me about this morning—the one where you were standing in Fey'Bahren watching kitlings dying in the egg and you heard me vow to Sybharukai that I would find a way to save them—that was no dream. The tairen *are* dying, Ellysetta, and if we cannot find a way to stop it, the Fey will die with them. I asked the Eye for the key to saving the tairen and the Fey, and it sent me to you."

Selianne pushed open her home's small side gate and walked through the tidy garden, untying the strings of her straw bonnet as she approached the lace-curtained kitchen door. Her troubled thoughts returned as they had all afternoon to Ellysetta and her pending marriage to Rain Tairen Soul. Though Selianne could see Ellie was all but glowing with happiness, she simply couldn't bring herself to share that joy.

Ellie was too dear a friend, and Selianne had read too much about the dangers of magic and the dread power of the infamous

Rain Tairen Soul for her to consider this marriage a happy occasion. Far better if Ellie *had* wed that brute Den Brodson—or even the lecherous old gilding Master Norble Weazman. At least the harm *they* could do would only be physical. The Fey could control people's minds—and gods only knew what else—with their terrible magic.

Selianne opened the side door and let herself into her small, sunny kitchen. "Mother?" she called as she hung her bonnet on a peg by the door. "Bannon, Cerlissa, Mama's home." The kitchen was empty, and she couldn't hear the children. "Mother?"

She walked down a short hallway to the main room and froze in sudden fear. A man stood over the sleeping bodies of her children as they lay on a blanket laid out before the hearth. Her mother stood motionless beside the hallway entrance, wearing a vacant look.

The man turned, his vivid blue-green eyes finding Selianne without hesitation, and a wave of ice washed over her. Though she could place neither his name nor his face, the sight of him seemed dreadfully familiar—like a vision from one of the dark nightmares that had plagued her these past few days since the Fey had come to Celieria.

A smile spread across his handsome face. "Ah, Selianne, there you are. We were beginning to worry."

Her hand clutched at her chest where a cold ache began to throb. She took a frantic half step towards her children, then gave a choked cry and stopped again at the sight of the wavy black blade in the man's hand, its sharp point gleaming a deadly threat.

"Who are you?" Her voice shook with fear. "What do you want?"

"What do I want?" The man's eyes darkened to a terrifying shade of black, endless, bottomless, soulless black that began to sparkle with malevolent red lights. "Why, you, my pet."

Before Selianne could react, her mother stepped in front of her, lifted an open palm, and blew a cloud of sparkling white dust in Selianne's face. She gasped in shock, then choked as the powder filled her lungs.

A strange, sapping lethargy crept over her. Her vision blurred, and she swayed. Her hands reached out, and she heard her own voice, sounding curiously distant, mumbling in confusion, "Mama?"

Kolis Manza watched the girl succumb to the *somulus* powder, and despite last night's endless orgy, he felt the familiar stirring of desire. She was undeniably lovely, with her blond hair and deep blue eyes. Even amongst the beauties of the High Mage's palace, she would hold her own.

"Come here, Selianne." Patient, smiling, he waved her towards him. Unlike her Eld-born mother, she'd not been soul-bound in childhood, so Kolis used drugs and careful weaves of Spirit and Azrahn to place Selianne in a dream state and plant directives that would guide her thoughts and actions without her knowledge. Like the directive that amplified her fear and distrust of the Fey, and the directive that would soon command her to deliver Kolis's wedding present to her friend, and the one that brought her to him now. In her current trancelike state, she knew and obeyed her master, even though he'd carefully removed all memory of his visits from her conscious mind.

Beautiful eyes unfocused, she approached, stopping only when he indicated she should and obediently holding out her left arm. On all three of their previous meetings, he had blooded her from that arm—and after the first blooding he'd taken the pleasure of drinking directly from her flesh after opening the vein with his dagger.

"No, my dear." Gently he clasped her hand and raised it to his lips, pressing a kiss on her fingers. "I'm in the mood for a change." He guided her hand to the ties of her bodice, accompanying the gesture with a weave of Spirit that roused memories of her husband from her mind.

Selianne's lips curved in a sensual smile as she loosened the ties that held the fabric of her gown. Soft, pale flesh found freedom. Kolis raised his dagger to one plump breast and sliced the tender skin beside her nipple as he murmured the ritual words. When the jewel in the pommel glowed a rich, satisfied red, he replaced the blade with his lips, suckling her, laughing as the sweet, warm taste of mother's milk joined the salty, sweet flavor of her blood.

***

"The tairen are dying and the Fey, with all your vast powers, can't find a way to save them—but you think *I* can?" Stunned, Ellie slumped back against the thick, knobby trunk of the fireoak behind her. Her fingers dug deep into the hard furrows of the bark. She stared at Rain in utter shock. Whatever she'd been expecting him to say, it hadn't been that. "How can you possibly believe such a thing?"

"It isn't as farfetched as it seems," he replied. "What's killing the tairen attacks only kitlings in the egg. None but tairen can enter the nesting lair, so I am the only Fey to set foot in Fey'Bahren since the Mage Wars. You, however, are my true-mate, and the tairen will welcome you as kin. You can get close to the eggs, as none of our *shei'dalins* have been permitted to do."

"And what good will that do? I'm no *shei'dalin*."

"Ellysetta, you healed Bel's soul with a touch. You mitigated my own torment with a simple embrace. Marissya is our most powerful living *shei'dalin*, yet in a thousand years she's never achieved so much. And you did it without even trying—and with no training of any kind. There's no doubt in my mind that if anyone has the power to save the tairen, you do."

She stared at him, aghast. "I can't even get through a state dinner without mucking it up. Instead of saving the tairen, it's more likely I'd doom them to a speedier extinction!"

"You just need to learn control, *shei'tani*. I can help teach you that."

Bright Lord save her. "I really don't think that sounds like a good idea. Isn't there some other way? Maybe you could go back to this Eye of Truth and tell it you want another answer."

Rain gave a wry laugh. "*Nei*. Even if the world itself hung in the balance, I doubt I could summon the courage to ask the Eye for another seeing. It wasn't pleased with me the last time, and the Eye has a very . . . effective way of making its displeasure known."

A vision of Rain screaming in torment flashed through Ellysetta's mind. A muted memory of pain stung her senses. Her hands curled instinctively into fists and her spine went stiff. "This Eye . . . it *hurt* you when you asked it for help?" Her voice was low, almost a growl.

The humor dancing at the edges of Rain's mouth deepened to satisfaction, and his eyes began to glow. He closed the distance between them. "I did not ask. I demanded. Quite rudely. The Eye punished me for my arrogance, as was its right." He brought her fists to his lips and kissed the clenched fingers. "Look at you, ready to fight the Eye of Truth, one of the Fading Lands' greatest powers, for the harm you think it did me. And you still believe you are a coward?" He smiled and shook his head. "It may take more to rouse the tairen in you, *shei'tani*, but never doubt it lives in your soul, and it is fierce indeed."

Pride and approval radiated from him, wrapping her in warmth and soothing away her fierce reaction to the Eye's rough treatment of him. But even his approval could not soothe the choking tightness in her chest. The fates of both the tairen and the Fey rested on her shoulders, and he expected her to somehow miraculously save them.

"You do not stand alone in this, Ellysetta," Rain said, clearly sensing the emotions swirling about her like a fearful cloud. "This task belongs to both of us. All I ask is that you help me find a way to save my people."

She looked up into his beloved face, so beautiful, so sincere. All her life she'd dreamed of him, all her life she'd wept for the sorrows he'd endured and prayed that the gods would give his soul peace. And now here he was, standing before her, asking for her help.

How could she possibly deny him?

She drew a deep breath, wrapped what little courage she possessed tight around her like a warming shawl, and nodded. "I'll do everything I can, Rain, though I'm not at all sure what help that will be."

"Approaching the line is the first victory of battle, *shei'tani*. Learn to celebrate your small braveries. They light the way to greater courage." He raised her hands to his lips. "It is my honor to be your *chatok*, your mentor, in this first dance."

Despite her knocking knees, she firmed her jaw and lifted her chin. "So where do we start, *chatok*?"

His low laugh rippled across her senses. "As with all adventures, we start with the first step. Something small, something simple. Before you can truly control magic, you must first learn its patterns. We'll start with the commonest patterns of all: the inherent magic that exists in all living things."

Her brows rose. "You believe all living things possess magic?"

He smiled. "Of course, Ellysetta. Life is the magic. It is Fire, Earth, Air, Water, Spirit, and Azrahn combined. Energy, substance, consciousness, and soul."

"This tree"—she pointed to the broad trunk of the fireoak behind her—"is conscious?"

"Not as you and I would know it, but *aiyah*, it is. Do not all trees know to send their roots towards the best source of water? Do they not all bend their branches to find sunlight?"

"That's just the natural way of things. Branches grow where there is more sunlight because they cannot survive without it, not because they want to."

"Have you never touched a thing and felt its magic?"

"No."

"I have. When I was a boy, just before my Soul Quest, when my own magic was awakening within me, I spent bell after bell walking the streets of Dharsa and the plains of Corunn, touching all manner of things to see if I could detect the magic within them, to see if I could make them respond to my presence."

She tried to imagine Rain Tairen Soul as a boy, but couldn't. "Did they respond?"

"*Aiyah*." He smiled, a tiny echo of a long-ago boy's satisfaction. "Even then, before I had tapped the wellspring of the Tairen Soul power within me, they knew and welcomed me.

The trees would rustle their leaves. The grass would bend towards me."

"It could have been the wind."

He gave her a disgusted look. "How can you be such a devotee of Feytales yet still be such a nonbeliever? It was not the wind, I assure you. Here. I will demonstrate." He moved around her in one graceful motion and laid a hand on the rough trunk of the fireoak. His eyes didn't glow the slightest bit to indicate he was working magic, but as Ellie watched, the thick canopy of branches bent slowly downward, towards him. All the other trees continued to rustle in the wind. "You see?"

"You aren't using magic to make the branches do that?" She had to ask, just to be sure, even though she could detect nothing.

"*Nei*. I am just touching the tree and asking it to acknowledge me, to share its magic with me." He took his hand from the trunk, and the branches sprang back into place. "Come. You try it. Put your hand on the tree like this." He guided her hand to the tree and gently pressed her palm against the bark. "What do you feel?"

"Bark."

He sighed. "Besides that." He eyed her sternly. "You think you are funny."

She gave him a small grin. "That was funny. Admit it."

"I admit nothing. Be serious. Just for a moment, *pacheeta*, then you can poke fun at me some more."

She smoothed the humor off her face and cleared her throat. "All right." She stretched out her fingers and pressed her hand more firmly against the trunk of the tree. "I'm being serious, but I don't feel anything but a tree."

"Close your eyes. Concentrate. Think about where your hand meets the tree, about what you feel beneath your fingertips, beyond the bark. There's energy, magic. It's like a pulsating glow, a soft light. It's warm and alive. Can't you feel it?"

"No." There was the sound of the river in her ears, the feel of tree bark beneath her hand, the cool breath of wind on her face. But she didn't feel or see any pulsating magical life force emanating from the tree.

"You're cluttering your mind with other thoughts, Ellysetta. You're still too focused on the physical. Block out what you hear, what you feel through physical touch. Those things are unimportant." His voice dropped to a low murmur, and he began speaking to her in Feyan, a chant of words she didn't completely understand but found oddly calming all the same.

The sounds of the river faded away. The breath of the wind on her skin was only a faint, distant sensation, soothing, relaxing. She could no longer feel the bark of the tree beneath her hand. She was floating in a well of warm darkness that changed slowly to a landscape of glowing lights pulsing with a multitude of colors and intensities. She could make out the shapes of everything around her, but it was as if she were seeing them through different eyes. Rain stood before her, a shimmering rainbow of lights—red, white, lavender, green, blue, black—all dimmed as if he were wrapped in a dark veil.

Beside her, the fireoak stood tall and strong. It was no pulsating glow. It was a brilliant light, blazing with vibrant shades of green and blue, marbled with veins of lavender, red, and black. It was beautiful, glorious.

"Do you see it?" Rain asked.

"Yes." Her tongue felt thick, as if she were trying to speak while half asleep.

"Do you see where your hand touches the tree?"

"Yes."

"Then call the light of the tree to your hand. Imagine it flowing into your fingers and up your arm. Ask the light to come to you, to share its magic with you."

With her eyes still closed, she looked at the glowing life beneath her hand. She wanted to know what that brightness would feel like rushing through her own veins. She opened her senses and asked it to flood her with its beauty.

The light of the tree rushed towards her in a blinding flash, shooting up her arm. Startled, Ellie cried out and yanked her hand away from the trunk. Her eyes flew open. Rain leapt forward to snatch her to his chest and fling a protective barrier around them as fireoak branches snapped and rained down from above, blanketing the ground around Ellie and Rain.

When the shower of tree limbs ceased, Rain looked at the destruction at his feet and glanced up at the tree. Not a single branch remained. The once-lush fireoak was now a thick, denuded pole thrusting up from the ground.

"I think we need to teach you moderation," he murmured.

"What happened?" Ellie looked at the tree in dismay. "Did I do that?"

"*Nei*, it wasn't really you, Ellysetta. You weren't weaving magic. You only asked the tree to respond to you. But you must have asked very, very strongly." He shook his head.

"Can you fix it?" She couldn't bear to leave the poor tree like this.

"*Aiyah.*"

As Ellie watched, Rain's eyes began to glow with summoned power. He gestured with his hands, and silvery white threads of what Ellie now knew was Air wrapped around one of the branches and raised it high overhead. Bright green Earth threads knit the branch back in place. Rain continued, branch by branch, until the fireoak was once more whole and undamaged.

When he was done, Ellie thanked him and whispered a heartfelt apology to the tree, not daring to touch it again lest she feel it quivering like a frightened puppy.

"That was good," Rain said.

"Good? I almost killed the poor tree!"

"But you did not. I want you to try weaving magic."

"I don't think that's a good idea. I just destroyed a tree without even trying to weave magic. I shudder to think what I might destroy if I *was* trying . . ."

"*Shei'tani*, trust me. You promised me you would accept instruction."

"I promised to accept instruction when we reached the Fading Lands," she countered. "We're not there yet."

He opened his mouth, then shut it. A rueful smile tilted up one corner of his mouth. "When you wager with tairen, take care with your words." Then his expression grew serious. "This is important, Ellysetta. I will not allow you to harm yourself or anything else, but you need to understand what magic you possess, and you need to learn to control it. Both our bond and the tairen depend on it."

She hesitated in indecision. On the one hand, she was terrified of the magic she seemed to possess. On the other hand, she was desperate to learn how to control it so she could stop herself from weaving it accidentally or with unexpected consequences as she had last night and with Adrial this morning.

"All right," she agreed. "Teach me."

CHAPTER FIVE

Terkaz, Blood Drinker, slake your thirst.
Frathmir, Flesh Eater, feed your hunger.
Boraz, Bone Grinder, mill your dust.
Choutarre, Soul Taker, claim your due.

—Feraz Witchspell

"We'll start with something simple," Rain said. "You've already shown you are strong in Air, and it is weightless and easy enough to direct for what I have in mind. Sit here." He indicated a grassy spot beside the Sarne River.

Ellysetta sat where he directed.

"Now we'll borrow a little bit of the river and shelter both it and us from the current and the breeze." He lifted his hands and wove a curtain of still Air around them and a small portion of the river near Ellie's feet. She started to dip her toe in, but he stopped her.

"*Nei*, do not touch the water. The surface must be perfectly still for this exercise." His eyes glowed faintly and a pale blue light shone around his hands. A moment later, the small portion of the river before them was smooth as glass. "There. Now I want you to try to weave enough of a breeze to make the water ripple."

"How do I do that?"

"Find the silence inside you. Just a moment ago, when you asked the fireoak tree to respond to you, you found the silence and through it you could see the weaves that make up all living creatures. The silence is the source from which your magic springs. You call the magic from there and let it flow through your body. And when it fills you and becomes you, then you can direct it as you do your own limbs. The process takes effort at first, but eventually the path will become as easy to find when you seek it out as it currently is when you travel it instinctively."

Once again he guided her through the meditative exercise to find the silent, shining place where the world was lit with glowing threads of magic.

"All around you is Air. You will see it as a soft whiteness. Summon it to you."

"I see it, but how do I summon it?"

"Much the same way as you asked the fireoak to share its essence with you. Open yourself to it. Imagine that you are a cistern and magic is the water that must flow to fill you."

Ellie gave it a try, but no shining white light answered her call. "It's not working."

"I will show you what I mean; then you can try again."

The shadowy world evaporated in an instant when Rain set aside his sword belts and settled behind her. He pulled her back against him. Tingling warmth raced up her spine as his body pressed against hers. He surrounded her. His thighs cradled hers, his arms covered her own, his fingers interleaved with her own.

"What are you doing?" Her voice came out a bit thready.

"If you were my *chadin*, my pupil, I would be able to enter your mind to observe your efforts and guide you. Since our bond is currently unfulfilled, I cannot enter your mind yet, but by holding you close this way, you will be able to feel what I do as I call and weave Air. I'm hoping you will be able to emulate my efforts and perform this exercise on your own." Against her cheek, she could feel him smile. "And besides, *shei'tani*, not a moment passes that I do not seek an opportunity and excuse to touch you."

Pleasure shuddered over her. "If you think I'll be able to concentrate with you snuggled up against me like this, think again," she warned him.

His lips brushed her ear. "It is good to know you are not un-affected by my touch." His low voice whispered across her skin, echoed in her mind. "But do try to concentrate, *ajiana*. When we are done, I will reward us both."

Her heart began to pound. How did he expect her to focus when he said things like that?

He began to murmur in Feyan, quiet, liquid syllables, words she couldn't make out that played in her mind like a peaceful song. The sound of his voice flowed over her and warmth seeped into her skin, making her feel drowsy. His fingers, long and capable, stroked her hands. The starch in her spine wilted, and she relaxed against him, tilting her head back against his shoulder.

"Now, Ellysetta, I will call Air. Can you feel it gathering in-side me?"

"Yes." The Air stirred almost imperceptibly as it responded to Rain's call. The magic didn't come to his hands, as she had always thought it would. Instead, it filled him from within, welling up and permeating his body, until the Tairen's Eye signet on his right hand began to glow faintly.

"I do not need much Air. The strength of the weave de-pends on the amount of magic called and the way in which it is woven. For now, I only need a gentle breeze, so I call just a little Air and release it in a loose weave. All the elements have their own natural patterns. Weaving magic is learning to bend those patterns to a particular purpose."

Ellie felt the power concentrate in his hands, fed from the inner spring within him. His pale hands grew luminous as the energies gathered in anticipation of release.

"A breeze is a soft, sinuous pattern, with very little distur-bance in the threads." His fingers flicked out, and thin fila-ments of white energy flowed out in lazily undulating lines. When the weave touched the stilled portion of the river, the water's surface rippled in response.

"Did you feel how I released the Air?"

"It felt like a sigh."

"*Aiyah*. Small Water weaves feel like laughter. Small Fire

feels like a blush. Your mind instinctively knows the patterns, you simply must learn how to weave them at will." With his hands still touching hers, he called Water and once more stilled the pond. "Now you try to ripple the water's surface."

Ellie took a breath, clenched her jaw, and tried to call the Air to fill her.

"Do not fight for it. You want to summon the Air, not overpower it. Draw it to you. Breathe it in." His fingers stroked hers.

She tried to do as he said, but nothing happened.

"Keep trying," Rain insisted. "Imagine the wind blowing past you. When learning to call magic, it helps to imagine the element in its natural state."

Ellie concentrated. Once again Rain murmured his encouragement. She imagined a breeze blowing across her face and through her hair. She imagined herself breathing the Air into her body until her lungs filled, imagined breathing it back out across the river, making the water ripple. Again, nothing happened.

"I can't do it."

"You're still fighting your magic. Relax, *shei'tani*. Let it fill you." His hands moved down to her waist. "Breathe," he whispered in her ear.

She dragged a deep breath into her lungs.

"Good. Now feel the magic gather within you." He stroked her belly, making tight heat curl within her.

Hunger was welling up inside her far faster than magic, and suddenly all she could think about was carnal weaves and the hard heat of Rain's body pressed against her back.

"Let the magic flow throughout your body until it becomes as much a part of you as your own flesh and blood." Rain's hands stroked upward on either side of her rib cage, brushing against the sides of her breasts in a way that made her breath catch in her throat.

She almost moaned aloud. *Dear gods, please let me complete this exercise before I leap upon him and demand a different kind of lesson.*

"And now," Rain said, "release it."

Flames shot from her fingertips. Water sizzled, and the river's surface rippled.

There was a small silence. "Well, *shei'tani*, you do wield Fire, after all."

Ellie refused to look at him. "That wasn't Air. I thought I called Air."

"You did. I felt it gather in you, but you obviously released Fire instead. I must have put the idea in your mind when I told you that Fire feels like a blush."

No, Ellie thought. He'd put the idea in her mind when he was running his hands all over her body and breathing in her ear.

"Or," Rain said, "I put the idea in your mind when I was stroking you."

She swallowed. "I thought you said you couldn't read my mind."

He laughed softly against her cheek. "That's not what I'm reading." His hands cupped her breasts through the warm, corseted silk of her new gown, and his thumbs brushed across the tight, sensitive peaks of her breasts.

Tongues of flame seared her. Ellysetta gasped. "Rain . . ."

"I think we are done with our first lesson, and I did promise to reward us both." His voice dropped to a husky murmur and his lips tracked tingling kisses down her throat. The Air weave around them dispersed, and the warm summer breeze swirled over them, fragrant with the scent of daisies and the verdant freshness of the glade. He lowered her to the soft, thick grass and leaned over her. His long, dark hair draped down around them like veils of ebony silk. Warmth infused the pale perfection of his face, melting all remnants of cold aloofness, leaving stark, burning beauty, unshielded need, and the fiery intensity of his eyes.

His hand trailed up her arm, the fingers light, dancing across her skin from elbow to shoulder, around the bend, then down to brush the soft curve of her breast beneath the saffron silk of her gown. The pad of his finger traced a spiral of increasingly small circles on the silk, traveling a scintillating path up the gentle swell. Anticipation tightened in her belly with each completed circle.

«Ku shalah aiyah to nei, shei'tani,» he whispered in her mind. Bid me yes or no. Each word was a caress as erotic as the sweet torment of his circling finger.

Never in her life had any man stirred her senses, not even the most celebrated Dazzles of the court over whom so many other young Celierian maidens sighed. No man until Rain. And with him, it was as if all the longing of the ages had been stored up inside her, waiting for his arrival to break free. One look, one touch, one whisper of his voice, and Ellysetta, who had never known the slightest desire for any man before him, went up in flames. Already she was aching for him with the same fierce passion that had fueled her weave last night.

Bid him yes or no, he asked. As if she could ever—would ever—give any possible answer but one.

"Aiyah." Consent emerged as a thready whisper, barely audible. The hunger was so strong, she could scarcely breathe. She lifted her hands to his hair, filled her palms with black silk, wished she were brave enough to reach for more.

"You have no idea the beauty that fills my eyes when I look upon you." With infinite care, he drew back the edges of her bodice to bare the soft fullness of her breasts. His fingers traced the contours of the small globes, then cupped them gently, thumbs whispering over pink nipples. The peaks leapt instantly to attention. His gaze flicked up, burning with lavender fire, locking with hers in a look so deep it shook her to her core. *«You dazzle me, Ellysetta.»*

Her mouth went dry. Liquid fire gathered in a rush of desire.

His gaze dropped to her lips. His mouth followed, pressing nibbling kisses. The tip of his tongue traced the seam of her lips, teasing, tasting. The warm, moist strokes made her gasp in delight, and he deepened the kiss, exploring the secrets of her mouth, laying claim to them. He took her breath into his lungs and gave her back his own.

Still his fingers circled her breast, teasing, tormenting. Her hips shifted restlessly, her arms wrapped around his shoulders, clinging tight. Her back arched, pressing her breast more fully against his palm in a silent plea. «*Rain . . . Rain, please.*»

"I heard your thoughts last night when you spun your Spirit weave," he whispered. "I heard what you said. I felt each word like a brand on my skin." His lips found the pulse point on her throat and pressed a kiss there.

She shivered as the wicked warmth of his tongue stroked the hollow of her throat. For once, the mention of her disastrous weave did not embarrass her. All she could think of were the feelings infusing her body, the wild need rising inside her. "What did I say?"

"You said, 'I want.'" His lips tracked up her throat, tracing a fiery path across the soft skin.

Oh, yes, she wanted. Him and no other. She always had. She always would.

"'I need.'"

He took her hand and guided it to his own chest. Earth magic tingled in electric arcs. Black leather vanished. The burning heat of pale, luminous Fey flesh filled her palms. She ran her hands over his chest, relearning every curve and rock-hard muscle she had discovered last night, testing the eager leap of his flat nipples as her nails drew lightly across them.

"'I ache.'"

Slowly—far too slowly—he drew back. The silk of his hair whispered across her skin. Cooler air rushed in where his warmth had been, sending a fresh flood of tingling sensation sweeping across her exposed skin. Her breasts felt swollen, the nipples taut and begging as his hands continued their teasing erotic play.

"'I burn.'"

Keeping his eyes locked with hers, he bent his head to her breast, and despite the flags of heat that flooded her cheeks, she couldn't look away. She watched him take her in his mouth. Oh, gods. Her lashes fluttered down as her eyes rolled back in exquisite pleasure. Her hands came up to clutch his shoulders, holding him fast as he worked all manner of enchantment that needed no aid of magic.

She was on fire. Living flame beneath his hands.

«*Burn with me.*» He sang in vivid tones that reverberated through her being. Incandescent notes of dazzling hues, so vivid each was a sensory explosion. Tairen song. His song. Resonating in her soul.

Undulating waves of Spirit burst from his hands, flying out in spiraling, rapidly accelerating weaves that spun away reality and replaced it with a flawless illusion of the two of them lying together in a lush riverside glade, surrounded by the rainbow-tinted mists of a dozen spectacular waterfalls. Gone were her saffron dress and his black leathers. Their bodies were naked and twined together, and there was no guilt, no stern Celierian modesty, no shame or regret to their passion.

She feasted on the sight of his body, so pale, so perfect, sinewed with ropes of lean, defined muscle beneath luminous skin. She stroked his flesh and breathed in the rich aroma of magic and Rain, a sensory memory she would never forget.

He was everything she'd ever dreamed of—every hope, every wish, every secret prayer she had ever whispered to the gods. A fierce, relentless warrior, bred for battle. A deadly defender, willing to sacrifice his immortal life to protect those in his care. A noble hero, a passionate lover. And when he looked at her with such intensity and devotion, he made her feel as if she, simple, plain Ellysetta Baristani, was more dazzling than the sun, more beautiful than every star in the heavens.

When she was with him like this, she could almost feel the retreat of the ominous shadows that had haunted her all her life.

In the Spirit weave that bound them, his body moved upon hers, slid into hers. She felt her own body stretch to accommodate the thick, burning length of him, the muscles clasping him tight, drawing him in deeper. He filled her utterly and perfectly, as if some long-absent part of her had finally found its place and made her complete.

Slowly, teasingly, he began to move. A long, leisurely withdrawal that made her moan a protest, a quick, surging plunge that made her gasp. "Rain!"

He laughed, loving the feel of her, the wild abandon of her response. Both in his weave and in his arms, the electric arc of passion leapt from her flesh to his, a rush of sensation and emotion that built between them with harmonic intensity. For all her innocence and tight-laced Celierian upbringing, she could not deny her hunger for him, nor stifle her body's overwhelming response. For him there was no greater joy than watching her bright, verdant eyes cloud with pleasure and feeling the rippling shudders of her body as a climax seized her. His naked chest pressed against hers. The soft fullness of her breasts was crushed against him. Skin to skin, he could feel what he did to her, both within the weave and without, and nothing—not even the thrill of soaring the freedom of the skies—had ever felt so magnificent.

Each thrust of his hips echoed the melody of his song. Pleasure and torment swelled in heightening waves. Even though he held the weave, each touch, each gasp, each shuddering explosion felt vivid and real, shaking him to the core of his soul.

He took her mouth as his Spirit body drove her to one last, powerful climax. His own control shattered, and his body clenched taut. Fierce shudders swept over him as passion exploded in blinding waves.

Together they lay there, breathless, dazed, their bodies still quaking with tremor after tremor until the wild beating of their hearts finally slowed. Above them, the summer sky filled their eyes with a bright, clear, cloudless blue, and the Great Sun blazed with searing intensity.

<hr />

Kolis Manza drew privacy wards around his bedchamber at the Inn of the Blue Pony and removed the black Mage blade from its sheath at the small of his back. On the table beside him lay a vial of blood from one of the dead whores, her severed finger, and a small silver dish. Kolis speared the finger on the dagger's sharp point, drizzled the blood over both blade and finger, then set the grisly offering on the floor with a grimace.

He'd much rather open the gateway without the paraphernalia, but that required such an immense blast of Azrahn that every Fey within a five-mile radius would come running to find and slay the summoner. Though Kolis longed for the day the Mages could cease their clandestine activities and rule openly, he was too much a realist to fancy a forty-to-one fight between himself and the Fey.

Stepping back, well clear of the silver dish, he muttered the words of the Feraz witchspell he'd long ago committed to memory: "Terkaz, Blood Drinker, slake your thirst. Frathmir, Flesh Eater, feed your hunger. Boraz, Bone Grinder, mill your dust. Choutarre, Soul Taker, claim your due." He took another long step back and completed the invocation. "Guardians of the Well, I summon you. Accept this offering and grant safe passage through your domain."

Within the silver dish, the finger and the pooled blood began to smolder. A small black pinprick formed in the air above. Dark shadows swept out of the tiny opening, hissing and circling around the offering. Demons. The incorporeal forms of the Guardians of the Well of Souls swirled and then swooped upon the offering like ravening beasts, demon fangs clicking, demon mouths slurping. In seconds the bloody finger was gone, flesh, blood, and bone utterly consumed, the black dagger drained of one of its captive souls. And behind the spot where the offering had been gaped an expanding dark hole in space, a gateway into a black nothingness that flickered with red lights.

The Well of Souls lay open, and Kolis felt the now-familiar tingling weakness in his limbs as trickles of the pure, untapped power of the Well escaped into the living world. He was not worried that the Fey would sense it. Tests over the years had proven they could not. Demons could, of course, but then demons were captive spirits summoned from the Well of Souls. If a doorway to the Well opened on the other side of the world, demons would know.

As he approached the gateway, Kolis glanced back to verify that the oilskin pouch containing a second offering lay on the nightstand where he'd left it for one of his *umagi* to activate when he returned. As the Eld had learned over the years, the Guardians were capricious, and without the offering and Feraz witchspells, exits from the Well never opened precisely where they were supposed to.

Retrieving his dagger from the floor, Kolis stepped through the gateway into the blackness, then turned to murmur a Feraz witch-word. Behind him, the doorway collapsed upon itself, and all light from the outer world winked out. Utter blackness enveloped him, snuggling close like a cold lover. He stood for several moments to let his eyes adjust to the dark. The jewel in the pommel of his dagger glowed like a red beacon in the darkness, casting a circle of dim light around him, illuminating a path through the shadowy realm.

He held the glowing dagger high and summoned the sweet coolness of Azrahn. His eyes closed in brief pleasure as the dark power swept through him. Azrahn, the second mystic, the soul magic, the unmaker, the most powerful of all six magics. The Fey feared and shunned it. They were foolish and shortsighted. The Elden Mages, on the other hand, embraced and mastered Azrahn, and they would triumph because of it.

Kolis reached out with Azrahn and guided himself through the Well towards Eld. The journey would not take long. Three bells at the most.

<hr/>

Ellysetta and Rain were in the air over Celieria City, circling round for their descent when the debilitating weakness swept over Ellysetta. She slumped in the saddle, only the leather restraining straps holding her in place while her fingers clutched feebly for a handhold. Like the deadly venom of an ice spider, the paralyzing cold sapped all strength from her body and left her limbs shivering helplessly. Her heart pounded with low, sluggish thuds, each beat an aching blow against the frozen drum of her chest.

Even in tairen form Rain sensed her emotions, because his wings suddenly spread wide to slow their flight and his great tairen head twisted around so he could fix one glowing, pupil-less eye upon her. *«Ellysetta? What is it? What is wrong?»*

Already the icy feeling had diminished and strength was returning to her limbs. *«I'm fine,»* she assured him. *«It's nothing. Just another ghost treading on my grave.»*

«That seemed much worse than before.»

With the knot of fear still lodged in her throat, she couldn't lie. *«It was.»* Much worse, in fact, as if some previously existing buffer had been peeled away so the frightening sensation could access her more directly.

Rain's tairen face took on an expression she could only call grim. *«Hold on, shei'tani.»* He waited just long enough for her fingers to tighten on the saddle; then his wings tucked in and he plummeted the remaining distance directly towards the small, bricked garden at the back of her family's home. He Changed in midair while she, with a little cry of surprise, slipped down a slide of Air into the waiting arms of her quintet.

"I want twenty-five-fold shields around this house all hours of the day—and around her whenever she goes out," Rain commanded the quintet as he strode the short distance to her side. "The wandering soul attacked her again." To Ellysetta, he added in an equally unequivocal command, "You will tell us whenever you feel this thing again. Something is hunting you, *shei'tani*, and my instincts tell me these wandering souls of yours are somehow related."

"All right." She met his fierce gaze and wondered how much of her fear showed on her face. Always before, she'd dismissed the shivery feelings as frightening but inconsequential episodes—nothing nearly as troubling or terrifying as her nightmares or seizures. But after last night's terrible dream, she couldn't hide behind that self-deception anymore.

You'll kill them, girl. You'll kill them all. Gooseflesh prickled Ellie's skin as the Shadow Man's mockingly triumphant declaration echoed in her ears.

What if she wasn't demon possessed as Mama feared, or some Fey foundling hunted by the Mages as Rain believed? What if the Shadow Man had been telling the truth—that she was an unwitting carrier of some malignant evil—and all the recent events were just signs of that cursed seed within her finally coming to life?

All her life she'd sensed a dark, fierce something deep inside her, a terrible something that frightened her even more than the Shadow Man. She'd battled it from earliest childhood when the terrible seizures and visions consumed her. Even now, she could feel it, crouching, a subtle tension coiled deep and tight, waiting for an opportunity to spring.

"Oh, Ellie, good, you're back." Mama's voice drew Ellysetta away from her dark thoughts. She looked up to find her mother standing by the back door. "Master Fellows is here."

"Thank you, Mama." Ellie forced a smile to her lips. "I'll be right in." She took a deep breath, lifted her chin, and headed inside to greet the queen's Master of Graces.

When Rain would have followed Ellysetta inside, Bel put a restraining hand on his arm. "A moment, Rain," he murmured. He waited until the door closed behind Ellysetta before speaking. "I've not heard from the two warriors I sent to Norban."

Rain's spine stiffened. "Sian and Torel?"

"They've not checked in since yesterday afternoon, nor answered my weaves."

Rain knew the two Fey. Both were responsible men and good warriors. Not likely to miss a scheduled report—and even less likely to ignore their commander when he called. "Keep trying. Torel's brother is with us in the city, is he not?

"*Aiyah*, Tiar is here."

"Have Marissya go to him." If Torel was alive, Marissya would sense feelings along the link where even brothers could sense only thoughts. If there was nothing, Tiar would need the comfort of a *shei'dalin* to help him control his grief until he returned to the Fading Lands where he could deal with his loss properly. "And dispatch a quintet to Norban to look for them."

Rain joined Ellysetta inside. Master Fellows, the queen's elegant, impeccably dressed Master of Graces, was already there, murmuring his approval as he circled Ellysetta and eyed her saffron gown with a critical eye.

"Not bad, my lady. Not bad at all. Some might say the clothes don't make the queen, but as I've always maintained, they certainly do help her radiance to shine." Gaspare Fellows tutted over the dagger at her waist. "That, however, I recommend you do without."

Ellysetta's hands closed around the hilt of Bel's bloodsworn Fey'cha. "No." The denial popped out before she could stop it, and she took an instinctive step backwards, closer to Rain.

He laid a calming hand on her shoulder. "It's a Fey queen you're training, Master Fellows. The blade stays. It's a symbol of great honor and an invaluable protection."

"I see." The Master of Graces frowned but gave in. "Well, the dagger stays, then, of course. All cultures should honor their customs." He cleared his throat. "And how did last night's dinner go?"

A betraying blush flooded Ellysetta's cheeks, and she cast a desperate glance up at Rain.

Master Fellows pressed his fingers to his lips. "Sweet Lord of Light. That badly?"

"Ellysetta did very well." Rain took Ellysetta's hand and gave it a reassuring squeeze. "Any . . . difficulties . . . were outside of her control and did not reflect badly on her."

"Difficulties? Ah. I had noticed something strange in the palace air today." Master Fellows paused, but when it was apparent no further explanation was forthcoming, he smoothly changed the subject. "Well, let's just make sure there are no difficulties in future. The best way I know to do that is to ensure your presentation is so queenly none will dare reproach you. Your next scheduled public appearance is Prince Dorian's betrothal ball. You'll need to be able to dance and converse with flawless polish." His finger wagged a caution. "I warn you, these next days of preparation will be far more difficult and demanding than our previous sessions. There's much more for you to master, and I will be a harsh taskmaster. My lord Feyreisen, if you will, please." He tapped his temple.

Rain summoned Spirit and wove a light weave to gather the instructive images from Master Fellows's mind, and for the next several bells, Rain devoted himself to guiding Ellysetta through her newest exercises in the Graces, using Master Fellows's detailed mental instructions. But throughout the lesson, his mind kept returning to Bel's perturbing report about Sian and Torel.

Two experienced warriors sent north to investigate the mystery of Ellysetta's existence were missing. Even without Shadow Men and wandering souls and Adrial's illness, that was cause for concern. Fey warriors did not simply . . . disappear. One too many troubling events had happened—and all of them circling far too close to Ellysetta for his liking.

When Ellysetta's lessons were concluded and Master Fellows had departed, Rain wasn't long behind him. He stopped at the warriors' barracks to check on Adrial—who was awake and claiming he was fit enough to return to his position in Ellysetta's quintet—then joined Marissya and Dax in their palace suite.

The *shei'dalin* confirmed Adrial's self-assessment. "I couldn't find anything wrong with him, Rain. Your *shei'tani* expunged his memories. They are completely gone, with no trace for me to follow."

"He wants to return to his duties."

She hesitated, then said carefully, "He's a good man, Rain. And I found no hint of evil in him. Whatever afflicted him, I don't think it was Eld."

"Would you want him in your quintet?"

"Let him stay here for a few days so I can watch him," Marissya said. "If he shows no signs of trouble, then let him rejoin her quintet. There are enough warriors on guard around her home to watch him closely. If you are uncomfortable with that, then yes, he can join mine. Ellysetta can have Soren. His skills are a close match to Adrial's."

Dax frowned at his truemate. A mated Fey would face an army of Mages, demons, and Drogan Blood Lords with less fear than the thought of harm besetting his *shei'tani*.

"I will think on it," Rain replied. "What of Torel?"

Marissya's eyes filled with sorrow, and she shook her head. "I could find nothing. He and Sian are gone. I wove peace and sleep on Tiar, but he should not remain here. Torel and he were close, and he's taking his brother's death badly."

"Send him home, then," Rain said. "With a quintet to ensure he finds his way. The last thing we need at the moment is a Fey warrior running around Celieria seeking blood vengeance." He turned to Dax. "How many Celierian supporters did we lose after last night?"

"Six of the thirty we were hoping to sway have told us outright they won't support us, and two of the lords we were counting on have now turned against us."

Rain scowled. "They fear our magic, yet they would let the Dark God's own servants pour across their borders? Where is the sense in that?"

"Don't expect sense from them, Rain," Dax said. "It's been a thousand years since they saw the true face of evil. They've grown complacent, so accustomed to peace and freedom they think nothing can ever take it from them. So they see enemies where they should see strength and friendship, and they plot to make friends of our enemies in order to better control us."

"Were you not the one who just a few days ago suggested we should allow the trade and use it to send spies into Eld?"

"I know. I know." Dax heaved a frustrated sigh and scrubbed his hands through his hair. "And at the time, I thought I was right. But Marissya and I have just spent the last three days with Dorian's courtiers, and the better part of today interrogating the lords openly. There is a disturbing distrust and even outright animosity towards us. The *dahl'reisen* attacks in the north are partly to blame, but Marissya and I both think it's more than that."

"Then you are beginning to believe the darkness I sense in Eld is real? That the Mages are indeed at work once more?"

"I'm beginning to think it's a strong possibility. Lord Teleos has arranged a private dinner for you and several of the nobles tonight at his city residence. And Lord Barrial sent word that he's available to meet with you."

"Excellent." Rain was very interested in the Celierian Great Lord who wore a Fey Soul Quest crystal and housed twenty-five of the feared *dahl'reisen* on his lands. "Is there anything else?"

"Lord Morvel has withdrawn his betrothal offer."

Rain gave a humorless bark of laughter. "Well, that at least is as much good news as bad. Ellysetta will be relieved, and in truth, so am I. There is no compassion in that human ice pick's soul. He will never be a friend of the Fey." He drew a deep breath. Much as he didn't like Morvel—or most Celierian nobles for that matter—he couldn't afford to lose what few potential allies he had. "I'll speak to Morvel tomorrow and try to smooth things over.

"As for the rest," he added, "Bel has sent a quintet to investigate Sian and Torel's disappearance. Let's send another two north to look into the other attacks. If *dahl'reisen* really are to blame, we need to put a stop to it."

CHAPTER SIX

Rain followed Cannevar Barrial's manservant to the northwest corner of the walled palace grounds where Lord Barrial and his four sons were occupied with archery practice.

The Great Lord wore golden brown leathers cut in plain lines that might have made him seem a simple man were it not for the glowing luster of the leather and the glint of decorative gold studs. His dark hair was caught in a leather band at the nape of his neck. His face was in profile, his concentration complete as he drew back the taut sinew of an Elvish bow. He did not wear a bowman's finger rings, Rain noted and was duly impressed when the border lord still managed to draw the bowstring back behind his ear. Not an easy thing for a man to manage when the bow was Elvish and crafted of indomitable hartshorn wood.

"I'll be with you in a moment, my lord Feyreisen," Lord Barrial said, proving that his concentration was not so complete as Rain had thought. Still, the Celierian never took his eyes from the tiny circular target far, far in the distance, and when he let loose the bowstring, his notched arrow flew swift and true to its center.

"Impressive shot." Rain nodded at the carved bow in Barrial's hands. "And a fine bow. Made by craftsmen of the Valorian Mountains, if my memory of Elvish symbols serves me."

"Your memory is good." Lord Barrial smiled. "Galad Hawksheart gifted this bow to me at First Hunt when I turned sixteen." Behind him, Lord Barrial's sons each let fly with his own arrow, and to the last, each hit his target dead center.

"Hawksheart?" Rain's brows rose. The Elf King was not unknown to him. He'd led the Elves into battle during the Mage Wars and guarded an ancient Elvish prophecy called the Dance. "You keep fine friends, Cannevar Barrial. Do you call a Song in the Dance?"

Lord Barrial laughed. "No, thank the gods. I just shake my feet to the tune like the rest of the world." He handed the bow to his manservant. "My relation to Hawksheart is a simple one: We share ties of kinship through my mother's family. I spent my childhood in Elvia after my parents were killed."

"Ah." This man grew more interesting by the moment. Royal Elvish blood, *dahl'reisen* friends, and a *sorreisu kiyr* around his throat. Cannevar Barrial might not call a Song in the Dance, but Rain would bet his last blade he at least played a Harmony.

Lord Barrial stepped away for a moment to murmur something to his oldest son. The young man nodded, and a few chimes later, he and his brothers began to pack up their gear. Lord Barrial walked back to Rain. "I understand you're dining with Teleos tonight,"

"I am. Will you be joining us?"

"No, I promised my sons I'd take them hunting since Council is out of session for the next two days. We're riding for Kingswood in a few bells." He grimaced and confided, "I'm avoiding Lady Thea. She, unfortunately, was the nearest unattached woman when your truemate spun her weave last night, and I think she read more into what followed than there was."

"My truemate's weave, Lord Barrial?" Rain tried to sound confused.

The border lord arched a canny brow. "I've enough Elvish in me to know magic when I see it. Especially when it grabs me by the cock and doesn't let go for seven scorching bells. If you recall, I was sitting directly across from your lady. As she was the only one not shedding clothes and those crystals of hers were glowing, it wasn't hard to identify the guilty party."

"Ah." Rain fought the urge to scratch a sudden itch behind one ear. At least, Lord Barrial seemed to be taking the weave in stride. "My lady has an unusually strong . . . affinity for keflee, and a strong gift in Spirit. Add to that five *sorreisu kiyr* and a bit too much pinalle, and . . . well, you saw the results. There was no ill intent, I assure you. She did not know what she was doing." He met Lord Barrial's gaze and held it steadily. "I would consider myself indebted, Lord Barrial, if you would keep the source of the weave a secret between us. Ellysetta already has a steep enough path to climb to gain acceptance from the noble Houses."

Lord Barrial grinned. "No debt needed. The memory of Morvel chasing his wife round the room like a chicken is more than enough payment for my silence." He laughed and clapped Rain on the shoulder, "Come, walk with me, and ask your questions. I'll give you what answers I can."

"Tell me about the *dahl'reisen*," Rain prompted as they walked through an avenue of stately, arching fireoaks.

Cannevar smiled. "I thought that might be among the first of your questions. Oh, I've heard all the rumors and listened to the 'proof' Sebourne and several others offered yesterday in Council, but I still find it hard to believe. *Dahl'reisen* have protected my family for centuries. And for all the bogey stories about him, Gaelen vel Serranis avoids contact with mortals."

"At the dinner, you said you'd met him."

"*Ta*. Twice. The first time was when I was a lad of five. Elden raiders attacked my family as we were returning from a wedding celebration at a distant cousin's estate. They killed my parents and were coming after me when a man appeared out of nowhere. He wore Fey steel and killed ten Eld in moments, as swiftly and skillfully as I've ever seen any being kill."

"You are sure it was Gaelen vel Serranis?"

"Black hair. Pale blue Fey eyes with all the color and

warmth of glacier ice. A scar bisecting his right eyebrow. Here"—he held out a hand—"take the memory to confirm it." When Rain hesitated, Cann said, "It's all right. I know the Fey can read thoughts through touch."

"I will not search," Rain vowed, "and I will try not to touch more than surface thoughts. Just think of the man you saw. Try to picture his face in your mind." Rain reached out to clasp the Celierian's hand.

The moment Fey pale skin slid over darker Celierian bronze, Cann's thoughts began to flow into Rain's consciousness. They didn't come in a flood, which proved Cann had stronger mental barriers than most of his countrymen, and most of the thoughts that did trickle through were related to Gaelen and the current situation: *Why do the dahl'reisen protect my lands but attack others? Why did Gaelen vel Serranis save my life and come to warn me that darkness is rising in Eld? Is there something behind Rain Tairen Soul's visit that—*

The last thought was cut off abruptly, and Cann quickly filled Rain's mind with a very strong image of a Fey warrior's face.

Even expecting it, Rain felt his gut clench at the image of the infamous, familiar face of the once-celebrated Fey warrior: Gaelen vel Serranis, now called the Dark Lord. It was Gaelen whose blood-drenched vengeance for his twin sister's death had catapulted the world into the Mage Wars. Long black hair framed a stern, humorless face dominated by piercing, ice-blue eyes. A long, curving scar started two inches above the right temple and slashed across his forehead to bisect his right brow. No Fey became scarred except *dahl'reisen*, and, except for deep, mortal wounds, even they only scarred when they made the kill that tipped their souls into darkness. Rain remembered Marissya's shriek of agony when her brother returned to the Fading Lands with that telltale mark on his face. He remembered the bleak despair on Gaelen's face when she and the rest of the Fey women fled from him and the unbearable pain of his doomed soul.

Rain released Cann's hand, and the image faded. "If that was the Fey you saw, it was indeed Gaelen who saved your life as a child."

Cann nodded and murmured softly, "I remember how fast he moved, how quickly and effortlessly he killed the Elden raiders. The last thing I remember, he was crouching over me, telling me I was safe. I must have passed out then. When I woke, I was alone. There were no bodies, no blood, just an empty field, a scorch mark on the grass, and my father's ring on a chain around my neck." Cann twisted the heavy signet ring on his right hand. "I still wish he'd left their bodies, so I could have had something to bury."

Rain knew the pain of loss all too well, and he knew the hollow ache of a loss that left nothing to hold, no way to say final good-byes. "Gaelen would have burned the dead so their souls could not be called back by Elden Mages," Rain said, wanting Cannevar to have at least that small comfort. "He did what was best for them, and for you."

"Did he? I never realized that."

"There is much your people no longer know, particularly regarding magic and magical races. The Eld freely use Azrahn, the magic we Fey have forbidden amongst ourselves. It is a dark and dangerous magic, too easily misused and too seductive a power for even Fey to wield without risk of abuse. You Celierians think we warn you against the Eld just because they and the Fey decimated one another a thousand years ago, but that is only a small part of the reason for our distrust of them."

The avenue of oaks opened to a small stocked fishpond. Rain bent to pick up a small stone and sent it skipping across the surface of the water. "Why would the Eld have killed your parents?" he asked.

Lord Barrial shrugged. "Why do they do half the things they do? They raid. They kill, unless the border folk kill them first." He sent a stone skipping several man-lengths past the ripples of Rain's, then smiled at Rain's arched brow.

Rain shook his head. "The Eld are not so indiscriminate. They rarely do anything without a purpose, and that purpose is usually guided by Mage hands. Was your father wearing the Tairen's Eye the night he was killed?" He picked up another stone and let it fly. This stone skipped fourteen times across the pond, bounced up the bank on the opposite side, and startled a flock of geese into flight.

Cann laughed and threw up his hands in surrender. "You win. And, no, my father only wore the crystal on ceremonial occasions. You think that's what they were after?"

"It's possible. Tairen's Eye is coveted by anyone who wields magic."

The crystal was priceless to those who dabbled in magic, due to the power it contained and its ability to focus and even amplify the wearer's own magic. In the hands of a skilled Mage, Tairen's Eye was lethal, especially a *sorreisu kiyr*, which could give the Mage access to a Fey's soul. Tairen's Eye could be corrupted with Azrahn to create *selkahr*, the black jewel of the Mages.

"Do you have the crystal with you now?" Rain asked.

Wariness replaced the amusement in Cann's expression. "Why do you ask?"

"If I am right, it is a *sorreisu kiyr*, a Fey Soul Quest crystal. It will retain the identity of the warrior who owned it first, and that may help me understand why the *dahl'reisen* and the Eld have taken such an interest in your family."

With obvious reluctance, Lord Barrial tugged the crystal free of his leather tunic and slipped the chain over his head. Rain took the shining stone between his fingers, feeling the tingle of the harnessed magic that made Tairen's Eye so rare and so valuable. He took a breath and opened himself to the crystal, asking it to offer up its secrets.

Power surged through him, ancient and strong. Great power, laced with shadows that made him grit his teeth. The crystal had belonged to a *dahl'reisen*, and not one who'd gone easily to the dark. Not a stranger either.

With a quiet gasp, he returned Lord Barrial's pendant to him. "It is the *sorreisu kiyr* of Dural vel Serranis," Rain said. "Gaelen and Marissya's cousin who never returned from the

Mage Wars." He met Lord Barrial's shocked gaze. "Elvish may not be the only magical blood that runs in your family, Cannevar Barrial. It's possible you're also kin to the Dark Lord."

He lay in the stench of a *rultshart's* den, the remains of the den's previous inhabitants piled in charred heaps near the cave's small opening.

His breathing was labored, his vision swimming. The Fire he'd called to empty the den had sent him into spasms of agony. He'd managed to drag himself into the cave before losing his senses, and it was only now—almost a whole day later, judging by the amount of light shining in—that he'd roused again with enough strength to put coherent thoughts together.

On the dirt beside him, two *sorreisu kiyr* gleamed in the dim light. Next to them lay a wavy black *sel'dor* dagger. The dark gemstone in the Mage blade's hilt glowed with hints of ruby light as it lay in the muddy mix of blood and dirt.

The Hells-flamed dagger liked the taste of his blood.

Gaelen vel Serranis laughed low and without humor. The dagger was the first thing in centuries that had warmed to him in any way.

Evil called to evil, or so they said, and Gaelen was certainly in a position to know. After all, he was the soul-damned *dahl'reisen* known as the Dark Lord, bogeyman of the Fey. He was the dread warrior who had willingly given himself into the shadowy, death-thralled existence of the *dahl'reisen* in order to wreak bloody vengeance on the Eld and spark the wars that had nearly ended the world. He was well and truly soul-lost, unredeemable. Evil.

But despite having more than earned the dark crown of the *dahl'reisen*, he still had a ways to go before he matched the unmitigated evil of the Mages, thank the gods for what meager blessings they still saw fit to bestow upon him. There still remained some stubborn, unquenchable flicker of Fey honor deep within him, and he clung to its faint light with all the strength of his blighted soul. Even now, though he would never again set foot on Fey soil, that honor demanded he protect his homeland.

Several days ago, Gaelen's network of spies had told him of the presence of two Fey traveling north towards Norban. He'd come to investigate, only to discover that a party of Eld apparently had the same idea. Gaelen had tracked them to the forest, to the hut of the woodsman Brind Palwyn. The Eld had killed the woodsman after torturing him for information, but in his rush to stop the Fey from reporting their news, the junior Mage—barely more than an apprentice, or he would have known better—had foolishly left the body intact.

Gaelen had used Azrahn to call Palwyn's soul from the dead, questioned him, then cremated his body so no other could do the same. Though the Fey had eradicated Palwyn's memories, his soul still remembered his subsequent brutal questioning at the hands of the Eld, and Gaelen had drawn those intact memories from him.

The High Mage of Eld had a daughter.

A red-haired, green-eyed daughter like the Celierian girl who'd called Rain Tairen Soul from the sky, lost in the woods of Norban more than two decades earlier.

When he'd first learned of the Tairen Soul's truemate, Gaelen had envied Rainier vel'En Daris the gods' apparent forgiveness, but now he realized the gods had forgiven vel'En Daris nothing. They'd only devised a new, more grievous torture for him—and a new, more deadly threat for the Fey.

Gaelen touched the two *sorreisu kiyr* that had belonged to the Fey warriors Sian vel Sendaris and Torel vel Carlian. He drew the names from the crystals, then traced a sign in the air over them, an ancient warrior's symbol to wish the dead Fey's souls speedy passage into a peaceful next life.

He had not known the two Fey, but he would have saved them if he could. He'd been too late, though. Again. He'd seen the last one fall, bravely and with honor as a Fey warrior should. Gaelen had slain the remaining handful of their attackers, including the apprentice Mage, but he'd taken numerous barbed *sel'dor* arrows in the process and three of the Eld had laid his flesh open with their swords before he'd managed to strike them down.

Despite the pain it caused him to call Fire with *sel'dor* piercing his flesh, he'd cremated the Fey warriors' bodies. He hadn't attempted to call their souls from the dead to learn what they'd reported to the Fey, though he could have woven Azrahn with minimal pain despite being *sel'dor* pierced. It would have surprised most Fey, including all but a handful of *dahl'reisen*, to witness his restraint. Even now there were still a few crimes the Dark Lord would not commit. Calling a Fey soul back from the dead was one of those.

The Eld he'd burned without soul-summoning as well, because their souls were already bound to their master and calling them would have alerted the High Mage to Gaelen's presence. Not a wise course of action when he was *sel'dor* pierced and bleeding his remaining strength into the dust at a fairly alarming rate.

He'd stumbled his way deeper into the forest until he found the *rultshart's* den. He'd burned out the den's inhabitants and dragged himself into the small, dank shelter before losing consciousness.

So here he was, wounded, weak, and lying in the foul stench of a *rultshart's* lair as he tried to summon the energy necessary to save himself. Part of him wanted to just close his eyes and bleed his life out. But another, stronger part of him fought the urge with a tairen's fierceness, all fang and claw and wild instinct to survive. That was the part that had kept him alive even after a thousand years as a *dahl'reisen*, banished forever from the beauty of the Fading Lands and the warmth of the Fey.

Why he'd been driven to cling to his miserable life so long, he did not know, but now, at last, he had again a clear and driving purpose.

The High Mage had a daughter.

Soon she would wed Rain Tairen Soul and the Fey would escort her back to the Fading Lands. Like the ancient legend of the great, cursed treasure that bore pestilence within its golden chalices, by bringing the High Mage's daughter safely through the Mists, the Fey would escort their own destruction into the Fading Lands. She would doom them all, including Gaelen's only remaining sister, Marissya. He couldn't allow that to happen.

The High Mage's daughter must die.

Slowly, in a process made awkward by the slipperiness of his blood and his own lack of strength, he worked his way free of his weapons and his black leather tunic. The wounds filled with *sel'dor* shrapnel weren't bleeding—the cursed Eld metal drank blood like parched ground drank water—but the long, bone-deep gash on his thigh and the two wounds where Eld blades had skewered him had soaked the bandages he'd applied last night and were once more bleeding quite profusely. He didn't have the strength to remove the *sel'dor*, but he couldn't let himself continue to bleed.

Gaelen pulled a black-handled Fey'cha from his belt and called a trickle of Fire to heat the blade until it glowed. *Sel'dor* twisted even that weak weave into agony. Gritting his teeth, he pressed the fiery blade against the worst of his wounds and fought back a wave of nausea as the smell of his own burning flesh reached his nostrils. He managed to reheat the blade and cauterize two other wounds before losing consciousness yet again.

❧

Vadim Maur stared hard at his apprentice. A small tic worked at the lower corner of his right eye, the only visible sign of his anger. *Well, that*, Kolis thought, *and the thirty-degree drop in temperature in his office chamber.* He wasn't about to ask about the angry red burn marks scoring the left side of the High Mage's pallid, cadaverous face. No doubt one of his many experiments had gone badly, but Kolis wasn't fool enough to remark upon it.

"She is a master of Spirit?" Vadim asked, his voice a chilling hiss.

"Without a doubt, master. Last night, she spun a Spirit weave that completely controlled over two hundred minds—Fey included—for over seven bells. None of them was aware of what she was doing until it was too late. She wasn't even consciously weaving. I've never seen the like. I was there in the body of my *umagi* Jiarine Montevero, and she has enough hearth witch in her that I could see the flows. They came from Ellysetta Baristani."

"And *your* mind, Kolis? As you were close enough to see this weave, did it control your mind too?"

Kolis flushed and dropped his gaze. "I am ashamed to admit it did, High One. Even knowing it was a weave, I could not deny its dictates."

Silence fell. The room temperature plunged again, and frost crackled on every surface. "So, she's a master of Spirit as well as Fire . . ."

Kolis's eyes widened as Vadim Maur's hand twitched towards the scorch marks on his face. Ellysetta Baristani had done that? Dark Lord's Scythe! How was it possible?

The High Mage's silver eyes began to darken with spinning clouds of black and red. "Not at all the ungifted wretch my pets have long tried to convince me she was."

Even knowing that his master's anger was not directed at him, Kolis felt the chill of it ice his veins. The captives would regret their duplicity. The walls of Boura Fell would soon echo with their screams. Despite himself, the Sulimage could almost feel pity for them.

"You will bring Ellysetta Baristani to me." The wintry command snapped Kolis back to attention.

"I anticipated your request, master." In a quick rush of words, he explained about the gift he had prepared for Ellysetta Baristani. "I've already arranged for its delivery, and ensured there will be no way to trace the gift back to either my *umagi* or myself."

The High Mage tapped a contemplative finger against his lips, and the room began to warm as the worst of his anger passed. "The idea has merit, but you lose much control once the package leaves your possession. What is your alternate plan in case this one fails?"

Kolis swallowed and cautiously admitted, "I haven't fully prepared it yet."

"The key to success, Kolis, is planning for failure."

"I know, master, and I have arranged for my newest *umagi* to serve as the Baristani girl's Honoria, in the hope that she could be of greater service to me. I thought perhaps an abduction at the wedding, should the gift not work as intended."

The High Mage shook his head. "The Tairen Soul will be there. It is too great a risk."

"Yes, Great One, but it seemed the best option. I considered having my *umagi* open a portal during the Bride's Blessing, when they are sequestered in the cathedral's Solarus for the purification, but she would be outnumbered and unlikely to succeed." The only people permitted to accompany a bride into the Solarus during the Bride's Blessing were the priest, the bride's mother, and the Honoria—and neither Lauriana Baristani nor Greatfather Tivrest were Mage-claimed. For all his posturing and arrogance, the archbishop was a man of deep faith, and he had staunchly resisted every one of Kolis's attempts to turn him.

"I'm pleased you considered an attack during the Bride's Blessing; it was my first thought as well. The isolation makes for a perfect opportunity." Master Maur smoothed the silk-lined velvet cuff of his purple Mage robes. "And though you would be correct about the unlikelihood of your *umagi's* success, assuming she was our only agent in the Solarus, I've already considered that problem and devised what I believe is a very workable solution." One silvery brow lifted. "Did you know that Ellysetta Baristani was once under the care of the Church exorcists?"

"No, master, I didn't know that."

"Mmm, well, she was. I received word just a few chimes ago from Primage Keldo. His *umagi* in Hartslea discovered it." The High Mage sat back in his chair and steepled his hands beneath his chin. "Apparently, young Ellysetta suffered regularly from violent 'seizures' in her childhood. The Church determined she was demon possessed and convinced her parents to approve an exorcism. According to Keldo's *umagi*, the girl's father had a change of heart before the exorcism could be completed, and the family fled Hartslea rather than give her up to the priests."

"That's very interesting, master." Kolis tried to infuse a tone of appreciation in his voice, even though he didn't see how the information helped them. "The mother is still quite devout and openly hostile to the Fey. I've been playing on her fears, hoping to use her to separate the girl from her guards, but so far she has steadfastly refused my bait."

"Your man in the north, the priest, he is an exorcist, is he not?"

"Nivane? He is. It was how I first Marked him." Like many of his northern-bred brothers, the young priest had been born with a remnant gift for weaving Azrahn, and when he'd unwittingly woven it while attempting to exorcise one of Kolis's *umagi*, he'd granted Kolis a foothold in his soul.

"Parts of the Grand Cathedral are extremely ancient," Vadim Maur continued, "built in an age when Demon Princes were a considerable threat. The initial purpose of the Solarus was purification—but not for brides. It was a chamber used almost exclusively for exorcism."

"I've never heard that before." Now the appreciation in his tone was genuine as Kolis's mind began to race with possibilities.

"The knowledge was lost long ago. I only discovered mention of it in an ancient Merellian text. As part of its initial purpose, the Solarus was built to withstand even five-fold weaves." The High Mage pressed his steepled fingers against his lips and smiled. "The entire room is a cage built to hold demon-possessed magical creatures. There is no better place in all the world to steal a Tairen Soul's mate."

CHAPTER SEVEN

"Greetings, My Lord Feyreisen, Lady Marissya, Lord Dax." Welcome shining in his green Fey-bright eyes, Great Lord Devron Teleos held out an arm and exchanged a warrior's handclasp with Rain and Dax as the Fey entered the spacious entry hall of his city residence shortly after sunset. The Celierian was paler than his pure mortal countrymen and darker than his Fey kin, his skin a golden ivory that glowed with Fey luminescence, his shoulder-length hair black as a raven's wing.

Rain murmured a greeting as he took quick stock of his surroundings. In a few swift glances, he noted the location of every entrance and exit, and the vast array of Fey, Elvish, Celierian, and Daneal weaponry on the walls. His gaze caught on one particular display: a full complement of Fey steel, gleaming with a mirror-bright polish no passage of time would ever dim.

"Ah, I thought you might find those of interest," Teleos said, nodding at the weapons. "They were Shanis's blades."

"I recognized them." Rain had spent many a year fighting beside his old friend, watching him wield those blades with deadly efficiency. Etched with the symbols of the mighty v'En Celay line, the legendary Fey Lord Shanisorran v'En Celay himself had commissioned the steel as a warrior's gift to his namesake, Shanis Teleos, a descendant of his brother's line. "I am surprised to find them hanging on a wall in Celieria City. Fey steel was meant for war, not decoration."

Teleos smiled, unoffended. "My father always considered Shanis's steel too valuable a family treasure to risk. He never used them, and a hundred years ago, when the Eld raids along the borders were getting worse, he had them moved here, to keep them safe."

Conscious of the eyes and ears around them, Rain met Teleos's gaze and said on a thread of Spirit, «*When you come to train at the Warrior's Academy in Dharsa, bring them. Shanis's blades deserve the honor of battle.*»

Teleos bowed slightly and swept out an arm. "Please, come, all of you. Most of the others are already here." The Great Lord led the way into a large adjoining parlor where some two dozen of the nobles Rain had met the night before were waiting. "My Lord Feyreisen, these are some of my oldest friends and most trusted colleagues in the Council, families with whom the House Teleos shares a long history." Teleos gave a faint smile, green eyes bright with some secret satisfaction. "It is my pleasure to introduce you again to Great Lord Verakis and his wife, Lady Ceiliana. Great Lord Nin and his lovely new bride, Lady Aleen. Great Lord Darramon and his wife, Lady Basha, Lord and Lady Fann, Lord and Lady Barlo."

As Teleos led Rain around the room, introducing him to each of his guests, Rain began to understand the reason for that satisfaction in Teleos's gaze, and his appreciation for his new friend grew exponentially. He'd underestimated the man, thinking his Fey appearance would make the other nobles less likely to trust him. Instead, it was plain the Teleos family had carefully built and maintained a powerful network of allies within their homeland.

This small gathering of lords represented some of the most strategic estates in Celieria as well as half a dozen industries of key military importance: Great Lord Darramon, the fifth most powerful lord guarding the Eld border; Lord Fann, famous for his Swan's Bay shipyards; Lord Nin, a celebrated naval hero, whose mighty Queen's Point fortress guarded the mouth of Great Bay; Lord Clovis, a captain of industry, whose coal-and-iron-rich lands supplied more than half of all Celieria's steel and iron; Great Lord Ash, a southern border lord whose handcrafted bows and superior bowmen rivaled even Elvish perfection. Teleos and his wise ancestors had established long-standing ties with all the powers necessary to build and equip an army for the defense of Celieria.

«An impressive network of friends.» Rain commented. *«Shanis would be proud.»*

Teleos smiled. *«It was his idea. When the Faering Mists went up, he said one day Rain Tairen Soul would return and that when he did, House Teleos should be prepared to aid him.»*

«Shanis arranged this?» Rain's gaze swept the room again at the network of Teleos's allies, and he realized he was looking at a gift from a long-dead friend.

Teleos met Rain's gaze, his Fey eyes steady. *«Tairen defend the pride.»*

The familiar Fey maxim had been Shanis's favorite. Sudden emotion surged, and a muscle worked in Rain's jaw. *«They do indeed, my brother.»* He took a deep breath and donned the familiar mask of stoic Fey calm as he turned to meet the guarded, suspicious gaze of the nobleman standing nearby. "Lord Darramon, a pleasure to meet you again."

The Great Lord arched a dark brow. "Is it?" The man's gray eyes grew flinty. "I'm here purely as a favor to Teleos. If not for our long-standing friendship, I wouldn't have come. The Lords of Celieria are not toys for your amusement, My Lord Feyreisen. Either you honor our right to free will, or the Eld won't be your only enemies on this continent."

Rain bowed. "I apologize for what happened last night, Lord Darramon. I can assure you it was a complete accident." He kept his gaze focused on Darramon, though he could feel the scrutiny of the other lords and ladies and knew they were listening intently to the exchange. "When a Fey discovers his truemate, as I have done, his emotions—and his magic—are not as settled as they usually are. It is a hard thing for a Fey to admit his discipline is not as strong as it should be, but there you have it."

Darramon gave a short laugh. "So you apologize and expect all to be forgiven?"

"Not at all," Rain replied soberly. "I accept full responsibility for what happened, and I will accept any consequences of that responsibility. But do not, my lord, accuse me of intentionally spinning that weave to control Celierian minds. Using magic to usurp another being's free will is an Eld tactic, not a Fey one, and that's exactly the sort of abuse of power I'm here to caution you all against."

Darramon's wife, a frail beauty with brilliant blue eyes and dark russet hair, put a hand on her husband's arm.

The Great Lord's eyes flickered towards her for a moment, and then he gave a curt nod. "I will hear what you have to say, My Lord Feyreisen. But what was done was done to my wife as well as me, and that trespass I find much harder to forgive. She has not been in the best of health."

Instantly solicitous, Rain turned to Lady Darramon with sincere concern. "My lady, if you will permit, Lady Marissya would be honored to be of service to you. There are no better healers among the Fey. *Teska*, please. It is the least we can offer."

Marissya stepped forward, scarlet silks rustling. "Indeed, my lady. If Lord Teleos would offer us a private chamber, I will attend you immediately."

"Of course," Teleos said. He gestured to a nearby manservant. "Marton, please show the ladies to my mother's suite."

"Basha—" Lord Darramon began.

"No. It's all right," Lady Darramon told him. "I have never doubted the Lady Marissya's goodwill, and I won't start now." The Great Lord's wife gave Marissya a wan smile. "I would appreciate whatever aid you can provide, my lady."

Darramon watched his wife go with a troubled frown, but his expression hardened when he looked back at Rain. "Don't think this will make me listen with a more favorable ear."

"My lord, I would not dream of it." Rain gave a final, precise bow. "An open mind is all I ask for."

Lord Darramon wasn't the only guest who responded coolly to Rain's overtures, but to his surprise, numerous couples welcomed him with warmth. That baffled him at first, but as the evening progressed and Rain watched those same couples exchanging long glances and subtle touches and smiles before dinner, he began to understand.

He glanced at Dax and saw the same amused realization in the Fey lord's eyes. *«Perhaps we're going about this the wrong way,»* Rain suggested. Despite the earlier tension with Lord Darramon, a thread of laughter tinged his weave. *«Maybe Rowan was right and we should be approaching all the elderly lords who might swap a vote in exchange for a bit more . . . rejuvenation.»*

Dax choked on his pinalle.

Swallowing a grin, Rain plucked a bite-sized morsel of roast quail in pastry from a passing tray and popped it in his mouth. If nothing else came of tonight's dinner, at least he could give Ellysetta the relief of knowing that not all Celieria's lords had found her weave an unwelcome enchantment.

Marissya and Basha Darramon returned before the guests were called to dinner. Darramon's wife, while still frail, had much better color, and she walked with a surer step.

«A malignancy,» Marissya informed Rain and Dax as the guests followed Teleos into the dining room. *«She will require far more than a few brief chimes of healing. I soothed her fatigue and did what I could to help her body fight the advance of her disease, but unless she comes to the Fading Lands or half a dozen of our strongest healers go to her, she will be dead this time next year.»*

«Well,» Dax said. *«Cruel as it sounds, if we want his vote, that seems one sure way to get it.»*

The *shei'dalin's* spine stiffened. *«Shei'tan, I know you cannot be suggesting we bribe him with his wife's life.»*

«Marissya, you accepted long ago that you can't heal every dying mortal. We're in a fight for our lives. If the promise of healing Lady Darramon helps secure Lord Darramon's vote, we would be fools not to consider it. Besides, if the Eld gain free access to Celieria, she's dead

already—or worse, used as a tool to force her husband to comply with the Mages.»

Rain gazed across the table at the tender concern and open love stamped on Lord Darramon's hard face as he bent his head to murmur something to his wife. What if Rain were in Lord Darramon's place and Ellysetta were the one dying? What wouldn't Rain do to secure her health? What wouldn't he give?

Tension coiled in his gut at the mere thought of it, and the tairen growled a fierce warning. Dax was right. The promise of healing Lady Basha would secure Lord Darramon's vote in an instant. A man who loved his wife as deeply as Darramon clearly loved Basha would never let something so trifling as the cast of a ballot stand in the way of her health.

A wily king would use that leverage to his own advantage.

After dinner, the guests retired to Teleos's conservatory. Servants bustled around offering tea, keflee, and a selection of flavorful liqueurs, and the discussion turned in earnest to the Eld Trade Agreement.

Great Lord Verakis, holder of a very large and strategic West Midlands estate, was a sober man, thoughtful, educated, and deliberate in his thinking. His lands lay directly in the path of the Garreval. If war came, the Eld would march through Verakis on their way to the Fading Lands, and luckily for Rain, the lord knew it. The calm, well-reasoned discussion provided the impetus Rain needed to draw even the more reticent lords into discourse.

"My lands are nowhere near the Garreval and of little strategic importance," objected Lord Dunn, a small central Celierian landholder.

"Perhaps not strategic by location, Lord Dunn," Rain corrected as he recalled the information Master Fellows had imparted to Ellysetta this afternoon about the House Dunn, "but even Eld armies need food. The quality and abundance of your crops make Dunn a ripe prize."

"My lord, really," Lord Nevis Barlo objected. The man was

another small landholder with estates located south of Celieria City. "You're talking as if Mage conquest is a certainty—when in fact no proof exists to support your claim."

"I know the Mages, Lord Barlo," Rain replied. "I am intimately familiar with what they will do for power. If the Mage Council has been reconstituted, have no doubt about it, conquest *is* a certainty. Perhaps not this year, perhaps not the next, but it will come. Mages are patient adversaries. They will wait until you grow complacent, and then they will strike."

"My Lord Feyreisen." Lord Callumas Nin, the Great Lord and naval hero who held Queen's Point, cleared his throat. "All of us are here because we are willing to listen to what you say. But let us talk facts, not conjecture—no matter how well-founded you believe that conjecture might be. You want our votes to keep the Eld out of Celieria. The Eld want our votes to let them in. We know what the Eld are offering: gold, trade, an unlimited supply of *keio* to cure any future outbreaks of plague. What is it the Fey are offering?"

Rain nodded, pleased by the glimmer of progress—even though what mortals called diplomacy was just a polite term for bribery. "A good question, my lord. As your ancestors learned long ago, the Fey have much to offer, and our gifts come with none of the strings the Eld attach." He accepted a small goblet of pinalle from a passing servant and leaned forward. "We have warriors of a skill no mortal will ever match, my lord, swordsmasters to train your men and fight alongside them should the need arise. Healers to tend your sick." He met Lord Darramon's eyes. "Magic to help ward your holdings. Sails that amplify the wind to make ships move faster." He took a sip of his drink. "Does any of that interest you, my lord?"

Lord Fann, the shipbuilder, sat up a bit straighter. "Magic-enhanced sails?"

Lord Nin's response was more reserved but no less interested. "Tell us more."

Rain signaled to Dax. The Fey lord launched into a detailed discussion of what the Fey and their magic could provide. As he spoke, Rain caught Lord Darramon's gaze and wove a private thread of Spirit between them. *«Your wife is dying. Without healing, Marissya says she will be gone this time next year.»*

The goblet of pinalle in the Great Lord's hand trembled, and sweet blue wine splashed over the rim to run, unnoticed, in rivulets over his shaking hand. His face turned pale beneath its tan. He had not known. Suspected, perhaps, but not with certainty.

Rain felt sorry for the man. The news was clearly a terrible blow. *«I will not risk the safety of our women by sending them far from the Faering Mists, but if you bring your wife to the Garreval, I will arrange for our healers to tend her there.»*

If I grant you my vote. The response was a thought unbacked by power but easily read.

«I would be lying to say that did not cross my mind,» Rain said, *«but nei, this a Fey gift, offered freely as a gesture of our goodwill, no matter how you cast your vote. I will post a quintet at the Garreval to wait for you. You have two months from today to bring your wife to them. If it is within the power of our healers to cure her, they will do so.»*

The border lord's lips moved, forming a single word. *Why?*

«Just bring her,» Rain answered brusquely, *«and do not delay. If you do not come within two months' time, we will assume you have declined our offer. The quintet will return to the Fading Lands and your wife will live or die as the gods see fit.»*

⟡

Ellysetta sat on her windowsill, looking up at the waning Mother and Daughter moons as they crawled across the night sky. Within the visibly shimmering twenty-five-fold weave surrounding the house, the world seemed utterly tranquil, yet tension still coiled inside her. The house was quiet. Mama and Papa had turned in earlier, and though Ellie could feel the press of weariness urging her to bed, she was afraid to sleep. What if she dreamed again? What if she dreamed worse than she had last night?

Bel had assured her that the twenty-five-fold weaves would keep out all known magical attacks, but her disquiet would not settle. Last night, the Shadow Man had found her. Who knew what terrors he might now unleash? Behind her, three lit candle-lamps cast bright circles of golden light around the room, chasing shadows to the darkest corners, but the flickering lights offered little in the way of reassurance.

Was it her imagination, or had the room grown colder? Ellie shivered and pulled the knitted shawl closer around her shoulders.

Suddenly her entire body went tense. What was that moving in the courtyard? She cupped her hands around her eyes and peered through the window, then sat back with a groan as she realized it was only Kieran, practicing his bladework in the moonlight.

"Oh, for the Haven's sake, Ellysetta, you're being ridiculous." She scrubbed her hands over her face and jumped to her feet, snatching up the heavy volume of Tarr's *History of Celierian Noble Houses* from the pile of books on her nightstand. After Master Fellows's lessons on the peerage this afternoon, she'd had Bel escort her to the library to fetch a selection of books that she hoped would help her build a better rapport with the nobles next time she met them. Since she wasn't getting any sleep tonight, the least she could do was spend the time doing something productive.

Crawling into bed, she propped the pillows up behind her, set the heavy book on her thighs, and began to read about the exploits and achievements of the past lords and ladies of Celieria. Unfortunately, Tarr's writing style, while a perfection of detailed accuracy, was lamentably dry. Triumphant victories—dizzying, incredible feats that had left her breathless when she'd read about them in volumes of Fey poetry—became about as vivid and engrossing as watching plaster set when recounted by the erudite scholar Master Tarr.

She persevered, determined to become an asset rather than a liability to Rain, and hoping to take her mind off her fears. Perhaps if Tarr had been a more engrossing writer, it would have worked. As it was, she jumped at each rattle of the windowpanes and creak of a floorboard, and every flicker of a shadow on her bedroom walls made her heart pound with fear. Halfway through chapter five, "The History of Great House Orly," a noise outside brought her rigidly alert. She stifled a scream as a shadow passed over her window.

"*Shei'tani?*" Rain stood on the small patch of shingled roof outside her window. Glowing green threads of Earth spun out from his fingertips and her window swung inward. Fresh night air, crisp with the scent of magic, wafted in on a cool breeze. He leapt with graceful catlike ease over the windowsill and landed without a sound in the center of her room.

Ellie clutched a hand to her throat, feeling the rapid beat of her heart beneath her fingertips. "What are you doing here?" She set her heavy book on the nightstand beside her. "I thought you were with Lord Teleos this evening."

"Bel told me you were still awake, so I left early." Two steps brought him to her side and he caught her hands in his, lifting them to his lips. "Fly with me, *shei'tani?*"

His long dark hair spilled over his shoulders, and his Fey-pale skin shone against the inky blackness of his leathers. Her heart pounded faster, but this time not from fear. Would there ever come a day when the sight of him did not leave her breathless?

Without hesitation, she went. Out the window, up to the rooftop, without a care for her bare feet or nightgown, she followed him.

"Trust me?" he asked when they stood on the crest of the roof, looking out over the sleeping city.

She answered without hesitation. "Of course."

He smiled and it was as if clouds parted before the sun. His teeth gleamed dazzling white, and his perfect masculine beauty softened to stunning appeal. When Rain smiled, even Light-maidens would weep with joy.

He drew her to him and his mouth covered hers in a long, sweet, melting kiss that made her legs fold beneath her and her hands clutch the broad strength of his shoulders to keep from falling. He laughed softly against her skin and tracked kisses up her jaw to her ear, then whispered in a voice of pure enchantment, "Don't be afraid." That was all the warning she received before he flung her skyward.

She soared up as if she were weightless, spiraling on a column of Air, breathless but unafraid. The twenty-five-fold weaves surrounding the Baristani house peeled back before her like the petals of a blossoming flower. Her arms flung out, and she turned her face up to the sky, letting Rain's magic carry her as high as it would. As she reached the apex of her ascent and began to gently fall back to earth, Rain's tairen form rose up beneath her and she landed neatly in the cradle of the saddle.

Magic spun around her in velvety clouds, and when it cleared, she looked down and laughed in delight. He'd changed her cotton nightgown to long, flowing robes that looked as if he'd woven them from starlight. Each whisper of movement made the cloth shimmer and gleam.

«I was feeling romantic,» Rain said with a chuff of tairen laughter. *«Hold on.»*

Ellie's hands gripped the pommel as his wings spread wide. Together, they soared skyward, into the dark heavens.

They flew for nearly a bell, for no purpose except the joy of flight, soaking in the silent beauty of the night, basking in the silver light of the Mother and Daughter moons. They skimmed effortlessly across the moonlit waters of Great Bay, dipping down so low Rain's wingtips slapped the water, leaving a symmetric trail of rippling circles behind them. They soared across the rolling vineyards on the north coast and over the dark, forested hills. They flew until the restlessness deep inside Ellysetta faded into peace and her fear of nightfall was a forgotten memory.

By the time they returned to the house, the moons had already passed their zenith. Rain landed lightly on the roof, but when he started to escort her back down to her bedroom window, she stopped him with a hand on his wrist.

"Would you mind very much if we stayed up here for a while?"

"Here, on the roof?" She nodded, and he shrugged. "Of course, if you like."

She sat on the steeply angled roof and leaned her head back to look up at the stars. They seemed so much farther away now than they had while flying, and the shimmering glow of the Fey's protective weaves dimmed some of the fainter stars from view. "I've spent many nights up here since I was a child, staring up at the stars, dreaming. It always seemed so peaceful."

He sat beside her. "What sort of things did you dream of?"

"Oh, what most young girls do, I imagine. Fey tales. True love." She gave a small, self-conscious laugh. "You."

"Good dreams, I hope." His thumb brushed lightly across her lower lip.

"Of course." Her voice came out breathless, just as it always did when Rain's eyes looked at her that way. Selianne would likely call it sorcery, but Ellie knew it was simple, besotted love. She drew a deep breath and tried to settle herself. "How did the dinner with Lord Teleos go?"

"Not bad." He told her about the assembly of nobles Teleos had gathered, and about the warm reception he'd received from several of the married couples. She blushed furiously but couldn't help a sigh of relief to learn that not everyone considered her weave a disaster.

When he told her about Lady Darramon's illness and the offer he'd made to heal her, Ellie's heart turned over. "Poor Lady Darramon," she said. "Poor *Lord* Darramon. I'm glad you didn't use her illness to try to win his vote."

"It was probably a mistake."

"Kindness is never a mistake, Rain."

His lips curved in an expression that seemed more grimace than smile. "That should be true, *shei'tani*, but when it comes to mortal politics, good deeds are rarely rewarded."

Her head cocked to one side. When it came to mortals, especially noble mortals, he was so cynical. "If you believe that, why didn't you do what Lord Dax suggested?"

Rather than answering, Rain drew his knees up and began twisting the large Tairen's Eye signet on his hand, watching moonlight set off a shimmering rainbow within the crystal's dark ruby depths.

"Rain?" His hesitance surprised her. She leaned over to lay a hand on his arm. Beneath the warm, supple leather, his bicep felt smooth and hard as river rock.

"I thought about it," he admitted in a low voice. "Darramon is a powerful Great Lord. We could have used him to secure another dozen votes at least. He would have paid any price to save his wife. His thoughts in that regard were too obvious to miss."

"So why did you offer to heal his wife without price?"

Glowing lavender eyes caught hers in an unbreakable gaze. "Because if you were the one dying, I would want someone to offer the same gift to me."

Ellysetta's breath caught in her throat. He'd never told her he loved her, never said the words. But his gift to Lord Darramon came as close to that declaration as she could imagine. It gave her hope that one day, the words would follow.

"You did the right thing, Rain," she assured him softly. "Love should never be used as a weapon."

He kissed her, a long, lingering kiss that combined intoxicating passion with exquisite tenderness, then leaned back against the angled roof, pulling her down with him. She lay upon his chest and listened to the beat of his heart while his fingers stroked through her hair.

"Rain . . . what will happen to you when I die?"

Black brows drew together in a sudden fierce scowl. "You will not die, *shei'tani*. I will not allow it."

She propped her chin on her hands and looked down into his face. "I don't necessarily mean killed—though after these last few days, neither of us can rule out that possibility. I mean die. Even if I'm only part-mortal like Lord Teleos, eventually I *will* die." She recalled what Rain had told her that first night of his claiming, when he'd followed her to Celieria's National Museum of Art. *If the Eld managed to kill you, I should not survive it.* At the time, she'd only considered the consequences of an unexpected, violent death, but talking about Lady Darramon reminded her that, like it or not, all mortal lives ended.

"Ah." The aggression faded from his expression. He reached

out to brush a curl from her cheek. "Don't worry about that, Ellysetta. Neither time nor sickness will ever claim your life unless you wish it."

Her eyes widened. "You can grant immortality?"

He shook his head. "The Fey are not truly 'immortal.' We die just like men if we receive a grievous wound and cannot be healed in time. What we are, more specifically, is eternally in our prime, untouched by age or infirmity. Our bodies have a natural ability to constantly heal themselves. It is why we do not age after reaching maturity, and why we do not scar. Here, watch."

Sitting up, he took a black Fey'cha from his chest straps and lightly scored the back of his hand. She stifled a cry of protest at the thin red line of blood that welled up in the wake of the blade's point, but when Rain wiped the blood away, she could see the skin had already mended.

Ellysetta reached for his hand, stroking the unmarked skin as she followed Rain's revelation to its obvious conclusion. "Fey *shei'dalins* are expert healers."

"*Aiyah*, they can perform for mortals what nature does for the Fey."

"Why have I never heard of that before?"

He shrugged. "It is a gift we have long worked to hide from the world. Too many ancient Fey texts in our Hall of Scrolls tell of *shei'dalins* enslaved and tortured by despots who demanded everlasting life. It is one of many reasons we guard our women so fiercely."

"Of course. You'd have to. Eternal life." She gave a dazed laugh. "Just think of all the possibilities. The twins can take all the time they want to find a man they truly love."

Rain frowned. "You misunderstand, Ellysetta. This gift is not one I can extend to your family. We grant it only to those who share the matebond with a Fey."

Dreams of sharing the centuries with her family crashed abruptly. "But they're my family," she protested. "You can't think I'd want to live forever without them?"

"Everlasting life would be the greater cruelty, *shei'tani*. Mortal souls were not fashioned to endure the darkness of the ages. They become . . . twisted and bitter."

"Is that the fate in store for me?"

"*Nei,* never. The *shei'tanitsa* bond ensures eternal strength for both our souls, until the gods call us home. But a mortal soul unanchored by a matebond has no such protection." When she continued to frown, he added gently, "You know as well as I do your mother would never accept that gift at such a price, even if we could offer it to her."

Ellie's gaze fell. He was right. Mama would never risk corrupting her soul.

Rain drew her into his arms. "This much at least I can offer: If your family comes to the Fading Lands, they will live free of illness and the effects of age until the end of their time."

"Thank you, Rain." She knew how jealously the Fey guarded their borders, Rain more than most. Not since the end of the Mage Wars had the Fey opened the Fading Lands to any but their own kind, but his offer still seemed small consolation. Her parents were the beacons in her life, standing bright and strong even against sometimes terrifying darkness. She couldn't imagine facing centuries of life without them.

"I have upset you."

"No, you haven't . . . not really. All mortals know they must eventually face the fact of their parents' deaths, but it's never been a thought I could bear without crying."

"If I could offer you more, I would."

"I know." She rose to her feet. "It's late. I should probably go to bed."

"Of course." With a wave of his hand, her shimmering gown changed back to her plain, cotton night rail. He helped her slip back in through her bedroom window. "Will you be able to sleep now? Your fear is gone?"

She bit her lip. "You knew?"

"I knew." He laid his palm over his heart. "I felt it here, through the first thread of our bond. It's why I left Teleos's dinner. I could not stay there once I sensed your distress. You should have asked Bel to call me earlier. I would have come."

"I didn't want to be a bother."

"You could never be that." He nodded towards the bed. "Shall I stay with you again, as I did last night?"

"Would you?" The hopeful question popped out before she could censor it. Immediately embarrassed, she hurried to demur. "I'm sorry. You don't have to. Really. I'll be fine."

His brows rose. "You think spending another night holding you in my arms is an onerous task? Surely I did not leave you that impression." Without waiting for an answer, he swept her up into his arms and deposited her on the bed, then deftly stripped off his weapons belts and leather tunic before joining her. His arms slid around her, pulling her to the warm security of his chest, and as her eyelids began to droop, she felt the press of his lips against her hair.

"Sleep, *shei'tani*." His whisper spun over her like an enchantment. Without a whisper of protest, she did, and for the first time in weeks, she passed the entire night in dreamless peace.

CHAPTER EIGHT

I live
I fight
I bleed
I die
    For love.
I am Fey.
  —*I am Fey*, a warrior's poem by Evanaris vel Bahr

Dressed in a form-fitting coat and trousers, with a waistcoat woven of Tuelis Sebarre's precious spider-silk in shades of blue and green to accent his vivid eyes, Kolis Manza climbed Celieria's palace steps. Appreciative female gazes followed him as he went, but he ignored them. When he donned the persona of Ser Vale, Queen Annoura's Favorite, the Sulimage was used to drawing feminine attention.

Everything was progressing on schedule. The butcher's son, Den Brodson, was packed and heading up the North Road to put Master Maur's plans for Ellysetta Baristani in motion, Selianne was delivering Kolis's gift for the Feyreisa, and Kolis's newest pamphlets were already papering the streets of the South End, their incendiary accusations stirring the mobs into a frenzy. Now, as Vadim Maur and Kolis had agreed last night, it was time for Jiarine Montevero to earn the gifts and titles Kolis had bestowed upon her.

Kolis made his way towards the back of the palace, where the grand ballroom opened to marble terraces overlooking sprawling, immaculately groomed gardens and fountains. King Dorian and Queen Annoura were hosting a luncheon to introduce their son's soon-to-be betrothed to the lords and ladies of the court.

A large white canopy had been erected on the lawn to keep the warm summer sun from overheating Annoura's noble guests. Snowy linen tablecloths fluttered in the slight breeze. Long serving tables offered an abundance of culinary delights: plum-stuffed hummingbirds artfully arranged in fields of candied flowers, roast peacock displayed in a fan of brilliant feathers, spit-roasted boar served on a bed of sautéed greens, iced fruits, and tiny vegetable sandwiches. A small string orchestra played beneath a blue-and-cream-striped canopy.

Annoura sat on a gilt chair beneath the largest canopy next to Prince Dorian and his future bride, Lady Nadela. The *shei'-dalin*, robed and veiled in unrelieved scarlet, was seated nearby, with her black-leather-clad Fey quintet behind her. Dorian and Lord v'En Solande stood some distance away in a smaller, less festive gathering of lords that included Teleos, Clovis, Nin, and Fann. Kolis had no doubt what they were discussing.

He caught a nearby page and handed him a folded, sealed note. "Deliver this—discreetly, mind you—to Lady Montevero, that lady in blue standing near the queen." He tossed the boy a gold coin for his troubles and headed back into the palace to a small reading library to wait.

A quarter bell later, the library door inched open and Jiarine slipped inside, locking the door behind her. Sky-blue sapphires and diamonds glittered at her throat and wrists, accenting the pretty blush in her cheeks and the soft powder-blue silk of her gown.

"That blue suits you, my sweet." The color lent a deceptive air of innocence to a woman who was anything but. He dragged her to him and tsked over the bruises on her throat hidden by carefully applied layers of powder. "Those buffoons at the dinner were careless with you. You should have insisted on better manners. But then, I know you didn't mind, did you, pet?" He smiled and stroked a finger along her jaw as the color in her cheeks deepened.

She yanked her face away and scowled at him. "You didn't tell me what that Feraz spell would do," she accused. "Why didn't you warn me?"

He lifted a brow, but let her impertinence pass. There would be time enough later to teach Jiarine the expected subservience of an *umagi*. "My dear, I didn't know. The *talis* doesn't cause a specific reaction; it only enhances its target's emotions and rouses a magical response. If she'd been cold, the room might well have ended up coated in ice."

"You left me. You left me there to them."

"I don't favor men. Especially not foul, drooling *bogrots* like Lord Bevel. Not even while existing in your sweet body." His hand trailed down her throat and followed the low scoop of her gown's neckline. Her breasts swelled against the bodice's narrow bands of fabric. He saw the hint of another bruise disappearing beneath the fabric and knew those marks on her throat weren't the only ones she bore.

"Who had you, Jiarine? Give me their names." His hands stroked across her bodice in feather-light, teasing brushes.

She shuddered and closed her eyes.

"Their names, pet. Bevel I know. Who else, hmm?" He knew her well enough to know there'd been more than one.

"Purcel." The admission grated its way past clenched teeth.

"Purcel?" Kolis chuckled. "You're a stronger lure than I suspected. The man's a walking corpse. I doubt he's been able to raise more than a finger in a decade." His mind raced through reams of data he'd committed to memory long ago. Purcel's estates were rich with iron and coal, and his foundries placed him second only to Lord Clovis as Celieria's greatest producer of steel. Vadim Maur would be pleased to gain such a conquest. "Who else?"

Kolis's hand slid into her bodice and lifted one breast free. The creamy skin, porcelain-fine and pale as milk, was marred by dark, finger-sized bruises and curved lines that looked like teeth marks. Her nipple was tight and pebbled. He brushed his thumb across it and watched her flesh jump in response. "Who gave you these little bites?" He bent his head and traced one of the bite marks with the tip of his tongue.

She gasped and grabbed his shoulders. "Ponsonney."

"Ah . . . yes, I've heard that about him. Did he show you his walking stick?" He licked her nipple and grazed it with his teeth. She rewarded him with a sudden wave of heat and the musky-sweet scent of her arousal.

"Yes," she gasped.

"Did he use it on you?" He raised her skirts and ran his hand up over the silk of her stockings, past the beribboned garters to the soft, bare skin of her inner thighs. Her hips jumped forward.

"Yes." Her voice was tight and choked.

"And did you like it?" Wetness soaked his hand as he stroked her. She rose up to the tips of her toes in an unconscious move to give him better access. Her hips began a familiar rhythmic grind against his hand.

"Yes!"

Kolis smiled and worked her with his hand and mouth, enjoying the eager way she responded to his touch and the scattered images and remembered sensations from the other night that filtered from her mind to his. She'd let them use her in every way a man could use a woman, and she'd reveled in it, begged them for it, wept and pleaded for their hands, their mouths, their cocks inside her. He bit down on her nipple at the same time as his thumb pressed hard on the small bud of straining flesh until she cried out and came in a sudden, jerking rush.

"Good," he purred when her spasms slowed to small shudders. "I want their votes. Get them for me. And I want Mull and Great Lord Harrod too. Do what you must." He clasped her shoulder and pressed her down to her knees before him. Without instruction, her hands went to the buttons of his trousers. Of all his *umagi*, Jiarine was the one whose insatiable appetites most closely matched his own. "I know how"—his voice broke off and he gave a faint groan as her mouth closed around him—"persuasive you can be." It was his turn to close his eyes.

A half bell later, Kolis stood watching from behind a marble column as Jiarine rejoined the courtiers gathered beneath the large canopy. She moved around the crowd with easy grace, pausing at the queen's side to murmur something in Annoura's ear that made the queen smile. After one brief glance over her shoulder, Jiarine lifted a flute of iced pinalle from a passing servant and strolled across the lawn towards Great Lord Harrod.

Kolis stepped away from the column into plain view and waited for Queen Annoura to catch a glimpse of him. He knew the moment she did. Even from a distance, he could see her body go motionless. He held her gaze for a long, hypnotic moment, long enough to refresh her memory of sultry Ser Vale's appeal, then turned away, knowing she would be thinking of her Favorite for the rest of the day. Temptation, as Kolis had long ago learned, worked best when delight was just out of reach, and despite Annoura's resistance, her hunger for forbidden pleasures was growing stronger with each passing day.

❧

Lauriana sat across from Selianne Pyerson at a small window-front table in Pimbold's bustling keflee shop on King's Street, where she and Selianne had come after the day's devotions. A small blue-and-silver-wrapped gift—Selianne's wedding present to Ellysetta—lay forgotten on the table between them. Lauriana's reflection in the window showed a face as stricken as her heart felt upon hearing Selianne's whispered news . . . rumors whispered in confidence from a friend with palace connections.

Ellysetta had been part of some . . . some *carnal banquet* at the palace two nights ago. The results of a spell woven by the Tairen Soul.

"I'm sorry, Madame Baristani." Selianne reached across the table to clasp Lauriana's hands. "I didn't know what to do, but I thought you should know."

"No, Selianne, you were right to tell me." Pulling her distracted thoughts back to order, Lauriana patted the younger woman's hand.

"I'm frightened for Ellie, Madame Baristani. I'm frightened of what's happening to her, of what will become of her when the Fey take her away. I know you've always been a beacon of strength for her. I fear what will happen when she doesn't have you to guide her." Selianne lowered her eyes and hesitated, as if gathering courage to speak. "My mother has a friend . . . a sea captain . . . He's agreed to offer Ellie safe passage on his return voyage. He can take her away to someplace where she'd be safe from the Fey."

"What?" Lauriana snatched her hands away and drew back to regard Selianne with shocked disbelief. Two days ago, awash in tears, Selianne had shared her fearful concerns about Ellie being exposed to the corruption of the Fey, but Laurie hadn't realized her worries would take her down *this* path. "Selianne, I know you mean well, but—"

"Please, Madame Baristani, hear me out. He can take all of you. Your whole family. There would be no repercussions and you'd all be safe . . . together and free of the Fey."

"No repercussions? Oh, kitling, by the king's own command, before the Supreme Council and with half the court as witness, we pledged Ellysetta's troth to the Tairen Soul. If we fled our bound oath, we'd all be outcasts, exiles. And the Fey would never give her up so easily. We'd be hunted for the rest of our lives."

Tears sparkled in Selianne's blue eyes. "I'm only thinking of Ellie. I can see her changing before my eyes, and it frightens me. I'm afraid of what the Fey are doing to her."

"As am I," Lauriana agreed grimly. "But we cannot right a wrong with a more grievous wrong, Selianne. No matter how tempting or justified it may seem. Every teaching in the Book of Light tells us that is the first step down the Dark Path."

"But what else can we do, Madame Baristani?"

Lauriana stared helplessly at the younger woman. Her eyes felt dry and burning, and the small luncheon they'd shared churned uncomfortably in her belly. "I don't know."

She was still worrying over it a bell later as she walked home, her arms full of packages she'd collected from various tradesmen. Her steps slowed as she neared the corner of West Avenue and Poppy. An unshaven man in a moth-eaten coat stood on the corner beside the lamppost. He held a large sign that proclaimed "The Shadows Are Among Us" and cried out for Celierians to repent their sins and seek the Light.

Lauriana grimaced. Shadow Seer. One of the crazed religious zealots who saw the end of the world in every cloud and flickering lamp. His sort gave true followers of Adelis a bad name.

She shifted closer to the street to give the man a wide berth, but as she passed him, he leapt at her and grabbed her arms. She gave a shrill scream of fear. Her purse and packages tumbled to the cobblestones. The man thrust his face so close to hers, she could see the spidery red veins in the whites of his wild eyes.

"He's here!" the man cried. "The demon-beast of the Dark Lord. He'll steal her soul, mother! Save her! Only you can save her!"

"Here now, let that woman go." Several men rushed to Lauriana's aid, prying her from the ragged Seer. "Get on back to the slums, you crack-skull." Two of the men shoved the Seer down the street, while a third bent to gather Lauriana's fallen belongings.

"You all right, madam?" A fourth man with kind eyes helped her to her feet.

"I . . . yes." Lauriana pressed a shaking hand to her face and battled back the threatening hot rush of tears. "I'm fine. Thank you. Just a little shaken." She took the packages and her bag back from the third man. "Thank you all," she repeated. Gathering her composure as best she could, she turned down Poppy and headed towards home.

She couldn't stop herself from glancing back over her shoulder. The Shadow Seer stood to one side of the cobbled road, watching her. His mouth was moving. She couldn't hear what he was saying, but she knew the words all the same. *Only you can save her.*

Deeply troubled, she made her way back home. Rain and Ellie were still out on their "courtship bells," those long, unchaperoned periods of time when they flew off to engage in gods only knew what kind of mischief together. Sol was certain the Fey-oath the Tairen Soul had sworn would keep their daughter and her virtue safe, but Lauriana wasn't nearly so trusting. Especially after Selianne's dreadful revelation.

At home, she carried her packages upstairs and set them down on her bed. As she did so, a sheet of paper fluttered to the floor. She bent to pick it up and frowned at the smudged block print of the headline that proclaimed: "Beware the Shadow Lord, Corrupter of Souls!"

Oh, for the Haven's sake. That Shadow Seer must have thrust one of his religious tracts in her bags. She'd never been a woman to pay the Shadow Seers much mind. She'd always been too intrinsically orthodox in her devotion to the Bright Lord to find their fanatical mysticism appealing.

Lauriana started to toss the pamphlet away, then stopped. What if, for all their wild-eyed madness, the Seers were right about the Fey? Hadn't Selianne just told her of the unholy carnal spell the Tairen Soul had woven over Dorian's court?

She scanned the text. Most of it was the hysterical drivel she'd come to expect from the Seers, but there was a line or two that hit a little too close to home regarding the beguiling lure of evil, and how the most dangerous of all the Shadow's servants were the kind that approached cloaked in beauty and false goodness. She reread those lines several times and shivered. The description of the Shadow's servants fit Rain Tairen Soul and the Fey perfectly.

Two bells later, Lauriana sat in silence, knitting with fervor and sneaking grim glances at the Fey king as he led Ellysetta through the steps of an intricate court dance Master Fellows insisted she must learn before the prince's prenuptial ball.

The corrupter of innocents moved with inhuman grace as he twirled Ellysetta in a series of elegant pirouettes. He looked so shining and pure and beautiful, not at all like the serpent of iniquity she knew him to be. Luring Ellysetta to carnal banquets. Endangering her soul. As the priests always said, the swiftest road to sin was down the path of pleasure . . .

Ellie glanced over, frowning a little. "Mama? Is everything all right?"

Conscious of the Tairen Soul's sudden interest, Lauriana blanked her face and did her best to blank her emotions as

well. "I'm fine, kitling." She forced a smile. "Just a little aggra-
vated by some of the tradesmasters I had to deal with today."

Deciding it was best not to sit in the Fey's presence with her
thoughts in such a turmoil, she set her knitting aside and went
upstairs to her room to finish sorting through the packages
she'd brought home.

She emptied the contents of the largest bag on her bed.
Along with the boxes of gratitudes and wedding programs she'd
picked up from the printer, the small blue and silver gift
Selianne had given her tumbled out. Selianne had asked Lauriana to put it somewhere that Ellie would be sure to find it and
open it herself, without an audience. ("It's a little something
from one married friend to another soon-to-be-married
friend, Madame Baristani," Selianne had whispered with a
faint blush.) Lauriana had forgotten about the gift, but now,
looking at the reflections shimmering in the shining silver ribbons, she felt compelled to tuck it safely away in Ellie's room as
quickly as possible.

She carried the gift down the hall and set it on Ellie's dressing table. When she turned back towards the door, a strange
light-headedness struck her and her vision went blurry. She
stumbled out of the room and put her hand against the hallway
wall to steady herself until the dizziness passed.

"Lauriana, you ninnywit. What did you think would happen
after not eating all day?" Her constitution wasn't as hardy as it
had been in her youth. She returned to her bedroom and
splashed cool water on her face before heading downstairs to
fix herself something to eat.

As she passed Ellysetta's open bedroom door, a glint of blue
and silver caught her eye and she paused, scowling with exasper-
ation.

Now, who had put that gift there in Ellie's room? How
many times had she told her daughters and the Fey that all
wedding gifts needed to be kept together downstairs. Argh!
She might as well talk to a stone wall, for all the good it did
her!

Lauriana had a *process* in place. If gifts were tossed willy nilly and opened at random rather than being carefully logged and recorded, she had absolutely no hope of ensuring the proper gratitudes went out to the appropriate people. And considering that half the gifts came from influential and noble families, such an oversight could besmirch her family's reputation and harm Sol's business. What nobles would buy their goods from an ingrate who couldn't even be bothered to thank them for the graciousness of their gifts?

She snatched up the package and marched downstairs to deposit it on the hall table, alongside the three dozen or so other gifts that had arrived today.

The front door opened. Dajan vel Rhiadi, the Fey who stood guard at the Baristani front door each day, entered, his arms laden with more packages that had been inspected by the Fey.

"On the table with those others until we make more room in the parlor," Lauriana rapped out. She stood, arms crossed over her chest, glowering, while Dajan did as he was told, then lectured the bewildered man soundly about the importance of following her precise directions for handling the wedding gifts.

« Trouble comes, General. »

Gaelen vel Serranis groaned as the persistent thread of Spirit penetrated his consciousness. Alternating fever and chills had left him weak as a babe, while his numerous wounds and the *sel'dor* embedded in his flesh reminded him of their presence with waves of pain that pounded him mercilessly.

« Report. » It was all he could do to form and send even that one word on Spirit, and gathering energy enough to send it spinning out into the world felt like spikes driving into his brain. Of all the magics, Spirit was the most difficult to weave while *sel'dor*-pierced. Earth ran a close second, followed by Fire, then Air and Water.

« Eld troops are moving along the border. » The information came from Farel vel Torras, Gaelen's chief lieutenant and most trusted friend, if it could be said that *dahl'reisen* trusted or befriended anyone.

«*Invasion?*» This time, the pain of weaving Spirit was so intense, Gaelen couldn't completely choke back his scream. He fell back against the rotting leaves of the *rultshart's* den, panting. The *sel'dor* shrapnel still buried in his flesh burned like live coals.

«*Possibly.*» There was a brief pause, and then, «*They're building up along the western borders.*»

Closest to the Fading Lands. Which implied that whatever the Eld were planning, it involved an attack on the Fey.

Rain Tairen Soul was in Celieria City. And so was Gaelen's sister, Marissya.

And the High Mage's daughter was with them.

Farel must warn the Fey—both of the serpent coiling on their doorstep and the one hiding in their midst. He must send *dahl'reisen* to slay the Eld demon's get before she could pass through the Faering Mists and unleash her father's evil.

Gaelen knew it was a terrible risk. Rain would die the moment his claimed mate was slain—no Fey, not even Rain Tairen Soul, could survive his truemate's death—and nothing would give the Eld a greater advantage than the death of the last Tairen Soul. But what choice did Gaelen have? Once the High Mage's daughter passed through the Faering Mists, her father could use her to strike deep at the very heart of the Fading Lands, and the *dahl'reisen* would be helpless to stop him. The Fey would be destroyed. Marissya would die.

Bracing himself, Gaelen summoned his remaining strength and once more threw himself against the *sel'dor*-spawned razors that slashed him as he tried to send the command. This time, not even his tremendous will could conquer the agony. His weave dissolved even as it formed. Despite centuries of training and experience, he screamed. It was a raw, sharp-edged roar of sound. As much fury and desperation as it was pain.

He fell back against the rotting leaves, panting and clinging feebly to consciousness as agony swept over him in dizzying, debilitating waves.

He wanted to curse and rail, but he dared not let even that much of his precious, rapidly dwindling supply of energy escape. His mind was already racing to find another solution. Evaluate, adapt, execute. Fey warriors were trained to think on their feet, to find ways around seemingly insurmountable obstacles.

Without Gaelen's command, the *dahl'reisen* would do as they had done for the last thousand years—protect the Fey from a distance—but none would communicate with the Fey directly, and none would dare approach Celieria so long as Marissya was there. Since he couldn't weave Spirit to issue the command, he would have to go in person. He would have to be the one to ensure the High Mage's spawn never set a single cursed foot in the Fading Lands.

But first he had to find the strength to get up.

Ah, gods, he hurt. His body had nothing left to give him. Nothing but excruciating pain, a heart full of *dahl'reisen* hate, and the memories of a time when he'd walked the Bright Path, not the Dark.

Get up, Fey. Warriors don't lie sniveling on the ground just because they're hurt. Do you think the Mages will give you time to recoup your strength? They'll slaughter you where you lie and piss in your skull. Get up, boy! In his mind, he could still hear the fierce, harsh bark of his *chatok*, the great Shannisorran v'En Celay, shouting at the young *chadin* Gaelen. How many times in those long years of training had the great Shan, Lord Death, pushed him beyond endurance? *Pain is life, boy. Fey warriors eat pain for breakfast. We breathe it. We embrace it. We jaff it on a cold night just to keep warm. Get up, boy! Get up, scorch you!*

Gaelen staggered to his feet.

His wounds shrieked. Agony roared up his limbs, immolating him with its fiery wrath. He bared his teeth and swallowed the tortured scream that fought for release, turning it inwards and feeding the energy back into his body. Fey ate pain for breakfast. Fey embraced it. Fey breathed it in and jaffed it on a cold night just to keep warm.

What are you, chadin? Shout it out! Let me hear you!

I . . . am . . . Warrior!

I . . . . am . . . Fey!

Or, rather, once he had been.

Clutching his side, Gaelen forced himself to walk. His steps were shambling at first, each shuffling motion detonating a fireburst of pain all over his body as cauterized flesh ripped open and shrapnel shifted within torn muscle, but soon the individual pains numbed to a single, dull agony, and that he could control. Shambling steps accelerated to a long stride, then a moderate jog. The pace was a far cry from his normal land-eating run, and his feet fell heavily on the earth, but it was forward progress.

The journey might kill him, the destination certainly would, but that was better than dying from infection and blood loss amid the foul ignominy of a *rultshart's* den. Besides, though he'd not come within half a continent of his last living sister in over a thousand years, he would willingly give his own life and the life of every *dahl'reisen* under his command before allowing the slightest harm to come to her.

With every step, Gaelen focused his substantial will on one single goal: He had to get to Celieria City. The High Mage's daughter could not be allowed to live.

CHAPTER NINE

Ellysetta hummed a bright Fey tune as she bustled around the Baristani kitchen, cooking up a hearty breakfast of peppered eggs, honey-cured bacon, and fried sweetcorn cakes with butter. Since that last nightmare after the palace dinner four nights past, not one bad dream had plagued her. Not even the slightest passing twinge. Each night after her parents went to bed, Rain snuck into her room and the Fey spun twenty-five-fold weaves around the house. Between the two of them, they had managed to keep out who or whatever was responsible for her nightmares.

She hadn't realized what a dreadful burden those dreams had become. Without them, it was as if a great weight had been lifted from her soul, leaving her truly happy and lighthearted in a way she couldn't remember ever being before.

Of course, she thought with a secret smile as she set the breakfast table, Rain was as much to credit for that as her lack of dreams. In addition to the daily courtship gifts—a crown of exquisite Pink Button daisies made from white and pink diamonds, a small crystal lamp that burned fragrant oil, a music box with a tiny dancing couple that twirled when the music played—he'd sent her more than a dozen little gifts each day.

Small, silly things meant to make her laugh or smile, each accompanied by a note penned in his own hand.

If that weren't enough, they'd spent the last day's courtship bells in a beautiful meadow in the hills overlooking Great Bay. There he'd lain with her in the sweet grass beside a cascading waterfall and shown her with both his body and his brilliant command of Spirit just how devoted he truly was. Even now, the memories of it made her skin tingle and brought her near to swooning.

She fanned herself and pressed a glass of iced water against her face to cool her flushed cheeks. Her wedding day—and night—couldn't come soon enough.

Rain had devoted equal care and guidance to her magical tutelage, too. Though she still couldn't summon real magic on a regular basis—and never a weave stronger than what Rain called a level-one skill—she'd become rather adept at asking living things to share their essence with her. She could make grass wave and water ripple in flows following her fingers, and when she passed her hands above Rain's bare flesh, not touching him but asking his body to share its magic with her, she could make his every muscle tremble and his eyes glow bright as the Great Sun.

The only unpleasantness in what would otherwise have been halcyon days were the continued unrest in the city and Mama's increasingly open bitterness towards the Fey.

Just yesterday, news of another *dahl'reisen* attack in the north had worked a mob of Celierians and Brethren of Radiance followers into near hysteria. They'd marched on the palace and gathered outside the gates to demand the expulsion of all Fey from the city. "Bride stealers!" they had shrieked. "Child killers! Servants of Shadow!" The hostility was so strong and virulent that even Lady Marissya's attempt to weave peace on the crowds had failed. In the end, a full complement of King's Guards rode out to arrest the more violent protestors and disperse the crowds.

The unrest had left many of the noble lords skittish. Even with the support that Lords Teleos and Barrial had helped assemble, Rain was finding it difficult to garner the final votes they needed to ensure the Eld borders would remain closed.

The ceiling creaked as feet trod the floorboards in her parents' room above. Ellysetta glanced up, frowning. Mama was almost as bad as the rabble-rousers. In the last few days, her previous grudging acceptance of Ellysetta's pending marriage had changed to suspicion and even outright hostility.

Ellie told herself the proximity of so many Fey was simply taking its toll on her mother's nerves—she'd never trusted magic or those who wielded it—but her reaction seemed stronger than that, almost as if something was amplifying her fears.

Shoving the grim thoughts aside, Ellysetta flipped the corncakes onto a serving plate, set them and the rest of the food on the table, then stepped back to admire her handiwork. Everything was ready and very nearly perfect. The eggs and corncakes were steaming, the bacon crisp and fragrant. The flowers she'd arranged for the centerpiece were bright and colorful, though perhaps the tiniest bit droopy.

She bit her lip. Rain had already taught her how to ask living things to share their essence. Yesterday he'd also taught her how to share a little of her own back. After a quick glance around to make sure she was alone, she closed her eyes to gather her thoughts, then, concentrating, passed a hand over the flowers. The stems straightened and the petals perked up.

Smiling, pleased with herself, Ellie turned to grab the salt and pepper off the stove—and froze. Her mother was standing in the doorway, staring at her. Ellie's heart skipped a beat.

"M-Mama. I didn't see you there!" Had her mother seen her fix the flowers? Deciding to brazen it out, she forced a bright smile. "You were still sleeping when I woke, so I made breakfast." She waved a hand at the table.

"I haven't been sleeping well," her mother murmured, still staring. She glanced from Ellie to the table and back again, her eyes dark and watchful. "Ellie, kitling . . . is there anything you'd like to tell me?"

Ellie's eyes widened. She blinked once, twice, and swallowed

e sudden dry lump in her throat. "Uh . . . no. Nothing."
hat was no lie. The last thing in the world she *wanted* to do
as tell her mother Rain was teaching her magic. There were
me things her mother was just better off not knowing.

She cleared her throat. "Have a seat, Mama. Everything's
ady. I was just about to call everyone to eat." She turned back
the stove and fumbled with refilling the salt and pepper
akers, taking that brief moment to marshal her composure.

She heard her mother pull out a chair and take a seat. *Thank
u, Bright One,* she whispered silently, giving a brief, grateful
ok skyward. She set the shakers on the table near her
other's place and jumped when Lauriana's hand closed
ound her wrist.

"I love you, Ellie. You know I only want what's best for you,
n't you?"

Ellysetta wanted to weep. She knew. She could feel her
other's desperate worry and deep love as strongly as she
nsed Rain's emotions when she touched him. But she also
new how appalled Mama would be if she discovered Ellie had
en practicing magic.

"I know, Mama." She bent down to kiss her mother's cheek
d hug her. "I love you too. More than I can ever say."

"You'd tell me if you were in trouble, wouldn't you? Or if
e Fey encouraged you to do something you knew was
rong?"

Ellysetta pulled back. "I'm not in trouble, Mama, and I'm
ot doing anything wrong. Please, stop worrying—and be
appy for me. I've dreamed of Rain Tairen Soul since I was a
ttle girl, you know that."

Before her mother could reply, the twins trailed in, squab-
ling over which of them would get to wear the pink hair rib-
ons today. Papa followed close behind, and the Baristanis bent
eir heads to say grace and eat. When they were done, Mama
ok the girls down to a neighbor's house for lessons while
apa headed off to his shop.

Never, Ellysetta promised herself as she watched her mother
alk down the street and disappear around the corner. Never

again would she practice even the smallest form of magic within a mile of her mother.

Feeling as though she'd dodged a mortal blow, she turned her attention to her morning lessons with the Fey. Adrial and Rowan had resumed their places in her quintet, and this morning they led the session with an introduction to the legendary Warrior's Academy in Dharsa and the centuries of training and testing a Fey warrior had to complete before he could serve on a *shei'dalin's* quintet.

"*Sel'dor* is a black metal that disrupts Fey magic," Adrial was saying. "Our enemies know this. That's why the Eld use barbed *sel'dor* arrows and blades designed to break off in our flesh. And we, of course, know that. So Fey warriors are trained from youth to fight through what would otherwise be debilitating pain, and to be an effective and lethal fighting force even wounded and without magic. It is a slow process. One that takes centuries to master, and we continue to perfect it all the years of our lives."

The prickle of hay straw stabbed and itched Gaelen unmercifully, the irritation amplified by the endless jostle of wagon wheels bumping over the rutted country highway. He stifled a groan as the wagon hit a particularly deep rut and bounced him hard against the unforgiving edges of a nearby crate. The *sel'dor* shrapnel peppering his back and arms shifted, shredding new muscle as it dug deeper, but he clung to his weak invisibility weave with dogged determination.

For three days and nights he'd made miserably slow but determined progress towards Celieria City. He'd lost countless bells to unconsciousness when exhaustion, pain, and blood loss took their inevitable toll, but he'd persevered. Running when he could, walking and even crawling when that was all he could manage, he'd pushed on. Last night, when he'd grown too weak to continue, he'd hitched a ride with an unsuspecting farmer heading south to deliver crates of canned goods and fresh produce to Vrest. The ride had been hard, his sleep sporadic, but at least he'd gotten a little rest without losing all forward progress.

The wagon slowed, and the sounds of distant activity reached Gaelen's ears. He forced open bleary eyes and dragged himself to peer over the edge of the wagon. Up ahead, he could see the clustered buildings that formed the outskirts of Vrest.

Time to abandon his ride. He'd barely managed to hold the simple invisibility weave with the amount of *sel'dor* still in him, and though it had worked to hide him from a farmer pre-occupied with driving his team, he couldn't risk having sharper-eyed citizens of Vrest detect him. A wounded Fey with a telltale scar across his brow would draw too much unwanted attention, and if news of his approach reached Celieria City before he did, the Tairen Soul might well flee with his soul-cursed, Mage-sired mate before Gaelen could get close enough to kill her.

Slowly, each motion an agonizing exercise in discipline and determination, Gaelen lifted his body up and straddled the sides of the wagon. As the cart neared a small, bridged creek bed, he pushed himself off and went tumbling down the embankment. Each bump and hard jostle sent agony ripping through him. His invisibility weave failed, and he dragged himself to cover beneath the bridge and wedged himself up high to avoid detection.

Gods, that had all but slain him. He flopped back against the shadowed embankment and drew breath in short, sharp gasps. Beneath his skin, lumps of *sel'dor* burned like acid.

He fumbled for one of the black Fey'cha strapped across his chest. Two hundred miles still lay between Gaelen and his prey in Celieria City. Healthy, he could have run it in less than ten bells, but in his current condition, he'd be lucky to make it in ten days.

Time to lose a little more of the black metal the Eld had dispersed so freely. When he reached Celieria City, he'd give the High Mage's get a little red Fey metal in return.

＜━━━◆━━━＞

Vadim Maur's flowing purple robes whispered in the tomblike silence as he descended to the deepest level of Boura Fell. His hair, long and bone white, shone bright in the flickering lamplight of the dark corridor, a beacon for the two men and the leashed flame-haired woman, Elfeya, who walked silently behind him.

Three days had passed since he'd last called the Celierian girl. He'd found her, but she'd managed to rebuff him and lock her mind away from him. For the last three nights he hadn't even managed to locate her, let alone call her. The failure infuriated him.

Kolis's ensorcelled gift hadn't worked either. The cursed spell still hadn't even been activated! Vadim's plan to capture the girl during the Bride's Blessing was looking more promising by the day. Fortunately, he'd had already put those plans in motion. He wasn't a Mage who believed in leaving things to chance.

Victory came to those who planned for it.

And punishment—swift and severe—came to anyone who stood in his way.

At the end of the level's longest corridor, two burly men stood guard by a large *sel'dor*-plated door. They held barbed *sel'dor* spears in their meaty hands.

"Open it," the High Mage ordered.

One of the guards grabbed the key ring at his waist and unlocked the door, swinging it open and standing aside to allow the Mage and his followers to enter.

The room was dark. Vadim lifted a hand, and Fire ignited the sconces throughout the room. Light blazed, illuminating a huge, cavernous space hewn from the black rock of Eld. Veins of *sel'dor* ran through the rock, a natural damper for the magic released here. The room was a scientist's delight, a laboratory stocked with a vast array of implements and pharmacopoeia to aid in the High Mage's centuries-old quest for knowledge. In the center of the room a wide table, fitted with *sel'dor*-barbed restraining straps, was bolted to the floor.

So much had been tried. So much had been learned. Almost enough, but not quite.

A large *sel'dor* cage sat against the far wall. Within it, a naked man cringed at the sudden brightness of the room.

Beside the High Mage, Elfeya made a soft, quickly muffled sound. A sob. The Mage smiled with pride. Even after a thousand years, Elfeya still had the ability to weep. It was a testament to his careful handling of her, the great care he had taken with both his pets. So many other Mages had lost their captives to madness, broken them with frivolous torture, but Vadim Maur had yet again succeeded where others failed.

The man in the cage went still. His head came up, nostrils flaring. His leaf-green eyes were drawn to the woman. Elongated pupils narrowed to slits, then opened wide like a hunting cat's. His eyes glowed for the briefest of moments, a predictable flare of power that made him gasp when the *sel'dor* manacles piercing his wrists and ankles twisted the power into agonizing pain.

Elfeya cried out and flinched even as he did.

The man launched himself at the barbed bars of his cage. His fingers wrapped around them, heedless of the sharp, jagged metal slicing into his flesh. He shook the bars violently in a grip that still retained incredible strength even after so many centuries of imprisonment. Even though the bars were made of barbed *sel'dor*, if the man's wrists and ankles had not been *sel'dor* pierced—and deeply—nothing could have held him in the cage.

He bared his teeth. He howled his rage. He howled his desire.

The woman trembled.

Vadim Maur laughed. Really, they were endlessly entertaining. And so easy to control, once you knew the trick of it.

"Come here, my pet." The Mage held out a hand, and although Elfeya's golden eyes blazed hatred—that had not dimmed in the last thousand years either—she came to him. She didn't flinch as he put the razor-sharp *sel'dor* blade to her throat. The black jewel in the pommel of the dagger began to glow with subtle red lights. It had tasted her blood before.

"Take him to the table," the Mage commanded, and the two servants he'd brought with him moved reluctantly to the *sel'dor* cage and the mad creature within.

As they unlocked the cage door, the prisoner sprang towards them, only to stop abruptly with a harsh cry.

The *sel'dor* blade had sliced into the woman's throat, just deep enough to cause pain. The High Mage smiled as he watched her golden eyes beg the manacled prisoner for death, laughed as the prisoner gave her a tortured look from eyes that now held despairing sanity. Subdued without a hand or a hint of magic laid on him, the prisoner allowed himself to be led to the table, and the servants strapped him down.

The Mage could have restrained the man with any number of weaves, but this way was so much more satisfying.

When the man was cuffed to the table, Vadim ran a finger over Elfeya's wound to close it. He touched the *sel'dor* rings that pierced her ears. Ten rings in each ear, set with tiny bells so she never forgot they were there or who had pierced her. Matching belled manacles lined with sharp spurs to dig into her flesh circled her ankles, and masterfully crafted *sel'dor* bands of surprising delicacy and beauty clasped her upper arms with hundreds of deeply piercing teeth.

She was the only woman in his care ever to need such extensive binding. Her power was that great. But the strongest, most unbreakable bond Vadim used to control her was the man lying on the table.

Three burly servants and a small, ragged girl entered the room carrying a large basin, several buckets of hot water, soap, and a cloth. The servants lowered the basin to the floor and filled it with the buckets of water. The girl stood there, holding the soap and the cloth, her eyes lowered. She was dark-haired, no older than ten or eleven. There was something familiar about her, though the High Mage couldn't have said what it was.

"What are you waiting for?" Vadim snapped at the child. "Bathe him."

The girl raised her head and looked at him. Large, startling silver eyes surrounded by a fringe of black lashes stared at him from beneath slashing dark brows and unkempt hair. Cold eyes, ancient eyes—*his* eyes.

Then he realized who she was. The granddaughter of his great-grandson, or something like that. One of his numerous progeny. Vadim couldn't remember her name, but it didn't matter. She had been born utterly without magic. A worthless lump of flesh, good for nothing but serving her betters.

His hand shot out and smacked across the face with a sharp crack, enough force behind the blow to knock the child to her knees. "Insolence is not tolerated, *umagi*. Lift your eyes to me again and I'll pluck them from your head."

Without a sound, the girl picked herself up off the floor. Eyes lowered with appropriate submissiveness, she stepped towards the chained Fey, dipped her cloth and soap in the basin, and began to bathe the years of grime off the prisoner's skin. The three burly servants who had accompanied the girl into the room unshackled one of the prisoner's wrists and feet at a time so the child could reach his back.

When she was finished, the servants lifted the basin of water and emptied it on the man strapped to the table. He gasped for air and shook his head to clear the water from his eyes. Water and grimy suds streamed off the table and ran in soapy rivulets towards the drain in the center of the room. The girl toweled most of the moisture from the man's body and the table; then she and her fellow servants gathered the buckets, bowed to Vadim Maur, and left.

The High Mage ran a hand through Elfeya's silky curls. Such bright, distinctive hair. She really was an incredibly beautiful woman. He'd not brought her to him for several years now because she'd been so fragile and had needed time to recover her physical and mental strength. She was stronger now—his visit to her earlier this week had proved that. His fingers stroked her neck. She didn't glance at him, didn't shiver, didn't even catch her breath. She merely stood there and endured, her eyes locked with the eyes of the man on the table.

"You may go to him now," the Mage told her, knowing that everything in her body, everything in her soul was drawing her to that man, even as her brain—educated by centuries of torment—screamed for her not to give in to her desires.

Torture was so much more excruciating when the memories of pleasure were fresh in one's mind. Fear was so much stronger when one remembered what, exactly, one stood to lose. If these two had robbed him of his greatest triumph all those years ago, as he suspected they had, their punishment would be worse than anything they had yet endured in his keeping. And they would have this time together, this small bit of happiness, to make the pain all the more exquisite.

"Touch him." The High Mage bent close to her ear and whispered, "I know you want to. How long has it been? Three years? Five?" And he knew she would know exactly how many years, months, days, bells, even instants had passed since last she'd touched this particular man. "Look at him. Look how his body begs you to touch him." The man on the table was fully, helplessly aroused, no more able to fight his body's instincts than she was. "Go to him. Touch him. Mate with him as you are aching to do."

With a low cry, the sound of a soul in torment, Elfeya flung herself forward, racing across the room to the imprisoned man. She grabbed his face between hands that trembled. Tears rained down her face, falling upon his lean cheeks and merging with the answering tears that streamed from the corners of his eyes. Her flame-colored hair spilled across his chest like liquid fire. She kissed him with frantic, helpless need and sobbed into his mouth, *"Ver reisa ku'chae. Kem surah, shei'tan. Kem surah."*

Lauriana went about her errands in a dazed fog, her body automatically carrying her from shop to shop while her mind kept playing and replaying those brief moments in the kitchen when she'd entered and seen. . . . what? She wasn't exactly sure what she'd seen. It had happened so fast, and she'd been tired after yet another night spent tossing and turning and waking from dreams she couldn't remember but which left her with an awful feeling of impending doom.

Had Ellie moved the flowers . . . or had they moved themselves, as it had seemed at first glance? She didn't know. But she couldn't shake the feeling that it was magic. That Ellysetta, her sweet kitling, had been weaving evil, unnatural magic, just like the Fey she'd always been so enamored of.

Oh, gods, why had she ever let Ellie nurture her fascination with the Fey? She could have stamped it out years ago, but she hadn't. To see the way little Ellie's eyes shone when Sol told her Fey tales of princesses and magic Fey giftfathers and the heroic quests of legendary Fey warriors of old . . . not even Lauriana's deep aversion to magic had been impetus enough to rob her daughter of those happy moments. What was the harm, she'd thought, in letting a child enjoy a few stories?

You reap what you sow, Lauriana, and just look what your indulgence has wrought. A daughter betrothed to the worst Fey of them all . . . a daughter who is turning her back on everything you taught her and abandoning the Way of Light.

The thoughts preyed on Lauriana's mind, beating at her relentlessly.

In desperation, she headed to the small West End chapel where she and her family worshiped, hoping Father Celinor might be able to offer some sort of guidance.

She should have known better. The young priest was as enamored of the Fey as Ellysetta.

No sooner had she begun to explain her fears than he'd begun defending the Fey, extolling their virtues and cautioning her not to condemn them for the extraordinary graces the gods had granted them.

"We are all the gods' creatures, Madame Baristani," he said. "Magic exists in the world because the gods deemed it should be so. Would you despise a flower for its perfume? No? Then why would you despise the Fey for possessing the magic they were born to have?"

"You're from the south, aren't you, Father?"

He looked a bit surprised, but nodded. "Yes, from the Tivali Valley, near the Elvian border. I've spent more than a few years in and around the company of magical races, and on the whole I've always found them to be honorable and worthy folk."

"Well, I'm from the north," she countered, "from Dolan

near the Eld border. And I know for a fact that not all all magics are good. Nor are all gods, for that matter."

"I'll grant you that," he agreed. "The Shadow Lord is evil, as are his followers—but we're not talking about Shadowfolk. We're talking about the Fey, and they have always been noble creatures. Not perfect—no living creatures are—but they do strive to be good. They follow the Way of Light."

"How do you know that, Father? No human has set foot in the Fading Lands in a thousand years. None of us know what goes on behind the Faering Mists."

He rose to his feet and held out a hand to help her up as well. "I'm afraid I can't help you there, Madame Baristani. What I can do is offer you the use of the chapel's Solarus. It's not as grand as the one at the Cathedral, but I still find peace there when I am troubled."

It wasn't the advice she'd hoped for, but it was apparently the best he had to offer. She followed him to the chapel's small Solarus and stepped inside. The door closed behind her, granting her privacy, and she moved to the altar at the center of the round room. Overhead, the mirrored ceiling and tiny dome set with numerous windows shone light down on the small statue of Adelis perched on the altar slab.

With a sigh, Lauriana knelt, bowed her head, and began to pray. For more than half a bell, she prayed. Sometimes kneeling, sometimes pacing, sometimes weeping, but the peace she sought was more elusive than smoke.

Father Celinor didn't understand. He'd never seen the ugly side of magic. Not even Sol, a northerner like herself, truly understood. He'd lived his early years in the sheltered town of Callowill while she'd grown up in Dolan, a small and unfortunately strategic logging hamlet nestled in the shadow of two great forests, Greatwood and the dark Verlaine.

Far too many fierce, magical battles of the Wars had been fought on Dolan's doorstep, and the terrible by-products of those clashes haunted Dolaners still. They knew firsthand the evils of magic. They suffered the attacks of lyrant, the vile, mutated descendants of long-tailed treecats corrupted by black

Magery. They witnessed the horrors of children born with ungodly powers, and suffered the agony of giving them up for the good of the town because they knew a worse fate awaited them all if they did not.

Lauriana's own sister Bessinita, a normally laughing, sweet-natured child of two, had been abandoned in the dark shadows of the Verlaine after she'd thrown a fit of childish temper while playing with a neighbor's child. That fit had sparked a fire that burned down the neighbor's house, nearly killed the neighbor's wife, and left the neighbor's child badly scarred.

So when Lauriana had found Ellysetta sitting under that tree north of Norban so many years ago, she'd known exactly what it meant. She'd known she should just turn and walk away. But the child's cap of ringlets and big, solemn eyes had dredged up such tearful memories of sweet Bess that Lauriana couldn't bring herself to walk past.

She'd made a bargain with the Lord of Light. If He would keep the child's magic leashed, Lauriana would raise the little girl in the Way of Light and do everything in her power to ensure that the child never strayed from the Bright Path.

She'd asked Him for a sign, and a shaft of sunlight had broken through the canopy of trees and shone directly on the baby, illuminating her curls like a halo of gold and flame. That was when Lauriana knew she'd been meant to find this child, that she'd been meant to save her as she could not save her sister Bess.

She'd kept her side of the bargain. She'd raised Ellie in the church, loved her with all her heart, and taught her to fear and reject magic. And though it had been like driving knives into her own flesh, she'd even turned her precious child over to the exorcists when those evil childhood seizures seemed proof that darkness was winning its bid for Ellie's soul.

And now the sweet baby girl whose soul Lauriana had vowed to save, the daughter she'd raised in Light, was turning her back on all that her mother had taught her, lured by the beautiful illusion of the Fey.

Lauriana wanted to weep and scream and snatch her precious

child out of harm's way, but she could not. King Dorian had declared Ellysetta to be the Fey king's bride, and there was nothing Lauriana could do about it. A woodcarver's wife could not flout the will of one king, let alone two. She had Lillis and Lorelle to think of, too.

"Please," she whispered, looking up at the shafts of sunlight shining in from the windows of the Solarus's tiny dome. "Please, help me. Show me how to protect her. Give me a sign."

But this time, the Bright Lord remained silent.

Weary and full of despair, no less troubled than when she'd begun her prayers, she exited the Solarus. Father Celinor stood near the doorway, his blue eyes gentle and compassionate.

"She's a good girl, Madame Baristani," he said. "I don't think you have to worry about her losing her path among the Fey, no matter what the pamphleteers and rabble-rousers are claiming. Once tempers calm and people starting thinking again instead of reacting in fear to these *dahl'reisen* threats, they'll remember that the Fey are soldiers of the Light."

"I hope you're right, Father," Lauriana murmured.

He patted her hand. "Trust the Bright Lord to protect the souls in his keeping."

She nodded with obedience but no sincerity and took her leave. Outside on the street, her doubts and fears rose up again, and she went about her errands in a cloud of despair, desperate to find a way to save Ellie but helpless to know how to go about it. She even, gods help her, considered approaching the Brethren of Radiance, but the moment she came within sight of their wild, wailing followers, she turned and fled. Desperate she might be, but not desperate enough to trade magic for madness.

All the while, the Shadow Seer's warning rang hauntingly in her ears: *Save her, mother. Only you can save her.*

When she left Maestra Binchi's shop on Queen's Street after finishing the final fitting of her gown for the wedding, she broke down into helpless tears. She'd just tried on the most beautiful gown she'd ever worn, custom-tailored for her by the country's leading Maestra of fashion. It should have been one of the giddiest, most exciting experiences of her life, a prelude to the even happier event of her oldest daughter's nuptial celebration. Instead, as she'd stood there, draped in exquisite, costly silks, all she could think was, *Will I dance in silk and jewels while I send my daughter to her doom?*

A familiar voice called her name, "Madame Baristani?"

She looked up, scrubbing her tears away with the palms of her hands. Selianne was standing on the sidewalk, not far from Maestra Binchi's shop door. She carried a bag filled with parcels and was watching Lauriana with a worried expression.

"Madame Baristani, are you all right?"

"Oh, Selianne." She began to weep again. Here was someone who shared both Lauriana's love for Ellie and her fear of the Fey. Here was someone she could talk to, someone who would understand. "No, kitling, I don't think I am all right."

Selianne stepped closer and slipped a comforting arm around Lauriana's shoulders. "Come with me, Madame Baristani." She glanced around at the storefronts surrounding them. "There's Narra's tea shop. Why don't we share a nice pot of tea, and you can tell me what's troubling you."

<hr />

Two bells later, Lauriana knelt beside Selianne and Ellysetta at the altar in the Grand Cathedral of Light, her head bowed in prayer, sneaking glances at Greatfather Tivrest. For the first time in days, she felt a glimmer of hope.

"I think you should speak to the archbishop," Selianne had suggested after Lauriana poured out her litany of fears in Narra's tea shop. "He's a sensible man, and a godly one. He's even powerful enough in the church to challenge King Dorian to protect the souls in his care. Talk to him. Tell him everything you've told me. I'd be surprised if he can't help."

Now, looking at him as he stood at the altar, stern and strong in his faith, she knew Selianne was right.

The archbishop was no blind admirer of the Fey like Celinor, nor a wild-eyed fanatic like the Fey-hating Brethren of Radiance. He was a sensible, orthodox man, a disciplined soldier of the Light, and a noble as powerful as any in King Dorian's court.

If any man could help her save Ellie, Greatfather Tivrest could.

He sketched the sign of the Lord of Light and intoned the final blessing of today's devotions. "Arise, daughters," he said when he was done, "and walk in Light."

The three women rose, and the air of formal ceremony faded.

"Well, that's that, then," Selianne said, rubbing her hands together and flexing the fingers that had been clasped in prayer for most of the last bell. "Tomorrow is the Bride's Blessing. Are you ready, Ell?"

Ellysetta nodded. "I think so."

"Nervous?"

"A little."

"It gets worse when it's time for the actual wedding."

They all laughed, including Lauriana. Ellie's expression grew a little more solemn. "You seem to be feeling better now, Mama."

"I am." From the corner of her eye, Lauriana saw the archbishop turn to descend from the altar. She pressed a quick kiss on Ellie's cheek, then Selianne's. "You girls run on. I'm just going to have a word with Greatfather Tivrest." She hurried towards him. "Your Grace? Can you spare a moment, please?"

"I wonder what that's about," Ellysetta murmured to Selianne.

Her friend shrugged. "Wedding stuff, most likely. I'd better be going. Gerwyn's out of town, so Mama's watching the children."

"Still? He's been gone for days."

Selianne nodded glumly. "I know. I miss him terribly."

Ellysetta felt the tingle of magic as the Fey tore down the barriers around the isle, then a familiar rush of emotion and power. What was Rain doing here? He'd always waited until she returned home before he collected her for their daily courtship bells. "Sel, Rain's here."

Poor Selianne looked as if someone had jabbed her with a knife. "I, uh . . . I think I'll go out the back." She turned and fled.

Ellysetta watched her disappear. She supposed it was a good thing, after all, that Selianne wasn't going to attend the wedding. It wouldn't look good to have her Honoria faint from fear of the groom during the ceremony. Of course, it would look even worse to have the groom murder the Honoria because he read her mind and discovered she was part Eld. At least, she and her best friend had been able to share this much—and thank the Bright Lord that Rain's dire predictions about the Mages consuming Selianne's soul had not come true.

She gave a quick, fanning wave, marshaled her thoughts, and hurried out of the cathedral into the bright sunlight where Rain stood waiting on the manicured lawn.

"Did you miss me so much?" she asked, a teasing smile on her face.

"Have I been such a poor suitor that you must ask?" His teeth flashed in a smoldering smile, and his voice lowered to a throaty purr. "I shall endeavor to do better."

Oh, my. She knew that look, that tone. Her cheeks flushed scarlet.

He laughed softly and moved close so that his body almost touched hers, but didn't; energy zinged between them all the same. Teasing her.

Her eyes narrowed. Two could play that game. He'd even taught her how. Mindful of being in a public place, she didn't use her hands. She just closed her eyes, concentrated, and sent her essence rolling over in him in pulsating waves. His breath hissed on a sharp intake, and she smiled in satisfaction as she felt the rewarding stun to his senses.

When he caught his breath, he regarded her with glowing, half-closed eyes. "If I'm very, very good, *shei'tani*, will you do that again when we're alone?"

She laughed. Without a care for their public location or the worshipers walking past them, she flung her arms around his neck and kissed him soundly.

The teasing passion in his eyes softened to a different, more tender emotion, one that made her heart skip a beat. His hand trailed down the side of her face, brushing back spiraling tendrils of hair. "Come, *shei'tani,* dance the skies with your mate."

He didn't escort her outside beyond the city walls as he usually did. Instead, he Changed right there on the cathedral lawn, much to the outrage of the priests who saw him. Ellysetta barely noticed. She settled into place on Rain's back and together they sprang into the sky.

❦

"You see what I mean, Your Grace?" Lauriana pointed out the window at the disappearing shadow of the Fey king's tairen form. "He calls his magic right here, on holy ground, with no respect for our beliefs or our ways. He's encouraging Ellie to try magic as well. I'm sure of it. She's so in love with him, she'll do anything to please him. I fear that in time she'd even turn her back on the Bright Path if he asked it of her."

Greatfather Tivrest turned away from the window and paced across his private office, his brows drawn together in an expression that was half scowl, half thoughtful deliberation. "It is perhaps providential, Madame Baristani, that you came to me today to discuss your fears." He glanced up, apparently having come to some sort of decision. "Will you follow me, please?"

He lit an oil lamp from his desk and led her to a small, windowless room adjoining his office. Long velvet drapes hung from floor to ceiling to ward off the chill of the ancient stone walls, and a small altar sat in one corner, its stone surface cluttered with dozens of red candles. The room still smelled of smoke and sago flowers as if someone had been burning those altar candles only recently.

Moving to the left wall, he parted the drapes to reveal a small metal door that he proceeded to unlock with a key he pulled from a pocket inside his robes. The door swung inward, opening to a narrow, curving stone stairway. A dim glow of light shone up from the darkness below

"You are not the first to approach me this morning concerned about the safety of your daughter's soul," he said as they descended. "Three brothers from the north came to see me as well." The stairs opened up to a small room furnished with a simple wooden table and chairs. The room's occupants—three men in scarlet robes—rose to their feet and turned to greet them as Lauriana and the archbishop entered.

"This," Greatfather Tivrest said, indicating the older of the two, "is Father Lucial Bellamy, head of the Order of Adelis. And this"—he gestured to the younger, white-haired priest at his side—"is Father Nivane, one of the brothers in his service. And the father standing in the shadows over there is Father Brevard." Father Brevard did not move from the shadows, nor remove the hood concealing his face.

Lauriana had never met any of the three men before, but even without the Greatfather's mention of their Order, the first glimpse of their scarlet robes had told her who—or rather what—they were.

Exorcists.

CHAPTER TEN

"No." Lauriana's feet began to move of their own volition, backing away from the men in their bloodred robes.

"Father Bellamy heard of your daughter's betrothal to the Tairen Soul," the archbishop said. "He came here to Celieria City as soon as he received the news. He says her name is not unfamiliar to his Order."

Lauriana's frightened gaze darted from one priest to the other. "I—" Her throat tightened, choking off her voice. Her knees went weak, and she reached out to grab the wall for support.

"Here, come have a seat before you fall." The archbishop put a supporting arm around her and led her to one of the empty wooden chairs. He pulled up a second, sat beside her, and patted her hand with a gentleness she hadn't known he possessed. "This isn't an interrogation, and I didn't bring you down here to cast blame or frighten you. You came to me for help, and I'd like to provide it, if I can. But first, I need to know what happened in Hartslea all those years ago." He bent forward, his blue eyes solemn, sincere, free of even the slightest hint of reproach. "Is it true your daughter was diagnosed as demon-possessed when she was a child?"

Lauriana swallowed hard and nodded. "Yes." She forced herself to speak, telling him about the seizures and the doctors' eventual diagnosis.

"So you sought assistance from the Order."

She closed her eyes briefly in pained remembrance and nodded. It had been the hardest decision of her life. "I did. Sol didn't want me to, but I insisted. They came to our house with their prayer books and needles . . . It was awful, what they did to her. She screamed and screamed." She could still see little Ellie's face contorted in agony, hear her shrieking and crying out for her mama and papa to save her, to make the pain go away.

"I know the rites can seem brutal," Father Bellamy said softly, "but they are necessary. Demons do not easily release their prey."

"But the exorcism wasn't completed," Greatfather Tivrest prompted.

She shook her head. "Sol couldn't bear it. He stopped it and threw the priests out. We left Hartslea. We prayed and prayed, and eventually the episodes stopped on their own."

"Did they?"

She couldn't hold his too-knowing gaze. "For the most part. It's been more than five years since she last had a seizure. She only gets an occasional nightmare now and again—at least until the Tairen Soul came to town."

"Her nightmares have increased?" Father Nivane asked suddenly.

She cast a wary glance his way. "Yes."

He exchanged glances with Father Bellamy. The older priest nodded. "Madame Baristani," Father Bellamy said gently, "once a demon claims a soul, it does not leave until it's driven out. It may lie dormant for a while, but it is still there." He laid a hand on her shoulder. "You must authorize the completion of the exorcism."

She lurched back, yanking her hand from the archbishop's, then leapt to her feet and turned to face them. "No." Her heart pounded against her ribs, and her lungs felt starved of breath. She began to back away, towards the stairs.

"My dear lady, your concern and deep love for your daughter is obvious. And it is obvious that your own love and dedication to the Bright Lord has been of invaluable assistance in keeping her on the Bright Path, but you cannot abandon her now, in her time of deepest need."

"You don't understand. My husband made me swear on the Book of Light that I would never turn Ellie back over to the exorcists. I can't betray my solemn oath."

"The Bright Lord would never ask you to keep an oath to surrender your child to evil," the archbishop replied. "Your husband was wrong to demand you make such a vow. I grant you dispensation to do the right thing."

Lauriana shook her head with frantic emphasis. "Sol would never forgive me. It would destroy our family." Mild-mannered and loving though he was, Sol had a spine of tempered steel and an unswerving sense of honor and loyalty. He could forgive many things, but not a personal betrayal of the sort they were proposing. "Even if Sol did understand, the Fey wouldn't. They'd kill anyone who touched her. The Tairen Soul won't even let the queen's Master of Graces hold her hand in dance lessons, for the Haven's sake! They'd slaughter us all . . . these exorcists . . . you . . . me . . . maybe even my entire family." She ran trembling fingers through her hair. "No, it's madness even to contemplate such a thing."

"Madame Baristani," Father Nivane interjected, "would you change your mind if you knew we could conduct the exorcism without anyone knowing it ever happened?"

"How on earth could you promise that? She shares a bond with the Tairen Soul. He . . . senses things. And all the Fey can read minds. They'd know the instant you touched her."

"No, they wouldn't." Eagerness lit the younger priest's pale eyes. "We recently discovered a forgotten text in the Church archives that proves we can conduct the exorcism without the Fey's knowledge. They could be standing right outside the door and not sense it."

"Most victims of demon possession have no memory of the

exorcism once it is complete," Father Bellamy added. "The Fey would never know. Your family would be safe."

The archbishop stood, adding his voice to theirs. "Madame Baristani . . . daughter . . . I know this is a difficult decision, but it's the right thing to do for your child."

She backed away, shaking her head. It was too dangerous. No matter what they said, she didn't dare risk it. "I appreciate your concern, Greatfather—more than you'll ever know—and I know I was the one to come to you asking for help, but this isn't the help I was looking for. I was hoping you could simply convince the king to dissolve the betrothal. Once I can get her away from the Fey, things will go back to normal and she'll be fine."

"There's no possible way I could break your daughter's betrothal. Not only was it decided by the Supreme Council, but between the king and the Tairen Soul, they've made it a matter of state. Even if I had such authority—which I don't—haven't you been listening to Father Bellamy? Your daughter isn't fine, and never will be until the exorcism is complete."

"And I've told you I can't authorize an exorcism. I just can't." Lauriana turned and rushed towards the stairs, but before she could set foot on the first step, a hand caught her wrist in a steely grip. Father Nivane held her fast.

"Think of your daughter, woman. Think of her soul. How can you make such a self-serving, cowardly decision and call yourself her beacon?"

"Nivane!" Father Bellamy rapped out. "You forget yourself. Unhand Madame Baristani at once." Turning a conciliatory face to Lauriana, the chief exorcist approached, hands outstretched in a gesture of peace and entreaty. "Madam, forgive my young Brother. He has long fought the agents of the Dark, and such work requires a certain fervor. It is easy, sometimes, to forget that others are not so acquainted with the perils of evil as we."

She pressed back against the wall. The stone felt icy against her skin. "I know what evil is, Father, believe me."

He searched her eyes and nodded. "I do believe you, daughter.

I can see in your eyes that you have confronted it before." Sorrow and compassion lay in his, and the simple kindness she saw made her start to weep. He obviously regretted what he was asking her to do, and knew how difficult a decision it was. "We cannot force you to do this, but will you at least promise to consider it? You can give us your answer tomorrow."

"I—"

"You cannot stop her marriage," he added, "but you can save her soul. And isn't that what you've wanted all along?"

Lauriana nodded, tears trickling from her eyes. "Yes."

"You've been a good mother to her, and an exceptional beacon. Without you, she no doubt would have been lost long ago. For her sake, will you promise to consider our request?"

Nivane bowed, his expression penitent. "Forgive my outburst, Madame Baristani. It was unbefitting my vocation. I want only the best for your daughter. Here, please, take this." He removed a golden pendant from around his neck and held it out to her. The pendant was a golden sun, set with an amber crystal. "It's a charm, blessed by some of the Brothers of the Order to ward against magic. I know the Fey have surrounded your home. This will help protect you and your thoughts against them."

Bellamy laid a hand of thanks on Nivane's shoulder. "Madame Baristani, if you still wish to refuse tomorrow morning, simply send the charm back to Greatfather Tivrest here at the cathedral. We will know you have declined our offer, and we will depart with no one the wiser. Neither your family nor the Fey will know we approached you."

Lauriana reached out slowly and took the pendant from Nivane. The metal felt warm to the touch. "I will consider everything you've said, and give you my answer in the morning."

In his room at the Inn of the Blue Pony, Kolis Manza smiled with satisfaction as he sensed the amber crystal change hands from Nivane to the Feyreisa's mother. The Feraz witchspell anchored to the stone didn't suppress thoughts but rather siphoned off the loudest of them and channeled them to the

receptor crystal Kolis wore around his neck. Short of a deliberate Spirit assault on Lauriana Baristani's mind, the Fey would
not be able to hear her thoughts, while Kolis, on the other
hand, sat like a little fly on the periphery, hearing everything
louder than a whisper.

Rain and Ellie flew farther and faster than they ever had. As
they'd departed Celieria City, she'd asked the innocent question, *«How fast can you fly?»* and with a wicked tairen laugh,
he'd shown her.

He'd wrapped them both in a cocoon of magic and shot so
high they could see the deep twilight cusp of the sky and the
dim shine of stars gleaming just beyond the blue heavens. No
breeze stirred in the shield of Air around them as they flew, and
Rain's wings weren't even moving. They were swept back,
fully extended but held close to his frame while magic alone
propelled them forward at tremendous speed.

"That was incredible," she breathed when at last they landed
and Rain Changed back to Fey form. "How fast were we going?"

Rain smiled. "Very fast. We're halfway to Queen's Point."

Her jaw dropped. "Halfway to—but Queen's Point is more
than five hundred miles from Celieria City!"

"A little over four hundred as the tairen flies. I could have
gone further, but then I would have had to feed to replenish
my strength, and tairen dining can be a little unsettling to those
unused to the sight."

She thought of Love and the kitten's penchant for leaving
the gnawed, half-eaten bodies of mice and lizards lying about,
and her stomach took a queasy lurch. How easy it was to forget that tairen were, first and foremost, predators, with a predator's instincts and a predator's habits. "What do tairen eat?"

"When they're hungry? Anything that moves."

"And are you . . . er . . . hungry now?"

He threw back his head and laughed. "Only for a meal we
can both share. In fact, why don't you set it out now while
I spin the protection weaves." After a quick glance at their

surroundings to find what he needed, he spun a rapid Earth weave. A folded blanket and a small basket appeared beneath a nearby pella tree.

Leaving her to lay out the blanket and basket of meats, cheeses, and various fruits and salads, Rain wove a large five-fold dome around them and secured the threads firmly in place. Not even here, on the beaches of Great Bay two hundred miles from Celieria City, would he relax his guard. Whatever was hunting her—be it Mage, demon, or *dahl'reisen*—would have no further opportunity to prey on her as long as he could prevent it.

He joined her on the blanket to share their meal. When they were done, he leaned back on his elbows and watched her walk towards the gentle surf lapping at the white sand. She stretched her arms up high over her head and lifted her face towards the warmth of the Great Sun, all but purring as the ocean breeze ruffled her hair and filled her lungs with the wild, fresh scents of the sea.

The sight of her standing there in the bright waves reminded him of the long-ago days of his youth when he, Rainier-Eras, Tairen Soul of the Fey'Bahren pride, would join his soulkin to swim in the warm, sparkling waters of Tairen's Bay and later bask on the silvery sands to dry his wings in the ocean breeze. His father, Rajahl, would bask as well, but never far away from his son and always with one watchful eye open, while Rain's mother, Kiaria, would lean against her mate, her slight Fey body shining and pale against his tairen darkness, her eyes closed, a smile of utter contentment on her face.

Ellysetta lifted her skirts and dipped a slender foot in the water. A wave crashed, sending spray and sand flying to soak the hem of her gown.

"That is not quite the right attire for a visit to the ocean," Rain said. He summoned Earth and wove it. Her heavy silk dress shifted, becoming a light, flowing white robe and gown that blew back in the breeze and molded to her body in ways that made his heart beat a little faster. She glanced down and gasped, and her arms slapped into place to cover all her most interesting bits. He grinned. The robe and gown were sheer and he had not spun undergarments.

She scowled. "This is not what I would call being 'very, very good.'"

"That is a matter of perspective, *shei'tani*. From where I'm standing, it looks very, very good indeed."

"Ninnywit."

"Happy mate," he corrected. He spun Earth again. His weapons disappeared and re-formed in a neat pile on a blanket spread beneath the broad fronds of a nearby pella tree. His leathers were transformed to a robe and loose trousers as flowing and sheer as her garments. Unlike her, he didn't try to hide his bits, not even the one growing more interesting by the moment. Her eyes went wide. "And impatient groom," he added with a shrug and another grin.

It felt good to stand in the sun and laugh with his truemate as though neither of them had a care in the world. Too good, almost. The gods were rarely so kind for long.

He jumped to his feet and held out a hand. "Come swim with me."

She hung back. "If I get in the water in this outfit, the cloth will turn completely transparent."

"I know, and I'm looking forward to it more than you can imagine."

Her cheeks turned a pink so bright it put the pella tree's blooms to shame.

He laughed and swept her up into his arms, twirling her around in circles several times. "You bring me such joy." He kissed her until they were both breathless, then tugged her once more towards the waves. "Come. Swim with me."

"You're serious."

"You've never seen the ocean as a Fey sees it. I'd like to share the experience with you." That was part of what he had been doing during their courtship bells, sharing with her the joys of being Fey. Showing her in every way he could that for all the difficulties and danger that came with being his mate, there were great rewards, too.

She hesitated for a moment, then put her hand in his and let him lead her into the surf.

Yet another little act of courage. There'd been so many in the last few days. She was still so innocent—she likely always would be in some ways—but beneath that innocence was a spirit of adventure. For years, Ellysetta had suppressed every hint of it, wanting desperately to be the modest, obedient daughter she thought her parents expected, but now, like a tairen kitling driven by an instinctive yearning for the sky, she was learning to spread her wings and fly. He encouraged her, true, but the effort, the desire, was all hers.

He tossed his robe to the sand, leaving only the thin trousers covering him from waist to ankle. She stared at him for several long moments, a look he could only describe as hunger on her face, and then, with a slow deliberation that nearly drove him mad, she shrugged off the outer robe he'd woven for her, leaving only the simple shift, held up by two narrow straps. The tops of her breasts rose above the bodice, alluring curves that drew attention to the small points of her nipples thrusting against the thin fabric. The bodice flowed down into fuller skirts that swept across her ankles and trailed behind in a short train.

It was Rain's turn to stare, and his look wasn't merely hungry—it was ravenous.

She lifted a brow, cast a siren's look over her shoulder, and dove into the waves.

"Spit and scorch me." Shaking himself free of his dazed paralysis, he closed his mouth and dove after her.

A simple weave of Air and Water let them both breathe under the water and see with as much clarity as they did on the surface, and together they explored the secrets of the world hidden beneath the waves. Sunlit reefs not far off the sandy shores gave way to deeper waters with mysterious caves and undulating fields of shimmering kelp alive with darting fish and other sea creatures.

In the glittering aqua depths, Ellysetta's hair shone like waving fans of coral. Her sheer gown was molded to her and the skirts fluttered languidly in the current, teasing him with flashes of smooth, pearly skin—a thigh, a calf, the delectable curve of her buttock, and the soft, rounded fullness of her breasts tipped with the darker circles of small, puckered nipples. He swam slightly behind her to torment himself with the view.

As he watched, she knifed downward through the water, her hand reaching out towards a school of rainbow-colored fish swimming near the kelp beds. They scattered quickly when her questing fingers came too close. Bubbles of air billowed around her as she laughed and chased after them again.

Even with the long—and very pleasingly transparent—skirts of her gown trailing behind her, she swam as if she'd been born to it like the Sea Folk who inhabited the warm waters of the western ocean. He would take her to meet them too. As delighted as she was by this small bay, he knew she would adore the Sea Folk, with their glittering tails and long, flowing hair that came in all the shades of the sea.

«Look!» Ellysetta called.

She reached down to the sandy ocean floor and lifted a large shell the size of both his hands. It was oval-shaped with long spikes curling back from the mouth, and it had a wide, broad lip colored a deep opalescent blue, with streaks of green and purple. The snail that had once occupied the shell was long gone.

«Isn't it beautiful?»

He looked at her smiling face and shining eyes. *«You are beautiful.»*

Her smile faded as he swam closer. He reached for her hand and pulled her up from the ocean floor until her body was pressed lightly against his and they were floating, weightless, beneath the surface of the sunlit waters. He kissed her, offering her all his joy and devotion.

Rain summoned Earth, and the tantalizing, translucent fabric of her gown parted beneath his hand, falling away to bare the perfection of silky skin and gentle curves. She *was* beautiful. Her long, bright hair, like flame on the water, floated about her, as lovely as any Sea Maid's, her limbs long and slender. Her small, round breasts fit perfectly in the palms of his hands. He bent his head to draw the soft bud of one nipple into his mouth, and the dark skeins of his hair floated in the current, teasing her other breast with feathery brushes.

Her fingers curled in his hair, gripping his head and holding it to her. The tingling laps of his tongue, the teasing brush of his hair . . . *mercy*! She was weightless, floating in warmth and sensation. Nibbling kisses trailed down her belly and lower. Her eyes flashed open. *«Rain?»*

He smiled and lifted his head from her breast but did not release the Spirit weave that pressed tantalizing kisses all around the soft, flame-colored curls between her legs. *«Las, shei'tani. Let me give you this. I promise you will like it.»* The Spirit weave moved lower, directly into those curls. Her eyes widened, but she didn't ask him to stop. Taking that as encouragement, he ducked his head to capture her lips. His tongue dove into the sweet, soft cavern of her mouth just as his weave dove into the softer, more secret cavern between her thighs.

Good, sweet Lord of Light. Ellysetta's eyes closed as wave after wave of unimaginable pleasure bombarded her senses. Heat and pressure built, every stroke of his tongue matched by an even more devastating stroke of his weave. Her hands gripped his shoulders, fingers digging into the lean muscle. He hadn't been bragging about his mastery of Spirit. Even though she knew which touch was him and which was his weave, both felt equally, devastatingly real. The muscles in her legs and belly drew tight. *«Rain . . . Rain, please . . .»* His Spirit flicked with warm, insistent pressure over a spot that seemed to control every trembling nerve in her body. She cried out and her senses shattered.

Holding her trembling body to his, Rain spun a powerful jet of Water, propelling them towards the surface of the ocean, and they burst through the cresting waves like dolphins leaping from the depths. The momentum carried them forward onto the beach, where a rapid weave of Air cushioned their descent. He landed lightly on the sand, Ellysetta in his arms, a scant two steps from the blanket he'd spread out beneath the pella tree.

He knelt on the blanket and lowered her gently beside him. Water streamed from his hair, dripping salty wetness. With a wave of his hand, he dried them both.

She stared up at him with a look of dazed wonder. "That was . . . was . . ."

He smiled. "I am glad you liked it." His eyes were glowing, burning. He'd given her release but taken none for himself. Need still pounded inside him.

Ellysetta's breath caught in her throat, and a new spiral of desire wound tight in her womb. He was so beautiful, so fierce, and yet so achingly gentle with her, always making sure the choice was hers and freely made. He had a power so vast he could have bent her to his will with scarcely a thought, but he used none of it to persuade her.

She sat up and laid a hand on his bare chest, marveling at the silky smoothness of his luminous skin, the power contained in so much beauty. He froze, kneeling beside her as her hand trailed down his side, over his ribs and the rippling, defined muscles of his abdomen. The front of his trousers shifted as the hard length of flesh still hidden beneath them pulsed against the fabric, as if reaching for her.

Her own brazenness amazed her. She was kneeling beside him, utterly naked and not the least bit embarrassed by it. Instead, she wanted him naked too. "Take these off." She trailed her fingers across the waistband of his trousers. "I want to see you."

He waved, and the thin cloth dissolved into wisps of insubstantial mist.

Ellysetta caught her breath. She wasn't completely unfamiliar with the male form. Between the paintings of the old masters in the museum, her giggling discussions with Selianne after she'd wed, and Rain's own Spirit weaves, she knew the basics of what to expect. Even so, nothing had prepared her for the reality of Rain or the rush of fierce desire that filled her at the sight of him.

He was beautiful. Everywhere. Especially there, where his sex rose up from a nest of dark curls, a thick, silken column of alabaster flesh topped with a broad, slightly rosy, rounded crown. She reached out, needing to touch him, to feel that part of his body so different from her own. Her fingers closed around his shaft, and her thumb brushed across the velvety head. His skin here was so soft . . . and so hot, burning like a flame in her hand. His sex pulsed in her palm, and with her fingers still curved around him, she stroked down the silken length, then back up. Tingling bursts of energy shot up her arm, leaping from his body to hers.

He lunged, catching her by surprise and bearing her back upon the cushion of fine sand. His body, the entire full, deliciously naked length of him, pressed against hers. Skin to skin, hot and heavy, a seductive weight that made her legs part and curve up around his thighs in instinctive invitation. His body gave one great, trembling quake, then froze, every muscle locked solid, hard as steel.

"Merciful gods, *shei'tani*." His eyes closed and he pressed his face into her neck. "Don't do that again."

"But I want you, Rain. I want this." She reached for him again, but he caught her hand in an iron grip.

"*Ellysetta* . . ." His voice was a rough scrape of sound, ragged with need. "I want you too, *shei'tani*. And I need to mate with you now. *Teska*, let me spin the weave." He groaned as the tairen surged against its bonds, reaching for her, roaring against its confinement.

A shocking wave of hunger crashed over Ellysetta—fiery, voracious, overwhelming. She shuddered in its grip, feeling the hunger invade every cell, twisting want to clawing need. It rose up, fierce and demanding. She needed him. Now, inside her. Completing her in truth the way he'd completed her so often now in Spirit.

"No weave," she commanded, her voice low, bordering on a growl. "Just you and me, as we were meant to be."

Dear gods. Every muscle in his body clenched in agony. "There's nothing I want more, *shei'tani*. I crave it so fiercely, it would frighten you to know." He dragged in a deep breath. The gods could not have devised a more insidious torment than this: Ellysetta, wholly untouched by any sensory enhancement, not just urging him to take what every instinct of his Fey and tairen souls was screaming for him to claim, but commanding him to. "*Teska*. I swore an oath to your father. I cannot break it."

Now he could scarcely believe he'd been so stupid as to make such a vow. No mortal had a right to govern what was shared between a *shei'tan* and his mate. When Sol Baristani had pressed Rain for his oath that there would be no mating before marriage, Rain should have refused. But he'd wanted the guarantee of time alone with Ellysetta each day, to court her slowly and win her trust so the bond between them could form.

"I didn't swear that oath," she protested. "When you wager with tairen . . ." She squirmed against him, her hips wriggling until his heart nearly exploded in his chest.

She was going to kill him. Without a blade, without a spell, she was going to be the ruin of him. Within, the tairen roared and lunged against its bonds, raging, furious, driven mad by the need to claim its mate.

"*I* swore it," he rasped. "I've already bent my oath as far as I can. This would break it."

Her eyes flashed. For a moment he feared she would demand what he had no more strength to resist, but instead she said, "Then spin your weave, *shei'tan*. Now."

Spirit rushed from his hands in twin rivers of magic so dense and shining, the whole world took on a glowing lavender tinge until the weave settled to illusory perfection. He spared only the smallest fraction of his concentration to spin his leather breeches back into place in the desperate hope of keeping his honor intact. His hands and mouth he gave free rein, falling upon Ellysetta's sweet body with ravening hunger just as the Spirit Rain caught the Spirit Ellysetta in a fierce, hungry embrace.

She reached for him with greedy hands and growled in frustration when they found the warm barrier of his leathers rather than the heated naked flesh she wanted. Her fingers dug into the waistband and tugged. "Take these back off," she insisted, then cried out as his mouth closed around the sensitive peak of one breast, setting her blood on fire.

Hands, mouth, teeth, tongue, both real and magic, worked their way down her body, finding every sensitive spot, tormenting every nerve ending until every fiber of her body came alive with hot, electric sensation. The muscles in her thighs began to tremble, then to quake as in both body and mind her passion exploded in a breathtaking rush. But even before the first shudders ceased, he began working his magic again, driving her to a second, more powerful climax, then a third.

"Rain, dear gods, you're going to kill me." Tremor after tremor shook her, the pleasure intense and ceaseless. She could no longer tell what was real and what was illusion. Her hands gripped his shoulders, nails digging into his skin. "Come to me."

"Not yet." His face was fierce, his eyes blazing like the sun, as he began driving her with relentless determination towards yet another orgasm.

She didn't want this again. She wanted him, not making her fly apart, but flying apart with her. Conscious thought shredded, and wild, insistent instinct rose in its place. She reached for the rigid bulge of his sex, cupping him through the heated leather. Using the technique he'd shown her, she shared the essence of herself with him. Energy leapt from her body to his in a streaming rush: hot, electric, exquisite. He gasped, nearly losing control of his weave as the dazzling force poured into him.

"Now," she insisted.

Flames scorched him. She wasn't begging any longer. She was commanding—and not only by sharing her essence. With the same instinctive, unintentional yet astonishingly powerful weave of Spirit he'd seen her use before, she was *pushing* him, urging him to fulfill her. Compelling him.

He could not deny her. In truth, he didn't want to even if he could.

In his weave, Rain's body sank deep into hers, and she cried out at the glorious fullness of it, the feeling of wholeness and completion. Their Spirit bodies began a fierce rhythm, limbs twining, hips rising and falling in unison.

Rain's throat strained as the need grew and skin stretched taut over bunching muscle. Every soft cry wrenched from her lips was a flame cast upon tinder. He poured himself into his weave, poured his magic across her senses.

Without warning, the wild force of her own untamed magic erupted around them both. Spirit threads dense with power exploded from her, writhing, twining, merging with his weave, driving him with the same relentless mastery as his Spirit drove her. Spirit Ellysetta locked her legs about his hips and rolled on top of him. His breath caught as he looked up at her: wild, glorious, fiercely female, her eyes blazing, her hair a nimbus of living flame around her. An ancient warrior goddess from the time before memory.

She rode him, her silken hips rising and falling, her inner muscles clasping him so tight each movement was an agony of delight. His weave surged around her and he gave himself up to hers. Nothing else in the world existed except him and her, and this breathless dance of Spirit that grew faster and wilder, until pleasure shattered them both and their cries merged with the rhythmic crash of the surf tumbling across the sands of Great Bay.

<hr />

"I don't know what came over me," Ellysetta muttered yet again as she and Rain alit in the cobbled courtyard at the back of her family's home. The hot blush in her cheeks hadn't faded since they'd left Great Bay.

"I don't know either, but I hope it comes over you again. Soon." Rain grinned and dodged her slap with a warrior's rapid reflexes.

His grin faded quickly when he caught sight of Bel standing grim and silent in the back doorway of her parents' small home. The look in Bel's eyes was one Rain recognized, and it never boded well.

"Ellysetta." Rain lifted her hand and pressed a quick kiss in her palm. "Give me a moment, *shei'tani*. I'll be in shortly."

She frowned at them both, realizing something was up, but then nodded and stepped past him into the house.

When she was gone, Bel spun a quick privacy weave. "I've heard from the quintet we sent to Norban. They found Sian and Torel's steel, along with scores of barbed *sel'dor* arrows, scattered over what was obviously a battlefield."

Rain's mouth tightened. The news wasn't unexpected—they'd already presumed the worst—but the *sel'dor* arrows . . . Barbed *sel'dor* arrows had been the Eld soldier's weapon of choice against Fey for millennia. "Has Dorian been informed?"

"Marissya brought him the news a bell ago. He says it's not enough proof to act. That anyone could have made the arrows—or even dug them up from an ancient battlefield."

Anger and frustration curled in Rain's belly. Dorian was determined not to see the truth before him—as if by ignoring the signs of the growing Eld threat, he could make it simply go away.

"There's more," Bel said. His face was grim. Whatever more there was, it wasn't good.

"Tell me."

"One of the men they were seen talking to in Norban—a pubkeeper—is missing, too, and is now presumed dead. Sebourne's already calling for an investigation of the Fey."

Rain closed his eyes. That was all they needed. More weapons in Lord Sebourne's anti-Fey arsenal.

"That's not the worst of it, Rain. Our warriors found another Fey'cha where Sian and Torel were slain. A red blade, bearing the mark of Gaelen vel Serranis."

"Does Sebourne know *that*?"

"*Nei*, thank the gods. None know but our warriors. I told them to destroy it."

Vel Serranis. Again. Had the *dahl'reisen* slipped so far down the Dark Path that he'd thrown in with the greatest enemy of the Fey? Had he slain all those Celierians in the north, murdered Sian and Torel, and sent that boy to stab Ellysetta after all? Rain's heart clutched at the thought.

Gods help Celieria *and* the Fading Lands if the *dahl'reisen* and the Mages had joined forces. And gods curse Rain for an unworthy fool if he didn't get Ellysetta and Marissya both out of Celieria and to the safety of the Fading Lands without further delay.

"Thank you, Bel." Rain dispersed Bel's weave and went inside, heading immediately to Ellysetta's side.

Sensing his turmoil, she brushed her fingers across the back of his hand. Tendrils of peace and concern wafted over him. "What is it, Rain?"

He stroked her fingers with his own and lifted them to his lips for a kiss. "Do you trust me, Ellysetta? To do what is best for you and your family?"

She searched his gaze, then nodded. "Yes, of course I do, Rain."

"Then there is a thing I would ask of your father, but I want your approval first."

<hr/>

"I wish to be released from my pledge to wed Ellysetta next week, so we may instead wed tomorrow, after the completion of the Bride's Blessing." Rain announced the request baldly as he, Ellysetta, and her parents sat at the small Baristani kitchen table. Bel and the rest of the quintet had taken the twins into the parlor to occupy them with unwrapping the last few dozen wedding presents and give Rain a measure of privacy for his discussion.

"Tomorrow?" Lauriana protested. "You can't possibly be serious!"

Sol frowned in sharp concern. "Why the hurry?"

Rain glanced down at his hands. His fingers flexed, wanting to wrap around the comforting grip of sharp Fey steel and confront the faceless danger he'd sensed for so long. "At twelfth bell tomorrow, Celieria's Council of Lords will convene for the final debate and vote to open the northern border to Eld. You know I've been working all week to prevent that from happening, but unless half a dozen lords change their minds or the king invokes *primus*—neither of which is likely—we know the vote will pass.

I want Ellysetta out of the city and on her way to safety before the sun sets on a Celieria that welcomes Mages within its borders."

"Safety?" Lauriana challenged. "You think we're foolish enough to believe that's what waits for her in the Fading Lands?"

"More safety there than here," Rain said.

"That's a matter of opinion."

"Madame Baristani, have you forgotten that someone tried to kill your daughter last week—or that something attacked her through her dreams just four nights past?"

"You Fey are magical creatures. Who's to say you didn't stage both attacks just to convince us Ellie's in danger?"

"Mama!" Ellysetta protested.

"Laurie!" Sol scolded at the same time.

Rain's eyes flashed dangerously. "Do not dare suggest the Fey would ever harm Ellysetta. Every warrior in this city— every warrior in the Fading Lands—would die to spare her the slightest wound. Two already have."

Sol stared at Rain in shock. "What?"

"I sent two Fey north to find out what they could about Ellysetta's origins. They were murdered." He covered Ellysetta's hand with his own. She'd been upset when he told her the news, but it had helped to convince her of the seriousness of the threat. He hoped her parents would be equally understanding. "I received confirmation of it today when we returned from our courtship bells."

"Murdered . . . by whom?"

"We believe it was the Eld, which means if the trade vote passes—as it appears it will—the same folk who murdered my men will have much easier access to Ellysetta and your family."

Unblinking brown eyes regarded him solemnly. A long moment passed in silence.

"Sol!" Lauriana protested. "You can't seriously be considering his request."

"How would you feel, Laurie, if she were hurt—maybe even killed—because we were too selfish to let her go?"

"Will it feel any worse than when we send her to the Fading Lands and she loses her soul to these godless sorcerers because there's no one there to be her beacon?"

"Mama!"

"Laurie!" Sol stared at her as if she'd grown two heads. "What's gotten into you? The wedding's already been agreed to. She's going to the Fading Lands. The only question is whether she goes tomorrow or a few days after that."

Lauriana bolted up from her seat at the table and rushed out of the kitchen. Sol gave Rain an apologetic look and followed his wife.

"Mama didn't mean it," Ellysetta said. "She's just been . . . upset recently."

Rain sighed. "She never wanted this marriage to happen. She made that clear from the start. I'd just hoped that she would have begun to accept the idea by now."

"I thought she had, to begin with," Ellysetta said softly, coming to wrap her arms around him. "But I guess she needs a little more time. After we're wed, when things calm down enough that we can come back for regular visits, she'll see for herself that living with the Fey isn't destroying my soul. She'll come around then." When Rain didn't respond, she drew back to look up at him. "We will come back, won't we, Rain?"

He hesitated, then said, "I've already told you your family will always be welcome in the Fading Lands."

Her spine went stiff. Her arms dropped away and she stepped back, putting distance between them. "Are you telling me once we leave, I can never return?"

"If the borders are opened to the Eld, it would be too dangerous."

Her face went stony and inscrutable even as irritation sizzled across his senses. "Well," she said after several long seconds of silence, "I guess you'd best do everything you can tomorrow to make sure the borders remain closed, then." Her jaw grew firm. "Because if my family is here, I will be coming back. Whether you like it or not."

She stepped past him and marched into the other room,

heading for the stairs. Unwilling to let her storm off, he followed and grabbed her wrist. Tumultuous emotions—hurt, anger, distrust, even an underlying current of fear—rushed into him as his flesh touched hers.

"I don't do this to hurt you, Ellysetta." His whisper had a sharp edge. "Would you rather I take the free will of every noble in Celieria and bend it to my own? I've tried everything else to convince them, but they won't believe the Eld are as great a threat as I know them to be."

"Then make them believe it," she snapped back. She yanked her hand away from his with such force that she knocked over a stack of wedding presents on the hall table, sending gifts skittering across the floor. Muttering a mild curse, she knelt to pick them up. "You're a Master of Spirit. I know for a fact your weaves feel entirely and vividly real."

"All Fey have sworn never to manipulate Celierian minds with magic." Rain knelt to retrieve a small silver-ribbon-bedecked blue box that had fallen beneath the table.

"I'm not suggesting you manipulate them," she snapped. "I'm saying *show* them what the Mage Wars were like, just as you've shown me the Fading Lands. Convince King Dorian to let you address the Council directly, before the vote. Make them see the results of Mage evil for themselves, firsthand. Here, give me that." She held out her hand for the small package.

As he passed it to her, their fingers touched, and she flinched at the contact. Grimly he stepped back to put a little distance between them.

Inside the parlor, Rain heard Lorelle ask, "Lillis, what's wrong with Love?"

There was a loud hiss, then a screech, followed by a short cry of pain. Love came tearing out of the parlor, skittering across the hardwood floor, little paws pedaling as she made a sliding turn, scrambled up the stairs, and disappeared.

Rain peered into the parlor. Lillis sat in Kieran's arms, her hand bleeding from deep furrows while the young Fey examined the wound. "What happened, Kieran?"

"I don't know." There was shame on his face for allowing one of the females under his care to come to harm. "The cat just went crazy." He glared at the other warriors. "Which one of you was calling magic?"

Rain glanced at each of his men, all of whom were shaking their heads and denying that they had done anything to set off the kitten. He turned back to Ellysetta, who wasn't paying the slightest attention to her sister but was instead focused entirely on opening the package in her hands. A chill stole over him. "Ellysetta?" He started towards her.

Before he could reach her, she lifted the lid of the box, revealing the small music box within. Now Rain could feel the subtle Spirit weave that had sent Love running. And as Ellysetta touched the music box, he also sensed the first cool, sweet blossom of Azrahn.

He leapt the remaining distance, tearing the package from her grasp and flinging it to the farthest corner of the room. The music box spilled out onto the floor, and the two black crystals in its lid began to glow with flickering red lights. A tinny melody began to play, and a shadow rose in the air, a chilly darkness that began to take shape.

He thrust Ellysetta behind him. "Bel! Get her out of here!" He didn't look to see if his command was obeyed, but kept his attention focused on the dark thing in the living room. Demon. A being who'd willingly surrendered his soul to evil before he died.

Rain felt the tingle of magic behind him as Ellysetta's quintet raised a five-fold shield to protect her. There was a brief scuffle—for some reason she was struggling against the five warriors who were trying to force her out of the room. "Ellysetta, go!"

The front door crashed open and a dozen Fey flooded into the room.

Taking advantage of Rain's brief distraction, the demon hissed and shot towards Ellysetta and her quintet.

The commotion brought Lauriana and Sol rushing down the stairs. "What in the Haven's name is—" Lauriana's furious question broke off, her face going blank with shock at the sight of magic blazing and the demon streaking towards her daughter. "Gods protect us!"

"Ti'Feyreisa!" With a fierce cry, Dajan, the young warrior who stood guard outside the Baristani door, leapt in the demon's path. Fire blazed in a red nimbus about him, and he threw himself forward to meet the demon's oncoming rush.

"Nei, do not!" Rain's sharp warning was too late.

The first dark edge of the demon pierced Dajan's Fire shield as if it weren't even there and touched the Fey's skin. The warrior went gray as the deadly creature siphoned his life's essence from his body. His lifeless form fell to the floor, and the demon screamed in triumph.

Whispering a quick prayer for the Fey's soul, Rain reached for his power, quickly plaiting Air, Fire, Earth, Water, and Spirit into a single, solid fist of power that he rammed towards the creature.

The demon was no longer there.

Rain froze, power flashing around him, eyes scanning the room in rapid sweeps, but he could not see the creature.

The cool sweetness of Azrahn whispered across Rain's flesh again, raising the hairs at the nape of his neck. The whisper became a stunning rush of power, filling the room with a gagging, sickly sweet stench. A dark rift appeared in the air above the music box. With a tiny cry, Ellysetta fell to her knees inside the protective bubble shielding her. Then, to Rain's horror, she staggered to her feet and lurched towards the growing black maw.

Rain slammed a new blast of power into the music box and the two black stones that were the focus of the Azrahn. The box exploded; the crystals shattered. The rift collapsed, and Ellysetta halted, shaking her head as if she were coming out of a trance.

From the ceiling above, an unearthly shriek ripped the air. Rain looked up. A barely perceptible shadow that blanketed the ceiling from corner to corner condensed into a fathomless pool of darkness. It shot across the room towards Rain. He wove power a third time, using the four elementals and one mystic to form a single shining blade so dense with magic that it was a solid thing in his hand.

He spun away from the demon's oncoming rush, missing it easily as his body moved into the light, fluid patterns of Cha Baruk, the Dance of Knives. As he came out of the spin, his blade bit into the creature's dark form. It howled and condensed a little more, shrinking in order to maintain its strength.

A second blade formed in Rain's free hand, a long, thin blade the length of his forearm. "Come, dark one. Dance with the tairen if you dare."

The demon lunged again, this time towards Ellysetta rather than Rain.

Rain leapt, blades flashing, slicing the creature to half its original size, drawing its dark rage to himself and away from Ellysetta. "Your master was foolish to send you for my mate. You are little more than a child of the darkness. No match for the Tairen Soul. Come. Accept your death and find peace as you should have when first you died."

The demon rushed at him. Rain stood his ground and plunged both shining blades into the center of the dark being. Throwing open the barriers in his mind, Rain called power to him and channeled it down his arms, down the magic-woven blades, into the bitter black heart of the demon. The essence of life crashed into the embodiment of death. The demon wailed, a screeching cry of denial and fury. Its dark form flashed bright for a blinding instant, then was gone, leaving nothing behind but a scorched gash in the wooden floor.

Sol stared at his daughter, the dead Fey, and the destruction of his home. He swallowed hard and met Rain's eyes. "I release you from our contract."

"Sol!"

The woodcarver put a hand on his wife's arm. "Hush, Laurie. We can't protect her, and you know it. Our only hope is that the Fey can." He turned back to Rain. "Marry her and leave tomorrow, if you think that's best. Just, for the gods' sake, keep her safe."

CHAPTER ELEVEN

Live well.
Love deep.
Tomorrow, we die.

—Fey warriors' creed

"What happened? What was that thing?" Ellysetta stared in horror first at the place where the demon had disappeared, then at the dead Fey lying on the living-room floor. Mama and Papa had taken the twins out back while the warriors put the Baristani home back in order and took care of Dajan's body.

"That was the proof Dorian has been wanting," Rain told her grimly. "That was a demon, summoned by Azrahn. The Elden Mages are here, and already at work."

"What?" Her head jerked upwards. A sudden stabbing pain behind her eyes made her cry out and press the heels of her palms to her temples.

Rain's concern, sweet and fierce, enveloped her senses. "You are injured." A spate of rapid Feyan followed, commands snapped out with a force that had warriors scurrying to obey.

"*Nei* . . . no, I'm not injured. But my head feels like someone is jabbing a knife in my brain." What had happened to her? One moment she'd been arguing with Rain, and the next, she was surrounded by her quintet watching some horrible black, formless creature attack him. And Dajan, the bright-eyed warrior who usually guarded her front door, was lying gray and dead on her family's living-room floor. "You say the Mages sent it? For me?"

"Aiyah." His eyes, pale and piercing, searched her face. "Do you not remember?"

"No." She frowned, trying to recall. "You and I were arguing. I turned and knocked over a pile of wedding presents. You helped me pick them up. The next thing I remember, Bel was holding me while that thing . . . that demon . . . was attacking you."

"You don't remember opening the gift?"

"What gift?"

He lifted a hand and gestured to a point across the room. The remains of the music box and a collection of strange black chips rose into the air and flew into his hands. "This one."

"I've never seen that before. Are you sure this came from the Mages?"

"See these shards?" He showed her the handful of black chips that looked like shattered crystal. "This is *selkahr*. Tairen's Eye corrupted by Azrahn and other Eld magic. The Mages make it. No other race knows the secret—not even the Fey. If this doesn't convince Dorian to invoke *primus*, nothing will."

"Rain." Bel murmured an apology as he interrupted. "Will you send our brother's body back to the elements?"

Rain's fingers closed around the *selkahr* shards, and the anger on his face faded briefly to grief, then stony blankness. "The honor is yours, my friend."

At Bel's signal, Ellysetta's quintet circled Dajan's body. In low, melodious voices they sang a spare, mournful elegy commending the dead Fey's bravery and honor, and summoned their power. She could see the magic in the air. Five separate strands—one from each warrior—folded into a single fiercely glowing ply that they used to form a shining net between them. Still chanting the death song, the warriors lowered the shining net. It settled over Dajan like a blanket of light, and the chant ended.

"Soar high, Dajan," Bel said, "and laugh on the wind. May you find joy before we meet again." He looked at the other four who each held a thread of the weave, sharing a silent communication. As one, they bowed their heads. The weave they had placed over Dajan's body flashed painfully bright for an instant. Ellie shielded her eyes.

When the light dimmed, the shining weave was gone, and so was Dajan. Nothing remained save a single round stone, Dajan's *sorreisu kiyr*, which Bel picked up and handed to Kieran. The younger Fey cupped the crystal in the palm of his hand, and his blue eyes glowed green for several long moments. A matching green glow surrounded the crystal. When the glow faded, he opened his hands to reveal Dajan's Soul Quest crystal, now set in an oval lozenge of gold filigree suspended from a gold chain.

"Dajan's crystal is yours now, Ellysetta," Bel said. "Fey custom dictates that when a warrior dies in the service of a *shei'-tani*, his *sorreisu kiyr* goes to her."

He placed the dark, shining jewel in her palm. It felt surprisingly warm, almost as if it were alive. Her skin tingled where it touched the crystal, and the pounding in her head seemed to grow fainter. She stared into the whirling rainbow of light flickering in the crystal's depths.

"Why didn't the crystal disappear along with Dajan's body?" she asked.

"Tairen's Eye is made of a magic beyond our powers," Rain said. "Fey can neither make nor destroy it."

"What am I supposed to do with it?"

"You wear it, *shei'tani*," Rain said, taking the pendant from her and slipping it around her neck, "in honor of the warrior who gave his life in your service."

There was a certain awful symbolism to that idea which didn't escape her. Fey warriors wore the soul of every person who died at their hands like a burning stone around their necks. Now, it seemed, she would wear the "soul" of every warrior who died protecting her as a literal stone about hers.

Rain bent his head to take her lips in a gentle, reassuring kiss.

"Ahem." The delicate clearing of a throat made them break apart. Master Fellows, looking bright as a newly minted coin in a perfectly starched linen shirt and ice-blue silk brocade breeches and coat, stood in the doorway. "I do apologize for interrupting such an obviously tender moment, but as we have only four short bells remaining to perfect Lady Ellysetta's mastery of the Graces, we don't have a moment to spare."

When they both regarded him blankly, Master Fellows frowned. "The prince's betrothal ball?" he prompted. "Tonight at eight bells?"

There was a strange, almost surrealistic feel to the remainder of the afternoon. Ellysetta danced in Rain's arms, and curtseyed and practiced courtly conversation with Master Fellows, while all around her, Fey warriors carted off wedding gifts and deftly stripped Ellie's bedroom bare and packed all her belongings in preparation for departure. Mama bustled about, scowling and snapping orders like an army general, as if that measure of control could restore normalcy to her household and conquer her fear of demons and other dangerous magical beings.

At the conclusion of their lesson, Master Fellows surprised Ellysetta with an unexpected compliment. "You have a natural, regal grace, my lady, and it has been the greatest of pleasures to teach you. Just remember, while some part of you may always be Ellie, the woodcarver's daughter, you are also Lady Ellysetta, the Tairen Soul's queen." He bowed and kissed her hand. "At the palace tonight, let Ellysetta reign."

Those words stayed with her the rest of the day. They were still echoing in her mind as she sat at her dressing table while one of the queen's junior hairdressers turned Ellie's long, unruly hair into an elegant confection of braids, poufs, and dangling curls.

Ellie glanced around at the barrenness of her room with a bittersweet sadness. She might once have been a woodcarver's daughter, but those days were already gone. She was a stranger in her own home now. All signs of her existence had been packed away and loaded on a wagon for transport to the Fading Lands.

"There now." The hairdresser, a woman in her twenties,

reverently nestled the crown of borrowed *sorreisu kiyr* into Ellie's hair and stepped back to admire her handiwork. "You are lovely, my lady."

Ellysetta stared at the elegantly gowned and coiffed woman in the mirror. "Am I?" she murmured. Her dress was lavender silk, the color of Rain's eyes, with a graceful billowing profusion of skirts and a flattering boat-shaped neckline that nearly bared her shoulders and dipped low enough to reveal the rounded tops of her breasts. Dajan's crystal gleamed against her pale skin. The woman in the mirror didn't look like a woodcarver's daughter. She looked . . . regal.

"Yes, ma'am," the hairdresser answered. "Lovelier than many of the court ladies, if you want the truth. You have fine bones and beautiful skin, and though your hair may be a bit difficult to tame, it's stunning once it's done right, even if I do say so myself. Like a crown of fire. I can't tell you how many noble ladies have asked for a dye to turn their hair your color."

Ellie laughed in disbelief. "You're joking."

"Oh, no, ma'am. I wouldn't be surprised if half the ladies at tonight's ball have red hair."

"Well, believe me, if that's true, it's because Rain Tairen Soul put a crown on my head and declared me Queen of the Fey, not because I'm beautiful."

"Ellie, Mama says to tell you it's time." Lillis poked her head in the door. Her eyes widened. "Oh, Ellie, you look beautiful. Like a Fey-tale princess."

The hairdresser raised her eyebrows meaningfully, and Ellysetta had to smile. "Thank you, Lillis." She stood and brushed the wrinkles from her skirts. "I suppose I'm ready."

She made her way downstairs and kissed her family good night before following Rain outside to the waiting carriage. Sol and Lauriana stood on the front stoop to watch the carriage roll down the cobbled streets towards the palace, flanked by leather-and-steel-clad Fey.

As the conveyance disappeared around the corner, Sol put his arm around his wife's shoulders. "She'll be all right, Laurie. The Fey will keep her safe."

"And her soul, Sol?" Lauriana asked. "Who will keep that safe?"

Leaving Sol frowning after her, she ran up the stairs to their bedroom and closed the door behind her. For several long chimes, she stood there, her back against the door, breathing deep and struggling for some sense of calm. She reached up to her neck and lifted the gold and amber pendant Father Nivane had given her from its hiding place in her bodice. Curling her fingers tight around the sun-shaped disc, she knelt beside her bed and began to pray.

<hr />

In the deepest levels of Boura Fell, Elfeya lay naked in the arms of her mate on the dirt floor of his cage. She had raised herself up on her elbows so she could look at his beloved face, searching the blessed lucidity of his green eyes. He was still there with her, completely rational and whole for the moment. Thank the gods.

«*The Great Sun rises in your eyes, beloved.*» His voice sounded in her mind, gentle, loving. The phrase was an old Feyan euphemism for "I love you," her mate's favorite because it played on the golden color of her eyes. Once, so many, many years ago, the woman would have smiled when her *shei'tan* said those words. Now they made tears tremble on her lashes. She blinked, and the tears fell like raindrops on the pale flesh of his chest, tiny pools of salty wetness that mingled with the saltier wetness of perspiration.

These last bells the Evil One had granted them had not gone to waste. Even knowing that such beneficence was a prelude to horrors beyond imagining, once Elfeya had breached that first barrier of fear and given in to instinct and temptation, she and her mate had made no further attempt to deny themselves the slightest pleasure of their bond. Despite the leering eyes of their guards, watching as Elden guards had always watched across the centuries, she and her mate had shared each touch, each caress, without shame. There was little to live for but these brief flashes of pleasure in an eternity of darkness.

Perhaps that was why she wept.

Better to think it was that than memories of freedom and joyous love. Those memories only gave the Evil One a doorway to their souls.

She closed her eyes as her *shei'tan's* hand cupped her cheek. In a gesture Elfeya knew as well as she knew the beating of her own heart, he thumbed away her tears. She brought her hand up, her slender fingers caressing the greater masculine strength of his. Sensitive fingertips traced the slight roughness of his skin, the hard length of bone beneath the veil of flesh, the smoothness of nail beds with their ragged edges.

So strong, and yet so fragile. He was a creature of vast power, as was she, but they were both housed in delicate cages of living flesh and brittle bone that had been brought to the edge of death countless times over the last millennium. Even now, despite these few bells of sanity, she knew he danced the razor's edge of madness. The vast power to which he'd been born had been made even vaster by the unholy experiments of the Evil One, but it had come at a terrible price. Gods save the world if ever those *sel'dor* manacles came free.

Her fingers curved around his hand, fingertips roving lightly over his palm, over the rent flesh still bleeding from his attack on the barbed *sel'dor* bars of his cage. She turned her face to his palm and kissed the many small, deep wounds.

«If I am your sun, beloved, then you are my world. But for you, I am a light shining with no purpose in the dark.» They needed no Spirit woven between them to speak. As bonded truemates, their souls and thoughts were one. *Sel'dor* could not isolate them, though they had worked diligently to hide that fact. Despite the countless secrets the Evil One had wrung from their screaming, tortured bodies, this was one of the handful of truths they had kept to themselves. It was a small enough thing. Not nearly as important as the other secrets they had kept. *«Feel my light, shei'tan. Feel my love.»*

She drew in a breath and went to that other place, the hazily distant place where she floated in a sea of numbness. There, the pain of *sel'dor* was but a vague twinge, scarcely felt, as she wove invisible strands of healing Earth and sent them into her truemate's damaged hands, softly stealing away his pain though she dared not heal his wounds. The wounds on his hands were small enough that she knew she could heal them, but the Evil One would know she had.

They could still weave magic, though there were limits to what they could do before the pain became unbearable. They had tested those limits many times over the last ten centuries, even expanded them, though only once had they managed to work significant magic. Only that once had they managed to suppress the immutable *shei'tanitsa* instinct to ensure each other's survival and brought themselves near the brink of death to spin their weaves.

The Evil One had suspected something, of course, when the child had disappeared. But not enough. Not the truth. He had been secure in his knowledge that *shei'tanitsa* bound them as securely as the *sel'dor* piercing their bodies. But that once they had managed to thwart him.

«Does she still live free, beloved?» She'd not asked the question in years, but he would know. He was bound to the child through threads of the Evil One's blackest magic.

«Aiyah. She comes into her power.»

Though Elfeya had suspected as much since Vadim Maur's visit to her bedchamber-prison, the cold hand of fear still clutched at her heart.

«How much has she revealed?» Once the Evil One discovered the child's true abilities, nothing would save them from his fury. Elfeya remembered in vivid, agonizing detail the years of torture she and her mate had been subjected to when the Elden servant, in whose mind they had implanted unalterable commands woven with Spirit, escaped the High Mage's palace with her precious burden. That agony would pale in comparison to what he would do when he discovered the full extent of their deception.

«Only a little, but with her even a little is more than enough.»

«How is that possible? Our weave should never have failed so soon.»

«Her power is vast, Elfeya. Even unbound, we could never have hoped to hold it back for long.»

She raised her head and looked into the beloved bright green depths of her truemate's eyes. Once, countless lifetimes ago, she had been the greatest healer in the Fading Lands, a *shei'dalin* without equal. When she met him, he had been a legendary Fey warrior only one or two souls away from becoming *dahl'reisen*, a dark, dread lord whose steel had tasted the blood of millions, whose incredible soul had staggered and would have fallen beneath the weight of the hundreds of thousands of lives he had claimed had not her strength and her love brought him back from the edge of the abyss.

Together, they had been the strongest matepair seen since ancient times, representing the greatest concentration of power in all the Fading Lands, more powerful in their oneness than even a Tairen Soul, though without the ability to summon the Change. And all that power, all that strength, had been captured in a single moment when the Elden Mages took her in an ambush. A knife to her throat, a single slice into her vulnerable flesh, and the man who'd once been the Fading Lands' greatest warrior surrendered his steel and walked willingly into captivity.

The High Mage had kept them alive because they were useful to him, strong and powerful creatures upon which to test his vile experiments. But when he realized exactly what they'd helped escape from his grasp, no amount of experimentation would make up for his loss.

«*If he knows . . .*» She could not even complete the thought.

«*Then we die, Elfeya. If we're lucky.*»

There were far worse things than death, as both of them were now intimately aware, but still her eyes closed against a swell of fear and denial. Though she could have embraced her own death freely, nothing in the world could make her willingly embrace his. He was her *shei'tan*, her beloved, the half of her soul that she must protect at all costs. She would suffer any torment to ensure his survival.

Elfeya guided her truemate's hand to her breast and leaned down to kiss him. "Love me, Shan," she whispered against his mouth. "As if it were the first time. As if it were the last."

"Always," he vowed.

She took Shan into her body as so long ago she had taken him into her soul. Wholly and without reservation. As their bodies and souls entwined, the words of an ancient Fey warrior's creed came to her mind. *Live well. Love deep. Tomorrow, we die.* Never had she appreciated it more than at this moment. She smiled into her beloved's eyes and laughed as if they were free, because she knew it brought him joy.

They could not fight. They could not win. But with each moment left for them to live, they could love. That was the greatest gift the gods could ever give, and it was worth the price they would have to pay.

⁕

As the coach wound through the cobbled streets towards Celieria's royal palace, Rain took Ellysetta's hand and placed something in it that sent a tingle up her arm. She glanced down and caught her breath. The rich golden light of the setting sun gleamed and sparkled like magic across the heavy, incredibly beautiful bracelet in her hand.

Diamond brilliants and baguettes glittered in radiant sunbursts around a cabochon Tairen's Eye crystal, much larger and richer in color than Dajan's *sorreisu kiyr*, which she was wearing around her throat. The band was fashioned in the shape of two golden tairen holding the crystal aloft on the backs of their proud heads and outstretched wings.

"The crystal was my father's, delivered to me after he and my mother died."

"Oh Rain, it's beautiful." It was stunning. She started to give it back to him, but he stopped her, his hand closing around hers. She felt his surprise, his uncertainty.

"This gift . . . does not please you?"

"It's for me?"

"*Aiyah*, of course."

She drew a breath. "I thought you meant it was your father's Soul Quest crystal—"

"*Aiyah*, it is," he confirmed. "The *sorreisu kiyr* of my father, my dearest possession, which I give into your keeping. My parents were not truemated, so my mother never wore it, but I think my father would be pleased to have his son's *shei'tani* wear his crystal. Kieran made the bracelet today while you were packing. Will you accept it?"

She nodded, and he clasped the bracelet around her right wrist. Her hand—her entire arm—tingled. Rajahl vel'En Daris's crystal hummed against her skin, and the resonance of it seemed to generate an echoing vibration in Dajan's crystal. It swept up through her skin to the tiara in her hair, where one of the loaned *sorreisu kiyr* responded with its own shimmering power. Bel's crystal, she realized with eerie perception. .

Dajan, Rajahl, and Bel's Soul Quest crystals were all resonating in a joint harmonic that pulsed in time with the beating of her own heart. As if they—and she—were somehow joined.

"Rain," she whispered, "I can feel your father's crystal and Dajan's . . . like a heartbeat."

His eyes gleamed with catlike satisfaction in the Fire-light. "That is a good sign, *shei'tani*. Your magic recognizes the magic of the warriors whose crystals you wear."

"Bel's crystal is beating, too."

"He has bloodsworn himself to you. That bound his soul to your service. Dajan forged a tie between his soul and yours when he died trying to protect you."

"And your father's crystal?"

"The link is a reflection of your bond to me. It is good that you feel it so strongly."

"It feels . . . strange."

"That will pass in a moment as your body absorbs the resonance into itself."

She held her breath, and the energies quieted . . . still there, but less noticeable. Rain watched her, smiling. There was a deep-seated peace in him she'd never sensed before. "You seem pleased," she said. "Did your meeting with Dorian go well?" He'd sent the *selkahr* shards and word of the demon attack to the king, then gone to see him in person as soon as their session with Master Fellows concluded.

"It did. I will address the Council directly tomorrow. If I

cannot convince them, he has promised to invoke *primus*. One way or another, the borders will remain closed."

"But you still want us to wed and leave tomorrow."

"I do. Keeping the borders closed only stops the Mages from sending their agents freely into every city and hamlet. It does not mean the danger is past. I'm sorry, *shei'tani*, I know you would like more time, but I need you safe behind the Faering Mists."

"It's all right." She laid her hand over his. "As long as I can visit my family, nothing else holds me in Celieria. I'm ready to go to the Fading Lands with you. I'm ready to learn how to use my magic and do whatever I can to save the tairen."

"His esteemed majesty, Rainier vel'En Daris Feyreisen, The Tairen Soul, King of the Fading Lands, Defender of the Fey, and Lady Ellysetta Baristani Feyreisa, truemate of the Tairen Soul, Queen of the Fading Lands."

With her hand on the back of Rain's wrist, Ellysetta descended the curving staircase. She looked out over the sea of faces below, and all she could think was that the last time she'd descended this staircase, she'd ended up humiliating herself and everyone else at the dinner.

As Prime Minister Corrias approached to greet them, she saw his gaze flicker briefly over the wealth of Tairen's Eye crystals she wore. He bowed, and his forehead nearly touched the floor. "My Lord Feyreisen, Lady Ellysetta." There was respect in his voice. And a hint of fear. He had not escaped the other night's Spirit weave unscathed, then.

She murmured what she hoped was a suitable reply and breathed a little easier when Rain guided her past the prime minister, saying, "Come, *shei'tani*. We must greet our hosts, and give the prince and his betrothed our blessings."

Queen Annoura, Ellysetta noted when they reached the dais, was missing the usual predatory gleam in her eyes. Instead, there was wariness and chilly respect and—as with Lord Corrias—a hint of fear. *«She knows I spun that Spirit weave, doesn't she?»*

«Dorian told her,» Rain confirmed.

Surprisingly, the queen's reaction hurt. Ellysetta was used to the fear and distrust of the common folk of the West End, but she had not expected it from the queen of all Celieria.

Behind the queen and off to one side, stood the queen's ladies-in-waiting, including a beautiful young woman with dark hair and stunning blue eyes, whom Ellie recalled meeting briefly at the previous dinner. What was her name? Jiarine? She was staring at Ellysetta with a strange intensity. Jiarine looked away as soon as their eyes met, but the brief exchange of glances left Ellysetta frowning. There was something unsettling about the lady.

King Dorian greeted her with a crooked smile and false heartiness. *«I trust we'll have a less eventful evening tonight, Lady Ellysetta?»* he added, surprising her by weaving his thoughts on the common Fey thread. *«I'm getting a bit old for that much excitement.»*

She blushed and promised to avoid the pinalle and keflee. After sharing a few more stilted pleasantries with the king and queen, Ellysetta and Rain moved to the left of the dais where Prince Dorian and his betrothed sat on smaller thrones.

The couple stood as they approached. The prince gave first Rain, then Ellysetta a quarter bow, and Lady Nadela made a curtsey of similar respect. There was no fear in either of their gazes, only youthful arrogance and a touch of resentment. Oddly enough, that made Ellysetta relax. The arrogance of Celierian nobility was something familiar and understood.

She stood silent as Rain laid his hands on the young couple and said, "The blessings of the Fey upon you, Prince Dorian and Lady Nadela. May you enjoy long life, prosperity, and the continuation of your line." He stepped back. *«Now you give them your blessing, Ellysetta.»*

She gave the couple an apologetic look. "Though the Fey have accepted me as one of their own, I wouldn't feel right offering you their blessings. I do, however, believe in the grace and mercy of the gods. If you'll permit me, it's their blessing I'd like to request on your behalf."

Prince Dorian and Lady Nadela shared a glance, then the prince nodded. "Of course."

Ellysetta smiled, relieved. "Thank you." She reached out and took the couple's hands in hers. "May the gods bless you, Prince Dorian and Lady Nadela, with a long life, a strong love, and the happiness of many healthy children." A strange, tingling warmth hummed through her, and her vision took on the fecund green glow of Earth. The tingling sensation concentrated in her chest, then traveled down the lengths of her arms and into her hands, where it flowed out of her fingertips and was gone, leaving only a cozy warmth and slight weariness.

She blinked and shook herself to clear her head. The prince and his bride stood before her, swaying slightly. The Tairen's Eye crystal on her wrist shone with glimmering rainbow lights that dimmed even as she glanced at it in surprise.

A hand touched her elbow. Approval and joy and gleaming hope flooded her senses as Rain guided her away from the royals.

"That was no level-one weave," Kieran said.

The warriors shared glances amongst themselves. "The gods are her key," Bel murmured.

"What is it?" she asked. "What did I do?"

"You spun a *shei'dalin's* weave upon them," Rain told her. "You gave them health. And long life. And fertility."

"I did?"

"*Aiyah.*"

"How did I do that?"

"We've all seen you spin powerful weaves before, despite the barriers that seem to block your magic most of the time. We've finally realized how you do it. The gods are your key. You call upon them just before you weave instinctive magic." He cocked his head to one side. "Your mother raised you to believe that magic was evil but miracles from the gods were good. So when you need a small miracle, you call upon the gods, and they answer by releasing the magic within you. That's your key."

"You called upon the gods just before you made my heart weep again," Bel said. "And when you took Adrial's memory.

"And again just now," Kieran added.

Ellysetta saw the surprise and certainty in all their faces. A thousand scenes flashed across her mind: her effectiveness at kissing away the pain when one of the twins came to her with a small wound; her ability to soothe her mother's agitation; the ease with which she found lost objects and even lost children on occasion; the way she could make herself all but invisible in a crowd when shyness overwhelmed her. The way she'd prayed and prayed for sisters—precious twins—to love.

She, Ellysetta Baristani, had made all those things happen. She may have offered herself as the vessel through which the gods could work their small glories, but the magic that made it possible had come from within. She had been working magic all her life. Just as Rain had claimed from the start. She stared up at him in shock.

"Magic isn't evil, *shei'tani*. Nor are those who wield it, if they wield it for good." He brushed the backs of his fingers across her cheek. "Will you dance the Felah Baruk with me, *shei'tani*? On the terrace, beneath the Mother's silver light?"

The Felah Baruk, literally the Dance of Joy, was the Fey dance of courtship and devotion. "Bel and Kieran showed me the steps, but I'm afraid I don't remember them all."

"It will be my pleasure to teach you."

She placed her hand on his wrist. "Then lead the way, *shei'tan*." She loved the way his eyes sparked as she called him that: true-mate, husband, beloved. Hers.

They passed the armed guards standing sentry by the large, arched doorways and walked across the marbled terrace to the balustrades overlooking the palace gardens.

Rain glanced over at Kiel. "Ask the musicians to play the Felah Baruk." The blond warrior slashed a quick bow and hurried back inside the palace ballroom. Moments later, the bright, soaring strains of the Dance of Joy spilled out through the terrace doors into the night.

Rain held out a hand, and Ellysetta took it with a smile and a curtsey.

"You mustn't laugh if I miss a step," she told him. But even as she spoke, she found herself moving gracefully, instinctively, in the patterns that symbolized Fey courtship and bonding. She turned slowly, swaying. He circled her, tall, dark, stern, his eyes burning. "You're guiding me," she whispered as she lifted an arm, passing a hand like a veil before her face, then extending it to Rain in a silent invitation.

"A little." He touched her hands, fingers threading through hers, clasping her hand. She turned, twirling so that his arm circled her waist and she backed against his chest. "Do you want me to stop?"

"*Nei*." She looked up, bending her head back so she could see his eyes. "It's nice, actually." He was feeding her the motions of the dance, guiding each step, but with so subtle a touch that she could almost believe it was memory, not Rain, leading her through the steps. She didn't try to fight him, she just opened her mind and surrendered command of her body to him, and they danced as if they had danced a thousand times before.

<hr />

He was home! Blessed merciful gods, he had been forgiven his sins. He was home! Gaelen vel Serranis stood in the tall grass of the plains of Corunn. The sun beat down on his head and gleamed on the golden spires of the Tairen Soul's palace in Dharsa, and the strains of the Felah Baruk flowed like healing magic over his body. The notes were faint, as if they were far away, but he heard them for the first time in over a thousand years, and his heart soared.

Marikah! Marissya! I'm home!

He saw them clearly, his sisters, as beautiful as life could ever be, two stars of the morning sky, running towards him with laughter and love shining on their faces, their hair unbound and flowing like banners of dark silk. Marissya, the gentler of the two, with deep, bottomless, ocean-blue eyes and hair as brown as the fertile earth. Marikah, his twin, with jet-black hair and pale blue eyes that would have seemed as cold as his own except for the love and laughter that always warmed them. His sisters ran towards him through the tall grass, their arms outstretched to welcome him. He saw Marikah's mouth form his name. He reached for her, and she faded, leaving him to embrace nothing but air. A frown drew his brows together as memory, fragmented and shifting like sand, disturbed his happiness. Marikah was . . . dead?

Nei! Nei!

But even as he shook his head and cried out in denial, Gaelen saw the scene that had played in his mind a million times. His twin Marikah lay against an intricate mosaic of blue and gold tiles, her gown an ever-deepening scarlet, matching the dark pool of thick liquid that spread beneath her, an Eld assassin's blade plunged deep into her heart. She turned her head and reached out . . . not to Gaelen but to the man who lay dead beside her. The Celierian. The mortal she had chosen as her mate.

Marissya stood still in the grass, clothed in *shei'dalin* red, her eyes accusing. *She was yours to protect and you failed. You are dead to us.*

Condemnation blew an icy wind through his soul, and he was freezing, teeth chattering.

Gaelen's eyes opened to the darkness of night. Stars twinkled in the sky overhead, paled by the light of the moons. Dimly he realized he was lying in the dirt at the edge of a field. He was not in the Fading Lands. Marikah was dead and he was *dahl'reisen*, soul-lost.

But he could still hear the strains of the Felah Baruk.

A low groan rattled in his throat as he rolled over on his belly and lifted his head. His vision swam, but he saw the glow of a walled city he both knew and despised.

Celieria City.

Outside on the terrace, the air was warm and sweet, perfumed with the scents of the palace gardens. Ellysetta danced with Rain until the last note of the Felah Baruk died away.

"Good evening, My Lord Feyreisen, Lady Ellysetta." A deep baritone voice spoke just behind her.

"Lord Barrial." Ellysetta's fingers tightened around Rain's

wrist as she turned to face the border lord. Here was the one person she'd actually liked from the dinner the other night, and she found herself holding her breath as she waited to see how he would greet her.

"Lady Ellysetta." He bowed deeply. When he rose, the faintest of smiles curved the man's lips. "No offense, but I trust you will not be drinking pinalle tonight?"

Ellie blushed. "No, my lord. I don't think I shall ever drink it again. Certainly never in combination with keflee."

"Now, that would be a waste of a fine opportunity." Lord Barrial arched a dark brow. "Wouldn't you agree, My Lord Feyreisen?"

Rain smiled, though a bit ruefully. "Indeed, though it certainly depends on the time and place of the opportunity."

Lord Barrial laughed, then moved a little closer and lowered his voice. "Teleos tells me you had a bit of trouble with the Eld today. A demon?"

"*Aiyah*, and the Mages finally made a mistake. They used *selkahr* to summon the creature, and left me with the proof I needed to convince Dorian. The borders will not open tomorrow, even if the vote passes. Dorian has said he will invoke *primus*."

"Well done, my friend." Lord Barrial clapped him on the back. "That is good news. Now you've only to pray that nothing else happens to muck things up before tomorrow's vote."

"Ah, here you are." Lord Teleos stepped through the terrace doors. "Good evening, Rain, Lady Ellysetta." The Fey-eyed border lord bowed his head, his dark, unbound hair swinging free about his shoulders. A stranger stood beside him, clad in robes that shimmered with otherworldly beauty and seemed to shift in color from blue to green to gold. "Have you met Elvia's ambassador? Lord Arran Bluewing, may I present the Tairen Soul, Rainier vel'En Daris, and his truemate, Lady Ellysetta Baristani."

The Elvian bowed. Long, silken, brown hair woven in myriad tiny plaits brushed against elegant tapered ears. His eyes were dark green, the color of the deepest forest, his skin almost

Fey-pale, but with a golden luster rather than a silvery luminescence. The ambassador turned his deep gaze on Ellysetta, and she stared at him in wonder. She'd never met an Elf before, and there was a strange, compelling mystery about him, as if those eyes saw things no others did.

He murmured something in a language that sounded like waterfalls in sunlight-dappled forests. She didn't understand him, but his words made Rain, Lord Barrial, and Lord Teleos stiffen in surprise. Rain's hand closed around her elbow and drew her closer to his side. He replied in the same language, but when he spoke, it sounded like raging rapids. Unperturbed, the ambassador turned his gaze on Rain, spoke again just as calmly as before, then bowed and took his leave.

"What was that all about?" Ellysetta asked.

It was Lord Barrial who answered. "He said your Song in the Dance has begun." He and Lord Teleos turned to look at her in surprised unison.

"Elvish mysticism," Rain muttered, shifting closer to her. "It means nothing, Ellysetta, except that you are the truemate of a Tairen Soul."

"And destined to change the world," Lord Barrial added, "as all who call a Song in the Dance do." He frowned at Rain. "And your Song must still be singing, Rain, if Galad Hawksheart wants the Fey to visit him in Deep Woods. He doesn't lightly issue such invitations."

"Well, Lady Ellysetta, you are all surprises." Lord Teleos shook his head. "But what else would one expect from the truemate of a Tairen Soul?" His smile faded, and he turned back to Rain. "In any event, I didn't come to bring the ambassador—he just divined where I was going in that way Elvish folk do and followed along. I came to tell you that Lord Krahn has arrived with his lady and heir. You and the Feyreisa should come to greet them, and there are several other lords I think you should meet who only arrived in town today. Sebourne's already making the rounds."

"Dorian has promised to invoke *primus*," Lord Barrial told him.

"Ah." Teleos's brows rose. "Excellent. The *selkahr* convinced him?"

"It did," Rain answered.

"Good. Good." Teleos rubbed his hands together. "Still, it never hurts to sharpen all the blades in the arsenal, does it? No telling what else the enemies of Celieria and the Fading Lands may yet hold in store. These are unsettled times."

Rain's eyes narrowed with sudden interest, and Ellysetta felt a brief, quickly contained rush of aggression. "Indeed." He held out his wrist to Ellysetta. When she put her hand upon it, he gestured with his free hand towards the crowded palace ballroom. "Lead the way, Lord Teleos. The Feyreisa and I would very much like to meet all Celierians still willing to honor your country's ancient ties to the Fey."

Ellysetta didn't know how long she and Rain spent greeting the lords and ladies of Teleos's acquaintance, but the time passed with surprising speed. Unlike the more jaded members of the royal court, most of these nobles spent a goodly part of each year on their far-flung estates, well removed from the intrigues and prejudices of the court. Most of them also came from the west, closer to the Fading Lands, and they greeted Rain with considerably more warmth than many of their peers.

Rain was pleasant and charming in a way Ellysetta rarely saw him with Celierians. For her part, she tried her best to follow Master Fellows's advice and remember that tonight she was not Ellie, the woodcarver's daughter, but Ellysetta, the Tairen Soul's queen. Drawing upon Master Fellows's training, her own vast knowledge of Fey legends and lore, and the histories she'd read in Master Tarr's voluminous tome, she managed to carry on appropriate conversation and avoid any embarrassing gaffes.

A number of foreign dignitaries mingled with the Celierian guests. Cool-eyed Capellans, bronzed Sorrelians, another three Elves in addition to the ambassador, representatives from all the mortal, immortal, and magical lands with whom Celieria held relations. Every one of those foreign dignitaries made a point of greeting Rain and Ellysetta as well. Soon it almost seemed there were two reception lines—one for Celieria's royal family and another for Rain Tairen Soul and his mate.

That fact didn't escape Queen Annoura's notice. Though her expression remained serene and welcoming, her hand clenched tight around her silver lace fan.

Jiarine Montevero bent towards Annoura's ear and whispered in a scornful sneer, "Do you think they even realize this is Prince Dorian's prenuptial ball and not the Tairen Soul's? Look at them lining up to play toady to a peasant."

The fan in Annoura's hand snapped. "Lady Jiarine," she said in a toneless voice. "My fan seems to have broken. Please, fetch me another."

"Of course, Your Majesty." Jiarine took the destroyed fan and headed for the queen's apartments, a satisfied smile curling her lips.

❦

Midway through the evening, the silver-coated servant at the top of the stairs announced a late-arriving couple. "Lord and Lady Collum diSebourne."

A broad smile warmed Lord Barrial's face. "Please excuse me, My Lord Feyreisen, Lady Ellysetta, my lords and ladies." Barrial executed a swift bow. "My daughter and her new husband have finally arrived."

Ellysetta watched him stride towards the grand stairs where a young woman was descending on the arm of a handsome, haughty-looking Celierian lordling. Lord Barrial's daughter had her father's chestnut hair, caught up in a profusion of thick, lustrous ringlets that spilled down the back of her deep rose gown. Her heart-shaped face seemed made for the dazzling smile that broke across it when she caught sight of her father. She rushed down the last few stairs and fell into Lord Barrial's arms for a laughing embrace, and Ellysetta felt her own heart swell with empathetic joy.

Beside her, Rain stiffened. "What is he doing?"

She followed his gaze and found Adrial standing near the

edge of the ballroom. Adrial's brother Rowan came bursting through the terrace doors and started shoving his way through the crowd towards him.

«*Bel,*» Rain snapped, his Spirit voice harsh as a whip.

Before Bel could move, Adrial gave a raw, choked cry, and Ellysetta's feelings became a tumult of emotions so intense that tears flooded her eyes. "Adrial?" she took half a step towards him, just as Rain jerked to attention and Rowan cried out, "*Nei,* Adrial!"

Before anyone could stop him, Adrial crossed the room in a blur of speed to stand before Lord Barrial's daughter. When his shadow fell over her, the young woman went totally still. The smile faded from her face and she slipped free of her father's embrace.

"Talisa?" Lord Barrial frowned at his daughter in open confusion, but she was not looking at him. Her gaze was locked on the Fey-pale, Fey-beautiful face of Adrial vel Arquinas.

She stared at Adrial, her eyes wide and dazed. "I know you," she said. "I've dreamed of you since before I can remember. I dreamed of you only days ago."

"Talisa?" The young lord who was her husband moved closer. "Who is this man? How do you know him?" His voice was heavy with suspicion.

His wife didn't appear to hear him. "I waited for you," she told Adrial softly, "but you never came."

"I am here now, beloved." In a voice husky with emotion, Adrial declared, "*Ver reisa ku'chae. Kem sera, shei'tani.*" He held out his hands, palms up.

Slowly, Talisa Barrial diSebourne reached out.

"By the gods, you will *not!*" Lord diSebourne snarled and grasped his wife's arm to yank her away from Adrial.

In a flash, Adrial lunged for him, lethal red Fey'cha clutched in each hand, murder on his face.

"Rain!" Ellie cried. "Stop him!"

Before the first syllable left her lips, bright shields sprang up around Adrial and around Lord Barrial, his daughter, and her husband. Ellie found her vision tinted as shields formed around her, too. With a push of Air, Rain thrust her protectively be-hind him even as the remaining warriors of her quintet closed tight around her.

In the same instant, dozens of Fey warriors appeared as if by magic, black-leather-clad shapes leaping from the balconies above, from the corners of the room, from the very woodwork itself, it seemed to Ellie. One moment the room was a sea of glittering pastel courtiers, the next, it was a dark abyss of black leather, grim faces, and naked steel.

CHAPTER TWELVE

King Dorian jumped to his feet as his personal guard swarmed around him and Queen Annoura, weapons at the ready. Beside them, Prince Dorian clutched his affianced bride.

Adrial lunged against the shield surrounding him, sparks of white and red flashing around him. "Release me! You have no right to keep a Fey from his *shei'tani*!"

Talisa was weeping, her hands reaching out to Adrial even as her father tried to pull her away. Her husband, enclosed in his own protective bubble, had drawn his sidearm, and violence glittered in his eyes. "And you have no right to touch another man's wife!"

"Peace." Marissya's voice was pitched low and tranquil.

"Don't you dare try your witch's tricks on me, Fey *petchka*," Lord diSebourne hissed. He called across the tomb-silent ballroom, "Is this what Celierians have become, sire? The lackeys of Fey magicians? My father told me what's been going on here in the city with these Fey. They murder our villagers— even our children!—and you do nothing. They steal a man's betrothed and you allow it. Will you also stand by while they steal a man's wife?"

King Dorian's face turned pale, then grew dark with wrath.

"You are overset, Lord diSebourne," he replied tightly. "Though your anger is understandable, you will marshal your tongue when speaking to your king."

"Sire, my family has lived and died protecting the borders for the last few hundred years. I am your loyal subject, but you either uphold a man's right to his wife or you do not. I will have your answer."

Lord Sebourne called out in support of his heir, "As will I, sire."

Lord Morvel echoed him, then another two border lords and a dozen other nobles followed suit.

Silent, watchful, Rain waited for Dorian's response. The Celierian king looked around the ballroom, his gaze moving slowly over the faces of the nobles who supported his rule, and over the still, pale faces of the Fey, once revered allies, now on the verge of becoming a polarizing force that could tear his kingdom apart. His eyes met Rain's for a long instant. When he spoke, Dorian's voice was clear, unhesitating. "Without a doubt, I support a man's right to his wife, Lord diSebourne. Above and beyond the claims of any others."

A noisy thrum of whispering voices followed his pronouncement.

Without the smallest change of expression, Rain bowed his head in the Celierian king's direction. "Nor would the Fey presume to think otherwise, Your Majesty. We honor your marriage rites as we honor our own matebonding. Both are inviolable."

"*Ve ta nei keppa!*" Adrial cried out. *You have no right!*

"*Ni ve ta!*" Rain snapped back. *Nor do you.* «*You will be silent. We will speak, but not here for the entertainment of these mortals. You will leave your truemate in her father's care, and you will come with me. Now.*» He razored a hard look at Lord Barrial and for the first time sent a thought straight into the border lord's mind. «*Keep your daughter safe, even from her husband. If he harms her, there will be death, and I will not be able to stop it.*»

Shock, indignation, and concern battled for supremacy on Lord Barrial's face, but Rain turned away. As long as the border lord guarded his daughter, this crisis might pass without bloodshed. Just to be safe, however, Rain issued a silent command, and five of the warriors in the room shimmered into invisibility. It wasn't that he didn't trust Cannevar, but no Fey would ever leave a truemate's safety entirely to the keeping of mortals.

Rain gestured, and the remaining Fey silently departed—warriors, Dax, Marissya and her quintet. Adrial didn't move. That was no surprise. But neither did the rest of Ellysetta's quintet.

Rain glanced down at his truemate, the faintest of frowns creasing his brow. Still enveloped in the protective shield, she stood behind him, motionless. Her gaze was fixed on Adrial and Talisa diSebourne, and tears spilled unchecked from her eyes.

❦

Ellysetta wasn't aware of watching, nor of weeping. She wasn't even consciously aware of her own flesh and bone. All she knew, all she could feel, was emotion. Soaring joy, shattering pain, a longing so fierce and so immense that it filled her entire being and made her tremble. And she could hear voices, their voices, somehow strangely a part of her.

«I waited for you, but you never came.»

«I am here now.»

«It's too late. I've already pledged my life to another.»

«Leave him. Come with me. You are my shei'tani. Your place is with me.»

«I am his wife. My place is with him.»

«I have waited eleven centuries for you. Does that count for nothing?»

Devastating sadness swamped Ellie's senses. *«I dreamed of you. With those others. With those women.»*

Oh, gods. An agony of self-recrimination, self-loathing, stole her breath. She was gasping. She was dying.

"Ellysetta!" Firm hands grasped her shoulders and gave her a quick, hard shake.

She came back to herself in a whooshing rush. Dazed, she stared up into Rain's face. His eyes blazed with fear.

"It's all right." She touched his hand and drew a deep breath, trying to still her racing heart. "I'm all right. But Adrial . . ."

Adrial stood trembling, and his face had turned a worrisome shade of gray. With an oath, his brother Rowan stepped forward and slammed one rock-hard fist into Adrial's jaw. The younger Fey crumpled, unconscious, into his brother's arms.

Talisa gave a small cry, but she choked it back quickly. With a presence of mind Ellysetta had yet to fully master, Talisa managed to collect herself and remain at her father's side as Rowan carried Adrial from the room. She stood as proud and aloof as the haughtiest Celierian noblewoman, even though Ellie knew her heart was breaking. It was shattering, in fact, splintering into a thousand tiny shards that shredded what precious happiness she had found in her marriage and her life.

Ellysetta shook her head, pulling back from the drowning lure of the young woman's emotions. Why could she now feel someone else's pain so clearly? First Adrial's, now Talisa's. She glanced up at Rain as he led her from the room. What was happening to her?

<hr/>

They gathered in Rain's chambers. Marissya's quintet wove the privacy wards around the room while Rowan laid his brother on one of the empty couches. Marissya sat beside Adrial and threw back her veils. Her face radiated concern as she laid her hands on him. Rain watched broodingly. After a moment, she stood.

"Physically, he is well. I have done what I can to ease his emotions when he wakes. But you know he won't leave Celieria now." She looked at Rain. "No matter what you, Dorian, or even Talisa herself says, he won't leave her."

"I know." No warrior would leave his truemate once he found her. "I've never known a married woman to recognize a *shei'tanitsa* bond."

"If this husband truly held any part of Talisa's heart or soul, she would not have. Not that that will matter to the Celierians. Lord diSebourne will not stand by while a Fey takes his wife. And his father will support him. Lord Barrial may as well."

"I know that too."

"It could mean the end of the Fey-Celierian alliance."

"Shall I kill Adrial now, then, and save us the trouble?" Rain said. Ellysetta gasped, and Rain bit back his temper. "The alliance is already lost. There's no way Dorian will declare *primus* now, and we don't have enough votes to keep the Eld out of Celieria."

"Who cares about politics?" Dax interjected. "Doesn't anyone besides me realize that for the first time in a thousand years we have not only one but two *shei'tanitsa* bonds recognized within ten days of each other? To Celierian women? Doesn't that strike anyone else as odd?" He glanced around the room at the other Fey. "No warrior has ever found a truemate outside the women of the Fey, yet a week ago, Rain, you found Ellysetta, and now Adrial has found Talisa. It defies all logic."

"At least there is some manner of explanation for Talisa," Rain said, remembering Cann's *sorreisu kiyr*. "There's Elvish blood in the Barrial line, and apparently Fey blood, too." He looked at Marissya. "Lord Barrial wears your cousin Dural's crystal."

She sank onto the couch where Adrial lay. "Dural?"

"I discovered it the night of Teleos's dinner. I wasn't certain they shared kinship, but now it seems impossible that they do not."

"But Barrial wasn't truemated to his wife," Dax protested. "The bond was purely mortal—clearly mortal or he would have died when his wife expired in childbirth. And if Lord Barrial is Fey, as you say, how could he sire a daughter outside the bonds of *shei'tanitsa*?"

Female Fey were only born to truemated couples, and even then such a blessing was so rare, a girl child's birth was cause for great celebration.

"I don't understand it any more than you do, Dax." Rain lifted his hands. "Talisa and Ellysetta are both from the north. Perhaps there is something there we have too long discounted. Perhaps something about the remnant magics from the Mage Wars, when combined with other magical blood, can make the impossible possible."

One thing seemed certain to Rain: Lord Barrial's heritage and Talisa's existence explained the twenty-five *dahl'reisen* camped on Barrial lands and the personal interest Gaelen had taken in Lord Barrial. There was vel Serranis blood in the Barrial line, and somehow, though he'd not been truemated to his wife, Lord Barrial had sired a daughter. A daughter who had never felt comfortable around *dahl'reisen*, as if she—like all Fey women—could feel the pain of their lost souls. The *dahl'reisen* had been protecting a potential truemate. And probably hoping that somehow the Barrial line might produce a truemate for one of them.

"Does it really matter how Talisa came to be Adrial's *shei'-tani*?" Rowan interrupted. "She is, and he will not leave her. No matter what you say, Rain, no matter what the cost to our relationship with Celieria, he will try to win her bond. None of us has the right to deny him that. If any wish to try, they'll have to take me first." He glared his challenge at them all.

Without warning, Adrial jolted back to consciousness. His body jackknifed into a sitting position, and his eyes scanned the room with fast, frantic sweeps. "Talisa—"

Rowan was at his brother's side in an instant. "She is safe. She is with her father."

Adrial clasped Rowan's arms, holding on tight, as if he needed his brother's strength to anchor his own. "The Celierian . . . diSebourne?"

"With his father."

"Gods, Rowan, it's not supposed to be this way. How could I not know she was there? How could I not have found her before she wed that man?" Adrial covered his face with his hands. "That night, at the pleasure house, she was there in my mind." His fingers raked through his hair in agitation. "I betrayed her even as I found her, and she was with me the whole time. She felt it all." He gave a harsh, choked laugh. "I don't even remember anything I did under that cursed Spirit weave, but she does. And she blames me for it."

Ellysetta gasped, and her hand flew to her throat as she finally understood the full extent of the sorrow that had been in

Talisa's mind. "Adrial . . ." She started to reach out to him, but he flinched away from her. "Adrial, I'm so sorry."

A hand closed over her shoulder, and fierce reassurance poured into her. "It is not your fault, Ellysetta." Rain's voice was firm. "It is no one's fault. Even without the weave, Adrial's *shei'tani* would still be wed to another."

Adrial stood abruptly. "Your pardon, Ellysetta. The Feyreisen is correct. I should not have implied that you were at fault in any way. I am . . . not myself." He turned towards Rain. "I must forfeit the honor of holding Air in the Feyreisa's quintet. I no longer have the right to guard her, nor can I return to the Fading Lands. My place is with my own *shei'tani*." He squared his shoulders and raised his chin in a faintly defiant challenge. "I cannot ask that you provide a quintet to guard Talisa, only that you do not try to stop me from doing what I must."

"Five guard her already," Rain answered evenly. "They are yours to command. No Fey will stop you from following your *shei'tani*. But, Adrial—do not shed Celierian blood. No matter the provocation."

"Not even to protect her?"

"Only if her life is in immediate danger. For no other reason."

Adrial nodded stiffly. "Agreed."

"And stay out of her husband's path. There will be trouble if he knows you're there."

"I will try."

"Do more than that."

Their gazes met over Ellysetta's head, and wills clashed for a brief, tense moment. Then Adrial bowed his head, and Ellysetta knew that for the moment, at least, duty to his people and his king would keep Adrial from provoking war.

Adrial took a step backward and bowed. "*Miora felah ti'Feyreisa*," he murmured as he rose from the bow. "May the gods grant you long life and fertility, Ellysetta Baristani, and may you find happiness in the Fading Lands."

Adrial met his brother's gaze in a brief exchange, then pivoted on his heel and left.

As the door closed, Rowan's shoulders slumped. "This should have been a joyous time."

Ellie's heart ached for Rowan almost as much as it ached for his brother and Talisa Barrial diSebourne.

He drew himself up and turned to face Rain. "I must excuse myself from the honor of holding Fire in the Feyreisa's quintet. I fight where I always have, at my brother's side. Besides," he added, "if Lord Barrial's daughter does not accept Adrial's bond and he is too far gone for *sheisan'dahlein*, then I must be the one to grant him peace."

"*Nei*, Rowan," Marissya protested. "We cannot afford to lose you, too."

"He is my brother. It is my duty and my right."

Rain nodded and held out an arm. After a brief hesitation, Rowan clasped it. "The gods be with you, Rowan, and your brother. I wait with joy for the day you both return to the Fading Lands."

"May the gods be so kind," Rowan murmured.

Then Rowan, too, was gone.

"*Sheisan'dahlein* is the Fey honor death, isn't it?" Ellysetta murmured. "Why would Adrial kill himself now that he's found his truemate, even if she doesn't accept their bond? And what did Rowan mean by granting Adrial peace?" Ellysetta glanced around the room, but one after another, each Fey gaze slid away from hers. She turned to her own truemate. "Rain?"

He was silent for so long that Ellie thought he might not answer her. Then, at last, he spoke, slowly, as if each word were dragged from him against his will. "When a Fey finds his *shei'tani*—as I found you, and as Adrial found Talisa—his soul is tied to hers. It cannot be undone, and he must win her bond in return or something we call the soul hunger will begin to drive him mad."

Ellysetta's stomach clenched. The Fey were creatures of power, some more dangerous than others, but even the weakest among them could wreak havoc if their magic was loosed upon the world without caution.

"As I told you earlier this week, all Fey have a bit of the tairen in them, a wildness that lives inside. It is very fierce, very power-ful. When the soul hunger comes, that bit of tairen slips its leash. Even those who aren't Tairen Souls become dangerous to them-selves and all around them. You know what a Fey can do when madness takes him. It cannot be allowed."

"So if Talisa doesn't—"

"If Lord Barrial's daughter does not accept the bond, Adrial must take his own life, or one of us must do it for him."

"And if *I* don't accept *our* bond?" She stared up at Rain in dawning horror.

"Then I must die, Ellysetta. By my own hand or that of an-other." He wasn't wearing his usual expressionless mask, but she could neither see nor sense anything but acceptance in him. The day he had come out of the sky to claim her, he had embraced her as his fate, not knowing whether she would bring him joy or death.

"Why didn't you tell me this before now? Why did you keep it a secret?" Since the beginning, she realized, they'd considered the possibility. They'd even built conditions to account for it into her marriage contract.

"It is what it is," Rain said. "We can't change it. Telling you would serve no purpose."

"No purpose?" She gaped at him. "I'm supposed to be your truemate. Don't you think I deserve to know that something I do or don't do can kill you? Don't you think I would *want* to know?" She crossed her arms over her chest. It hurt to re-alize he'd deliberately kept this from her. "What happened to all that trust you keep talking about? Or is it just me who's supposed to trust you, while you can keep hiding things from me forever?"

Spots of color flashed on his cheeks. "I had hoped there would be no reason to tell you. You seemed . . . willing to en-tertain the idea of loving me. I thought the rest would come in time."

"Who has sworn to kill you?" But she already knew. She turned to Bel.

"Rain and I are brothers in all but blood," he said.

"Could you really kill him? *Would* you?"

"If I must."

"How could you ever bring yourself to do it? You love him, almost as much as I do."

"It is not something we do lightly," Marissya said. "A Fey cannot take the life of another Fey without losing his own soul and becoming *dahl'reisen*."

Vadim Maur descended the final flight of stone steps to the bottommost level of his subterranean palace. Ten rings of power glinted at his fingers, and *selkahr* glittered darkly at his wrists. The voluminous deep purple folds of his robes dragged behind him. His sash had long ago become so heavy with the jewels of his achievements that he had ceased to wear it for all but the most ceremonial of occasions, and this was business, not ceremony.

He turned to the left of the stairs and walked down the long, shadowed hallway, past several dozen empty cells. Once, they had all been filled, as some of the cells in the right corridor still were, but over the centuries, all but a precious few of his Fey pets had died, and lately even *dahl'reisen* were hard to come by.

The guards outside the last cell at the farthest end of the long corridor opened the heavy *sel'dor*-banded-and-bolted door as Vadim approached. He stepped into the room and summoned light in the sconces high on the walls, illuminating the cage and the matepair within. Even before he'd entered, they had backed into a corner of their cage, and once again— predictable as time—the man had pushed his mate behind him. As if that puny gesture could protect her.

Vadim smiled without a trace of humor. "Shannisorran v'En Celay . . . my beautiful Elfeya . . . I am not happy that you've both been keeping secrets from your master."

The man tossed his head, throwing the long strands of hair out of his face so he could see his enemy more clearly. His broad, naked shoulders squared and his eyes issued an open, almost sneering challenge. "What secrets would those be,

Vadim?" Lord v'En Celay's voice was rusty with disuse, but the deep, rumbling tones of it were as proud as they had ever been.

Vadim knew the legends of Shannisorran v'En Celay. He'd been raised on them, as all Elden children were raised on stories of their enemies. He knew that the great v'En Celay, Lord Death, had been the most feared Fey warrior of his time, commanding thousands of his brethren in battle, leading them to victory in some of the world's most savage and bloody battles. The Mages had feared him as much as they feared the Tairen Souls. Lord Death was invincible, ruthless, impervious to pain, privation, and even defeat.

Until he had met and claimed his truemate.

In that one irreversible instant, Lord Death had become forever vulnerable. But until Vadim, no Mage had ever dared turn that vulnerability to its best advantage.

It was Vadim who had conceived the plan of capturing a matepair, for study, experimentation, and breeding. The other Mages had called him a fool, but he had persevered and plotted, winning several of the younger, less hidebound Mages like himself to his side. He had planned the capture of Elfeya, laid the trap, buried himself and five other Mages beneath the stink of rotting corpses while his fellow conspirators had driven the v'En Celay matepair into ambush during the height of the Mage Wars. It was Vadim who sprang the trap, Vadim who captured Lord Death and catapulted himself into the upper political ranks of the Mage Council. He had been the obvious choice to replace the High Mage Demyan Raz after that man's idiotic decision to murder Rain Tairen Soul's mate resulted in the decimation of the Eld race.

And it was Vadim, the High Mage, the visionary, who had devoted the last thousand years of his life to that aim so grand, so glorious that even now his enemies doubted he could ever succeed. Those doubters would soon bow down before his greatness. His ultimate triumph was at hand, and in just a few short bells, he would claim his prize.

Vadim smiled coldly at his too-proud captive. "What secrets,

Lord v'En Celay? Are there so many that you don't know the ones of which I speak?" Not waiting for a response, he purred the answer himself. "The child, Shan. The one you stole from me two decades ago. The one you and our lovely Elfeya somehow managed to convince me had no magic in her, though she's been claimed as truemate by the Feyreisen himself. My child, Shan."

CHAPTER THIRTEEN

Cold kiss. Bright steel. Sharp bite.
Black blood. Red death. My friend
  Fey'cha.
    —*The Blade*, a warrior's poem by Evanaris vel
                                              Bahr

"I have worked a thousand years for victory, and you have tried to rob me of it."

A whip of Earth lashed out, opening a slice of skin across Shannisorran v'En Celay's back, adding another runnel of blood to the countless wet trails already there. The man who had once been named Lord Death barely flinched. Over the years, pain had become a familiar friend. If Vadim Maur flayed the very skin from his bones, Shan doubted he would do more than groan even while his body writhed. Except for Elfeya. It was agony for her to watch his punishment, and her agony wounded Shan in ways the High Mage's worst blows never could. When he would have slipped forever into the hazy, sweet freedom of madness, she kept him anchored. The irony of it had not escaped him over the last centuries. In the true dichotomous nature of *shei'tanitsa*, she was both Shan's greatest blessing and greatest curse.

Vadim Maur knew it and used that truth to his best advantage.

A lash made of Earth was both painful and bloody, unlike Fire, which cauterized the wounds even as it made them. Elfeya had never liked to see Shan's blood running over his skin, not even before the Mage Wars, when most wounds had been slight nicks inflicted while he taught Fey younglings the complexities of the Dance of Knives.

«It looks worse than it feels, Elfeya.»

Love and sorrow flowed through him, healing and wounding all at once. *«I know, beloved.»* It hurt her to do nothing, not even take the edge off his pain, but they had long ago agreed that she should never attempt even the smallest bit of magic in the High Mage's presence.

Not that it would matter much longer. The child's true nature was stirring. The bonds he and Elfeya had placed on her were weakening just as the fear of her own magic they had regretfully instilled in her was waning. There was precious little time before she revealed what Shan and Elfeya had struggled so long to hide.

Rain Tairen Soul had claimed the girl as his truemate. He must protect her now that Shan and Elfeya no longer could. Shan had never known Rainier vel'En Daris well, but his father Rajahl had been a good man and a fierce warrior, a blade Shan had trusted at his back. Gods willing, his son would be the same, strong and fierce enough to face the Mages and win.

A sharp knife ripped into Shan's side, and he convulsed in sudden, breathless pain. Vadim had tired of toying with him and had begun the torture in earnest. Elfeya's silent scream made Shan's soul howl.

He felt a distant, troubled stirring. An awareness forged between himself and the child by Vadim Maur's darkest evil. Shan could usually block the link but he'd never been able to sever it, even when he knew firsthand the horrors it inflicted. He pulled back, holding the pain to himself and Elfeya alone, but the torture had only just begun. The pain would get far worse, and then he would not be able to keep his agony and rage from spilling over.

Oh, child, I am sorry.

The king's carriage bounced over the cobbled streets. Inside the royal conveyance, Ellie sat alone, huddled in one velvet-

cushioned corner, furious at the Fey for their ways, furious at
Rain for not telling her. Furious at herself for not thinking
enough to ask.

Every Fey tale she'd ever read was a story of balances. For
every light, there was a shadow. For every smile, there was a
tear. For every gift, a sacrifice.

If she did not complete the truemate bond, Rain would die.
And Bel, with his too-ancient eyes and carefully hidden hope,
would strike the killing blow, destroying both his best friend
and his own salvation. Rain and Bel both accepted the possibility without question and without complaint.

Perhaps life was more precious to mortals because they had
less of it to enjoy, but she didn't want even one more person
dying on her behalf. Certainly not Rain or Bel.

The carriage slowed as it pulled up before the Baristani
home. A moment later, the door opened, and Bel helped
her descend the narrow steps. She paused in the street to
look up at the welcoming lights shining from the windows of
her family home. Her parents were still awake, and the Fey
hadn't yet woven their twenty-five-fold weaves around the
house.

As she approached the front door, the familiar reek of onions
and bacon made Ellie's back stiffen. She knew that odor.

"You look a fine slut, Ellysetta Baristani, all dressed in your
fancy silks and satins." Den Brodson stepped from the shadows.

Fey blades hissed out of their sheaths.

"No . . . it's all right." Ellysetta waved her guards back.
They didn't cover their steel, but neither did they dismember
Den on the spot. What a shame the Fey hadn't included an
anti-Den thread in the Spirit weaves that kept the rabble-
rousers out of the neighborhood. Since his parents lived
nearby, he must be able to pass through the weave at will. She
lifted her chin and met her former suitor's sullen glare.
"What do you want, Den?"

"The bride your dishonorable, betrothal-breaking *rultshart*
of a father promised me would do, for starters."

Ellysetta bit back a searing retort. With her strangely

heightened senses, she could feel his anger, his hatred. His dark, acid emotions set her on edge. She struggled to remain calm. The evening had already been difficult enough without her adding to the disturbance. Still, she'd had more than enough of Den Brodson and his groundless claims. "My father is a fine and decent man. The betrothal was broken legally, in a court of law, and your parents are wealthy beyond their dreams because of it."

"My father was bribed, his mind twisted by that Fey sorcerer's tricks. There was nothing lawful about it."

"Your father saw more gold than he would earn in a thousand lifetimes, and he grabbed it," she corrected sharply. "There was no sorcery involved."

"You bear my mark!"

"No longer." She turned her head to show him her unblemished throat. "And I only bore it because of your deceit, so don't bray on about Fey sorcerer's tricks."

Den growled a nasty oath and spat on the ground. "Their magic may have removed the mark, but we both know who claimed you first, Ellie."

"Why did you want me as your wife in the first place? It's not as though you ever harbored any feelings for me, except the thrill you got in bullying me when I was a child."

"What do you know of my feelings?"

"Enough to know that you had no tender ones for me."

"I would have treated you kindly."

"Meaning you'd only have beaten me twice a week instead of daily." Her unsettled emotions coalesced into anger, and she glared at him. "You're a greedy little bully of a man, Den Brodson, with precious few kindnesses in you—if there are any at all. You've never loved anyone in your life, least of all me."

"Love?" He barked an ugly, mocking laugh. "Is that what this is all about? You think the Tairen Soul loves you?"

If he'd meant to hurt her with that, he'd failed. "No, I know he doesn't love me. But he needs me, Den, and that's enough for now."

"He doesn't need *you*. He needs your magic and he needs your womb, Ellie, to breed more Tairen Souls for the Fey. The fact that you come with them is just a little inconvenience he'll have to deal with to get what he wants. Keep that in mind on your wedding night."

She laughed with genuine amusement. "Was that supposed to hurt my feelings, you pompous little bloat toad? Half the women in this city—including most noblewomen in court—would kill to have Rain show them a fraction of the devotion he showers on me. Do you honestly believe any woman would choose *you* when she could have the king of the Fey?"

His face darkened, and he took a threatening step towards her. "*Petchka*. No woman talks to me that way."

He was on his back in the street before he moved another inch. Kieran knelt over him, a razor-sharp red-handled blade held at Den's throat, icy menace gleaming from blue eyes that normally shone with laughter. "Little sausage, I've lost all patience with you. If you live past the next minute, you will never come near the Feyreisa or her family again. Do you understand?" When Den nodded very carefully, Kieran gave him a slight smile that was even more frightening than the deadly look in his eyes. "*Kabei*, a wise decision. A first for you, perhaps?" Without taking his eyes off his captive, Kieran asked, "What would the Feyreisa like me to do with this annoyance?"

Before Ellysetta could answer, the front door of the Baristani home opened, and Sol stepped outside. "What's going on here?"

Ellysetta drew a deep breath. "Nothing, Papa," she said. "Den just thought it might be a nice night to make trouble. Kieran has convinced him otherwise." She met Kieran's gaze. "Release him," she ordered. "If he comes here again, take him to the palace and let the king's justice deal with him." She turned on her heel and climbed the stairs to enter the house, trying desperately to quell the fear rising inside her.

For one frightening moment when Kieran had asked what

should be done with Den, a terrible voice deep inside her had responded, *kill him*.

⟡

"There's no way Dorian can invoke *primus* now without risking open rebellion. *Krekk!*" Rain spun away and paced to the high, arched windows overlooking the carefully manicured acres of fountains and gardens at the rear of the palace. "I've been a poor Feyreisen. Too caught up in my own misery to do my duty."

"*Nei*, Rain," Dax countered. "If anyone is responsible for the deterioration of our relations with Celieria, Marissya and I are. We've come every year since the Mage Wars and never realized what was happening. We were too complacent, thinking vol Serranis blood in Celieria's royal family would ensure our alliance."

"You are not the Defender of the Fey. I am. The responsibility is mine." His jaw clenched. "You and Marissya should leave tonight. Take a hundred men and go. Ellysetta and I will follow as soon as we can complete the marriage rites." He gave a curt, humorless laugh. "At least her father agreed we could hold the ceremony tomorrow."

"We're not leaving until you do. We—" Dax frowned suddenly and turned to his truemate. "Marissya, you are not well?"

The *shei'dalin* had retreated to a chair in the corner of the room. She was rubbing her temples, her skin paler than usual. "There are too many strong emotions around me tonight. It has been very difficult to block them, and I haven't managed as well as I'd like."

Dax was at her side in an instant, curving his arm around her waist. "*Shei'tani*, why did you say nothing? Come lie down. You should rest."

She patted his arm and smiled wearily. "There will be time enough for rest when we reach the Fading Lands."

Concerned by the *shei'dalin's* pallor, Rain added his insistence to Dax's. "There is time now, Marissya. We can do nothing tonight to alter our course."

"I don't think I could sleep even if I tried. There's too much anger, too much sorrow. Such pain . . ." She closed her eyes.

Rain and Dax exchanged a worried look.

«Marissya!»

«Rain!»

The blasts of Spirit hit Dax, Marissya, and Rain simultaneously, the urgency unmistakable: Talisa's quintet calling for the *shei'dalin*, Rowan summoning his king. Rain, Dax, and Marissya bolted for the door and raced down the palace corridors towards Cannevar Barrial's chamber.

<hr />

The High Mage brought his whip down in a brutal blow, shredding flesh from bone.

Shan's body arched, every muscle seized in agony. His scream was a roar that echoed off the carved rock walls of his prison. Beside him, sobbing, Elfeya screamed too.

Despite his best efforts, pain blasted beyond his control, screeching down the link that tied him to the unfortunate girl in Celieria.

<hr />

Clad in a simple blue-gray nightshift, Ellysetta paced her room. Jeweled hairpins lay scattered like rain across her dresser, and her hair tumbled down her back in an unruly mass of curls and braids. Her silk ballgown lay crumpled in a heap in the corner, the golden Fey crown tossed carelessly atop it.

Kill him.

Except during her childhood exorcism, when pain had driven her to the brink of madness, she'd never consciously had such a desire in her life. Where had it come from? How could she ever have even thought such a thing, so coldly and with such frightening venom?

Kill him.

Dear gods, if her father hadn't come outside, she might have given voice to the thought, and Kieran would have obeyed her. Den would be dead. At Kieran's hand but by her command.

She pressed her hands to her temples. Her head hurt again. It was throbbing with a steady, squeezing pain that set her teeth on edge.

Without warning, agony slashed across her nerves, flinging

her to the floor. She clapped her hands over her ears to block out the screaming, but the horrifying sound came from within and would not be silenced.

The attack didn't last long, a handful of seconds at the most, and when it ended, Ellysetta scrambled to her feet and ran, racing down the stairs, past her startled quintet, and through the kitchen to the tiny walled garden at the back of her parents' house. There she stopped, hemmed in, heart pounding. Desperately she dragged in deep gasps of cool night air and shivered as the clammy sweat that had broken out across her body evaporated.

Calm down, Ellie. Calm down and get control of yourself.

It was hopeless, of course. Once an episode started, nothing could hold back the violent seizures that ensued. Demon possession, the priests had proclaimed when she was a small child. Something not right in her soul had left a doorway for evil to gain access.

~ ~ ~

The sounds of fighting reached Rain's ears long before he turned down the final corridor. He rounded the corner at a dead run to find Lord Barrial's door barred by Talisa's quintet, and scorch marks from blasts of Fire on the walls around them. Rowan lay dazed against one wall, and Adrial stood in a crouched fighting stance in the center of the hallway, teeth bared in a snarl, red Fey'cha in each hand.

Rain absorbed the entire scene in an instant and launched himself at Adrial. A five-fold weave spun from his fingers, knocking the venomous blades to the ground and melting them to harmless slag even as Rain slammed into Adrial. They landed hard on the marble floor. Adrial's collarbone snapped and he grunted in pain, but Rain still pinned him with both muscle and magic. Fey warriors were taught from early adolescence to fight through pain, through debilitating and even mortal wounds, to keep fighting until their hearts no longer beat.

A sudden driving pain and shrieking roar in his ears made Rain gasp, and he almost lost his hold on Adrial. When had the younger man learned to do that? Quickly Rain wove a block, tight threads of Spirit barricading his mind from illusionary and mental attack.

Immediately Adrial struck again.

The air around Rain thickened, and a breathless feeling invaded his lungs. Adrial was weaving the oxygen out of the air around his king. Rain narrowed his eyes and growled a warning. "Careful, Fey, or you'll make me do something you'll greatly regret." He rebuffed Adrial's weave with a firm, steady push of his own. It wasn't an easy task. The Fey's mastery of Air was as strong as Rain's own, perhaps even stronger since Adrial had spent his years honing his primary talent while Rain had worked to master five. But despite that mastery, Adrial was wounded, his concentration scattered by the recent *shei'tanitsa* claiming.

❧⟡❧

Gaelen groaned. His head was pounding and he couldn't be sure if the most recent fall had knocked him unconscious or merely dazed him. He opened his eyes and stared up at the narrow slice of starlit sky visible between the hulking buildings on either side of the dark alley. The twin stars of the Great Serpent constellation still shone almost directly overhead. He'd been merely dazed, then.

He took a breath and wished he hadn't. Something was rotting in the darkness, and it wasn't just him. He rolled over onto his hands and knees. A soft, bloated lump squished beneath one palm. All at once, his stomach revolted and his body convulsed in wracking heaves.

The spasms passed, the agony slowly faded, and his head drooped down between trembling shoulders. He panted in deep, uneven gasps.

If the Eld could see him now . . . the Dark Lord, weak as a babe, puking his guts up in a rank little alley. That would give those soul-twisted Mages a good laugh.

Gaelen started to wipe his mouth, then thought better of it when he caught wind of the better-to-remain-nameless muck coating his hands.

Gods, this was ridiculous. Pathetic. When he found the High Mage's daughter, his stench would bring her guards down on him long before he got within range of attack.

He rose to his feet, wobbled, and slapped a hand against the dark wall to steady himself. His feet shuffled forward and he staggered out of the alleyway into the dimly lit streets of one of Celieria's lower-class districts. Keeping to the shadows, he made slow progress through the narrow, winding streets. Old memories and instinct would have steered him towards the royal palace and Marissya, but he resisted the temptation of seeing his sister one last time. She was in the palace under guard of her *chakor* and close to a hundred Fey. In his current state, there was no way he would reach her alive to issue a warning. *Nei*, his first task must be to slay the High Mage's spawn.

He stretched out his senses, seeking the pull of Fey magic, the natural affinity that drew him to others of his kind. He sensed the concentration of the Fey in the palace, and another concentration in a humbler district of the city. Gaelen turned and staggered towards the West End, clinging to walls, forcing his feet to move step after dragging step.

He followed his senses into the heart of the West End until he reached a barrier that shone to his eyes with a faint lavender glow. Spirit weave. He examined the weave, recognizing the redirection pattern meant to keep unwanted mortals out. Beyond the barrier, he saw a faint lavender glow on a rooftop, then another atop a building just across the street. Fey warriors, cloaked in Spirit to hide them from mortal eyes. Guarding something. Guarding someone.

He stepped back into the shadows and marshaled his strength, managing a loose weave to hide his presence from them. It wasn't a strong weave—the *sel'dor* shrapnel in his body prevented that—but it was enough to make their eyes skim past him without seeing unless they knew just where to look.

Leaning back against a brick wall, he considered his options. He detected some fifty or more Fey guarding the small house. He was so weak, he would never survive a direct assault on the Fey. He patted the pocket of his torn and bloodstained tunic, feeling the bulge of the two *sorreisu kiyr* he'd removed from the dead Fey. They'd died, presumably, in the service of the Tairen Soul's mate, which would have forged some small tie to her. He would use that to draw her out, away from her guards, and then strike. But where?

A cool, fresh scent teased his nostrils. Water, clean and pure. The Velpin. Sudden thirst overwhelmed him. The river's magic-purified waters would cleanse him and soothe the worst of his wounds. The Fey magic permeating the Velpin's depths would revitalize his flagging strength. He would draw the woman to him there. He lurched to the left and shuffled painfully down a tiny side street, out of the path of the warriors and towards the cool renewal of the river.

⟡⟡⟡

Ellysetta wrapped her arms around her waist and tipped her head back to look up at the square of starlit sky that shone down through the crowded buildings. Dizziness assailed her, and her vision blurred. A second set of stars seemed to superimpose themselves over the first, wavering. She smelled something rank, something awful.

Sudden nausea gripped her, and she fell to her knees, retching violently in the grass beneath her mother's carefully tended orange tree.

When her stomach had emptied itself, she knelt there, panting.

"Ellysetta."

Bel touched her shoulder, and she turned on him, snarling like a wild animal. He actually backed away from her. "Leave me alone," she snapped.

"You are ill."

"No doubt you've already told Rain." Her tone was ugly, and she didn't care. A terrible anger had come to life inside her.

"He has blocked himself. I cannot reach him." Bel never took his eyes off her. "I thought you and I had become friends. Can you not talk to me?"

"Hasn't there been enough talk for one night?" Awkwardly, her bones aching as though someone had taken a stick to her, she rose to her feet. A breeze blew across her face, and she became aware of a faint chill on her skin. She lifted a hand, touched her cheek, and brought away cooling wetness. Tears. She was weeping and had not even realized it.

"Ellysetta," Bel insisted, "the Fey blame you for nothing, nor will we even if you don't accept Rain's bond. And we want nothing more from you than that which you are willing to give. The gods weave as the gods will, and we Fey accept what comes our way. You are a blessing to us all."

She ignored him in favor of the new need that drove her. Thirst. She was so thirsty.

Bel took hold of her shoulders, shaking her. "Ellysetta. Talk to me."

He was in her way. She frowned at him and he was gone. Gods, she was so thirsty she could drink a river.

❧❧❧

"She's in pain," Adrial cried, struggling to free himself from Rain's grip, "and they won't let me go to her!"

"You haven't the right to go to her," Rain answered. "And if you'd killed a brother Fey, you would have lost her forever. Adrial, think. It's the bond madness driving you. Believe me, I know. Find your center and hang on with both hands. Talisa is safe. Marissya is with her."

Rain didn't release the younger man until the glow of magic had left Adrial's eyes, and even then he remained watchful, not releasing the full measure of his power just in case he needed to summon it quickly.

"Let me go in, let me see her."

"Adrial—"

"She's calling for me." The torment in Adrial's eyes was plain to see. "*Teska*, Rain."

It wouldn't be long before Lord diSebourne learned of the fight outside Lord Barrial's chamber. Adrial hadn't been exactly subtle in his approach, and palace walls were notoriously thin, especially when it came to intriguing gossip. Still, if Talisa was calling for Adrial, and the husband wasn't here to prevent it, who was Rain to keep a *shei'tan* from his mate?

"Quickly, then," Rain murmured. "And if diSebourne comes, you go out the window. He can't find you with her. Be patient until we can find a way to get out of this without starting a war. Just as I had to stand in Dorian's court to appease his nobles, you must honor their laws and customs, too."

Their eyes met, two *shei'tans*, both unbonded but tied forever to foreign truemates. Adrial nodded and slipped into the room. Rain waved Rowan inside as well, in case Adrial might need the calming influence of his older brother. The others went to work erasing evidence of the confrontation before melting away into the shadows. Talisa's quintet followed Rain into Lord Barrial's chamber, closing, bolting, and warding the door behind them.

Talisa lay on a plum silk fainting couch, her cheeks wan, her eyes closed. Marissya sat beside her, healing hands splayed and glowing, but Dax was holding his truemate's shoulders, which Rain knew was a sure sign that Marissya was unwell. Dax only did that when his *shei'tani* needed his strength to augment or bolster her own.

Lord Barrial was pacing the room like a caged tairen. He halted abruptly when he saw Adrial come in and hurry to Talisa's side. "What's he doing here?"

"Talisa called him," Rain said.

"Talisa—" Cann stared at his daughter. "I never knew she could do that."

Rain saw Talisa's eyes open, saw the relief on her face when Adrial knelt and clasped her hand in his. "Chances are, neither did she. Though I'll wager that over the years you've had instances when you've known that she was hurt or in trouble."

"Yes, but I've always had a sort of link to the ones I love," Cann said.

Rain nodded, unsurprised. "We call it Spirit, one of the two mystics. All Fey have at least a rudimentary control Spirit."

"I'm Celierian, not Fey."

"If Dural vel Serranis is your ancestor, you're Fey enough. Serranis blood has always been strong. It's even produced Tairen Souls in the past."

Marissya sat back.

"Well?" Cann asked her. "What is wrong with my daughter?"

"What's wrong with my *shei'tani*?" Adrial echoed.

"There is nothing wrong with her." Marissya said. "The pain she feels belongs to another. As does mine. I should have known, but it's been so long since I felt it." The *shei'dalin* drew a deep breath and met the dawning realization in Rain's eyes. "*Dahl'reisen.* An incredibly strong one."

"Gaelen?" Rain asked.

"I don't know. I can't bear to open myself enough to find out. I've built as strong a block as I can, and still I feel his soul tearing at me."

"What possible reason would he have to come here?" Cann asked, frowning. "Surely he knows the Fey are here and that Marissya would sense him."

Rain thought of the two Fey slain when he'd sent them north and the rumors of *dahl'reisen* raids along the Eld-Celieria border. If Gaelen had joined forces with the Eld, there was one person in Celieria he could use to cause the Fey irreparable harm.

«Ellysetta.» Rain reached for her, then realized his block was still in place. He tore the weave down and tried again. His heart stopped. He could not sense her.

⟡⟡⟡

Bel groaned and picked himself up off the ground. His ears rang and his vision was blurry from the force of his head cracking against the stones that paved the narrow courtyard.

Let that be a lesson to you, Belliard vel Jelani. When the Feyreisa says leave her alone, listen to her.

Grimacing, he shook his head and leaned over for an instant until the dizziness passed. Ellysetta's thrust of Air had been quick and brutal, plowing into him like the whip of a tairen's tail, flinging him across the courtyard and slamming him into the wall on the far side.

It had been stupid of him to grab her. A boy who had yet to pass his first level in the Dance of Knives would know better.

«Bel?» Rain's voice whipped at the insides of Bel's aching skull. *«What's happening? I can no longer sense Ellysetta.»*

«She's here with me.» He glanced at the spot where she should have been, and froze.

Ellysetta was gone.

⦿⥤⥤⥤⥤⦿

A mile from his prey's house, when he was certain he was clear of detection by Fey sentries, Gaelen released the weave that hid his presence. He slumped against a wall, gasping as sweat rolled down his face. The *sel'dor* shrapnel burned like live coals in his flesh. He was spent, with nothing left to keep him standing but sheer force of will.

He didn't even have the strength to hold his torment in check. Though he wasn't fully broadcasting his pain, too much of it was slipping though his mental barriers. The warriors wouldn't sense it. Empathy was solely a Fey woman's gift, or curse, as was more often the case.

Marissya, forgive me.

She would know he was here. She had to feel him by now, and the pain would grow worse the longer he remained. He had to get to the Velpin, restore what strength he had left, and kill the High Mage's daughter before the Fey could find and slay him.

Pushing himself away from the wall, he started off again. He followed the Velpin's sweet scent unerringly through a maze of narrow cobbled roads and alleys, each shambling step bringing him closer to the promise of relief until, at last, the street opened to a grassy park and a tree-lined embankment overlooking the river. Stone steps led down to a ledge where the local women could do their wash.

Clutching at the wall, he eased his battered body down the steps. But he was too tired, his strength sapped. His dragging feet tangled. He tripped on the last step and toppled forward, plunging into the river. His head struck the side of the ledge, and his ironic last thought as the water closed over him was that at least the stench would be gone when his body was brought to Marissya.

⦿⥤⥤⥤⥤⦿

Why was she standing in the middle of the West End's river park in her nightshift?

Ellysetta turned in small, dazed circles, stunned by the feel of the soft grass beneath her feet and the cool night breeze, fresh with the scent of the river, on her face. The last thing she remembered was the initial warning pangs of a seizure, the strange double vision that had made her sick, and the terrible thirst.

She pressed a hand to her heart, frowning. She didn't feel the same as she usually did after an episode of demon possession. Her head ached—that was typical—but her body ached too, a hundred burning pains like tiny hot pellets scattered beneath her skin. She closed her eyes, and unfamiliar images flashed in her mind. Tall, waving grass, two girls racing towards her, laughing, arms outstretched. One looked like the *shei'dalin* Marissya, but younger. The other was oddly familiar as well, and the sight of her bright, pale eyes and happy smile made Ellie's heart swell with joy. Then the scene changed to something horrible.

Ellie's eyes snapped open and she fell to her knees, sobbing.

«Rain, help me!» The call was as much instinct as conscious thought.

«Ellysetta! Where are you?»

Relief nearly left her prostrate as the reassuring sound of his voice filled her mind. *«By the river, in the park near my home. Something's happening to me.»* She flinched as more images crowded her mind. *«I'm afraid.»*

«Stay there. I'm coming.»

«Hurry.»

«As fast as my wings can fly, shei'tani.»

From the river, she heard a faint splashing, a weak cough, and she crawled forward on her hands and knees, pulled towards the source of the sounds like steel to a lodestone. *«There's someone here. By the river. I've got to—»*

«Nei! Stay where you are.»

Dimly she heard the fierce roar of a tairen, saw a gout of flame scorch the night sky in the distance. But it was the dark figure in the water that claimed her attention, overriding her will and pulling her inexorably to his side. A man. As she stumbled nearer, she could see the cuff of his black tunic caught on a mooring hook, could feel his grim desperation as he struggled to keep from drowning in the river's steady current.

«*It's a man. He's hurt. In pain . . . oh, gods, so much pain.*» There was no way she could pull him out of the water. The best she could do would be to free his arm from the mooring hook and pull him to the relative safety of the embankment steps. She grabbed the dark-clad arm, surprised to feel leather beneath her fingertips. Celierians didn't wear leather tunics. That was when she saw the glint of steel flashing beneath the surface of the water. Blades crisscrossing a leather-clad chest. «*He's Fey!*»

«*Get away from him! Don't touch him!*»

«*He's got to be one of yours. He's wounded. Bleeding.*» Grasping the man's arm with both hands, Ellie planted her feet and pulled the dead weight of his body out of the main river current to the stone steps leading down into the water. "It's all right," she murmured aloud. "You're safe. We'll get you help." She reached out to turn him on his side. His head lifted. Piercing blue eyes, pale as ice, stared up at her, glowing faintly.

«*Ellysetta, nei!*»

The man's hands closed around her wrists. His bare skin, wet and cold from the river, touched her own. Agony like nothing she'd ever felt poured into her, and she screamed.

<hr />

The High Mage's lash bit into Shan's side just as something else bit into his soul. Bitter black agony screeched up the link between himself and the girl in Celieria, overwhelming all physical torture with something far, far worse.

Dahl'reisen. Soul lost. An emotional wasteland devoid of all but despair, pain, and the remnants of wrecked dreams. Once it had almost claimed Shan's soul, but Elfeya had saved him. Now it loomed again, pulling him in, an irresistible well of blackness.

Connected to him as she had been since the day of their bonding, Elfeya's shriek overlapped his, her fear and pain echoing and amplifying his own.

<hr />

Rain plummeted out of the sky. He'd begun the Change back to man-form as he started his descent, but the sudden onslaught of pain wrenched away his control. His body melted helplessly into human form and he crashed to the ground, slamming down hard, feeling the jarring crack of bone as several ribs gave way. He let out a short cry, but the pain of his injury was nothing compared to what he felt through Ellysetta. The howling bitter emptiness of the soul-lost, the anger without focus, the dead dreams and grim despair.

Time and reality shifted in a dizzying rush, and suddenly he was a young, fierce Tairen Soul, winging over a battlefield, raining deadly tairen flame upon the enemy, battering their protective Mage-shields. The battle was fierce and bloody. Fey warriors fell by the hundreds, but so too did the enemy. A desperate call alerted him. To the south, a troop of vicious Merellian mercenaries, led by three shrouded Demon Princes, were decimating Celierian infantry and Elvish bowmen at an alarming rate. Rain dispatched twenty-five quintets to aid his embattled allies even as he swooped low to scorch a small knot of Mages. The Mages threw up a shield in time to avoid death and managed to hold it despite the punishing fire he rained down upon them. Hissing, Rain banked left, flew high on an updraft, and circled around for another pass.

That was when the Mages' true battle plan was revealed. Three *dahl'reisen* demons coalesced into lethal, shadowy life, directly in front of the Fey line Rain had just thinned by his command to aid the Celierians and Elves. Soul-poisoned demon blades cut through the lines of seasoned Fey warriors like farmers scything wheat, and Mages followed in their deadly shadow. Within moments, they had broken through to the tents erected behind the battle lines, where *shei'dalins* worked to save as many of the wounded and dying as they could.

Sariel was no *shei'dalin*, but she had some minor healing talent and she could weave peace on any man, a skill that had its own special value in a place of death. A gentle girl, whose laughter was stolen by the ugly brutality of war, she'd not had time for more than a split second of horror and a single brief call before Fire and a black Mage blade claimed her life.

«*E'tan!*» Husband. Lover. Protector. Friend. Mate, but not

truemate. Abruptly, not even that. Not protector either. He was the one who'd thinned the ranks and left the women vulnerable to attack. Left Sariel to face her death.

Trapped in his memories, reliving the madness, Rain watched helplessly as the scene repeated itself. Only this time, as the Mage lifted his black blade, it was not Sariel beneath the knife. This time it was Ellysetta who stared up in horror as the sword descended upon her all too vulnerable neck. Ellysetta who screamed, "*Shei'tan!*"

Shadows flashed with glints of steel as scores of Fey warriors raced into the small park, weapons drawn. Bel was in the lead. He saw his king, his friend, fallen on the ground, shouting for Ellysetta, eyes locked on some scene visible only to him, a swirling cloud of magic gathering about him like a storm as he summoned the Change.

«*Marissya, we need you!*» Bel summoned the *shei'dalin* on a blast of Spirit, then barked commands to the five quintets, ordering them to surround their king. «*Weave your strongest cage around him. We can't let him fly. No matter what it takes to stop him.*»

Bel sprinted past his dearest friend, racing to aid the woman he'd pledged his soul to protect. She was on the steps, clutched in the grip of a *dahl'reisen* Bel knew and had once admired. She was screaming, a shrill wail of torment and terror.

«*Vel Serranis! Release her!*»

Dahl'reisen though he was, Gaelen vel Serranis was still Fey. Any Fey who took Gaelen's life would lose his own soul.

Bel never once paused as he pulled two wickedly sharp, red-handled Fey'cha free of their sheaths and leapt forward to kill the *dahl'reisen* who had laid hands upon Ellysetta Baristani.

Behind him, Rain's shouts changed to the chilling, full-throated roar of an enraged tairen.

Held in the viselike grip of the man she'd thought to save, Ellysetta's consciousness wavered uncertainly in a mirrored hall of madness. She was Ellysetta Baristani, yet not. She was a man, naked and howling beneath an Elden Mage's lash. She was a woman screaming as tears of blood poured from her eyes. She was Gaelen vel Serranis, descending into madness as he watched his sister, the person he loved beyond all others, die in one swift, shocking moment at the point of an Eld assassin's blade. She was Rain, locked in an agony of old memories and new nightmares, teetering on the brink of destruction.

She was herself, shrieking from the horrors that battered her mind, even as a violent rage swelled within her, fierce as any tairen's fury.

The pain must stop. *Would* stop.

Bel was in mid-leap when Ellysetta's screaming abruptly ceased and a fist of Air slammed hard against his chest, batting him to the ground. All breath left him, and the red Fey'cha flew out of his grasp.

«*Kill him!*» Bel shouted the command to his brother Fey, demanding the sacrifice without a second thought. «*He's got the Feyreisa.*»

«*Nei. You will stand down.*» The command came from Ellysetta, but her voice was different, resonant with power, her order irresistible. Blades fell harmlessly from Fey hands.

Behind Bel, the warriors guarding Rain gave a shout. "The Tairen Soul! He's free! Our weave is down! We cannot call magic!"

At first Bel thought it was Gaelen vel Serranis using dark *dahl'reisen* magic to control them all, but then Ellysetta turned her head ever so slightly towards him. Her face was expressionless, her eyes glowing.

Fear shivered up Bel's spine. "Ellysetta . . ." The soul that looked out at him from those glowing eyes was not the gentle spirit that had claimed his devotion. "Ellysetta, you must let us stop Rain. In his present state, he's a danger to us all." He tried to summon his magic, but nothing came to his call. He could sense the source within him, rich and powerful, but it was as if the flows of his magic had been redirected.

To her.

«*Aiyah, it must stop.*» With strength beyond her slender form, she turned the *dahl'reisen* on his back and ripped the wet leather of his tunic down the middle, baring the pale skin of his chest and the myriad bleeding wounds that marred it. She laid her hand over the *dahl'reisen's* heart, and a brilliant weave blazed to life, intricate and bright as the Great Sun. Bel raised a hand to shade his eyes against the stabbing brightness. The weave spread out like a net above the *dahl'reisen's* chest, then dropped, sinking into him, and every fingerspan of Gaelen vel Serranis's exposed skin glowed like a candle shade lit from within.

The *dahl'reisen* cried out, a sobbing, ragged sound. His body convulsed in a rigid arch, muscles clenched and straining. An anguished moan rattled out between gritted teeth, the sound of torment beyond bearing. And Belliard vel Jelani saw something he'd never believed possible.

The scar bisecting the Dark Lord's brow—the mark of his lost soul—began to fade.

Bel raised astonished eyes to Ellysetta. The picture of her at this moment would be indelibly burned into his mind for all eternity. Her eyes so fierce in a face of pure serenity.

Her body stiffened. Her head reared up, and her eyes blazed with a sudden flare of blinding light that lit the river's edge bright as day for a moment's span. Then the light in her eyes and the glow in vel Serranis's body winked out, gone as quickly as a snuffed candle flame.

"Rain . . . where's Rain?" Ellysetta's voice was a thin whisper; then she gave a tiny sigh and crumpled over the *dahl'reisen's* still form.

CHAPTER FOURTEEN

Vadim Maur backed away from his two Fey captives. The cold sweat of terror—something he'd not felt in centuries—trickled down his spine.

The v'En Celay matepair lay motionless on the dirty stone floor of their cage. The sudden blaze of light that had enveloped them was gone, and the broken shards of what had been *sel'dor* manacles and earrings lay scattered around their whole, unblemished bodies.

The High Mage backed out of the cage, slamming the door shut and locking it with shaking hands. He shouted for the guards waiting outside the chamber. "Get the manacles! Pierce them both. Hurry! Before the male wakes."

If Shannisorran v'En Celay woke unrestrained by *sel'dor* . . .

Vadim shuddered. The Fey lord had been unshackled only once since his capture, and then only to test the success of Vadim's experiments. The crazed beast that raged into life had slain four Mages and two platoons of guardsmen. A barrage of *sel'dor* barbed arrows had done little to slow him. A knife in the chest of the *shei'dalin* was the only thing that had finally brought him back under control.

The Fey lord and his mate flinched but never roused as the

guards snapped needle-barbed *sel'dor* manacles into place. Only then did the tension begin to leave Vadim's body.

What had happened just now? Where had that blast of concentrated power come from? Vadim had never known anything that could vaporize *sel'dor* within a Fey's skin. He'd never heard anything like the commanding voice in his mind that said, *"It must stop."* Even the memory of it made him shiver.

One of the guards paused a short distance away and cleared his throat. "What shall we do with the captives, Most High?"

Vadim took a breath and struggled to keep his voice level. "Have the servants tend them."

"Shall we separate them, Most High?"

He thought of the flash of power, of the astonishment of *sel'dor* disintegrating into harmless brittle shards. If that were to happen again while the v'En Celay matepair were together and conscious . . .

"Yes. Put the female back in her cell. Inform me when either of them rouses." Vadim waited for the guards to remove Elfeya from her mate's cell, then wove magic around the *sel'dor* bars. Whatever power had decimated the Fey captives' *sel'dor* piercings would not find it so easy to shred a six-fold weave, especially as that sixth thread was a thick rope of Azrahn. Just to be safe, however, Vadim added a shield of blackest Feraz witchcraft.

<hr />

«*Primary, to me. Ravel, choose twenty-five men to guard the dahl'reisen. The rest of you, see to the Tairen Soul.*» Bel barked the commands over the common Fey thread. The stunned silence and frozen stillness of the warriors in the park ended as Bel's orders spurred them into quick action.

Bel hurried down the remaining steps and gathered Ellysetta's limp body in his arms. Her skin felt cool and clammy to the touch, and her pulse stuttered rapidly beneath his fingers. "Kiel, check vel Serranis. Is he alive?"

The blond warrior knelt beside the prostrate *dahl'reisen* and laid a hand on his throat. "He's breathing and his heart's beating. He's alive." Then Kiel swore an astonished curse. "Spit and scorch me. Vel Serranis's *dahl'reisen* scar—it's gone!"

"*Aiyah*," Bel confirmed.

Kiel's gaze flew to the girl Bel held in his arms. "Did she—? Does this mean what I think it means?"

"*Aiyah*, she did. And I think it means exactly that. But restrain him anyway, in case I'm wrong." Bel shifted Ellysetta more securely in his arms.

"But how is that possible? How could she have restored his soul?"

"I gave you an order, Fey," Bel snapped. "Restrain vel Serranis now. Quickly, before he wakes." He carried Ellysetta across the park to where Rain lay motionless and laid her beside him. *«Marissya, where are you?»*

«Not far. What happened? There was so much agony, so much rage, and now I cannot sense anything.»

«I'll explain when you get here. Just hurry.»

When Marissya arrived, the sight of her brother Gaelen, unconscious and surrounded by an impenetrable shield, made the *shei'dalin* stop in her tracks. "Dear gods. Gaelen." She gave a small, choked sound and started towards him, but Dax held her back.

"*Nei, shei'tani*, do not go near him. See to Rain and the Feyreisa."

"Dax, his scar is gone and I cannot sense his pain. How can that be?"

"I don't know, beloved, but I do not trust it. Come away." Dax pulled her away from her infamous brother.

After a brief resistance, Marissya went with him. Rain needed her. He was just waking and she could feel his dull pain throbbing at her. He was her primary concern. His bones were broken, but, more alarmingly, his internal defenses were all but decimated. Ellysetta's torment had ripped through his shields and nearly driven the tairen into madness. His first waking thought was fear for her safety, and that fear made the tairen surge against the last thin threads of Rain's control. Quickly Marissya poured her strength into him, helping him to rebuild his tattered barriers as he came back to consciousness. Only once she was sure he could keep the tairen in check did she turn her attention to his broken bones.

She'd barely begun to fuse the bones back together when Rain grabbed her wrist, his eyes snapping open. "Stop."

She sucked in a breath and drew her hands away from Rain's side. "The bones aren't knit. You're not fully healed."

"Conserve your strength for Ellysetta. Something is wrong with her." Pain from his broken bones stabbed deep enough to draw a quiet hiss as he sat up, but he waved Marissya off and gathered Ellysetta's limp body to his chest. Lines of worry bracketed his mouth as he laid his hand on Ellysetta's bare skin. "I cannot sense her at all."

"Let me try to reach her." Marshaling her strength, Marissya summoned the full complement of her *shei'dalin's* powers, pooling magic within her until it filled her body and pulsed like the very blood that sped through her veins. She sent her consciousness into Ellysetta on a rich flow of healing magic.

The younger woman's life force was strong, her colors bright and vibrant, but the essence that was Ellysetta was absent. Marissya called to her softly, infusing her mental voice with hypnotic compulsion in an attempt to draw her out, but utter silence greeted her efforts. She called again, strengthening her summons,

«*Rain, call to her. Bel, you too. You have a connection.*»

As their voices replaced hers, she felt the faintest flutter of a response, quickly snuffed out. She sped towards the source of that faint response, and came to an abrupt, shocked halt.

What should have been the bright glow of Ellysetta's consciousness was hidden behind rope after rope of glowing magic. «*A weave. Lord of Light, bless us all. She's built a fortress around her mind. Rain, I've never seen anything like it.*»

It was a *shei'dalin's* Spirit weave, but in a pattern so dense and so complex that Marissya could not begin to fathom it. Cautiously she sent out a rippling tendril of her own power to test the barrier, and started with surprise as a shining thread fell away. She moved closer, and realized that the dense weave was actually many lighter weaves, layer after layer of Spirit that formed a deep thicket around whatever it was protecting.

<hr>

Consciousness returned to Gaelen, but not by one flicker of an eyelash nor a minute change in breathing did he let it show. Wariness honed by centuries of battle had made such still wakings second nature to him.

He was still alive. He'd laid deadly *dahl'reisen* hands on the Tairen Soul's mate, yet he still drew breath. How was that possible?

Surreptitiously he extended his senses to evaluate his surroundings, only to find them rebuffed by humming walls of power. Dense five-fold weaves surrounded him, caging him in.

He risked opening one eye and saw the warriors ringed around him, saw through the glow of their weaves the Tairen Soul clutching his mate's limp body against his chest. Marissya crouched beside them. His heart clenched as he drank in the sight of his sister, as beautiful as the last time he'd seen her beloved face a thousand years ago. Dax, Belliard vel Jelani, and Rain Tairen Soul knelt beside her, worry plain on their faces.

He'd not succeeded, then. He'd not slain the High Mage's spawn.

He braced himself for the cold fury, the *dahl'reisen* hate that had driven him here with such relentless, deadly determination.

It did not come.

Only then did Gaelen realize what else was missing. The pain. The anger. The despair.

He raised shaking hands to his face. Disbelieving fingers sought the cursed mark of the outcast, the brand of his lost soul.

It was not there.

Realization swept over him. Directly on its heels came horror, then devastating grief and guilt. He stared at the unconscious girl, the miracle he'd come to destroy, and tears he'd not shed in over a thousand years spilled helplessly from his eyes.

Dear gods, what had he done?

<hr>

Marissya sent out another thrust of power at the threads of the outermost weave. After a brief protest, they unraveled and dissolved. Encouraged, she moved on to the next.

Layer after layer, Marissya picked apart the woven strands of Spirit and released their stored energy. Progress was quick at first, but slowed as each successive weave proved to be denser and more resistant to her efforts. Time passed without notice. Weariness crept over her, and she found herself reaching for Dax's strength to supplement her own.

She dissolved a particularly troublesome weave and nearly wept at the sight of the next. Knit tighter than any she'd ever come across, it was a veritable wall of power. Intimidating. Un-breachable. Weariness and despair swamped her.

«Marissya!» Alarm colored Dax's call.

«I can't do it. It's impossible, and I'm so tired.» She just wanted to sleep.

«Marissya!» This time, Dax sounded distant, muffled. She was dimly aware of a tugging sensation, but dismissed it. She would sleep. Just close her eyes and sleep for a while.

A surge of power rippled through her, jerking her back to awareness with a faint protest. *«Nei, let me sleep.»*

«Later.» It was Rain, his voice hard and commanding. *«You are the shei'dalin. You must do this.»*

«But I can't. Look at that weave. It would take days to unravel.»

Another surge of power joined Rain's. *«The Feyreisa needs you, Marissya.»* That was Bel. *«We will give you our strength.»*

«It doesn't matter how much strength you give me. I can't do it. Don't you understand?»

⸻⟡⸻

"Let me help her!" For what seemed like the thousandth time, Gaelen pleaded with his stone-faced captors. "Scorch you all for your blindness! She restored my soul! Let me at least try to mend the harm I've wrought. Put red to my neck and kill me if I even breathe in a way you do not like, but let me help be-fore you lose her."

Ravel stared hard at his infamous captive. He didn't trust the *dahl'reisen*, but even he was shaken to his soul by the miracle Ellysetta seemed to have wrought. Tears were spilling down vel Serranis's cheeks. *Dahl'reisen* did not cry.

Ravel didn't know what to believe.

But Marissya's power was nearly spent, and the Feyreisa was not waking.

"Do it," Ravel snapped. "Teris, Cyr, put red to his throat. Jurel and Vonn, you take his back. If any of you sense the slightest inkling of ill intent, slay him. The rest of you, crack the weave but be ready to seal it again at a moment's notice."

A new surge of power rippled through Marissya. A brisk, powerful wind that swept across her awareness. «*Little sister . . .*»

Marissya felt her heart clench. «*Gaelen?*»

«*It is I, ajiana.*»

«*Gaelen . . . how—?*»

«*There will be time for answers later, ajiana, I promise. For now, take what I can offer you, finish your work, and return to your own self. I am here. Your mate is here beside me. We will not let you fail.*»

«*But, Gaelen, the weave is impossible. I don't even know where to begin.*»

«*It is a Spirit weave, Marissya, and it is defending itself against you. You are weary because it told you to be weary. Your power is spent because it told you to spend your power. It is impossible because it tells you to believe that. It's an illusion, little sister, as most Spirit is.*»

«*Gaelen—*»

«*You worry your mate, and though I've never liked him much, I cannot help feeling pity for him.*» He gave a laugh that had been rare even when Marissya was a child. The sound of it filled her with renewed strength. «*So do this thing, ajiana, and return to him.*»

Marissya felt her brother's determination bolster her, an endless supply of power and sheer will from which she could draw forever. He was a tower of strength. He always had been. He was her hero, the brother she had idolized all her young life.

«*Aiyah. I will do this.*» She directed her attention to the Spirit weave, focusing her concentration, gathering the strength of those connected to her and weaving their wills to her own. She attacked the weave, not with subtlety but with bold determination, cutting through steely threads of Spirit as if they were tailor's silk. The weave tried to defend itself, swamping her with fatigue and self-doubt, but she persevered until the last thread was severed and the barrier fell away in dissolving bands of power.

«*We did it!*» she crowed, laughing at the dimming, now-powerless threads.

«You *did* it, *little sister.*»

«*Gaelen . . . oh, Gaelen, I've missed you. I—*» Her voice broke off as her attention wandered away from the dissolving threads of Spirit and she caught sight of yet another weave.

«*What is it?*» Though no hint of worry colored Gaelen's mental voice, the mere question was enough.

«*Marissya!*» Dax did not try to hide his concern.

«*There's another weave.*» She breathed an awed sigh. «*You should see it. It's brilliant. Beautiful.*» Huge bands of power were woven in a tight sphere, the thick, multi-ply ropes of the weave shining white, blue, red, green, and lavender. «*Five-fold. Blessed tairen's fire, it's a five-fold weave and masterfully done.*»

«*Did Ellysetta weave it?*» Rain asked.

«*I don't know. I'll touch it to see if I can sense the maker.*»

Marissya approached cautiously, surprised that she couldn't sense power emanating from the weave. A five-fold weave with threads that thick should have throbbed with power. But this one would have been invisible if Marissya had not sent her consciousness into Ellysetta's body. It was—like so many things about the woodcarver's daughter—a mystery.

Marissya reached out with her senses, brushing gently against the outermost curve of the shining sphere . . . and gave a shrill cry as something attacked. She had a brief impression of blazing eyes and deadly fury before she found herself flying out of Ellysetta's body, returning to her own with a painful jolt that sent her sprawling backwards into the grass.

She groaned and heard the sound echoed by several others. Hands reached out, helping her to sit up. "I'm fine," she muttered, waving her quintet away. It wasn't exactly true. Her head felt as if someone had taken a hammer to it.

Dax and Bel were struggling to sit up, each rubbing his head.

Beside them, surrounded by glowing magic and naked poison blades, Gaelen was doing the same.

"Are you all right?" Marissya's question to them all was instinctive, even though she knew before they nodded that they had suffered no serious harm. Her gaze rested longest on Gaelen, drinking in the sight of him. She would have thought that after a thousand years as a *dahl'reisen*, his appearance would have changed. But he was Fey, immortal, held forever in the beautiful perfection of his prime, as familiar to her as he ever had been.

Love filled her and flooded her eyes with shimmering tears. "Gods' blessing on Ellysetta Baristani," she whispered to herself, giving the spread-fingered fanning wave of the Lord of Light. She turned to Rain. "The weave wasn't hers, Rain. The Spirit weaves were—all of them, even the most powerful ones—but the five-fold weave belonged to someone else. Someone put it there deliberately."

"What?" Rain stared at her in surprise. "But why?"

"If I were to guess, I'd say someone wanted to be sure she would never use her magic. Maybe they even wanted to prevent anyone from realizing she *had* magic."

"Why would anyone do that to her?"

"I don't know, Rain. But I can tell you this: If the strength of that five-fold weave is a measure of what it was made to contain, her magic isn't just strong, as we've suspected. It's a vaster power than I've ever known."

CHAPTER FIFTEEN

Ellysetta groaned and peeled open her eyes. The now-familiar headache was worse than ever, pounding sharply at her temples. A loud, confusing barrage of thoughts and concerns flooded into her. She had a blurred image of faces hovering over her; then hands reached out to touch her. The cacophony in her mind grew deafening. She gave a small cry and flinched back, coming up against a solid wall of blessed quiet. She huddled closer, seeking shelter, and Rain wrapped his arms around her. Warm peace, edged with fierce protectiveness, blanketed her, muffling the noise of the others.

«What is it, shei'tani?»

«I can hear them all. In my mind, all at once, I can hear them.»

"Shield yourselves," Rain commanded. "Your thoughts disturb the Feyreisa."

Immediately the voices quieted, though sensations of surprise and curiosity rose sharply.

"Ve ta dor," Marissya said. *"Ve ku'jian vallar."*

You are in pain. Allow me to help you. For the first time, Ellysetta understood how hard it was for Marissya to stand there, waiting patiently for permission to weave comfort, while Ellysetta's headache beat at them both.

«*Do not fear Marissya, shei'tani. She means you no harm.*»

"I know." Ellysetta frowned. That was no lie. She *knew* Marissya wanted only to heal the headache, nothing more. She knew it as surely as she'd ever known anything in her life. It was as if she could see into the other woman's mind, into her soul even, and find her intentions shining like a beacon.

Ellysetta looked at Dax, wondered what he was thinking, and the answer was simply *there*. He was worried for his mate; she was so weary, yet would not cease trying to heal Ellysetta. He distrusted Gaelen vel Serranis, no matter what the Feyreisa had done to make his scar disappear, no matter even that Marissya believed he had been returned to them without a taint of evil.

Ellysetta's gaze moved from Fey to Fey, plucking thoughts from their minds as easily as picking wildflowers in a meadow. Many thoughts bordered on reverent awe. She could take the scar from a *dahl'reisen* and restore his soul! She was a gift from the gods, or perhaps a god herself, sent to save them. She flinched away from those thoughts, even more quickly than she flinched from the darker suspicions of a few of the warriors, who were thinking that in taking the scar from a *dahl'reisen*, she had overturned the judgment of the gods and upset the balance of millennia of Fey law. To change that which the gods had ordained could never be good, no matter how wonderful it seemed at first.

Ellysetta sought out the *dahl'reisen* whose scar she had supposedly removed, found him ringed by watchful warriors. She skimmed his mind and discovered his thoughts were as easy to read as the others. Stunned disbelief was foremost in his mind, followed by joy at the unexpected treasure of standing in his sister's presence and causing her not even the slightest twinge of pain. Pale, ice-blue eyes met Ellysetta's. He knew what she was doing, knew she was plucking thoughts from the minds of all the Fey, knew she was in his mind now.

«*There is nothing I would hide from you, ki'falla'sheisan.*» His mental voice was calm and steady, a rock of unwavering acceptance, completely devoid of fear. «*My mind and my soul, which you have restored from despair, are open to you without reservation. Though I warn you there are memories of things that would make a shei'dalin weep.»*

Even with his permission, she shied away from sifting through his mind while he was watching her. She turned instead to Rain, but his thoughts were completely hidden from her. She touched his hand and sighed in relief when his concern touched her senses. That much, at least, had not changed.

At her touch he glanced down at her. *«Shei'tani, will you not let Marissya at least try to relieve your pain?»* A small frown creased his brow.

Squeezing Rain's hand, she turned to the *shei'dalin*. "If it will give you peace to heal me, then do so." For the first time, she wasn't afraid to accept Marissya's touch, because she *knew* the other woman only wanted to stop the pain that Ellysetta's headache was causing them both.

As Marissya raised her hand, Ellysetta realized she could actually feel her summoning her magic, could see the swelling glow as it responded to her call and watch her spin the power into shining thread that she then wove together in a visible pattern. Lavender Spirit, green Earth, and cool white Air whispered through her, soothing clenched muscles and throbbing nerves. Then it was done, and Marissya leaned back into her truemate's strength, utterly spent.

Ellysetta touched her temple. The headache was still there, but muted. *"Beylah vo."*

"It is my honor to serve the Feyreisa," the healer replied. Her gaze went again to her brother, and stayed there. "You have truly wrought a miracle. There is nothing I could ever do to repay you."

"He is healed, then?" Rain asked. "No hint of *dahl'reisen* in him?"

"He and my sister Marikah walked the earth a thousand years before my birth. Gaelen's soul was dark from war long before I knew him, but even that is gone now." She stepped towards Gaelen, waving away the instinctive protests of Dax and her quintet as she reached out and laid hands upon her brother. "He is as unshadowed as an infant." Suddenly, there were tears in Marissya's eyes, and she flung her arms around her brother, clinging tight.

Over his sister's shoulder, Gaelen met Ellysetta's gaze and his voice sounded in her mind, *«For this moment alone, I owe you my soul.»* His ice-blue eyes squeezed shut, and his face drew tight in lines of intense, barely checked emotion as he returned his sister's embrace.

Ellysetta turned her face into Rain's chest. "For once," she whispered, "it appears I may have done something right with this magic you've awakened in me."

He stroked a hand in her hair. "What you have done is a miracle, as Marissya says."

"*Ki'falla'sheisan* . . ." Most honored lady. The deep, baritone voice sounded behind her. The voice was slightly raspy, as if rarely used, but the tones were familiar. She'd heard them in her mind just a moment ago.

She turned. The man known and feared throughout Celieria as the Dark Lord swept into a graceful bow so deep that his brow nearly touched the ground. He straightened as gracefully as he had bowed, towering over her own not-inconsiderable height by more than a head.

"*Ki'falla'sheisan*," the Dark Lord repeated. "I am Gaelen vel Serranis, brother of the *shei'dalin* Marissya v'En Solande and once a proud warrior of the Fey. I have been *dahl'reisen* for the last thousand years, the most lost of all lost souls, but you have restored me."

"I am Ellysetta Baristani, Ser vel Serranis. And in truth I don't know what I did or how I did it, but you are welcome all the same."

"You are not what I expected. You are . . . innocent." The pale gaze sharpened, grew so intent that Ellysetta could almost feel his look like a physical touch, probing, as if he were searching for something. Then Gaelen's face cleared, and he dropped to his knees before her. "Ellysetta Baristani, truemate of the Tairen Soul, of my own free will, I pledge my life and my soul to your protection. None shall harm you while in life or death

I have power to prevent it." Slowly, so as not to alarm the many warriors ringed around them, he unsheathed a black Fey'cha and drew the blade across his palm. Fisting his hand, he let six drops of blood splash on the knife. "This I do swear with my own life's blood, in Fire and Air and Earth and Water, in Spirit and Azrahn. I do ask that this pledge be witnessed."

Utter stillness fell over the park. The Dark Lord knelt there before her, his head lifted proudly, his eyes never wavering from hers as the silence stretched out. A muscle worked in Gaelen's jaw. "She restored my soul. *Lute'asheiva* is my right."

"Your right?" Rain repeated. "You lost all rights the day you turned down the Dark Path. You laid *dahl'reisen* hands on my truemate, and that should have earned you death. Instead, she cleansed the darkness from your soul. That doesn't mean I trust you, *vel Serranis*."

Gaelen shifted his steady gaze from Ellysetta to Rain. "I serve no other master, despite what you may believe, and with my soul sworn to her service, I never shall." When still Rain did not witness the pledge, he added, "You should be leaping at the chance to witness my oath. *Lute'asheiva* guarantees I can never betray her."

"Rain?" Ellysetta touched his hand as the silence stretched out again.

He stared hard, with cold, cold eyes, at the former *dahl'reisen*. "If ever, even by accident, you betray her or bring her to harm, *vel Serranis*, your life is forfeit. Only I will not send Fey to kill you. I will send the tairen. And there will be no next life for you."

Galen's pupils lengthened to narrow slits. "I would have it no other way."

"Then your oath is witnessed." Rain said. The words seemed torn from him.

"Witnessed," Bel echoed, followed by the rest of Ellysetta's quintet, Marissya, and Dax, then all the other Fey in the park.

The blade in Gaelen's hand flashed bright, sealing the bond. He offered the blade to her, handle-first. "Your *shei'tan* is your first protector, *kem'falla*. Know that I am your second."

"Third," Bel corrected.

Gaelen met Bel's hard gaze with his own. "Third," he acknowledged, then smiled faintly. "For now."

Ellysetta accepted the proffered blade. "Thank you, Ser vel Serranis."

Bright green surrounded the former *dahl'reisen's* hands, then dimmed to reveal a platinum chain and sheath, which he extended to her. "To you I am Gaelen, *kem'falla.*"

"Why did you come here, vel Serranis?" Rain broke in. "You were *dahl'reisen*, and you entered a city occupied by a *shei'dalin*. Just for passing through the gate, your life was forfeit. Surely you knew that."

"I knew." The Dark Lord rose to his feet in one lithe movement. "I came to protect my sister. The Eld are preparing an attack. They may already be here."

A sudden gust of cool night wind swept through the park. Ellie shivered.

Gaelen's eyes narrowed. "Your *shei'tani* is cold, Tairen Soul, and weary." Green Earth blazed first in Kieran's hands, then a moment later in Gaelen's. "I will tell you what I know, but see to her comfort first." He held out a cape of soft blue wool. Behind him, the fur-lined velvet cloak that Kieran had just completed dissolved back into the elements.

Rain wrapped the blue wool around his truemate's shoulders. "Ellysetta and I will fly back to the palace. Join us there immediately, vel Serranis. I have many questions for you, and you have much to explain." He swept an imperious look at the Fey surrounding him. They stepped back to give their king room to summon the Change.

As he shimmered from Fey to tairen, the power that radiated from him washed over Ellysetta like a shower of hot rain. She shuddered, feeling her skin tighten with prickling awareness. Rain Tairen Soul turned his massive head and purred low and deep. His wings stretched out, rising high on his back, then spreading wide, fully extended in the male tairen's gesture of strength and dominance. She walked to his side and closed her eyes as Air swirled her upwards. Her hands buried themselves deep in the soft fur on his neck, and with a roar, Rain Tairen Soul leapt into the night sky.

As the Tairen Soul and his mate winged away, Kieran approached the man who was his uncle. There was a challenging light in the younger man's eyes. "I hold Earth in the Feyreisa's primary. It was my place to make her cloak."

The infamous Fey met Kieran's gaze. "You weren't fast enough. She stood there shivering while you fussed with fur and velvet. Extravagance has its uses, young Fey, but expedience is better. You serve the Feyreisa. Learn to serve her well in all things."

Kieran stiffened. "I was only a moment or two behind you."

"You stand outside the Fading Lands. A moment or two could mean her life."

"It was just a cloak to ward off the chill."

"And what will it be the next time? You've already failed her once. Where were you when she laid hands on the most murderous *dahl'reisen* who ever lived?" Leaving Kieran speechless, Gaelen vel Serranis turned and broke into a run, swiftly catching, then outstripping the other Fey as they ran towards the palace.

The five warriors of Ellysetta's primary shared a fulminating look, then burst into their own land-eating run, racing after the Dark Lord.

⚜

Rain and Ellysetta reached the palace first. Her quintet traversed the distance on foot with surprising speed and arrived well before any of the others. Ellysetta was sitting at the secretary in Rain's suite, penning a note to her parents, when Bel burst through the doors. The other members of the quintet followed so swiftly that all five warriors nearly ended up in a heap on the floor. They were breathless and flushed, perspiration trickling down the sides of their faces.

Kieran bent over, hands on his knees, and dragged air into his lungs. "Well done, brothers. We beat the smug *chervil*."

"You all look like you could use a drink." Cool and unwinded, Gaelen smiled at the new arrivals from the sofa near the window. "Water? Or perhaps something a little stronger to help you regain your strength?"

Kieran bared his teeth and snarled. Bel cursed quietly and straightened. "How did you manage it?" he asked, wiping the sweat off his brow with the back of his arm. "We passed you outside on the palace steps."

"Did you?" Gaelen rose with a single fluid motion. "Are you sure?"

"That was Spirit?"

Vel Serranis shrugged. "I *am* a master of it."

"As am I. If it was Spirit, I would have known."

"Mmm. But then, I do have at least a thousand years on you, Belliard vel Jelani. And countless lifetimes more experience."

With a casual arrogance that set Rain's teeth on edge, Gaelen promptly commandeered the small stone-topped bar in the corner and began handing out glasses of ice water and taunting evaluations of the quintet's shortcomings with equal measure. Judging from the fulminating looks in the warriors' eyes, they were none too happy to have the former *dahl'reisen* appoint himself their *chatok*, their mentor in the Dance of Knives.

"So the Eld are on the move, planning an attack, and you came to warn your sister," Rain said. "And how did you come by this information?"

Gaelen shrugged and left off taunting the others for the moment. He selected a crystal goblet and pulled the stopper from a flagon of pinalle. "My men reported Eld troop movements along the western border not long after I stumbled across an Eld raiding party in Norban."

"Your men?"

"The Brotherhood of Shadows. *Dahl'reisen* who still protect the Fading Lands." He poured a stream of pale blue liquid into his goblet, filling it generously. "We guard the borders against Eld attack."

"The rumors are true, then."

"Some are. I don't eat small Celierian children for breakfast." He lifted the goblet to his lips, met Kieran's angry stare over the rim, and smiled wickedly. "Infant Fey playing at being warriors are much more satisfying."

Rain's eyes narrowed. "Kieran is your sister's son, and a fine warrior. Young, but stronger in Earth than any other Fey in the Fading Lands. He holds a master's strength in Air and Fire as well, plus a fourth-level talent in Spirit and Water. If you prick him one too many times, vel Serranis, you will regret it."

"I doubt that. He may be my sister's son, but he has his father's reflexes."

"I'm so glad you've returned to us, Gaelen," Dax announced dryly from the doorway. "I'd forgotten what a pleasure it was to have you around." He, Marissya, and her quintet entered the suite.

Gaelen raised his glass to Dax. "You never were and never will be good enough for her, but at least you're Fey and possess some minor ability to ensure her protection and happiness. Not like that worthless mortal Marikah chose." He downed the rest of the pinalle in one swallow and set the goblet aside. "But enough of that." He raised a hand. The suite doors closed with a bang and bolted. Shining nets of Air and Spirit shot out from his fingertips to seal the room. It happened so quickly that even Rain was left blinking in surprise.

Galen arched a dark brow. "I am a master of Earth, Air, Spirit, and Fire, and a fifth-level talent in Water, mentored in the Dance of Knives by the great Shannisorran v'En Celay himself." He looked at Kieran, and his face hardened. "I was the sharpest blade in the Fading Lands, and still the Mages murdered my sister while she was in my presence and under my protection. One brief hesitation, one split second cost her life." He met Kieran's gaze steadily. "If I demand perfection, young Fey, it is because nothing but perfection will do. Not when protecting the Fading Lands, and certainly not when protecting a *shei'dalin* who has truemated a Tairen Soul and can bring the Dark Lord back from living death."

"You said you stumbled across an Eld raiding party," Rain interrupted. "Tell us what you know. Marissya, verify every word he speaks."

When his sister's hands closed around his arm, Gaelen lifted his chin. "Three days ago I found the remains of a Celierian woodsman just outside Norban. He'd been tortured and slain by an Eld raiding party led by an apprentice Mage. The Eld were seeking information about a red-haired child found there some twenty-four years ago." His gaze flickered to Ellysetta, touching on her flame-red hair. "I tracked the Eld, and found them in the final moments of a battle with two Fey."

"Truth," Marissya said. "That must have been Sian and Torel."

Rain frowned. "The Fey—Sian and Torel—they were slain?"

"*Aiyah*. One was already dead. The other took his last breath before I could reach him. They died with honor, as warriors should." Gaelen reached into his tunic and tugged two pendants free. "I have their *sorreisu kiyr* to verify my claim."

Marissya touched the stones and closed her eyes. "These are the crystals of Sian and Torel. And their death happened as Gaelen has said."

"Do you have any idea what the woodsman might have known about the Feyreisa that was so important a Mage would come to interrogate and kill him for it?" Rain asked.

"The woodsman's memories were gone," Gaelen answered. "Someone—your Fey warriors, by the look of it—erased them before the Mage got to him."

"If the woodsman was already dead, and Sian and Torel died before you reached them," Bel said quietly, "how is it you know they erased his memories?"

Gaelen hesitated. "You are observant, Belliard vel Jelani." He tilted his head in acknowledgment. "As I said, I'm a master of Air, Earth, Fire, and Spirit, and a fifth-level talent in Water. From what I can tell"—he met Rain's gaze without flinching—"I am also a fourth-level talent in Azrahn." Marissya gasped. Both her quintet and Ellysetta's suddenly looked alert and deadly. Gaelen bestowed a gentle smile on his sister and freely condemned himself. "I summoned the man's soul back from the dead to learn what I could before Firing his body."

"Oh, Gaelen."

"Use of Azrahn is a banishing offense," Kieran said.

Gaelen gave a bark of laughter. "That's not much of a deterrent when one is already banished for far worse, now is it, puppy? Besides, Fey law also forbids tampering with Celierian memories, so I am not the only one to break Fey laws when the situation warrants." He eyed Rain coolly. "I never expected to walk again in the Fading Lands. If you choose to deny me entrance because I called Azrahn as a *dahl'reisen*, so be it."

"I will not deny you entrance. But you will not call Azrahn again. It is forbidden."

Gaelen's jaw hardened. "I will do as I have always done. Whatever is necessary to protect the Fey."

"As you protected us when you threw us into the Mage Wars for vengeance's sake?"

"No less than you, when you scorched the world."

"Stop it, both of you," Marissya snapped.

"If the Fey stole the woodsman's memories, what kept you from calling *their* souls back from the dead to learn what they knew?" Kieran sneered.

The temperature in the room plummeted. The chill was cold anger, coming from Gaelen, followed a moment later by mocking acceptance. "Well, puppy, I did try, but by then I was *sel'dor*-pierced and my magic wasn't quite as manageable as it usually is."

"Untruth." Marissya smiled at her brother's quick scowl. "At least about trying to summon Fey souls. You *were* sel'dor-pierced."

"I caught a few barbed arrows while dispatching the last of the Elden raiders and the apprentice Mage who led them. I couldn't send Spirit; that's why I came to Celieria in person."

"There's no trace of *sel'dor* in you now."

"The Feyreisa must have removed the barbs when she healed me."

"She didn't," Bel said. "She touched you and lit you up like a candle, but she didn't remove any *sel'dor* so far as I could see."

"And yet the *sel'dor* has vanished from my flesh."

Everyone turned to Ellysetta. "If I did it, I don't remember it, and don't have any idea how to do it again."

"So . . . she truemates a Tairen Soul, restores a *dahl'reisen's* lost soul, and disintegrates *sel'dor* with a touch. Yet she is still here in this city rather than safe behind the Faering Mists? And Marissya as well?"

Rain bristled at the reproach. "Not because I wish it so, believe me," he retorted. "I am bound by honor and Celierian law. Her father and Dorian set aside her Celierian betrothal only on the condition that I wed her by Celierian custom, and the formalities of it take time. Were that not so, I would have taken her and returned to the Fading Lands days ago. Just as I would have commanded your sister to return the moment I learned that the Celierians have been negotiating a trade agreement with the Eld, and that she and Dax knew of it."

Gaelen speared his sister with a penetrating look that actually made the imperturbable Marissya flush, but whatever scathing remark was on the tip of his tongue went unsaid. He turned back to Rain. "The Eld are on the move. Whatever attack they have planned will come soon. You should leave now, in the night. Take your *shei'tani* and go."

"I've told you, I cannot. She does not complete the required prenuptial ceremonies until tomorrow. We wed and depart after that."

"Do not place honor above your *shei'tani's* life."

"That's the sort of thinking that led you down the shadowed path so long ago, vel Serranis. I will honor my vow. To do less makes me unworthy of her."

A knock sounded on the doors. Kiel opened them upon Rain's command. Marissya pulled her hand from her brother's arm, a small, instinctive courtesy to spare his pride, as Rowan stepped into the room.

"So it is true." Rowan pinned Gaelen with a hard glare. "How is it that you still live, *dahl'reisen*?" He held his hands close to his blades, tension and aggression vibrating from him with almost visible force.

"Peace, Rowan," Kiel murmured. "Gaelen is *dahl'reisen* no longer. The Feyreisa has restored his soul."

"So we heard, but I didn't believe it until now. It still doesn't

excuse him from bringing his taint into this city and tormenting my brother's truemate."

"Your *brother's* truemate?" Gaelen glanced from Rowan to
Ellysetta.

"Not Ellysetta," Marissya clarified. "Talisa diSebourne, Lord
Barrial's daughter." Gaelen's face went blank with surprise.
"You didn't know she could truemate?"

"*Nei*. How could we know? Lord Barrial's marriage bond
was a purely mortal one. We knew the girl was slightly empathetic but we never suspected anything more. If we had, we
certainly would never have allowed her to waste herself on Sebourne's heir."

"Then why do you have twenty-five *dahl'reisen* stationed on
Lord Barrial's lands?" Rain asked. "You knew Lord Barrial was
a descendant of your cousin Dural, that Fey blood—vel Serranis blood—ran in the Barrial family line."

"*Aiyah*, I did know that. Dural's disappearance was what
brought me back to Celieria seven hundred years ago. He was
gone without a trace, his mortal mate slain, his son orphaned.
And they weren't the only ones. All along the borders there
were tales of midnight raids and folk gone missing. It was then
I formed the Brotherhood of Shadows. We began patrolling the
borders, stopping the raids when we could. As for the twenty-
five *dahl'reisen* . . . they are there to protect Lord Barrial. Too
many of the raids over the years have targeted Dural's descendants."

"Why?"

"We don't know. Over the years, I've sent more than a hundred *dahl'reisen* into Eld to find out. None of them ever returned."

"So, back to my earlier question," Kieran interrupted with
an open sneer. "Why didn't you summon the souls of the Eld
you killed and ask them?"

Gaelen gave a small, tight smile. "The Mages soul-bind their
followers to them, boy. If you summon a soul owned by the
Mages, you might as well send a thread of Spirit straight to the
High Mage himself and set up a flare to light his way back to

you. Using Azrahn opens your soul for . . . things . . . to get in. I'd personally rather not have one of those things be a Mage."

"Azrahn?" Rowan interrupted. He speared Rain with an incredulous look. "Gaelen is a *dahl'reisen* who freely admits to wielding Azrahn, and you let him draw breath within the same room as the Feyreisa? Have you gone mad?"

"He has," Kieran muttered.

"Gaelen is *dahl'reisen* no longer," Marissya answered, flashing a dark look at her son. "The Feyreisa restored his soul. What would you have Rain do, slaughter him now that he is whole once more? Or banish him for something he did while living outside our laws?"

"The Dark Lord has bloodsworn himself to the Feyreisa." That dry remark came from Teris, the new holder of Fire in Ellysetta's primary.

Rowan's jaw dropped, and he turned a shocked look on Rain. "You *have* gone mad."

"Rowan." Marissya gave him a warning look. "Is everything all right with Talisa?"

Shaking his head with astonished incredulity, the warrior was slow to answer. "The husband came, demanding her return. Lord Barrial nearly drew steel on him before he would leave." He flicked a quick shuttered glance at Gaelen, then directed his attention to Rain. "It was all I could do to keep Adrial from slitting diSebourne's throat."

"Adrial is still with his *shei'tani*?" Rain asked.

"*Aiyah.*"

"Did the husband find him there?"

"*Nei,* Adrial had enough sense to cloak himself in Spirit before diSebourne entered." Rowan's jaw flexed. "Can you not speak to the king, Rain? Is there no way to dissolve the marriage, as your betrothal was dissolved?"

"Some other time it might have been possible. But you heard the nobles tonight. Dorian rests on the blade's edge of a rebellion. Even if dissolving a marriage were within his power, Dorian couldn't do it now. Not to benefit the Fey at the cost of his own subjects. Go back to Adrial; tell him to have patience."

Even as he said it, Rain knew the advice was worthless. No amount of patience would make Talisa a free woman. If she left her husband of her own volition, diSebourne could simply claim the Fey had used magic to control her mind. There were many Celierians who would be all too happy to believe it.

Rowan started to leave, then stopped at the door and turned to pin Gaelen with a fierce glare. "I'll be watching you, *dahl'reisen*, with red never far from my fingertips."

"It's heartwarming to be the object of such affection," Gaelen quipped when the door closed behind Rowan with a bang.

"What did you expect, *vel Serranis*?" Rain asked.

"Death," he said simply. "But I received salvation in its stead." He bowed in Ellysetta's direction and gave a fanning wave. "I will do everything in my power to prove myself worthy." He straightened, and his shoulders squared. "And you, Tairen Soul, should not make me the focus of your suspicions when the High Mage has fixed his eye upon your mate."

"I am quite aware of the Eld threat. But the attacks on Ellysetta and the recent host of troubles with Celieria all appear to have been orchestrated by *dahl'reisen*, not by Mages." Rain nodded to Marissya, who took her brother's hand again.

"I ordered no attack on your mate. Not by command or implication," Gaelen said.

"Truth," Marissya said.

"And yet your Fey'cha ended up in the hands of a street child who stabbed her with it last week." Rain lifted a brow. "How do you explain that?"

"I've fought along the borders for the last seven centuries. I've lost a blade or two in the process. One of those could easily have fallen into enemy hands." Gaelen frowned. "Since I did not order that attack, the most obvious suspects are the Mages, but that makes no sense. This High Mage is no fool. Why would he send a search party to Norban to torture a woodsman and slay two Fey for what they learned about the Feyreisa if he simply intended to kill her?"

"The blade was numbed," Marissya said. "Perhaps it was meant only to injure."

"To injure?" he repeated. "For what purpose?" Gaelen had walked the earth for twenty-five hundred long years. More than half that time, he'd spent fighting Eld. He knew their ways. And he knew the Mages never acted without purpose.

The Fey'cha was meant to implicate him, obviously. It was only a diversion, a false trail. But the attack itself . . . a numbed blade not meant to kill. Was that a false trail, too? Images whirled in his mind: the tortured woodsman, the two dead Fey, the Mage searching for a lost child who he claimed was the daughter of the High Mage of Eld. Another image superseded the others: a great and legendary treasure bearing pestilence in its golden chalices.

Gaelen's gaze swept across the room to fix on Ellysetta, and horror dug its talons deep in his belly. He'd come to kill her, and she'd saved his soul. She was innocent, as bright a soul as he'd ever seen. But what if there was darkness in her even she did not realize?

Conscious of Marissya's hand on his skin, he clamped a fierce hold on his thoughts. His face went still as stone. "You said there've been several attacks on the Feyreisa," he said to Rain. "What else has happened besides the stabbing?"

"She received an ensorceled gift yesterday," Rain answered. "When she touched the thing, it summoned a demon and opened some kind of . . . rift behind her."

"A rift?"

"Like the portals demons use to escape the Well of Souls, only much larger."

"Did anything come through it?"

"*Nei*. But she was being directed towards it by a Spirit weave."

The tension that gripped Gaelen abated slightly. If Ellysetta was indeed an unwitting agent of the High Mage, he would not set a trap to capture her.

Unless the demon attack was yet another false trail intended to speed her delivery to the Fading Lands. What better way to make the Fey rush her behind the safety of the Faering Mists than to make it seem as though her life were in danger?

No, no, he wouldn't believe it. His suspicions sprang from the last thousand years of living as a *dahl'reisen*, which he'd survived by suspecting a trap in every gift and seeking the enemy in every shadow.

She'd restored his soul, and he was bloodsworn to her service, bound to protect her above all others in life and in death. She was an innocent, a miraculous gift from the gods.

«What's wrong, Gaelen?» Marissya's concern swept across him.

He secured his wayward thoughts and emotions behind the barriers of his mind, where she could not access them except through forceful Truthspeaking. *«I do not like the sound of these Eld attacks.»* That was truth enough to reassure her.

"What is the Well of Souls?" Ellysetta asked.

"Celierians call it the Underworld," Rain answered. "It's the home of unborn souls and the dead who haven't yet earned passage to the next world. It's also the home of demons."

"The Eld have long used Azrahn and *selkahr* crystals to summon demons from the Well," Gaelen added, "but in the last few years, they've learned how to open a physical doorway between the Well of Souls and the living world." He felt the weight of every Fey's sudden, penetrating stare. They had not known about this new Eld accomplishment, then. "They use it to travel, and they're completely undetectable unless they use Azrahn to open the doorway. If the rift that opened behind the Feyreisa was such a gateway, it's possible the Spirit weave directing her could have guided her through the Well directly to the High Mage himself."

Rain dropped a hand to the hilt of the *meicha* at his hips. "Can they open a doorway anywhere? Into this room, for instance?"

"*Nei.* From what we've seen, either a third party must open the endpoint for them, or there must be a *selkahr* crystal bespelled to open the portal at a given time. I tried once or twice to open a doorway on my own, so I could learn more about the process, but the results were . . . rather alarming. What guards the Well of Souls doesn't like to be disturbed."

"You think the Eld will use these . . . doorways . . . to attack us here in the city?"

"Wouldn't you? Eld armies are massing along the border. If there are Mage-claimed in the city—and considering the attacks on the Feyreisa, there must be—the High Mage could use them to open enough portals to deliver an invasion force to Dorian's doorstep without warning."

"If that were the case, why wouldn't he already have done so?" Ellysetta asked.

"Perhaps he was not yet ready, *kem'falla*. Perhaps discovering your presence here in Celieria City has prompted him to act sooner than he would like. Or perhaps he postponed his planned attack to give his envoys time to capture you."

Gaelen turned back to Rain. "If the Eld sent a demon for the Feyreisa, they'll be back, and most likely in force. The High Mage doesn't tip his hand so boldly. He doesn't want to remind anyone what the Eld are capable of. He's been very careful to keep the Mages quiet, to project a friendly face to the world. And all the while, he's been rebuilding Eld power since the Mage Wars. He has spies and emissaries in every king's court around the world."

"And how do you know that?"

"Because I have spies and emissaries in every king's court as well. While the Fey have spent the last thousand years hiding behind the Faering Mists, licking their wounds from the Mage Wars, the rest of the world has taken the opportunity to rebuild, to grow strong again, to forge alliances that don't include the Fey."

Rain's lips thinned. "If you're trying to tell me I've been a bad king, save your breath. I know it all too well."

"That's not true," Marissya objected. "You've no right to judge him, Gaelen. You know nothing of what it's been like, of what he's been through, of what a triumph it was just to reach the first day when he could cling to sanity without the help of every *shei'dalin* in the Fading Lands. We haven't hidden behind the Faering Mists only to lick our wounds. We caged ourselves there to protect the world, too."

"Marissya, the Fey are weak. Their enemies are strong. The reasons don't matter. A wounded champion and an unarmed boy die just the same when the blade falls on their necks."

"*Setah*," Rain snapped. "We return to the Fading Lands tomorrow. Ellysetta and I speak our Celierian marriage vows after the Council vote. You will come with us, Gaelen. I want to know everything you know about the Eld and their plans. It is time for the Defender of the Fey to actually start defending them again. Until then, Ellysetta must stay here, safe in the palace under constant guard." Rain nodded to Marissya, and her hand dropped back to her side.

"Is that it?" Kieran demanded incredulously. "The questioning is over?" He pointed a shaking finger at his infamous uncle. "Before you grant him passage through the Faering Mists and celebrate his return in the streets of Dharsa, won't you at least make him tell you whether or not he and his 'Brotherhood' have been murdering Celierians?"

"Kieran," Marissya murmured, frowning at her son.

"No, Mother. He needs to answer. Our alliance with Celieria is in danger of destruction thanks to rumors of *dahl'reisen* murdering villagers in the north. We need to know whether he did it or not."

"Kieran is right," Rain agreed. He nodded, and with obvious reluctance, Marissya put her hand back on her brother. "Answer his question, Gaelen."

The former *dahl'reisen* hesitated, as if weighing his words, then shrugged. "*Aiyah*, the Brotherhood and I have executed a number of Celierians."

Marissya stifled a gasp. "Truth. Oh, Gaelen. Why?"

"They were Mage-claimed. We could not let them live to spread their evil."

"How could you know they were Mage-claimed?" Kieran challenged. "Did you personally see these peasants in the company of Mages, carrying out their will? Because we all know there's no way to tell who is in the service of the Mages until they act."

"That's not entirely true, young *jita'nos*."

"Your *dahl'reisen* have found a way to detect Mage-claiming?" Rain queried sharply. The secret, invisible power of Mage-claiming was one of the Eld's most deadly weapons.

"We have. Mage-claiming leaves marks on the claimed ones. These marks are invisible to the naked eye, even invisible to Fey vision, but they appear in the presence of Azrahn, like black shadows on the flesh over the claimed one's heart."

"Azrahn again," Kieran spat.

"Azrahn is just magic, boy. A mystic like Spirit. Despite what all Fey have been raised to believe, it isn't evil, and weaving it won't turn you into a servant of the Dark so long as you wield it wisely and with caution." He glanced at Ellysetta and knew he must learn the truth, if only to determine how best to protect her. "Look." Before the others could react, a small, shadowy spiral sprang to life in his palm, and a chill, sickly sweet aroma wafted through the room.

Marissya cried out and fell back away from her brother. Ellysetta cried out too, as much in warning as in fear.

Twelve red Fey'cha flew fast and true.

Not quickly enough to penetrate the rapid weave that surrounded Gaelen and stopped the Fey'cha in mid-flight.

Ellysetta clutched a hand over her chest where the shock of his sudden action had made her heart all but leap out of her chest. A cold, dull ache throbbed in her left breast. Her skin tingled from lack of oxygen and the sudden rush of fear, and her teeth began to chatter. Somehow she knew Gaelen meant no harm with his weave, but her terror didn't abate.

"Stop it, Gaelen," she commanded. "Stop it now." She pressed the palm of her hand hard over the fluttering wildness of her heart.

His eyes narrowed slightly. "As you wish, kem'falla." The former dahl'reisen bowed, and his Azrahn weave winked out.

"The rest of you, put your weapons away." Ellysetta's voice shook. By some miracle, her knocking knees did not collapse beneath her.

Slowly, with hissing reluctance, the Fey sheathed their second round of blades. A moment later, Gaelen's shields fell and the twelve red Fey'cha trapped by his weave clattered harmlessly to the floor.

As fast as Gaelen had moved a moment before, Rain moved

now. In a blur of speed he was at Gaelen's throat, his long fingers wrapped tight around the other's windpipe. "What was the meaning of that display, *dahl'reisen?*" Rain demanded. "Is it death you seek after all?"

"If I'd meant harm, you'd all be dead already," Gaelen answered. "I only meant to prove a point."

"By weaving the forbidden magic?"

"I wove Azrahn. Did I summon demons? Mages? Have I lost my soul again? *Nei,* none of those dire predictions came true. Because the magic itself is not evil."

"It is forbidden! It is the magic never to be called!"

"Only because ancient Fey who lived and died so long ago we hold no memory of them or their reasoning said it should be so," Gaelen shot back. "*Dahl'reisen* don't have the benefit of hiding behind protective barriers and indulging ourselves with self-righteous adherence to laws long past their use. We survive by wit and speed and will. And we've learned that to defeat our greatest enemy, we must understand that enemy's most powerful weapon."

With a growl, Rain released his grip on Gaelen's throat and thrust the older Fey away from him. "In the Fading Lands, we hold true to our honor and our laws. If you intend to live among us, you will do the same."

"And if you refuse to consider change, don't expect to survive the coming war," Gaelen countered. Muttering a curse, he spun on one heel and started to pace. Halfway across the room, he stopped and cast a hard, searching glance Ellysetta's way. His shoulders slumped a little, then straightened. "I didn't summon Azrahn a moment ago just to prove a point. I did it for a different reason. Because there was something I had to know."

"Something like what, *vel Serranis?*" Rain growled. "Whether or not we could cut you with red before you raised your shields?"

"*Nei,* that was not it." He smiled faintly. "But it is good to know you can't." Sobering, he crossed the short distance to Ellysetta and went to one knee before her. He clasped her hands in his. "*Kem'falla,* know that I am yours. I will never betray you. I will defend you beyond death itself. I would walk the Seven Hells if you asked it of me."

Ellysetta didn't know what to say. "*Beylah vo*, Gaelen. I am grateful for your kindness."

"Then forgive me, *ki'falla'sheisan*."

"Forgive you for what?" She frowned in confusion as Gaelen rose once more and took a step back.

"Vel Serranis?" Wary of the Fey's suspicious behavior, Rain stepped in front of Ellysetta and guided her back, away from the former *dahl'reisen*.

"The Eld who killed the woodsman and your Fey wasn't looking for just any red-haired child," Gaelen told the room. His eyes never left Ellysetta's. "And I did not come to Celieria City just to warn you of Eld troop movements along the border."

"I knew it!" Kieran muttered. "I told you we couldn't trust him."

"*Las*, Kieran," Bel hissed. "Let him speak."

Rain held up a hand to silence them both. "Why, then, did you come, vel Serranis?"

"In a moment. First let me say I no longer believe what I thought was true. And let me remind you all—you especially, Tairen Soul—that no great gift from the gods comes without an equally great danger. The price of the gift is the willingness and courage to embrace the danger. If you cannot accept the one, you are not worthy of the other."

"I need no lecture on the price the gods demand for their blessings. I have lived with those prices all my life," Rain said.

Gaelen bowed his head in acknowledgment. His expression grew still, becoming the blank, impenetrable stone mask of the Fey. "The Eld were searching for the lost daughter of the High Mage," he said baldly. He met Ellysetta's gaze. "And I came to kill her."

CHAPTER SIXTEEN

Though once with joy our garden greened
Love's blossoms fade round salted spring
My heart is lost, my hope is gone
And sorrow now my only song
        —Sorrow's Garden, a lament by Mara vol Elias

Ellysetta's quintet surrounded her in an instinctive reaction to
the perceived threat. But even as they flung up magic in her defense, their emotions slapped at her. Astonishment. Disbelief.
Fear.

Worse, much worse, was the way Rain withdrew his hand
from hers.

"It cannot be true," Rain said. But Ellysetta sensed his uncertainty, heard it in the faint vibration of his voice.

"I don't want to believe it either," Gaelen said. "But the possibility exists, and for her sake if for no other, we cannot ignore it."

"It cannot be true. It is not true." Rain turned and swept a
hand, palm up, towards Ellysetta. "Look at her. She is bright
and shining. No Eld could ever be so bright. Especially not the
daughter of the High Mage."

"The Eld are not born evil," Gaelen answered. "They are
corrupted by their environment and chained into dark servi-
tude by the Mages. The Mages bind the souls of Eld children
on the first anniversary of their birth and continue until they
own them utterly. But if she is the one they sought, she was
smuggled out of Eld as a child. The soul-binding was never
completed."

"Gaelen, you must be mistaken," Marissya said. "It's just another Mage trick, meant to manipulate us and cast doubt and suspicion where there can be none."

"That is entirely possible," he acknowledged. "But when I called Azrahn a moment ago, all of you reacted the way Fey do. She did not." He met Ellysetta's gaze again, his own filled with bleak sorrow. "She reacted like one who bears the Mark of the Mages."

Ellysetta flinched as though he'd struck her, and clutched a hand over her betraying heart. "No. No, it's not true." But even as she denied it, she recalled the cold, insidious voice from her nightmares hissing, *Girl . . . you can't hide from me forever. He'll kill you when he learns what you really are.* Even worse came the mocking sneer from last week's horrific nightmare, *You'll kill them all. It's what you were born for.* "Rain . . ." Tears welled in her eyes as she turned to face Rain and saw the horror and the revulsion in his stricken gaze. She reached out. "Rain, please." He flinched away, and her tears spilled over in hot lines that chilled rapidly as they slid down her cheeks.

Rain's jaw clenched tight. "Vel Serranis, you said Azrahn reveals the Marks."

"Aiyah."

"Then do it."

"No!" Ellysetta shrank back from Gaelen's approach.

"I will not hurt you, *kem'falla,*" Gaelen vowed in a sorrowful voice. "But we must know one way or another. Knowledge is better than blind fear."

Gods. She wanted to turn and run. She wanted to flee them all—even Rain—and hide some place where no one would ever find her.

«Courage, Ellysetta,» Gaelen whispered in her mind. *«A Mage Mark does not make you evil, but it does put you in danger. We cannot protect you properly if we do not know how badly your defenses have been compromised.»*

Courage? When had she ever had that? She avoided confrontations and hid from her own magic because she was afraid of what was inside her and always had been! And now Gaelen wanted her to stand there and let him bare the horrible, secret blackness of her soul to the man she loved?

«If you won't think of yourself, then think of your shei'tan,» he urged. *«Just the possibility of this Mark has raised doubts in you both. You'll never complete your bond without knowing and accepting the truth. Rain will die.»*

The mere thought filled her with fear greater than any she harbored on her own behalf. She stopped retreating. "All right," she whispered. "See if I bear this Mark."

"*Beylah vo, kem'Feyreisa.*"

Gaelen's hand rose, palm up. His eyes began to glow as he summoned magic. His pupils stretched wide, revealing the inner dark of his eyes, a deep blackness flickering with red lights.

A shadowy wisp of Azrahn swirled in his palm, and the sickly sweet chill of it pebbled Ellysetta's flesh. A cold, throbbing ache began in her chest, just above her rapidly pounding heart. Her fingers ached to clutch at the spot, to hide it, to repress it as she had all her life. She looked down at her chest. A single, despairing tear trickled from the corner of her eye.

There, on the soft, ivory swell of her left breast above her heart, revealed by the scooped neckline of her nightgown, a shadow lay upon her skin. A hideous, damning smudge.

⟁

Rain stared in horror at the mark on Ellysetta's flesh. If Gaelen was to be believed—and, gods help him, Rain did believe him—this was proof of Mage-claiming. The Eld had forged a foothold in Ellysetta's soul.

"Only one Mark," Gaelen was saying. "It could be worse. It takes a full six Marks to completely subjugate a soul."

Rain only half heard him. His mind was reeling. The instinct to kill anyone infected with Eld evil was so strong, his hand actually ached for the feel of red in his palm. And yet . . . this Mage-claimed woman was his *shei'tani*, his truemate, the miraculous bright and shining soul who had brought him out of the shadows of despair. She was the one he'd been sent to find and bring back to save the Fading Lands.

Wasn't she?

She stared at him, weeping, hands outstretched. Silently pleading with him for reassurance, for proof that he would not revile her.

Gods help him, he could not give her that.

He stumbled back a step, and then another and another, retreating from the promise and damnation she represented. Better to have died a thousand years ago than face this torment now. His hands rose to his face. His fingers curved like tairen claws. He ached to rend his own flesh from his bones, to rip out the helpless need and hunger that bound him to her.

He was the Defender of the Fey, sworn to slay the enemies of his homeland, and she was Mage-claimed. How could he let her live?

He was the Tairen Soul, last repository of the greatest of all Fey magics, and she was his *shei'tani*. How could he let any harm befall her?

How could she possibly be the key to saving the tairen and the Fey while bearing the foul taint of the Eld on her body and in her blood?

Madness tore at him. Howling fury and mindless rage fought to consume him. Only the smallest sliver of control kept him clinging to sanity, and Ellysetta's devastated emotions threatened to undermine that.

"Rain." Marissya called to him. Her *shei'dalin's* voice throbbed with power, with peace.

He fought it off. Marissya could not help him. Not this time. "I've got to go. I cannot stay here." His eyes met Ellysetta's and flinched away. He lurched for the glassed balcony doors and flung them open. "Keep her safe here tonight. Return her to her family in the morning." Without a single look back, he flung himself into the night sky.

"Rain!"

She called after him in desperation. Ellysetta. Truemate of the Tairen Soul. Daughter of the High Mage of Eld, Rain's most deadly and despised enemy.

With a scream of fury and a scorching blast of flame, Rain Tairen Soul raced into the darkness of the night.

⸺⸺⸺⸺

"Rain," Ellysetta whispered. He was gone, swallowed up by the night. He'd cut her off from his emotions, leaving her nothing, no tie to him, no way to reach him. She covered her face with her hands and wept.

"Come away, little sister." Marissya tugged her back from the balcony. But beneath the compassion, Ellysetta felt the *shei'dalin's* involuntary flinch. Even Marissya could not completely hide her revulsion at the taint in Ellysetta's blood.

She pulled her tattered emotions tight. "I should go home now. Tonight. There's no reason for me to stay here."

"There is every reason," Gaelen corrected. "You are still the Feyreisa, and you are still in danger." He nodded towards the window. "The Feyreisen will be back. He has no other choice. He will realize it soon enough"—he paused, then added softly—"once the soul hunger begins."

⸺⸺⸺⸺

Rain flew hard and fast towards the Fading Lands. Blind instinct more than conscious thought drove him towards the haven of Fey'Bahren and his tairen kin. For centuries they had guarded him when no other creature could, and he knew that when the soul hunger began to consume him and madness claimed him once more, the tairen would grant him final peace through the fiery embrace of tairen flame.

Ellysetta. Just the thought of her name made the tairen roar in fury.

When first she'd called him from the sky, he'd thought the gods had sent a miracle to save him. Now he realized they'd sent her to complete his damnation.

Daughter of the High Mage. Mage-claimed. Bound to his soul forever.

He would give his life before risking the Fading Lands with a Mage-claimed truemate.

Marissya and the Fey called frantically to him from Celieria, but he ignored them. Summoning a fierce tail wind to speed his flight, he raced across the sky towards the west. Towards the protection of the Fading Lands and the tairen's waiting fire.

The tairen had other ideas. No more than a few bells into his flight, a rich, resonant chorus of golden notes filled his mind, tairen song from Fey'Bahren, authored by Sybharukai, leader of the Fey'Bahren pride. The rich notes poured through him, not soothing and restful as they so often had been in the past, but crisp with power and command.

«We sense your approach, Rainier-Eras,» she sang. *«Why do you return alone? Where is the one you were sent to find? Where is your mate?»*

He had not spoken with Sybharukai or any other tairen of the pride since leaving the Fading Lands, but it did not surprise him that she knew of Ellysetta. Quickly, weaving as much information as he could into his tairen speech, Rain explained what had happened.

«You left her, your mate? You left here there, among the humans?»

«What else was I to do? I could not bring her to the Fading Lands.»

«Tairen do not abandon their mates.» Even across the vast distance between them, the great cat's disapproval vibrated down to Rain's bones. The glorious symphony of tairen speech rang cold with deep, discordant notes.

«Sybharukai, did you not hear me? She is Mage-claimed.»

«Mages,» Sybharukai sniffed. *«You think we fear them?»* She sent an image of claws indolently shredding rock. *«Did not a single tairen once drive Mage evil from the earth for a thousand years? Tairen do not abandon their mates. Tairen defend the pride. She is the one you were sent to find, Rainier-Eras. Bring her to us.»*

As the Tairen Soul, Rain was king of the Fey, but he was also a tairen of the Fey'Bahren pride . . . which Sybharukai ruled. Still, he resisted. She did not understand the dangers. She did not understand what she was asking him to do.

«It is to defend the pride that I must not bring her. She is the daughter of the High Mage of Eld, and she is Mage-claimed. He will use her to destroy us. Through her, he can even use me. I cannot allow that to happen.»

The great cat's response carried an image of Sybharukai's ears and tail twitching with irritation. *«Claiming a mate is never without challenge or risk. Only the strongest prove worthy. Such ways ensure the health of the pride. Bring her to us.»*

Rain's claws extended, curving and razor sharp. Venom pooled in his fangs, and licks of fire sparked in the night sky. *«I cannot. I will not.»*

«Rainier-Eras! Obey me! There is a reason you were chosen. Only she can save us, but only if you can save her. Do your duty, Tairen Soul! Guard her! Protect her! Bring her—»

Her voice was cut off in mid-sentence. For the first time in his life, Rain blocked the song of his tairen kin from his mind. He didn't need Sybharukai's censure to know his duty lay behind him, there in Celieria City. Without Ellysetta, the Fey and the tairen would surely die. But he also knew, with terrifying certainty, that if he did not turn from Ellysetta now, he never would. Even if that meant surrendering his own soul to the Mages.

And if the Mages gained control over a Tairen Soul, many more people than just the tairen and the Fey would perish.

<hr />

After Rain left, the Fey spent several bells bitterly debating what to do about Gaelen and his knowledge of what was happening to Celierians in the north. Marissya wanted to take him to Dorian and have him tell everything he knew. Dax and Bel vehemently disagreed.

Gaelen's presence was a double-edged blade. He could swear under *shei'dalin* oath that Celierians in the north were Mage-claimed, but if questioned, he'd also have to admit to leading the *dahl'reisen* and murdering Celierian peasants. Just having him in their company lent credence to Lord Sebourne's claims of *dahl'reisen*-Fey collusion.

In the end, Bel and Dax convinced Marissya it would be best to keep Gaelen's presence a secret, even from Dorian. The risk of revealing him was simply too great.

<hr />

Ellysetta spent the entire night curled up in a deep wing-backed chair in Rain's palace bedroom, staring out into the night, watching the Mother and Daughter cross the sky as the small silver bells of the night rang out in slow, lonely succession. A twenty-five-fold weave hummed around the room, enveloping her in buzzing power. Gaelen had offered to add Azrahn to the weave, saying it would protect her against the powers of the Mage Mark, but the others almost pulled red on him again for the suggestion.

What little sleep she got was tormented by new nightmares of Rain turning from her in revulsion, of Fey voices crying "Mage-claimed!" in the same way the accusers of all her previous dreams had cried "Demon-possessed!"

Worst of all, she dreamed of shining, grim-faced Fey legions throwing a thousand razor-sharp knives to pierce her, and of Rain Tairen Soul swooping down to scorch her with incinerating fire as she stood before them, crackling with dark power, her eyes bottomless pits of blackness blazing with red flame.

Powered by strong, unnatural winds from the west, the sky itself turned against Rain. Sybharukai was not pleased with his defiance, nor forgiving of his stubborn refusal to hear reason. Strong headwinds surged across the skies like waves on a stormy sea, doing their best to push him back towards Celieria City and Ellysetta, forcing him to wrest each mile from the sky through fierce, hard-powered flight.

Furiously he refused to turn back. The winds became a tempest. Towering thunderclouds blossomed. Buffeted and tossed about the sky, he kept his head turned into the wind and his wings stubbornly pumping. He flew for what seemed an eternity, with no idea how much progress—if any—he was making, but refusing to stop.

As he flew, drawing further and further from Ellysetta's healing presence, he heard the rising murmurs of voices—of the millions he'd slain—hissing their accusations, as they had for centuries. *Murderer. Destroyer.*

Worse were the forlorn, grief-stricken voices of the friends and innocents who'd died beneath his scorching fire.

I had a family, children!

My Sahra . . . we were to be wed come spring.

Rain, my friend, how could you do this to me?

They reproached him, wept for all their lost happiness, the lost days of life he'd stolen from them, reminding him that he—not Ellysetta—was the one with the true taint on his soul. If ever any creature deserved to be reviled and condemned, it was he.

He raged against the voices, wanting to protest, knowing he could not. Gouts of flame spewed from his muzzle, turning rain to steam as it showered down from the thunderclouds, but still, stubbornly, he flew.

It wasn't until much, much later, in the small bells of the night, that the clouds finally parted. And when they did, fresh fury swelled inside him. His wily tairen kin had used his stubbornness against him. He'd been so busy battering himself against their raging, tairen-spawned winds, that he hadn't noticed those winds had changed their course. Instead of blowing him back to Celieria City, they'd blown him hundreds of miles north, towards Eld.

Below him, the wide, long ribbon of the mighty Heras River cut across the landscape like a scar, and beyond that the dark, dense forests of Eld stretched out as far as his tairen eyes could see. It was the first time he'd laid eyes on the land of his enemy in a thousand years.

Bitter memories flooded him. Some his own, some memories he'd never seen before, sung to him on a vibrant new melody of tairen song flowing on the winds from Fey'Bahren.

«Look, Rainier-Eras,» the new song urged. *«Look and remember. And learn.»*

Vivid, bloody visions filled his mind, despairing visions of the terrible war he'd once fought, and the terrible price not only he but all the tairen and Fey had paid to end it. Devastating grief and loss. The grim determination and staggering sacrifice of so many Fey warriors, *shei'dalins*, mates, even truemates who'd lost their immortal lives battling the enemy they had mistakenly allowed to grow strong.

The tairen and the Fey had both been decimated in those

wars, a blow from which neither race had ever recovered. Of the survivors, thousands more had willingly, selflessly sacrificed themselves again to build the Faering Mists. They'd given their lives . . . not just to protect the Fey, as he'd always thought, but to protect him.

He saw it now so clearly in the tairen song that his heart nearly burst from the pain. Despite the consuming darkness in his soul—despite the millions he'd slain when he scorched the world—neither the tairen nor the Fey had reviled him. Instead, they'd died to give him life.

They'd died so he, Rainier-Eras, the last Tairen Soul and the least worthy of them all, would not perish.

Even Ellysetta, who called herself a coward, had faced the terrible blackness of his soul, and offered him what he'd been too craven to give her: acceptance and healing through the quiet, steadfast courage of her love.

«*Enough,*» he cried to the winds. «*I yield.*»

The unnatural, tairen-spawned winds died instantly. The skies cleared. «*If death is what you seek, it lies before you. We will not keep you from it. If life is your choice, you know where to find it, and you know what you must do.*» Sybharukai's final words resonated across the vast distance; then the tairen song, like the winds, fell silent.

Circling the calmed skies near the land of his enemy, Rain made his choice. His wing dipped. His tairen body wheeled north, into Eld.

CHAPTER SEVENTEEN

Ellysetta woke, exhausted, to the faint light of dawn. Still curled in the wing-backed chair. Still alone. No courtship gift lay beside her. No *shei'tanitsa* awareness warmed her senses. Rain had not returned.

Gaelen and Ellysetta's quintet were waiting for her when she emerged from the bedroom. They regarded her in silence, their Fey eyes full of compassion and remorse.

"Where is he?" she asked.

"We don't know," Bel admitted. "He isn't responding to anyone's calls."

Her chest felt as if a tight fist were squeezing slowly, inexorably around her heart and lungs. "It's over, then. He isn't coming back."

"He just needs more time," Kieran suggested. "He'll be back as soon as he starts thinking clearly."

"Of course he will," Gaelen concurred, "but we can't afford to wait for him. The High Mage is hunting you, *kem'falla*. You aren't safe here. You must accompany the Fey back to the Fading Lands. It's your only hope of survival."

"The Fading Lands?" She stared at him as if he'd gone mad. "You made it very clear last night that's the last place I can afford to go. I'm the High Mage's daughter, you said. I bear a Mage Mark. You even planned to kill me to stop me from entering the Fading Lands."

"That was when I thought you were corrupt. You are not. But you *are* in grave danger. Rain has left. We must assume the Mages know that by now. They will think to use his absence to their advantage, which means the attack will come soon."

Ellysetta turned away. At the moment, she didn't care if the Mages attacked. She just wanted the hollow pain in her heart to stop hurting. "My parents agreed to send me to the Fading Lands only on the condition that Rain marry me by Celierian custom in a Celierian church. Well, look around." She flung out her hands to indicate the room. "Rain's not here. It's hard to have a wedding without a groom."

"You can wed by proxy," Gaelen answered without hesitation. "It was common practice among kings of old when they took a foreign bride. Belliard will stand for Rain so the wedding can take place today and we can quit the city before the Eld have time to attack in force."

"Rain wanted the wedding to take place today, in any case," Bel added. "Marissya has the warrant he obtained from the king to ensure the archbishop's compliance."

She stared at them in sudden understanding. "You've both been planning this all night, haven't you?"

Bel and Gaelen glanced at each other and nodded in unison. "We are bloodsworn to protect you," Bel said. "No matter what happens between you and Rain, the *lute'asheiva* bonds Gaelen and I both made to you remain. Getting you out of harm's way is our greatest priority."

She almost started weeping again. What sort of cruel irony was it that Gaelen and Bel would be more steadfast than Rain? "Bel, answer honestly. Do you really think the Fey or the tairen will be safer with the daughter of the High Mage residing in the Fading Lands?"

"Whatever the High Mage is to you makes no difference," Bel answered. "You are the Feyreisa. And your soul is so bright, I cannot believe he could ever use you for evil."

"You didn't answer my question."

"You did not ask the right question," he replied. "Would the Fading Lands be safer with the daughter of the High Mage living within? Perhaps not. But would our queen be safer with the power of the Fey, the tairen, and the Faering Mists standing between her and those who seek her harm? The answer to that question is now and always will be *aiyah*."

There was certainty in his shining gaze, no doubt at all. She looked away. "I need to go home. I need to be with my family. I'll give you my answer after I've spoken with them."

Her quintet and Gaelen exchanged glances, then nodded. "We will take you."

Whatever hope Ellysetta harbored for parental comfort shriveled the moment she reached her family home. Her parents were waiting by the door, their faces drawn tight with more anger and disapproval than she'd ever seen.

"What have you to say for yourself?" Lauriana snapped the moment Ellysetta crossed the threshold. Fists planted firmly on her hips, she glared at her daughter. Beside her, Sol stood puffing rapidly on his pipe, a sure sign of his agitation.

"Mama?"

"Gone all night, doing gods only what what."

Ellysetta had spent the night in torment because she was the soul-cursed daughter of the High Mage, and Mama was worried about the appearance of impropriety? She would have laughed if she weren't so close to crying.

"Mama, please. You're upset for no reason. There was a . . . disturbance last night, and Rain thought I would be safer spending the night in the palace. Didn't you get my note?"

"Upset for no reason, she says," her mother growled. "An unmarried girl hies off to the palace to spend the night with a man, but her parents have no cause to be upset. Is this how we raised you? To act the slut for an immortal with a pretty face?"

"Mama!" She couldn't have been more shocked if her mother had slapped her across the face. Never had Ellysetta heard her mother voice such an ugly accusation, let alone aim it at her.

"Madame Baristani—" Bel began.

"Silence!" Lauriana's roar cut them both off. She turned the full force of her fury on Bel. "You Fey have no comprehension of decency. You've tarnished our daughter's reputation beyond repair! No decent man would have her now."

Bel stiffened, and Lauriana was angry enough to be pleased he was insulted. Ever since their arrival, these Fey had trampled on Celierian customs and honors, bit by insidious bit tearing away the lifetime of moral lessons Lauriana and Sol had worked so hard to instill in Ellysetta. Seducing her with their evil magic ways and deadly beauty. Endangering her soul.

"Nothing happened, Mama," Ellie said. "Rain wasn't even there—he left almost immediately after bringing me back to the palace."

"You were seen, Ellie!" her mother exclaimed. "You were seen entering the Fey king's suite at night in nothing but your nightgown! Look me and your father in the eye and tell us the Tairen Soul hasn't mated you, tell us he hasn't started you using magic. Tell us you've kept to the vows of your Concordia!"

Ellie went pale, then flushed bright, betraying pink.

Sol stiffened at Lauriana's side. "He promised me . . . he swore a Fey oath—"

"It wasn't like that," Ellie protested quickly. "Rain kept his oath. He swore to you he wouldn't mate with me, and he hasn't—not really—and the magic was just little things. He was trying to teach me to how to control my magic. We just—"

"You need not explain nor apologize for anything, *kem'-falla*. You have done nothing wrong." An unfamiliar Fey with piercing pale blue eyes stepped close to Ellysetta, towering over her in a manner that radiated protective devotion. But the moment he shifted his attention from Ellysetta to Lauriana, his entire demeanor became one of palpable threat. He stabbed her with a look of such coldness, she actually felt the blood chill in her veins.

"There are none who could guard your daughter's honor better than the Fey," he stated in a voice dripping with disdain. "Even were that not so, she is meant for greatness, not for playing broodmare to a mortal or being shamed by filthy minds too blind to see her brightness."

Lauriana stepped closer to Sol and instinctively clutched his arm. "Who are you?"

"My name," the man said coldly, "is Gaelen vel Serranis."

Lauriana had never paid much attention to Fey tales, but every Celierian knew the terrible history of Gaelen vel Serranis. "The Dark Lord?" Her tone rose, ending on a shrill note that made more than one of the Fey wince. She speared Ellie with a horrified look. "You brought the Dark Lord into my home?"

"Mama—"

"Madame Baristani—" Bel began.

"Out!" She pointed a shaking finger towards the door. "Get out of my house! You gods-cursed Fey sorcerers have put your last foot across my threshold. First it was magic, then demons and dead men and the ruination of my daughter's reputation. And now you *dare* to bring the Dark Lord himself into my family's home? I will not stand for it!"

"Mama, please!" Ellysetta held out beseeching hands. Never once in her life had she seen her mother in such a fury. Or so close to hysteria.

"Don't you 'Mama' me! I want these Fey out of my house. And gone from my doorstep. This instant!"

"Madame Baristani, it is too dangerous to leave you without any protection," Bel tried again. "The Elden Mages have—"

"OUT!" she shrieked. "GET OUT! Sol!"

Sol took the pipe stem from his mouth and put an arm around his wife's shoulders. Anger had turned his eyes hard and cold. "My wife is absolutely right. You Fey have abused our trust and brought the worst sort of evil to our doorstep. You need to leave. Right now."

"Papa!" Ellysetta protested.

"They go, Ellysetta. All of them. This instant. And they can consider the betrothal contract null and void, too. The entire flaming world can burn like the Seven Hells before I'll entrust the Fey with my daughter now." He jammed the pipe stem back into his mouth and clenched his teeth down hard.

"Papa! You can't be serious! The Fey are here to protect us. We're all in danger."

Neither the furious expression on her mother's face nor the sober determination on her father's wavered the least bit.

Ellysetta's lips trembled. She clamped them together and clenched her fists at her sides. She'd never defied her father before. She was going to defy him now.

"I will be leaving with the Fey today, Papa," she said. She met his gaze without flinching. "I'd rather go with your blessing and a Church-sanctioned marriage, but I'll go without both if I have to." She saw the shock in her father's eyes, and it almost gave her pause.

"You would choose the Fey over your own family?" her mother cried.

"If I stayed here without them, I'd endanger us all. I won't do that. I've already brought enough harm to this family."

Lauriana's expression went lax for one shocked moment, then hardened with determination. "If you walk out that door, Ellysetta Baristani," she declared in a tight voice, her face pale but resolute, "you will not be welcome back."

"Laurie," Sol muttered. He gave her shoulder a warning squeeze. "That's enough."

Lauriana yanked free of his grip and ran up the stairs in a flurry of skirts. The slam of her bedroom door rattled the glass table lamps in the parlor.

Sol turned back to Ellysetta, frowning. "I trusted you, Ellie, despite your mother's misgivings. And in return, what have you given us? Lies and deception. And now the Dark Lord. What sort of evil has Rain dragged you into?"

"It's not like that. Rain's been trying to protect me from evil, not drag me into it."

"Then how do you explain *him*?" Sol jerked his head towards the infamous Fey behind her and lowered his voice, "He's a dangerous man. The most murderous *dahl'reisen* who ever lived. I can't believe Rain allowed him within seven miles of you. I can't believe you brought him into this house."

"Gaelen's not a *dahl'reisen* anymore, Papa. I restored his soul."

Her father's pipe fell out of his hand and clattered on the floor. "You *what*?"

"That's what happened last night. That's why Rain took me back to the palace." She spread her hands, staring at the smooth, seemingly mortal palms. "There's magic in me—and not just the little bit you've always suspected. It scares me even more than it scares Mama, but I can't deny it any longer. And I'm going to have to learn to use it."

Her father's brow creased with dismay. He knew, just as she did, there would be no reconciliation between Ellysetta and her mother once she began using magic openly.

"I love you, Papa. I always will . . . but you and I both know I don't belong here anymore." Her throat closed tight, cutting off the last word. It was the truth, but saying it aloud was like stabbing a knife in her own heart.

"Ellie, no . . ." Tears rose to her father's eyes. "We can go away—leave the country if that's what it takes . . ."

"No, Papa. I've been running all my life, and you've been running because of me. It's got to stop. The Fey can help me in ways you can't. And they'll keep me safe."

"Is this what you truly want?" His eyes begged her to say no.

"It's what has to be." His shoulders slumped in weary defeat, and she rushed on before she completely lost her composure. "You agreed the wedding could take place today, immediately after the Bride's Blessing. I'll understand if you and Mama don't want to come, but I'd like your approval and blessing all the same."

"If I don't want to—? Oh, Ellie." Sol wrapped his arms around her and pulled her tight to his chest. The fragrance of fresh wood, pipe smoke, and polishing oil surrounded her—the scents she would always associate with love and protection. "Of course I'll be there. We both will. You're our daughter."

"Thank you, Papa," she whispered against his throat. "I'm so sorry for all the trouble I've caused." She closed her eyes, sent up a silent prayer, and tried to summon her power. The crystal on her wrist glowed, aiding her, and a whisper-thin thread of Spirit answered her call. She wove her thoughts into it and sent the thread into her father's mind. *«I'm going to order the Fey outside to stay, Papa.»*

She pulled back, meeting his eyes, and added, *«They'll remain invisible, so they don't frighten Mama, but I want you to know they'll be there, protecting you.»* She watched shock freeze his expression and stiffen his spine the moment he realized she wasn't speaking aloud but through magic. *«I love you, Papa.»* She sent that too, packed with every emotion in her heart, so he would know it was true.

Breaking his shocked paralysis, he snatched her back into his arms for a final, fierce hug. "I love you too, Ellie-girl. I always will."

Her chin trembled and her mouth worked to hold back the sudden sob that fought to get out. Quickly, before she broke into fresh tears, she extricated herself and started for the door. "I'll send someone for my things." She walked past Bel and left her father's house.

Gaelen and the others followed. Bel was the last to leave.

"Master Baristani"—Bel bowed to Sol—"the Fey regret causing your family distress, but please believe me, despite what your wife fears, the path Ellysetta walks now is the one the Bright Lord himself has prepared for her."

Sol nodded. "Just keep her safe."

❧

"Oh, now, that was well done," Kieran snapped as the door closed behind them. "Insult the Feyreisa's mother, terrorize her, and turn the whole family against us!"

Gaelen curled his lip. "What was I supposed to do? Follow your example and just stand there while that woman shamed the Feyreisa and made her weep?"

" 'My name is Gaelen vel Serranis,' " Kieran mimicked, then scowled. "Why didn't you just shout it to the entire neighborhood? Tairen's scorching fire!"

"She asked me who I was. I answered. Or do you suggest I should have lied?"

"Stop it, both of you," Ellysetta snapped. She speared Gaelen with a stern look. "Kieran is right. Marissya and Dax made it very clear the Fey can't afford any more notoriety at the moment. You no longer live outside Fey law. If you wish to serve me, as you have bloodsworn yourself to do, you must do so with honor. And that does *not* include introducing yourself by name to people like my mother in order to terrify them into submission."

"*Kem'falla*—" Gaelen protested.

"Don't bother to deny it," she snapped. Irritation was better than tears. Anger bred strength, and strength was what she needed. "I know why you did it, and you should be ashamed. Whether you like her or not, she is my mother and deserving of your respect."

Kieran smirked at Gaelen until a sharp glance from Ellysetta wiped his face clean. "And as for you, Gaelen is your uncle, your mother's beloved brother. He's your family. Learn to get along with him. You don't have to like him, but you might want to consider the fact that he's walked the earth more than twice as long as either of your parents, and he's spent the last thousand years battling the enemies of the Fey. He's probably forgotten more Fey skills than you've ever learned. Try giving him a little respect, and maybe you'll get a little back.

"The same goes for the rest of you," she added, expanding her glance to encompass all her quintet, "I'm sure there are skills Gaelen could teach us all, and we would be fools not to learn them."

Gaelen looked shocked. All her quintet looked shocked. The mouse had roared like a tairen, and none of them knew what to make of it. Ellysetta squared her shoulders. They claimed she was their queen. It was time for her to start acting the part.

"I can't go back. That means I must go forward, and considering where forward is taking me, I'll need all the help and skills I can muster. So instead of battling among one another, why don't you fine warriors of the Fey put your energies towards something constructive—like coming up with a plan to get me through today's Bride's Blessing and wedding ceremonies alive."

Long after Ellie's departure, Lauriana was still sitting in her room weeping and praying for guidance, but the Bright Lord had remained stubbornly silent. Sol had come up earlier to try to convince her that all would be well, but she sent him away. How could all be well when her eldest child was rushing head-long down the same perilous and evil-shrouded path of magic Lauriana had strived so long to save her from? With the Dark Lord at her side, no less!

She held Father Nivane's pendant in the palm of her hand. The amber crystal gleamed in the light shining in from the window. Perhaps, she thought, the Bright Lord was not an-swering her pleas now because he'd already done all his talk-ing, through the counsel of his servants.

Greatfather Tivrest and Father Bellamy had offered her a so-lution, a way to save Ellysetta's soul, even if Lauriana could not keep her here in Celieria, away from magic. She didn't even have to act. She had only to accept their offer by keeping this golden charm Father Bellamy had given her.

Giving a last, shuddering breath, Lauriana made her deci-sion. She rose to her feet, tucked the pendant back into her bodice, then sat down to pen a brief note to Sol, which she placed under her pillow for him to find if today did not go as planned. When she was done, she headed downstairs to heat water for a bath. It was time to prepare for the Bride's Blessing.

<hr>

Once more garbed as the elegant Ser Vale, Annoura's Favorite, Kolis Manza approached the chambers of Celieria's queen. He walked unchallenged past the two guards standing sentry at her door, through the Queen's Parlor into the adjoining bedroom, where two dozen elegantly garbed Dazzles stood talking qui-etly. Several of them cast long, appreciative glances his way, but he didn't spare them a look. His eyes were only for Celieria's small, beauteous queen.

She sat at her vanity, looking impressively regal in a gown of silver lace. Ladies-in-waiting re-pinned her hair and touched up her makeup in preparation for her attendance of the sea-son's last and most important meeting of the Council of Lords.

Vale sketched a deep bow and declared with seductive extravagance, "Your beauty rivals the shining brilliance of the Mother herself, My Queen."

Annoura had known the moment Ser Vale entered the room. She'd watched him in the mirror, told herself she would be cool to him. But still her breath caught and blood rushed with sudden heat in her veins as his throaty baritone slid over her skin like warmed silk.

"So," she declared, meeting her Favorite's gaze in her mirror, "you've returned."

"I know my presence displeased you, My Queen," Vale murmured, moving closer, "but I could not bear to stay away any longer. Forgive my impertinence. I brought you this small token of my devotion." He offered a bouquet of perfect creamy white roses tied with a bloodred ribbon. "Their loveliness pales beside your own."

She waved an impatient hand, dismissing the hovering ladies and the flock of Dazzles. "Leave us." The attendants and courtiers curtseyed and bowed and backed out of the room to the adjoining parlor, leaving the queen and her Favorite alone, with the door open to observe propriety.

Annoura did not move from the vanity nor even turn to face him. Instead, she waited where she was, forcing him to approach her. It was a small Trump she often played, so why, when she played it with him, did she feel like the nervous ingenue to his cool majesty?

"Take them," he whispered, holding out the roses so that their heady scent wreathed around her. "Tell me you forgive me."

His vivid blue-green eyes had always fascinated her. They had such mesmerizing depths. Feeling dazed and light-headed, Annoura reached for the flowers. She gave a hiss as a sharp thorn tore the soft skin of her finger.

"Curse my fool valet," Vale muttered. "He vowed he'd removed all the thorns." He knelt beside her, tossing the bouquet aside on the vanity and lifting her injured hand for his inspection. A pearl of blood welled up on her fingertip, scarlet against the pampered white perfection of her skin. "Forgive me, My

Queen." He brought the wounded finger close to his lips, then lifted searing eyes.

Her breath caught in her throat again. Wordless, unprotesting, she let him carry her finger to his lips and shivered as his breath swirled over her skin. The warm, wet rasp of his tongue licked the tiny wound and curled around her fingertip in wicked seduction. She shuddered, eyes half closing as sensation clenched every muscle tight and heat pooled in her loins. A strange, dark lethargy consumed her, dimming her vision, leaving only heat and pleasure and darkness.

A voice, soft and compelling, whispered to her, "The Fey have betrayed you, Majesty. The Dark Lord is in their service. He is here in Celieria City at this very moment, and the Fey are hiding him from you and the king. You must order the Dark Lord bound in *sel'dor* chains and thrown in the darkest pit of Old Castle prison. Quickly! Before it is too late."

Kolis watched the queen's lax, entranced expression crease in a frown as his words began to sink in. He could still scarcely believe the terrified thoughts he'd received from the Baristani woman's charm, but he didn't have time to investigate and couldn't take the chance she was wrong. Vel Serranis was too dangerous a Fey to leave guarding the High Mage's prize. He had to be removed from the equation.

The taste of Annoura's blood was fresh on Kolis's tongue, the first link forged between them . . . not as binding as a Mage Mark, but a bond nonetheless. He leaned closer, pushing with a force he'd never dared use on her before. "This proves the Fey and *dahl'reisen* are in collusion. They have been all along. They will destroy all that you've worked so hard to build. Celieria needs the Eld, to help it stand firm against the Fey. Only the Eld can help you save your throne. The Fey must be defeated. The agreement must pass."

✦❧

"The Council meeting has begun," Bel announced. "The weaves have gone up." He glanced around the palace suite and saw the tension in all the warriors visibly increase. The dangerous part of the day was about to start.

Ellysetta stood in the center of the room, garbed in a simple, unembellished blue linen gown with a modest neckline, her hair hanging to her waist in a cascade of bright, unrestrained curls. Gaelen knelt before her, fastening a pair of empty, steel-studded leather Fey'cha sheaths to her calves.

"I've tied an Earth weave to these sheaths and Bel's weapons belts," he was saying. "Your Fey'cha will re-form exactly thirty chimes after he surrenders his steel at the cathedral door. You can enter the cathedral unarmed—and answer truthfully that you haven't brought weapons into the cathedral, should the priests question you—but you'll get your Fey'cha back before you enter the Solarus. If anything happens during the Bright Bell, anything at all, just blood yourself with one of these blades. Bel and I will come running."

The rules of the church—which required that brides on the day of their Blessing arrive modestly dressed and completely unadorned as a symbol of their willingness to throw off outward trappings of wealth and vanity—meant Ellysetta could not wear her *sorreisu kiyr* jewelry or her Fey'cha belts. But the Fey weren't about to let her enter the cathedral Solarus without some manner of protection.

"The sash is done," Kieran said. He handed Bel a stiffened blue waistband that matched Ellysetta's dress.

Bel fastened the band around Ellysetta's waist. "How does that feel?" he asked.

"Good," she answered. Her four *sorreisu kiyr* were sewn into the band. She could feel them pressing against her skin, humming with reassuring power.

"How do *you* feel?" Gaelen asked.

The sudden rush of tears that burned in Ellysetta's eyes caught her by surprise, and she barely managed to keep them in check. Directly on the heels of sorrow came a rush of anger. How did she *feel*? Both her mother and her betrothed had reviled her, and she'd learned her birth father was the most evil man on earth. How did he *think* she felt?

She suppressed the tears and gripped the anger, hardening it into determination.

She took a deep breath. "I feel ready," she said, and saw pride shining on the warriors' faces. They thought she was being brave. Nothing could be further from the truth. She was operating on pure nerves, driven not by courage but by the sheer absence of any other viable choice. "Let's get this over with."

A carriage was waiting for her outside the palace steps, along with well over a hundred Fey in full steel. Bel helped her inside and signaled the coachman. The palace gates swung open, the coachman snapped his reins, and the carriage rumbled out of the palace grounds, turning onto the broad cobbled thoroughfare of King's Street. The Fey fanned out around the vehicle, magic shining.

They passed several small mobs of protestors and Brethren of Radiance followers, who booed and jeered the Fey, but the unspoken threat of sharp Fey steel kept the worst of the rabble-rousers in check.

Scarcely a mile from the cathedral, a man's voice cried out, "Halt in the name of the queen!" and the carriage came to an abrupt stop. Ellysetta stuck her head out the window and saw a small army of armored soldiers standing in the center of King's Street, blocking their path. Three even larger groups were approaching from the east, west, and the rear.

"We have a warrant for the arrest of the murderer Gaelen vel Serranis," the guards' captain announced as he drew near. "In the queen's name, I order you to surrender him to us."

Ellysetta didn't dare glance back at Gaelen, who stood near the rear of her carriage. How had they found out about him? He hadn't made any attempt to disguise himself, true, but though his name was as infamous as Rain's, without his notorious *dahl'reisen* scar she doubted more than a few people in Celieria would have recognized him. Her stomach took a sudden unpleasant lurch. Had her mother turned him in?

The captain extended to Bel a parchment bearing the royal seal. "I have been instructed to inform you that harboring vel Serranis will be viewed as an act of war."

Ellysetta thrust open the carriage door and jumped out, ignoring Bel's silently hissed command to stay where she was. She snatched the warrant and scanned it. Her eyebrows rose in outrage. The charges against Gaelen included murder, war crimes, and acts against the interests of the crown, many of them stemming from the Mage Wars a thousand years ago. "This is ridiculous!" she exclaimed. "Even if Gaelen was with us—and I'm not saying he is—I wouldn't give him up to stand trial for something that happened a thousand years ago."

"There is also the more recent matter of murdered Celierian citizens in the north." The captain took a more aggressive stance. "Lady, I am here to arrest Gaelen vel Serranis, who is known to be in your company. If you refuse to surrender him, I'm afraid I must take you into custody in his stead."

Bel stepped in front of her. "She is the Feyreisa of the Fading Lands," he warned in a cold, toneless voice. "She is no longer subject to the laws of your land. If you are fool enough to try to take her from us, you and your men will die where you stand." He did not blink. He did not raise his voice.

Behind the captain, his men shifted with visible nervousness and their fingers clenched more tightly around their blade hilts. Several of the guards even drew their swords. The captain himself stood his ground, though his face lost most of its color. "If that is the price of obeying my queen, ser, then that is the price I and my men must pay."

"*Setah.*" Gaelen stepped forward. "There is no need for threats or violence."

«*Gaelen, what are you doing?*» Ellysetta objected. «*Let me handle this.*»

«*Las, kem'falla. You cannot afford the delay.*» He met the captain's gaze with glittering, icy eyes. "I am vel Serranis."

Ellysetta didn't think it was possible for the captain's face to go even paler, but it did. He swallowed and clenched his jaw. "Gaelen vel Serranis, by order of the queen, I am placing you under arrest. Step forward, ser, and hold out your hands." One of the men behind him moved closer and held out a set of black metal shackles with shaking hands.

Beside Ellysetta, Bel gave a shudder of revulsion. "Were you also ordered to bind him in *sel'dor*?" he demanded.

"I was. The Dark Lord's power is too dangerous to leave unfettered."

No expression crossed Gaelen's face as one of the soldiers approached with the *sel'dor* manacles, but fierce protectiveness rose up in Ellysetta. She had restored Gaelen's soul. He had bloodsworn himself to her. He was hers. She'd not been able to stop her countrymen from torturing Bel last week, but she would not let the same thing happen to Gaelen.

"Captain," she protested, "if binding Gaelen's powers is what you require, the Fey can do it. There's no need for these." Before anyone realized her intent, she stepped between Gaelen and the approaching soldier and snatched the manacles out of the unsuspecting man's hands.

Fiery pain scorched her palms and shot halfway up her arms. A shocked cry broke from her lips. The *sel'dor* restraints fell to the cobbles, and she stared in astonishment at her hands. The skin was bright red and already swelling with nascent blisters.

Her quintet leapt to surround her. Blades hissed out of scabbards. Celierians and Fey faced each other, snarling, over bared steel. The Tairen's Eye crystals pressed against Ellysetta's waist tingled almost painfully in response to a sudden surge of powerful magic. Around her, each Fey held both steel and power at the ready, waiting for the signal to attack.

"Stop," Gaelen commanded. "Put down your weapons. I will go with them, bound in *sel'dor* as they demand." He stood unresisting as the soldier bent to retrieve the *sel'dor* manacles and locked them firmly around his wrists. "Trust me, *kem'falla*. This is for the best."

Ellysetta flinched at the sound of the lock snapping closed. "We'll go to the king," she vowed. "We'll have Marissya Truthspeak you while you tell him what's happening in the north. He'll have to believe you."

"There isn't time for that. Go. Do what you must. I will be fine." He didn't resist as the soldiers led him away. "Get her to the cathedral, vel Jelani!" he called over his shoulder. "And get those shields up as soon as you cross the bridge." To Ellysetta's shock, he threw back his head and laughed. *"Miora felah ti'Feyreisa!* And gods bless meddling Celierian queens!"

"Why is he laughing? What did he mean, 'bless the queen?' " She turned to Bel and found him staring after Gaelen with a peculiar expression on his face. "Bel?"

Bel turned back and flashed a quick signal to Cyr, who hurried to Ellysetta's side and wove Fire to draw the worst of the heat from her burned hands. Around them, the remaining Celierian guards backed carefully away, clearing the path to the cathedral.

"Look at your hands, Ellysetta." Bel's cobalt eyes gleamed bright. "The *sel'dor* burned you. Badly. And you weren't even weaving magic."

Her eyes widened in sudden realization. "*Sel'dor* doesn't burn Eld flesh."

"*Nei,*" he agreed, "it doesn't. Such a strong reaction can mean only one thing." A dazzling smile broke across his face. "Beyond a shadow of a doubt, Ellysetta, you are Fey. Full-blooded, immensely powerful Fey."

Whatever the High Mage was to her, he was definitely not her father.

<hr />

Selianne was already at the cathedral when Lauriana arrived. The younger woman was standing in silent prayer at a shrine of the lesser goddess, Asha, guardian of health, hearth, and family. As Lauriana approached, Selianne removed a golden pendant from her neck and placed it in the altar's offering bowl alongside the coins and jewelry left by previous supplicants.

"Someone in your family is ailing, Selianne?"

The girl gave a startled jump and spun around. "Madame Baristani! I didn't hear you come in." She clasped a hand to her chest as if to still her pounding heart. "Yes, I'm afraid my mother hasn't been feeling quite herself lately."

"Oh, dear, I'm so sorry to hear that. I hope it's nothing serious."

"A minor chest ailment. But after that nasty bout she suffered this past winter, I promised myself I'd make a point of praying for divine healing sooner rather than later."

Lauriana forced a smile and tried to tamp down her own nerves. She wanted to take Selianne into her confidence, but she didn't dare. Selianne had no necklace to keep her thoughts secure from Fey intrusion, and Lauriana couldn't risk the chance of discovery.

A whisper of soft leather soles on the marble floor brought her spinning around. The archbishop walked towards them down the center of the nave. As usual, his tunic was a pure, pristine white. But this morning, even the sleeveless robe worn over his tunic was white rather than blue, a symbol of his recently purified soul and his readiness to perform the sacred rites of the Bride's Blessing. "Good morning, Madame Baristani, Madame Pyerson."

Lauriana and Selianne both sank into curtseys and kissed his extended ring.

He turned his stern gaze on Lauriana. "Are you ready, Madame Baristani?"

She swallowed and nodded. "As ready as any mother can be on such a day."

"Put your heart at ease, madam," he offered with an uncharacteristic show of kindness. "It will all work out for the best. You'll see."

A muffled commotion sounded near the main cathedral entrance. Five Fey in full steel strode into the nave. A young man in the blue tunic and robes of a novitiate priest hurried after them. "Sers! You cannot enter the cathedral with weapons! It is forbidden!"

Lauriana recognized the Fey as one of the groups of warriors who guarded her home and her daughter. Their leader—What was his name? Ravel something—bowed and extended a sealed letter to the archbishop. "Greatfather, we come with the authorization of King Dorian, to secure the cathedral before the Feyreisa's arrival."

Lauriana's breath caught in her throat. Secure the cathedral? By the king's authority? Lauriana's vague worries coalesced into sudden, sharp fear. Had the Fey somehow realized what she and the archbishop had arranged? Had Father Nivane's charm failed and allowed them to pick up some wayward, betraying thought? Her hands knotted together, and fear buzzed in her veins, leaving her breathless and dizzy. *Calm down, Laurie, and think of something else.*

The archbishop snatched the parchment from the Fey's fingertips, ripped open the seal, and scanned the document.

"Your king," the Fey continued as the archbishop read, "has granted us the right to search both the nave and the Solarus where you will conduct the rites of the Bride's Blessing."

The archbishop's hand began to clench around the note, but he stopped himself before committing the petty treason of crumpling the king's missive. Instead, he collected his composure with visible effort and gave the Fey an icy glare. "Search, then, but be quick about it. I'll not have your weapons polluting the Bright Lord's house more than a moment necessary. Are you the leader of these men?"

Ravel bowed his head slightly in acknowledgment.

"Then only you—under my supervision—may search the altar, luminary, and Solarus. And you will not bring steel or magic to any of those holiest of places. *That* is not negotiable."

"Agreed." Without the slightest change in his expression, the Fey removed his knife belts and sword harnesses and swept a hand towards the altar, "After you, Greatfather."

Behind him, two of the Fey walked slowly around the perimeter of the nave, checking under altars and opening the rows of carved and gilded wooden devotionals to peer inside the private prayer rooms. The other two warriors went row by row through all the pews, lifting cushions, inspecting hymnals, and checking under the pews themselves.

Selianne huddled closer. "What do you think they're looking for?" she whispered.

"I don't know, dear," Laurie lied. She patted the girl's hand. "I'm sure it's just a precautionary measure to ensure Ellie's safety."

Ravel and the archbishop finished an equally in-depth

inspection of the main altar and the raised platform of the luminary, and began heading towards the Solarus. Lauriana couldn't tear her gaze away as the two men opened the heavy connecting door and entered the small, sacred chapel. She forced herself to remain calm, breathing slow and steady, working hard to marshal her thoughts. The archbishop didn't once look back her way, and his manner bespoke nothing more consequential than stiff affront at the invasion of the holy site entrusted to his care.

They remained in the Solarus for what seemed like ages. All the while, Lauriana waited for the accusatory cry. Time inched by . . . one chime . . . five . . . a quarter bell. Perspiration gathered on her upper lip and slicked her palms. Her nerves stretched to the breaking point.

Just as she grew certain of discovery, Ravel and the archbishop returned to the nave. Without a word, Ravel gathered up his steel, and all five warriors headed for the main entrance of the cathedral. He paused at the doorway. "Thank you for your time, ladies, Greatfather. The Fey regret any inconvenience, and we appreciate your gracious understanding and cooperation." He bowed quite deeply, then spun away and made his exit.

"Well," Selianne murmured. "That was exciting."

"Yes." Lauriana excused herself and hurried to the archbishop's side. "Greatfather?"

The cleric patted her hand. "Do not trouble yourself, daughter. All is well."

A few chimes later, Lauriana's ears detected the clap of approaching boot steps, and the familiar, despised tang of freshly woven magic soured her tongue.

Ellysetta and her Fey guards had arrived.

Ellysetta climbed the thirteen steps of the Cathedral of Light's Grand Entrance, and stood waiting while her quintet, with a great show of grudging acceptance, surrendered their steel to the young novitiate priest waiting by the cathedral door. Behind her, at all corners of the Isle of Grace, the Fey were spinning dense, impenetrable twenty-five-fold weaves that rose up around the Isle like a massive dome of shimmering, sunlit mist. Through the open double doors of the cathedral, she could see the archbishop's pristine white form standing at the far end of the nave. Selianne stood on his left side, looking pale and frightened, no doubt waiting for the Fey to scream "Eld spy!" and slay her. Mama stood on his right.

The sight of her mother made Ellysetta reconsider her suspicions about who had betrayed Gaelen to the queen. If Mama had done it, why would she show up for the Blessing? To willingly lock herself behind magic shields with a hundred Fey after turning Gaelen in for crimes against the crown seemed uncharacteristically reckless.

With her quintet following close behind, Ellysetta approached the altar. She stopped directly before her mother. "I didn't think you'd come."

Lauriana's lips trembled before she clamped them tight. "You're my daughter, Ellysetta," she replied. "If you insist on leaving with the Fey, I can at least see you properly blessed and wed before you go." Her jaw worked for a moment. "Don't think that means I approve of your choice. I don't."

Ellysetta nodded. Disapproval she could live with. The loss of her mother's love, she could not. Then, because she had to know, she lowered her voice to a whisper and asked, "Did you say anything about . . . the guest who came with me to the house this morning? Did you report him to the queen?"

Lauriana drew back in genuine surprise. "No!" Her brows lowered to a scowl. "Though I probably should have, come to think of it."

Though Ellysetta was far from accomplished with her Fey gifts, she couldn't detect any hint of a lie. Her mother was very nervous and tense—which made perfect sense, considering her intense dislike and suspicion of the Fey—but she hadn't been behind Gaelen's arrest.

Ellysetta exhaled a relieved breath. "Thank you for coming, Mama," she said. "I know it wasn't an easy decision for you, and I love you for caring enough to be here, despite your reservations." She wished she could weave time like the Fey wove the elements and erase the harsh words she and her mother had exchanged this morning. "You've always been my beacon. It wouldn't have felt right to receive the Bride's Blessing without you by my side."

Tears filled her mother's eyes, but when Ellysetta stepped forward, intending to embrace her, Lauriana turned away and choked out, "Please, Greatfather, let's get started."

Ellysetta's arms fell to her sides. The rejection hurt almost as badly as Rain's abandonment last night. But Mama was here, she reminded herself. Despite her doubts and obvious fears, Mama had come to stand at Ellysetta's side. Rain, wherever he was, hadn't even offered that much.

CHAPTER EIGHTEEN

Rain woke to the astonishing sensation of velvety horse lips moving over his face, and the loud sound of equine teeth munching in his ear. He peeled open one eye and stared into a horse's large, thickly lashed brown eye.

Above him, a dazzling bright blue sky stretched out. Below him was the soft, musty prickle of—he pulled a handful of the stuff up and stared at it—hay. He was lying in a haystack. In the middle of some farmer's field. With a big, heavyset shire-horse nibbling haystraw from his face and hair and munching loudly in his ear.

He shoved himself off the haystack, away from the horse's hungry, grazing mouth, and staggered to his feet. Gods, he hurt. Every muscle, joint, and sinew ached from the bitter, arduous bells he'd spent battering himself against last night's fierce, unnatural winds.

Sybharukai, bless her for the wicked tairen she was, had known exactly how to punish him for his stupidity while leading him roaring and fighting from rage back to reason. She'd beaten the fury out of him, shoved bilious truth down his throat until he gagged on it, then left him exhausted and filled with the bitter taste of humiliation, to make the final choice on his own.

Now, in the bright light of day, as he stood in the quiet peace of a farmer's field with Eld behind him and hope beckoning from Celieria City far to the south, he knew, with a certainty of purpose he'd long been lacking, that his choice was the right one.

For every great gift the gods demand a great price. Rain should have known the gods wouldn't grant him the stunning, unexpected miracle of a truemate without demanding something in return. Even Marissya had warned him of it on that very first night after he'd claimed Ellysetta. *You cannot shirk your duty, not to the tairen, not to the Fey, and definitely not to your truemate. Because, Rain, one other thing seems certain . . . whatever task the gods have set before Ellysetta Baristani, it is fearfully dangerous. Else she'd not need a tairen to protect her soul.*

What could be more dangerous to her than bearing the taint of the High Mage himself? Yet just as Ellysetta had flinched from her first encounter with the tairen, Rain had flinched from his first true test of courage as well. Worse, he'd fled and left her thinking she repulsed him.

She was not to blame for who her father might be, nor for any cursed Mage Mark set upon her in infancy. And Rain's first duty was not to the world, or the Fey, or even the tairen. His first duty was to her.

Gathering his strength, he spun a swift query on a weave of Spirit and sent it arrowing south towards Celieria. The answer that returned several chimes later came from a young Spirit master Rain did not know well.

«*The Feyreisa is at the cathedral. The twenty-five-fold weaves have gone up. Marissya and Dax are with the mortals in the Council. Those weaves have gone up as well. Marissya said if you contacted us, we should tell you to hurry.*»

«*I come,*» Rain returned with grim curtness. The weave dissolved as soon as the last crisp word was sent. His hands clenched into fists.

Ellysetta was safe, secured behind a powerful weave and protected by more than one hundred of the Fading Lands' strongest warriors. The Council, however, was another matter.

He'd promised her he would not let Celieria fall to the Eld. After his terrible betrayal last night, he was determined not to fail her again.

He had to get back to Celieria City. Now. Without delay.

Rain bent his knees and sprang into the sky. A frenetic cloud of gray mist and magic swirled around him. The familiar exultation of the Change shattered his senses, unmaking Rain, the Fey, scattering him to the clouds, then gathering him back up again as Rain, the Tairen Soul. Below him, the startled farmer in whose field he'd slept looked up from his plow, and in a small fenced pasture near his fields, a herd of cattle scattered in instinctive fear of the predator overhead.

Rain circled the farm and the penned cattle. The Great Sun was already nearing its zenith, and he was still hundreds of miles away from Celieria City. He would need to fly as fast as he could to get there in time.

He swooped down on the cattle pen once, twice, three times, thinning the small herd until his tairen belly was full, and then he swooped a fourth and final time over the haystack where he'd slept. Earth magic spun out, reaching deep into the rock below the field, finding what he needed and spinning it into his gift.

«*The Tairen Soul thanks you, Goodman,*» he called out to the farmer. «*I offer payment for your cattle and Fey blessings on your house.*»

Ropes of Air spun out behind him, generating a powerful tailwind that sent him racing across the Celierian skies at three times his normal speed. He swept through misty clouds like a gale, leaving them swirling madly in his wake.

Behind, in the field he'd just left, the farmer and his family laughed and danced around a haystack with exuberant delight and threw fistfuls of haystraw into the air. Haystraw Rain had just transformed into purest, gleaming gold.

❦

Following opening remarks given by Lords Sebourne and Teleos and half a bell of ineffectual salvos fired by half a dozen lesser lords, Lord Morvel, one of Celieria's twenty Great

Lords, took the floor to address the Council. He began by reminding his peers of his initial, magnanimous gesture of goodwill and acceptance towards the Fey—and the reason for his subsequent change of heart. Then he proceeded to expound upon the many economic benefits of demilitarizing the northern borders and expanding Celierian trade.

From her silver throne, Annoura listened to Morvel's bombastic posturing with half an ear and kept a surreptitious eye on the door to the chamber, watching for any sign that Gaelen vel Serranis's capture had been accomplished.

"The borders have been all but silent for the last hundred years," Lord Morvel concluded, his voice carrying easily across the length of the marbled chamber. "The Eld have extended the hand of friendship. Celieria must not cling to the narrow-minded exclusionism fostered by the fear mongering of the Fey and a few misguided Celierian lords."

A murmur of agreement rose up from several quarters of the room. "Really, Morvel?" Lord Barrial stood up in dissent. "The borders have been silent for a hundred years? Life must be quite idyllic over there in the east. Remind me to visit you when next I go on holiday." Several lords laughed. Lord Barrial waited for them to quiet, then continued in a more serious vein. "Unlike my very fortunate friend Lord Morvel, in my lands we still see regular raids from the north. The Eld I know are not kindly guardians of Light, but fierce and deadly enemies. Even with constant patrols and the help of the *dahl'reisen*, I lost more than thirty villagers last year along the Heras River—men, women, even children."

"Grim news indeed, Lord Barrial," Queen Annoura interrupted. "But how can you be certain the raiders are Eld? Witnesses from other estates say *dahl'reisen* are to blame."

"With all due respect, Your Majesty, I doubt *dahl'reisen* are behind the raids on my lands," he replied. "Gaelen vel Serranis himself made it very clear not two months past that he could have walked past my safeguards and murdered me or any member of my family at any time of his choosing. And he has not done so."

"Ah, yes," she murmured. "Gaelen vel Serranis, the Dark Lord. The same Fey who once thrust this country into a cataclysmic war that nearly destroyed the world. You would have this Council believe he is some tragic, noble guardian of the north, when all evidence speaks to the contrary. I have to wonder, Lord Barrial, if your blind faith in this Fey—who by all accounts is a murderous war criminal—has anything to do with the fact that you're his kinsman?"

The news brought the lords of the Council to their feet, voices raised in outrage.

King Dorian lifted the Bell of Order from its velvet cushion and rang it forcefully. Lord Corrias snapped to attention beside the king's throne. "Silence!" he called. "By the king's command, there will be silence in the chamber."

"Lord Barrial," Dorian commanded when the lords quieted, "please explain to the Council, as you have already explained to me, the exact nature of your kinship to Gaelen vel Serranis—a man who, I might add, is also my kinsman." He shot a look at Annoura, who arched a brow without remorse.

Lord Barrial bowed. "Thank you, sire." Turning back to address the Council at large, he said, "Her Majesty is correct. It appears Gaelen vel Serranis is indeed my kinsman. Though like our king, I am not his direct descendant. I recently discovered that a man the family archives record as Jerion Dural—whose grandson Pollis became the diBarrial from which my line descended six hundred fifty years ago—was in fact Dural vel Serranis, cousin to Lady Marissya and Gaelen vel Serranis."

Annoura listened with only half an ear. A young clerk serving as a runner to the Council was hurrying along the perimeter of the chamber, clutching a small sealed envelope. She watched his progress from the corner of her eye. The note passed from the clerk's hands to her Master of Affairs.

"When did you learn that your ancestor was Dural vel Serranis?" Dorian prompted.

"Just a few days ago, sire."

Lord Sebourne leapt to his feet. "Was that before or after the

Fey tried to steal my son's wife, Barrial? What have you agreed to?"

"Leave my daughter out of this," Cann shot back, "and don't you dare impugn my honor or my loyalty."

"You've done that yourself! From the beginning, you've supported Fey interests over those of Celieria. What have they bribed you with? Eternal life?"

"Must a border lord of Celieria now be bribed to defend the march? I do my duty, Sebourne! What of you and your cronies? Or has the glint of Eld gold erased all hope of reason?"

Sebourne's supporters once more leapt into the fray, pointing fingers and hurling accusations. Teleos and half a dozen others jumped up to rally round Cann.

Annoura's Master of Affairs handed her the clerk's note. She cracked the seal and glanced at the three simple words scrawled on the parchment: *We have him*.

She glanced back at Vale, whom she'd invited to serve in place of one of her regular attendants, who'd fallen ill. He was watching her, his vivid eyes intense. He gave a faint nod.

The bell rang again. "Silence and be ordered!" This time Dorian barked the command himself. "Lords, take your seats and be silent!" When the nobles subsided into grumbling compliance, Dorian turned back to Cann. "Lord Barrial, where does your allegiance lie?"

Cann stiffened his spine. "Where it always has. With you, sire, and with Celieria."

"Have you now or ever accepted any form of payment or reciprocity from either *dahl'reisen* or Fey in return for political favors?"

"Absolutely not."

"Have you now or ever put Fey or *dahl'reisen* interests above those of Celieria?"

"Never, my liege. I am, first and foremost, a Lord of Celieria."

"Lord Sebourne, since you leveled the accusation, I will ask you directly: Do you have any evidence to prove Lord Barrial is in the service of the *dahl'reisen* or the Fey?"

Scowling, Sebourne muttered, "No, sire."

"Then the only thing the revelation of Lord Barrial's ancestry proves is that he and I are distant cousins. I will hear no further accusations against him without evidence. Not even by intimation." Dorian's gaze came to rest on Annoura.

She arched a brow. "Then perhaps we would be best served directing our questions to Gaelen vel Serranis, himself." She turned cold eyes on Marissya v'En Solande. "Since my guard just arrested him here in the city, in the company of Ellysetta Baristani and the Fey."

The Council Chamber erupted.

A trio of white-robed acolytes emerged from the cleric-hall as Ellysetta rose from the cushioned bench before the altar of Adelis. The young boys filed up a small, spiraling stone staircase to a tulip-shaped balcony overlooking the luminary and began to sing.

Their voices rose up like silvery beams, carrying freely through the cathedral's vaulted nave, enhanced and amplified by its carefully engineered acoustics.

"Stand, Ellysetta Baristani," Greatfather Tivrest said, "and follow me to the luminary to offer Adelis your final devotions before the Bright Bell."

Gathering the folds of her linen skirts, she rose and circled round the altar rail to join the archbishop. As her fingers slid into his, she opened her senses and deliberately allowed his thoughts to flood into her. She even, gods forgive her, dared to skim his mind.

A barrage of focused, determined thoughts greeted her probing. *Shine your radiance upon her, oh, Lord. Banish the darkness from her soul. Guide her in the Bright Path and help her stand fast against the shadows. Shine your radiance upon her, oh, Lord.* Over and over the thoughts were repeated, and the only image in the archbishop's mind was of a bright, blinding light.

What she'd been expecting, Ellysetta really couldn't say, but she couldn't find anything dangerous or threatening in his dedication to saving her soul.

He led the way to the round, raised platform of the luminary and escorted her up the thirteen steps to stand on the large engraved golden medallion at the luminary's center, directly below the cathedral's great golden dome and the spire that housed the statue of Adelis. "Look up, daughter," he said, "and let the glory of the Bright Lord illuminate your path."

She tilted her head back. Above her, the interior of the cathedral's great dome had been painted to look like a summer sky, and the illusion was nearly perfect. A golden disk gleamed at the dome's center. As she watched, a pinpoint of light formed at the center of the disk. It widened rapidly, and a beam of light shot down from the center of the dome, enveloping Ellysetta and the archbishop in a shower of golden-white radiance.

"Kneel, daughter, and say your devotions."

Ellysetta knelt in the shining warmth of the luminary and felt her skin soak up the light. It tingled in her flesh, almost like magic. She closed her eyes and turned her face skyward towards the source high above. "Adelis, bless me. Keep me always in the Light. Shine your brightness on my path so I may never lose my way." *Help me, Lord,* she added silently. *Grant me the courage and strength to defeat the evil that hunts me.*

<hr />

"Marissya, Dax, Annoura—in my private chamber. Now!" King Dorian surged to his feet and swept towards the private room at the back of the Council Chamber in a billow of ceremonial robes. Fury etched his every step as he stalked away. He barely waited for the door to close before whirling on the three of them. "Is it true?" He glared at his ancestral aunt and her mate. "Have you been harboring the Dark Lord here in Celieria City, beneath my very nose?"

Marissya reached out. "Dorian, I—"

"Answer the question, damn you! And don't bother trying to weave peace on me. It will not work!"

"He came last night," Dax admitted. "But it's not what you think."

"It's not what?" Annoura challenged. "Aiding an enemy of

the crown? Abetting the murder of innocent Celierian civilians? Or do you still expect us to believe that the Eld, not the *dahl'reisen*, are responsible for the Celierian deaths in the north?"

Marissya and Dax exchanged guilty glances.

"Oh, gods," Dorian exclaimed. "He did do it. He did it, you knew it, and yet you said nothing." He stared at the pair of them as if he'd never seen them before. All his life he'd adored and idolized his legendary Fey relatives. He'd loved them even more than he'd loved his own parents. All his life he'd believed in one absolute: the honor and truth of Marissya v'En Solande.

"Dorian—" Marissya began.

"Be silent!"

"But, Dorian, the ones Gaelen killed were Mage-claimed. He swore it—by Fey oath, under *shei'dalin* touch."

For a moment Dorian's disbelief wavered. Fey oaths were inviolable and could not be sworn on a falsehood. And a Fey oath sworn under *shei'dalin* touch ensured that not only the words but the spirit of the oath were honest and true.

"A *dahl'reisen* swore a Fey oath?" Annoura sneered. "Under *shei'dalin* touch? Don't take us for such fools."

Dorian's jaw clenched. The brief moment of uncertainty was wiped away. "Annoura's right, Marissya. As you've told us many times before, *dahl'reisen* have set themselves beyond the bounds of Fey honor. Any oath of theirs is meaningless. And even if it weren't, the Fey would never let a *dahl'reisen* lay hands on a *shei'dalin* of the Fading Lands and live." His eyes narrowed. "Unless all that has been a lie, too."

"Fey don't lie," Dax stated, glaring. "We may not tell you everything we know, but what we do reveal, you can be assured is truth."

"How can I believe that now? You've both just been caught in open deception."

"Gaelen did swear a Fey oath, Dorian," Marissya interjected. "And he did swear it under *shei'dalin* touch—*my* touch. Ellysetta restored his soul. He is Fey once more."

Dorian gaped at her. "That's not possible."

"Until last night, I would have agreed with you. Such a miracle is beyond a *shei'dalin's* power—certainly beyond mine. But apparently, it's not beyond the power of a Tairen Soul's truemate." She took a step towards Dorian. Tears shimmered in her blue Fey eyes. "Last night, for the first time in a thousand years, I stood in my brother's presence. I embraced him. And I touched him with these hands"—she held up her hands—"while he swore a Fey oath that what he told us was true."

Doubt crept into Dorian's eyes once more. She looked so earnest, filled with such profound joy, he wanted to weep himself.

Annoura grabbed his arm and yanked him away from the *shei'dalin*. "Leave us, Fey!" she barked. "I will speak to my husband alone. Without your sorcery influencing him."

"Without my—?" Marissya choked back whatever words were on the tip of her tongue. She took a deep breath and visibly controlled her temper. "Dorian," she said in a much calmer voice, "*kem'jita'taikonos.*" Grandson of my sister's line. The appellation tugged at Dorian's emotions. She hadn't called him that in a very long time, not since he'd ascended the throne after his father's death. "Everything I've told you is true. I would never lie to you, and I would never try to manipulate your thoughts. Everything I've ever done has been to protect and help you, as I protected and helped your fathers before you. As I hope to protect and help your sons after you."

"I don't know what to believe anymore," Dorian muttered, turning away from Marissya's outstretched hands and entreating eyes. "Please, do as my queen says. Leave us."

Marissya's fingers curled in loose fists, and her arms fell back to her sides. Dax put a hand on her shoulder. "Come, *shei'tani.*" He gestured. The door leading back to the Council Chamber opened, and he escorted her through.

When they were gone, Annoura caught Dorian's hand. "You know you cannot believe anything the *shei'dalin* said. She lied about the Dark Lord. She hid him from you, here in your own palace, the seat of your power. The place you call home. She did that even knowing her brother was murdering Celierians in the north. You can't afford to fall for her *shei'dalin* tricks."

"But what if she's telling the truth? Even if the Fey and the *dahl'reisen* are in collusion, what reason besides Mage-claiming would they have for killing Celierian peasants?"

She gave a short laugh. "The treaty, Dorian. Think about it. Under your leadership, Celieria has prospered and grown strong. We have become the leading power in the mortal world. Yet the moment we consider signing a treaty that would give us independence from the Fey, Celierians begin dying in the north and Rain Tairen Soul appears after a thousand-year exile to stir up fears about a reconstituted Mage threat . . . a threat no one but he seems able to sense." She moved closer and took his hands. "Fear is power, darling. As long as we fear the Eld, the Fey can keep Celieria under their thumb, reliant upon them."

Dorian had lived his life amidst the intrigues of the palace. Courtiers smiled and pledged friendship and loyalty while plotting behind one's back. Everything Annoura said made sense, and if it were any other ally but the Fey, he would unquestioningly believe them capable of such machinations. But trusting the Fey was so ingrained in him, it was practically instinct now. Even when confronted with proof that threw all his beliefs into doubt, he didn't want to think them capable of deception.

Annoura caught his face in her hands and stared earnestly into his eyes. "I know how difficult this is for you, my love, but your country needs you to be strong. You must put aside your personal feelings for the Fey and consider what is best for Celieria. Banish the Fey from the Council Chamber so they can't manipulate our minds," she urged. "Have the guard bring Gaelen vel Serranis from Old Castle, bound in as much *sel'dor* as we can find, and let him stand for questioning by the Council. Let us discover *all* the facts, not just the ones the Fey want us to know. And then let the lords vote their conscience."

The loud murmur of voices fell silent when the door to the king's private antechamber opened again. All eyes focused on King Dorian and his queen as they approached the raised dais and took their seats in the matching gold and silver thrones.

"Lord Corrias," Dorian commanded, "escort Lady Marissya, Lord Dax, and the rest of the Fey to their rooms and see that they stay there."

"Dorian, *nei!*" Marissya protested.

He ignored her. "Send a runner to Old Castle. Have them bind vel Serranis in every ounce of *sel'dor* we possess, then bring him here, to this chamber, for questioning. The Council will reconvene in half a bell to hear the Dark Lord's testimony."

Her devotions in the luminary complete, Ellysetta knelt once more at the altar rail while Greatfather Tivrest held his golden scepter over her head and intoned the second blessing. When he was done, she rose and followed him to the large, heavily carved and gilded door that led to the Solarus. Behind her, the faint clap of Fey boots sounded against the nave's marble floors as her quintet came to stand beside the entrance to the sacred chamber.

Greatfather Tivrest harrumphed his disapproval of their presence and glared at them from beneath thick, dark brows. "You shall not enter the Solarus. Your comrade has checked it."

"And I will check it again before the Feyreisa sets foot inside," Bel insisted. His cobalt eyes held the archbishop's glare steadily until Tivrest stepped aside in grumbling defeat.

"Enter, then," he muttered. "But only one of you as before. Touch nothing, complete your search, and get out."

Bel bowed and entered the Solarus. Ellysetta stood waiting in the protective circle of her remaining quintet while Bel conducted his investigation. Several long chimes later, he returned. "The room is clear."

"*Beylah vo*, Bel." She laid a hand on his. "Thank you for everything." Against her calf, she felt the distinctive tingle of magic as her bloodsworn Fey'cha re-formed in secret. Taking a deep breath, she followed Greatfather Tivrest into the sacred chamber. Selianne and Lauriana followed close behind, and the great golden door swung shut.

"All right, then, Dark Lord. You've been summoned to the Council." The large, heavyset prisonmaster of Old Castle approached the holding cell containing his newest and most infamous guest. "Get in there, men, and make sure he don't flaming move."

Carefully, their faces set and pale, a dozen guards armed with pikes and swords inched into the cell and warily surrounded vel Serranis.

"Corbin," the prisonmaster barked, "bring those chains."

Behind him, his burly young assistant hurried forward, *sel'dor* chains rattling and clanking as he half carried, half dragged them to the cell and dropped them in a large, black pile near the door. Taking the first set of heavy ankle chains, he cautiously approached the prisoner.

"What are you waiting for? Put them on him."

The younger man swallowed and drew even closer. Cold sweat beaded on his forehead and he carefully knelt down before the Dark Lord and reached out to clasp the first *sel'dor* manacle around the *dahl'reisen's* booted left ankle.

At the first touch of the black Eld metal, the *dahl'reisen's* leg shot off a tiny explosion of sparks. Corbin cried out and fell backward, releasing the manacles. The *sel'dor* chains fell *through* the prisoner's booted foot and landed on the straw-covered cell floor. Above it the *dahl'reisen's* boot shimmered and sparked, wavering in and out of existence.

"Gods scorch the Fey!" the prisonmaster exclaimed. He spun on his heel, snatched up a *sel'dor* chain from the pile, and whipped it towards vel Serranis's body. The prisoner's torso gave off another shower of sparks as the chain passed straight through his body. "Our prisoner's a flaming Spirit weave. We've been tricked!"

Throwing down the chain, he ran down the hall, calling to the guards. "Send word to the king! Vel Serranis has escaped!"

❦

Bel turned to face the cathedral nave. He dragged a long breath of air into his lungs, testing the scents and tastes with every one of his Fey gifts.

"I know you're there, vel Serranis," he said to the empty air. "We're alone now. Show yourself." He took another, even deeper breath and turned to his right, facing the altar.

Scarcely a man-length away, the air began to shimmer. The white and gold marble of the great altar, covered with its blue watered-silk altar cloth, wavered. A faint shadow solidified into the fully armed, black-leather-clad figure of Gaelen vel Serranis.

"Spit and scorch me," Kieran muttered.

"How did you manage it?" Kiel demanded. "How did you break free of the *sel'dor*?"

"He didn't," Bel answered. "He never let the *sel'dor* touch him."

Gaelen cast Bel an approving glance. "Perhaps there is hope for you yet, vel Jelani."

"How did you do it?" Kieran demanded.

His uncle shrugged. "When the Feyreisa burned herself, I used the confusion to kick the real manacles under the carriage and spin a couple of convincing weaves. The manacles the guard picked up were Spirit, as was the Gaelen vel Serranis those Celierian buffoons took into captivity." He arched a brow at the astonished quintet. "My place is at the Feyreisa's side. Surely you didn't think I would let a few overreaching mortals keep me from fulfilling my bloodsworn bond?"

"I'm surprised you didn't sneak into the Solarus with her, then," Kiel said.

Gaelen shook his head. "The Bright Bell is a sacred rite, and far more ancient than even the Celierians realize. As I am neither Ellysetta's beacon nor her priest, my presence would have been a defilement."

Bel coughed something that sounded like "Tairen *krekk*" and arched disbelieving brows. "And the ward on the door that made your weave start to fail when you tried to pass through it didn't have anything to do with your decision?"

"Well," Gaelen acknowledged with a wry grin, "there was that."

Inside the cathedral's sacred chamber of meditation and spiritual purification, Ellysetta took stock of her surroundings. The large, circular room was as big as the entire first floor of the Baristani home, and it was constructed entirely of white marble. Scenes of Adelis and the other twelve gods bestowing their gifts upon the peoples of the earth had been etched in gold on the marbled walls. The room's sparse furnishings consisted of a small golden prayer bench positioned before an ornate devotional carved into one wall, and a circle of cushion-topped benches surrounding a raised white marble altar in the center of the room, directly beneath the room's towering domed ceiling. Six marble columns circled the perimeter. Gilded mirrors tiled the dome's interior, reflecting back every ray of light so that the smallest candle could have illuminated the entire Solarus and a full chandelier would have set the room ablaze. As it was, six small golden lamps made the room bright as day.

"Go to the devotional, daughter, and recite the six devotions of Light while I bless the chamber. Once that is done, we may begin your soul's purification."

With Mama and Selianne beside her, Ellysetta walked across the room to the carved devotional, knelt on the golden bench, and began to recite the devotions she'd learned as a child. Behind her, Greatfather Tivrest slowly circled the room, pausing near each of the columns to murmur a prayer and wave his scepter at the chamber walls.

Ellysetta's skin prickled with a now-familiar tingling sensation, and the words of the devotion caught in her throat.

The archbishop was weaving magic.

⚬~≈≈≈≈≈~⚬

"Gaelen vel Serranis has escaped from our custody." Dorian made the announcement with a heavy heart. Around him, the buzz of outrage was already rising to fill the Council Chamber. Any hope of questioning vel Serranis directly was gone, as was the faint hope Dorian had still harbored that he could discover the truth.

He glanced at Annoura, who was watching him with pride and approval. She gave an encouraging nod, urging him to reveal the rest, as they had agreed he must. "In the interest of a fair and open debate," he continued, "I must inform you that Gaelen vel Serranis admitted to slaying Celierian villagers in the north. According to the Fey, he alleged that the ones he killed were Mage-claimed."

The Lords of the Council burst into noisy debate and accusations. The Bell of Order rang several times, its peals drowned out by the din. After several chimes, when the volume of the shouting began to die down, Dorian granted Lord Sebourne the floor.

Sebourne turned to his fellow lords and Great Lords. "Since their arrival, the Fey have tried to make us doubt our northern neighbors and cast blame upon them for the murders that Gaelen vel Serranis has admitted to committing. They have sought to fill our minds with fears of Mages and threats to our freedom, while all the while their own exiled people were the true threat." He cast a slow, speaking gaze around the chamber. "Everyone knows the Mage Council was destroyed in the scorching of the world. What few Mages have survived were scattered to the winds, and there has been no sign of coordinated Mage activity in Eld ever since."

He waited for the raucous chorus of supportive cries and applause to die down before continuing. "If you still have doubts, then ask yourself this: How is it vel Serranis can allege that his victims were Mage-claimed when everyone knows Mage-claiming leaves no visible sign of its existence?" He let that sink in for a moment, then answered his own rhetorical question. "No, my lords, the victims of vel Serranis's murderous rampage were not Mage-claimed, they were just innocent peasants, simple, uneducated people who had the unhappy misfortune to be in the wrong place at the wrong time. These dubious accusations by the Fey are just the latest in a series of attempts to manipulate Celierian opinions and keep us frightened of nonexistent threats from the Eld. I urge you, my fellow lords, do not give in."

He turned to pin first Lord Barrial, then Teleos, with an unwavering look. "And if you find yourself still wanting to believe in the protection of the Fey, remember this: Our crops are failing this year. The late freeze destroyed the spring harvest in the north, while the floods wiped out half the wheat and corn in the south and east. The Fey, for all their vast magic, have done nothing to help us. Across the river, however, Eld has prospered. From our watch towers, we see daily caravans bursting with produce heading to market.

"Even if you don't trust the Eld, even if you cling to the old ways, can we, as responsible lords, turn our back on the opportunity to purchase food for winter? Do you think our starving tenants will care if the only meal on their table comes from Eld rather than Celieria?"

He spread his arms wide. "The Eld of non-Mage families are just people, like Celierians. Simple, mortal folk. They have come to us in peace and offered the hand of friendship. Can we not accept that they simply wish to live and prosper, as we do?"

"This is the opportunity to counter the influence of Fey magic upon us!" one of Sebourne's followers called out.

Lord Morvel stood up in agreement. "Lord Sebourne is right. Why do we concern ourselves with the memories of some centuries-old feud? The real question is, what is best for Celieria? Even if we did not need food for winter, where's the harm in giving the lords of Celieria an opportunity to profit from the export of our tradegoods to a new market?"

The doors to the Council Chamber burst open. A familiar voice called out, "To the contrary, Lord Morvel, Lord Sebourne could not be more wrong. The Eld are not your friends, and to think of them as anything but an enemy bent on your destruction is deadly delusion."

The lords shifted in their seats to stare at the newcomer, and a loud murmur of voices—some exultant, some outraged—rose up to fill the chamber.

Rain Tairen Soul had returned.

CHAPTER NINETEEN

❧

On mighty wings, the tairen soared through skies
  set flame by fiery roar;
Below, with bright and deathly grace, fought
  legions of the shining Fey.
So proud and fulsome fierce their stand 'gainst
  demon, Mage and witchly hand
That shei'dalins, in flowing red, wept for the brave
  immortal dead.
  —"The Battle of Eadmond's Field" from "Rainier's
    Song" by Avian of Celieria

It took a full ten chimes for Dorian to regain control over the
Council Chamber, and when at last the lords took their seats, he
turned to Rain, eyes snapping with temper. "My Lord
Feyreisen, the guards posted outside the doors of this chamber
were expressly ordered not to admit anyone. Yet here you are.
Explain yourself, ser."

"You invited me to address this Council, Your Majesty,"
Rain reminded him. "I have come to do so."

"Our invitation to speak was extended before we were
aware your people were harboring criminals wanted by the
crown. You know Gaelen vel Serranis was captured earlier this
morning, in the company of your truemate and the Fey?"

"I was informed of it a few chimes ago, as I approached the
city." He could see that the news had shaken Dorian's faith in
the Fey. «*I was not here when Dax and Marissya decided to keep
Gaelen's presence secret, Dorian, but in all honesty, I probably would
have done the same to avoid exactly this distrust and suspicion you
now harbor towards us.*»

"And were you also aware that the Dark Lord escaped before
he could be brought before this Council for questioning?" Annoura interjected. "Did the Fey perhaps have a hand in that?"

"The news does not surprise me. Vel Serranis has spent the last thousand years outwitting enemies far more wily and dangerous than a troop of King's Guards." He didn't even have to wonder where Gaelen would be. A bloodsworn warrior never wandered far from the woman to whom he'd sworn himself. *Unlike a certain unworthy truemate.* Rain grimaced. When this was over and he could go to Ellysetta, he knew he would have a long, hard road to earn back the trust he'd so cravenly thrown away last night.

Dorian was speaking again. Rain forced his attention back to the king and caught the last part of what he was saying. "—so, will you stand in vel Serranis's stead and answer any questions my lords ask of you?"

"I will not stand as a prisoner in *sel'dor* chains, if that is what you mean," Rain answered, "but I will answer the Council's questions as best I am able."

Dorian nodded. "Fair enough, My Lord Feyreisen."

"Your Majesty!" Sebourne protested. "You cannot be serious. We can't believe anything he says. The Truthspeaker is not here to confirm his words, and the Fey have already proven their gift for deception."

Rain glanced at the contentious lord and arched a disbelieving brow. "You wish to Truthspeak me? You spit on the Fey, attack us at every turn, yet still want to reap the benefits of our many gifts?" He laughed without humor. "The Fey have a word for foolish mortals like you. *Dravi'norah.* Maggot food."

"How dare you!"

"Calling a *rultshart* by its name is the least of what I dare, Lord Sebourne." Rain lifted one corner of his mouth, baring the edges of his teeth, and leaned forward. His pupils lengthened and widened as he sighted his prey. "You know very well the Fey are not half the enemy you claim them to be, else you'd not dare continue to taunt and torment us as you do, but I warn you, tairen are not so tolerant. Push me far enough, mortal, and this tairen will show his fangs." He turned his back on the man, ignoring his furious sputtering. "Ask your questions, King Dorian, then grant me the freedom to speak, as we agreed."

"Very well." Dorian ignored the furious Sebourne. "As you have reminded me, I did invite you to address this Council. Considering the gravity of the matter before us, we *will* listen to what you have to say, but first, let us address the matter of Gaelen vel Serranis. He admitted to slaying Celierians in the north. That is a fact not in dispute."

"Agreed. I was mistaken about that. Gaelen swore under *shei'dalin* touch that *dahl'reisen*, not the Eld, are indeed to blame for the dead villagers . . . but he also swore the ones he killed were Mage-claimed."

"As Lord Sebourne pointed out earlier," Annoura interrupted, "Mage-claiming is known to be undetectable. How can Gaelen vel Serranis be certain the ones he killed were, in fact, Mage-claimed?"

"Until last night, I believed as you do. No one—not mortal, Fey, Elf, or Danae—has ever known who is Mage-claimed until they act. But the *dahl'reisen* have discovered a way to do what we cannot. Gaelen says the ones he slew were in the service of the Mages. He swore it, under *shei'dalin* touch. I believe him, as should you."

Behind Annoura, Rain saw one of her little lapdog lordling's eyes go wide with fear. A similar but more somber concern was reflected in the faces of some of the lords who held land along the border. Unfortunately, those few were outnumbered by the many showing open doubt.

"There is more," Rain added. "Gaelen also warned us that Eld troops were gathering along the border."

"Oh, for the gods' sake," Sebourne exclaimed. "Must we listen to this propaganda? Gaelen vel Serranis—an admitted murderer—now claims he can detect the undetectable and see invisible Eld troops gathering across the Heras River. Your Majesties, this is an utter fabrication, and not even a credible one at that!"

"Is it?" Rain countered. "I, too, wanted to reject what Gaelen said. I wanted to hide from the truth, as Celieria has long been doing, but the tairen convinced me I could not. They reminded me that I have a duty, no matter how unpleasant or frightening it may seem, to defend the Fey and protect the world from Mage evil. They reminded me that I have a duty to my mate, and to her kin, and to the Fey-kin among you." He glanced at Dorian, Barrial, and Teleos, and said, "Tairen do not abandon their kin. Tairen defend the pride."

He turned back to Sebourne and pinned the man with a hard gaze. "I flew to the Eld border last night, Lord Sebourne. I crossed the Heras and scouted five miles deep into Eld, and what I saw confirmed Gaelen's claims. Those caravans bursting with produce you say you've watched pass by every day? They've been carrying more than vegetables. The Eld have been smuggling troops and armaments along the border, right under your noses. The villages have all been trenched and fortified. The Eld are preparing for war."

Several of the other border lords sat up a little straighter. How many of them, Rain wondered, had also watched the caravans from their own keeps and thought nothing of them?

Sebourne would not be swayed. "If the Eld have strengthened their defenses along the border, Worldscorcher, it's most likely because they learned that you"—he jabbed a finger at Rain—"are no longer safely locked away behind the Faering Mists!"

"That is a possibility," Rain agreed. "But can you afford to take the chance?"

Several seats down from Sebourne, Lord Darramon, one of the moderates of the Twenty, rose to his feet. "Even assuming the Mages have regrouped—and that is an unsubstantiated assumption—and even assuming the Eld have built up their troop strength along the border, why would they attack us now? Celieria has shown no aggression towards the Eld in centuries. What cause have we given them for war?"

Before Rain could answer, Teleos surged to his feet. "Why have the Eld ever attacked?" he called out. "For conquest. For power. For the glory of the real Dark Lord, Seledorn, God of Shadows."

"To destroy you and your defenses," Rain stated baldly. "Because Celieria is all that stands between them and the Fading Lands."

◆━━◆◆◆◆◆━━◆

"Why have you ceased your devotions, daughter?"

"I—" Ellysetta stopped herself before she asked the archbishop why he was weaving magic. "What kind of blessing is that, Father?" she asked instead.

He frowned in annoyance. "It is the traditional blessing of the Solarus required before the initiation of the Bright Bell. Now direct your attentions to your devotions, and allow me to continue. We cannot begin the Bright Bell until the chamber is blessed."

Ellysetta turned back to the altar and bowed her head. The familiar words fell from her lips by rote, but her attention remained focused on the archbishop as he circled the chamber.

She realized her mistake almost immediately. The archbishop wasn't weaving magic. It was the scepter in his hand. Just as the Fey had long ago cast a Fire-spell on the lamps of the city and a cleansing-spell on the waters of the Velpin, the archbishop's gold and crystal scepter—passed down through generation after generation of priests—contained magic. And the traditional "blessing" invoked the scepter's magic.

«Bel. Gaelen.» She wanted to tell them what she'd discovered, to ask if they could sense the weave, too.

Only silence answered.

She opened her senses, forcing down her own natural barriers in an attempt to examine the scepter's weave. What she found sent a chill down her spine.

Five-fold. The archbishop had enveloped the Solarus in a five-fold weave.

She was imprisoned in a cage of magic.

"Join me in the center of the room, daughter, so we may begin the Bright Bell of meditation and purification."

"Remove the blessing from the room, Greatfather."

The archbishop seemed genuinely surprised by the request. "I cannot unbless the chamber. And we cannot leave the Solarus until the Bright Bell is concluded. Now come, join me in the center of the room and prostrate yourself upon the Altar of Light."

She stood and faced him. "Not until you remove the five-fold weave you just constructed around this room."

Behind her, Lauriana gasped. "Ellysetta! Mind your tongue!"

The archbishop's face darkened. "I? Weave magic in this sacred chamber? How dare you accuse me of such blasphemy."

Her stomach clenched in a sick, terrible knot, but she stood firm. "Whether you intended to do so or not, Greatfather, you just wove a five-fold weave with that scepter. And I must insist that you undo it. Or give me the scepter, and I'll undo it for you."

He jerked the scepter back, well out of her reach. "You go too far, woman. Get yourself to the altar and beg the Bright Lord for forgiveness." One steely hand clamped around her wrist and he yanked her towards the altar.

The touch of his skin on hers bombarded her senses with the fury of thoughts he was projecting. Ellysetta didn't stop to think, she just plunged into his mind. Flinging open her senses, forging determination into an arrow of power, she forced past his deliberate barrage of thoughts and laid bare his mind.

Thoughts and memories assaulted her. Mama weeping, begging the archbishop for help to save her daughter's soul. His determination, his certainty that magic was evil and must be destroyed. His burning zeal to forge the young Fey queen into a beacon of Light for the Fading Lands. But first, he must strip her soul of the Dark Lord's magic. He must exorcise the demons from her soul.

A scraping groan of marble shifting on old, hidden tracks made Ellysetta's heart clutch. She spun to face the altar as its massive white bulk rolled backwards and slid into a deep pocket behind the marble wall to reveal a small, dark chamber at the top of a secret stair.

Greatfather Tivrest grabbed her in a tight, unyielding grip as three men in the hooded scarlet robes of exorcists stepped from the darkness into the white light of the Solarus.

"No!" She fought to escape the archbishop's surprisingly powerful grip. «*Bel, Gaelen, help me!*» Her Spirit weave dashed against the barriers enveloping the room and dissolved. She struggled furiously. Around the room, the flames in the sconces roared to life, leaping high, licking with angry, useless hunger at the marbled walls and ceiling.

The archbishop cried out, "She's burning me!"

One of the exorcists leapt forward and threw a dark rope round her shoulders. She cried out in pain as the hot rush of her magic curdled into agony. *Sel'dor.* The rope was threaded with it. She struggled, trying to free herself from the archbishop and the rope.

The second exorcist threw back his hood, revealing a stern face. "That's enough, girl," he commanded. "I am Father Lucial Bellamy, head of the Order of Adelis. We're not here to harm you. We're here to save your soul. But we can't have you endangering us all with your demonic powers." He pulled a pair of black metal cuffs from one pocket and approached.

"Mama!" Ellysetta cast a frantic, pleading look over her shoulder. "Mama, get help!"

But instead of looking shocked, her mother stood weeping, hands clasped tightly together.

"Mama?" Realization dawned too late.

"Don't fight them, kitling, please. Let them save your soul."

Ellysetta turned desperate eyes to her best friend. "Selianne?"

"I—" Selianne glanced at Lauriana, who shook her head frantically and grabbed Selianne's arm as if to stop her. When Selianne turned back, her face was set in a grim, fatalistic expression. "I'm sorry, Ellie. The Fey have bewitched you. This is for the best."

The exorcist snapped the *sel'dor* around Ellysetta's wrists. Pain drove her to her knees.

❧

"The Mages no doubt still remember how an alliance of Fey and Celierians once defeated them," Rain continued in the lull of silence, "and they will not want to make the same mistake twice. Why do you think they sent their ambassador to you with his offer?" He cast a long, sober glance around the chamber. "If they can convince you, our allies, that Fey magic and Fey might, which have always been used for good, are somehow more evil and threatening than the Eld; if they can convince you to accept their lies and false friendship and throw open your borders, you will soon find yourselves worshiping Seledorn and surrendering the souls of your children to the service of the Mages. They won't have to raze a single village to conquer you."

"Ridiculous fear mongering," Sebourne sneered. "Fabrications void of any hope of reliable proof. You lied about Gaelen vel Serranis. You lied about the murders in the north. You're lying about this as well. Your motive is obvious. Celieria has grown independent in your absence. We've become powerful in our own right. Your baseless claims and scare tactics are part of a pathetically transparent scheme to keep Celieria subservient to Fey power."

Teleos surged to his feet. "You fool!" he cried. "Have you not listened to a word he's said? We are in danger! The Fey do not lie! The enemy is at the gate, sharpening his blades!"

"The enemy," Sebourne replied sharply, pointing a finger at Rain, "is right there! This Tairen Soul has already shown himself willing to break Celierian treaties, manipulate Celierian minds, and murder his allies."

"Here, here, Sebourne," Morvel applauded. "Celierians won't cower in fear from Fey tales and bogey stories."

Rain stared in disbelief at the men leading the opposition. Had they forgotten so much? Had the last few centuries of peace erased the hard-taught lessons of the past from mortal memory? Fire sparked in his eyes. "I stand before you, a living witness to the Mage Wars and to the vast, unrepentant evil of Eld, and you call me a liar and dismiss my warnings as Fey tales and bogey stories?"

Show them, Ellysetta had urged. *Make them see Mage evil for themselves.*

His fingers curled tight. He'd already failed her once. He

would not fail her again. Magic gathered in a painful rush, burning his veins with its intensity. "Since I cannot make you listen, perhaps I can make you see. Behold! This is the past I remember, the past I lived."

Rain swept out his hands. Light shot from his fingertips, undulating beams that formed a glowing, expanding mass. The sounds of battle rose. The smell of burnt flesh, fresh blood, magic, and human sweat. Long-dead men and women—Fey, Celierian, Elf, Danae—unfolded in vivid, masterfully created life. *Shei'dalins* in flowing red veils worked beneath bright tents to save the wounded and weave peace upon the dying.

He could have simply immersed them all in the past, but he let his weave move slowly across the Council Chamber, enveloping the Celierian lords one by one until each of them stood on that ancient battlefield, every sight, smell, taste, touch, and sound re-created with breathtaking clarity. And as the Spirit weave took each lord, he poured into the man's mind vivid memories of all the events leading up to Mage Wars: the Eld machinations, the subtle corruptions, all culminating in the shocking brutality of a royal assassination, Gaelen's vengeance, and finally the ravaging ferocity of open war.

A blast of Mage Fire shook the earth. A score of pampered lordlings cringed in fear.

A fierce battle was under way. Several thousand Eld soldiers and two dozen Mages were defending a captured Celierian keep. Thick flows of dreadful magic rolled over the castle walls, forming a toxic, deadly mist that oozed across the battlefield towards the approaching army. Celierian soldiers shrieked as the mist enveloped them and their flesh literally fell from their bones. Armor tumbled in clattering heaps as the oozing, bloody bones of what had been men took one final, staggering step before crumpling in puddles of stinking slime. Not even the hungry demons howling across the battlefield would touch the foul soup that remained.

Fey, Elves, and Danae warriors raced towards the front line, magic sparking around them as they blew the acid mist back towards the keep and its surrounding dark armies. A hail of arrows dropped half the reinforcements as they bravely stood on the field and spun their defensive weaves. Demons consumed another two dozen in mere instants. On the ridge, trebuchets flung fiery missiles over the castle walls, and several hundred Elvish archers launched their own deadly accurate volley of arrows into the black-armored enemy ranks.

A deep, terrible roar sounded overhead. A shadow swooped over the warriors, bringing a hot, dark rush of air that carried the scent of tairen and fire and magic. Immense wings, spread wide as a city block, swept low over the battlefield as the giant winged cat dove in for his attack.

Rolling clouds of flame spewed from the tairen's great black muzzle, engulfing the line of robe-clad Mages. Shields sprang up around the Mages, but high-pitched screams erupted from the unfortunate unshielded soldiers nearby as flame clung to flesh and consumed with voracious appetite. Wings pumped, and the great cat reared back, holding the roaring jet of fire on the knot of shielded Mages.

A massive ball of Mage Fire shot towards the black tairen from his left flank.

"Rain! Behind you!" The shout came from several men all at once, Celierians and Fey, fighting together near the front of one allied line.

A second black tairen as large as Rain Tairen Soul swooped down, and a blast of tairen fire consumed the deadly Mage Fire before it reached Rain. The magnificent creature joined Rain, adding its powerful flame to the attack. Moments later, the Mage shields gave way, and half a dozen burning figures raced in frantic, futile madness from the inferno.

Eld horns sounded the call to retreat. Enemy soldiers poured over the keep walls and fled in chaotic disarray. A dozen tairen flew after the remaining Mages, flames licking at enemy heels, while Celierian and Danae infantry pursued the fleeing soldiers. From the surrounding forest, a hail of Elvish arrows filled the sky, raining down upon the fleeing troops. A black and silver line of Fey warriors blocked off the only remaining avenue of escape.

Scarcely a chime or two later, it was over.

In the ensuing silence, mortal, Fey, Elf, and Danae walked the battlefield, gathering fallen friends and comrades. They helped the wounded to the healing tents, and laid the dead in neat lines at the edge of the forest.

The two black tairen swooped down from the sky, metamorphosing at the last moment into tall, black-haired Fey warriors. Rain Tairen Soul and his father, Rajahl.

A Celierian wearing gold-chased silver armor wiped the blood off his sword with the hem of his blue cape and sheathed the blade at his side. Every Celierian in the Council Chamber recognized the crossed blades and crowned hawk of the Torreval royal family crest.

"My Lord Rajahl. My Lord Rain." Dorian II reached out to clasp arms with the two Fey. "Well fought, my lords."

Half a dozen mounted, mail-clad Celierian soldiers galloped in from the battlefield. One of the riders broke off from the group, guiding his horse towards the king and the two Tairen Souls. He pulled back on the reins and slid from the saddle with lithe, almost inhuman agility. His chest plate bore the Teleos family crest, a golden tairen rampant on the white field of a rising sun, honoring both their blood ties to the Fey and their devotion to the Church of Light.

"Your Majesty." The rider, Shanis Teleos, approached his king. He removed his helm, revealing Fey eyes of vivid green, shining bright in a face dark with blood and grime. Shanis dropped briefly to one knee in a swift, smooth bow. "The enemy is routed, sire." He straightened and turned to the Tairen Souls. "My Lord Rajahl, Rain." A smile flashed in his battle-grimed face as he and Rain exchanged handclasps. "My thanks for your help. We could not have claimed victory without you. Give us a quarter bell to recover our dead and wounded from the field before you burn the Eld."

"Be quick, my friend," Rain said. "An Elf scout spotted a suspicious caravan not two leagues from here. If there's a Primage or a Demon Prince among them, they'll soon be close enough to summon the souls of the dead. We don't have enough warriors to fight this army again in demon form. A quarter bell, and we fire the field."

"Understood."

"Sire!"

Dorian turned, a smile breaking over his face as he caught sight of the approaching knight. "Pellas! Cousin! I am glad to see you well and unhurt."

Lord Pellas, the king's cousin, didn't return his royal kin's smile. "I'm unhurt, yes, but our uncle's son Theron wasn't so fortunate. Come quick, sire. He lies near death. The *shei'dalin* does not think she can save him."

Dorian began to run.

As Dorian neared his waiting cousin, Lord Pellas's eyes darkened and the hand at his side curled tight around the long dagger at his hip, yanking it from its sheath.

"Sire! Beware!" Shanis cried the warning and leapt towards the king's cousin, blades flashing. He separated the assassin's head from his shoulders even as Rain and Rajahl's red Fey'cha thunked home with deadly accuracy in the man's chest.

"Pellas?" The king stared in horrified disbelief at the still-twitching, headless corpse of his cousin and at the blade still clutched in the dead man's hand.

"Did you not see his eyes just as he started to strike?" Shanis said. "They went black as night. I don't know how the Mages managed to turn him, sire, but he was Mage-claimed."

"I don't believe it. He's close as a brother to me."

Shanis pried the blade out of the dead man's hand. "This is a Feraz assassin's knife, sire. There is a hollow, poison-filled vein down the center of the blade. The tip is designed to break off inside the victim to release the poison." He planted a boot heel on the knife and snapped it in two. Three small drops of green liquid spilled onto the ground. The soil sizzled, wisps of smoke rising. Several handspans of trampled grass around the spot turned rapidly brown, then black.

"But . . . how is it possible? How could I not have known?"

"Do not torment yourself, King Dorian," Rajahl said. "'Tis likely the Mages stole his memories so he was not even aware himself. There is no warning of who is Mage-claimed, until they strike."

The Spirit weave faded. The ancient lords of Celieria melted into mist, and Rain turned once more to the nobles gathered in Dorian's Council Chamber.

"The Mages have returned. How many of them, I do not know. But I do know this: Where there are Mages, there are Mage-claimed. They could live among you, break bread with you, celebrate the marriage of your children, and share the most intimate moments of your life. And the instant the Mages call upon them, they will murder every member of your family while you sleep—slit the throats of the smallest sleeping babes—to please their masters.

"The Fey do not hunger for power—we never have—but the Mages do. Do not open the borders to Eld. To do so is to usher in your own destruction."

❧

Ellysetta crouched, panting. The fiery burn of *sel'dor* made every muscle tremble, but she forced her pain-wracked hands to move, fingers fumbling beneath her long skirts for the two bloodsworn Fey'cha blades strapped to her calves.

Her fingers closed round the hilts of both knives and she yanked them free.

"'Ware!" one of the exorcists cried. "She's got blades!" He kicked out, catching her manacled hands with the toe of his boot. The two Fey'cha flew out of her hands and skittered across the room.

Ellysetta scrambled back away from him, her skirts tangling around her legs, hiding her calves and the thin, parallel cuts oozing beads of red blood.

❧

Bel stood outside the Great Cathedral's Solarus door with the seemingly effortless stillness of a Fey warrior. Only his eyes moved, scanning the cathedral for the slightest hint of trouble. Beside him, Gaelen vel Serranis did the same.

At Bel's back, the utter silence emanating from the Solarus should have reassured him, but instead the tension humming through him intensified. He would have felt considerably better had Ellysetta sent him an occasional thought, just as the quintets stationed around the small island sent an update to him every ten chimes.

Suddenly every muscle in Bel's body stiffened. Beside him, Gaelen flinched as well.

Their eyes met in a fierce look, Fey First Blade to *dahl'reisen* leader, for once perfectly in accord. They turned in unison, hands raised, magic blazing to life, and loosed a joint five-fold weave powerful enough to turn the door into molten slag.

A concussion wave blasted back, flinging both of them and the rest of the quintet off their feet and smashing half a dozen pews into sawdust.

⚜

A soundless boom shook the Solarus, making the crystal chandeliers overhead shiver with a series of melodious, tinkling notes. Lauriana cried out in nervous fear.

The archbishop grabbed the edge of the altar to steady himself. "What was that?"

Father Bellamy cast a look at the Solarus door. "If I were to guess, I would say the Fey have realized what's going on in here and are trying to break in."

The archbishop blanched and took a nervous step away from the Solarus door. He cast an accusing gaze at Bellamy. "I thought you said they wouldn't be able to detect the exorcism!"

"They should not have. But either someone betrayed our plans or this young woman has found a way to breach the holy wards of the Solarus and alert her Fey friends to our presence."

The exorcist who'd kicked the Fey'cha out of Ellysetta's hand flipped back her skirt, baring the shallow, bleeding cuts on her leg. "The blades must have been bloodsworn," he spat. He shoved back his hood to reveal white-blond hair. "When she cut herself, she sent a call to the Fey who gave them to her."

"Let me go," Ellie urged in a shaking voice. "They'll kill you all for this. Let me go now, before anyone gets hurt." She stared hard into her mother's gaze. "Mama, I know you mean well, but this is wrong. I'm Fey. That's where my magic comes from, not from demons. I'm not evil. My magic isn't evil. Please, let me go before something terrible happens."

"Should we halt the exorcism?" Lauriana ventured.

"Where's your courage, woman?" one of the exorcists demanded. "Your daughter's soul is at stake. Surely that's worth a little risk on your part?"

"Do not fear, Madame Baristani," Father Bellamy soothed. He cast a repressive scowl at his underling. "The Fey cannot break through. This cathedral's Solarus was designed to withstand a direct assault by Mage Fire or a five-fold weave."

"I'm not concerned about myself, but I have two other children and a husband. There's nothing to protect them from Fey wrath. Greatfather Tivrest promised me the Fey would not know about the exorcism."

"Courage, madam. When we are done, the Fey will see your daughter is whole and unhurt, and they will have no reason to harm your family." Father Bellamy clasped a comforting hand on Lauriana's shoulder. "No great duty comes without risk, and saving your daughter's soul is the duty entrusted to you. Take comfort in knowing the Bright Lord rewards those who serve him with devotion."

✦

"My lords," King Dorian said, addressing the assembled lords, "the time has come to cast your votes. Lord Corrias"—he turned to his prime minister—"begin the roll call."

"Yes, Your Majesty." The prime minister opened his Council records book and turned to the voting logs. "The vote before the Council is the matter of the Eld Trade Agreement. Aye votes will tally in favor of passing the agreement into law. Nay votes will tally in opposition of the agreement. Lord Abelmar, how do you vote?"

In the upper reaches of the chamber, the young, recently entitled lord of a small fief near Swan's Bay rose to his feet. "Abelmar votes aye, ser."

✦

Bel sat up, rubbing his head. Flames scorch it; that had hurt. He and Gaelen should have put a hole in the wall large enough for a tairen to fly through, but considering the force of the recoil, it felt as though most of the energy had bounced right back at them.

«Ellysetta, are you all right?» He hauled himself to his feet. And froze in disbelief.

The Solarus door was not destroyed. It wasn't even scratched.

Gaelen growled a string of choice swear words. "The flaming room's been built to withstand a five-fold weave. It's warded against magic—and I'll wager beneath that gold finish, the door's entirely clad with *sel'dor*. Walls, too, probably."

«Fey! Ti'Feyreisa! Get those weaves down! Call Rain!» Bel flung the command outward to all his men on the cathedral's small island.

«Demons!» The cry came back across the common Fey weave. *«Rising out of the ground! Dozens of—»* The Fey weave dissolved abruptly.

An icy wind swept through the cathedral, and a faint, sickly sweet smell pervaded the nave. Cold, hissing laughter whispered in the gloom.

"Ah, *krekk*," Kieran muttered.

"We've got company," Gaelen said. He turned to face the long, shadowy nave, all five magics blazing to life at his fingertips. "Demon." Narrowed ice-blue eyes scanned the cathedral. "Make that two."

Bel's heart thumped heavily. It was a trap. And with the twenty-five-fold weaves surrounding the island, the Fey had woven their own cage.

He rapidly channeled every ounce of power he could summon into yet another weave. *"Chakor!* Five-fold weave, now!"

Even before he finished the first word, Kieran's powerful rope of Earth joined Bel's Spirit. Kiel's Water spun into the mix, then Fire and Air from Teris and Cyr.

«There's an active selkahr crystal by that small altar at the back of the nave,» Gaelen said. *«I'll circle around and destroy it so our friends here don't invite more company.»* The temperature in the room plummeted. *"Krekk."*

"What?"

"Add one very unfriendly *dahl'reisen* demon to the mix." Gaelen swore again. "Don't speak on the common path. He'll hear you. I've got to smash that crystal. Keep these fellows occupied."

Bel nodded. He'd fought demons before in the Mage Wars, but few of those deadly creatures were as dangerous as the spirits of *dahl'reisen* who'd surrendered their souls into dark service. "Go. We'll give you what cover we can. And hurry. The Feyreisa needs us." As Gaelen bolted off, Bel gathered his strength. "Remember, Fey . . . five-fold weaves only. Steel's useless. And for the gods' sake, don't let them touch you."

Bel didn't wait for the others to acknowledge his words. Two dark shapes gave a hissing screech and shot out of the shadows towards Gaelen. Bel grabbed command of the five-fold weave and flung a burning net to block their path. The demons shrieked as their formless evil sizzled against the shining webs of power.

***

«Rain! Bel! Gaelen! Someone help me!» Despite the *sel'dor* burning against her skin, Ellysetta flung desperate, pleading weaves of Spirit against all corners of the room, hoping the call might escape through some small chink in the magical cage imprisoning her.

"Be calm, daughter," Greatfather Tivrest said. "Do as Father Bellamy commands. Forsake your demon magic and put your faith in the Bright Lord."

"The magic my mother fears is my natural birthright, Father, not demon possession. You've got to believe me." She held his gaze. Her voice throbbed with earnestness and compulsion. Doubt entered the archbishop's eyes, and she pressed her advantage. "Look at me, Father. I'm telling you the truth. I was raised in the church. I celebrated my first Concordia here in this very city. I follow the Way of Light." Her breathing grew ragged as the manacles' burn intensified. "Let me go, Father. Don't do this to a child of Light."

A shadow darted in her periphery, followed by the crack of

flesh hitting flesh. Sudden, sharp pain set the side of her face aflame, bringing an abrupt end to her attempt at weaving a *shei'dalin's* compulsion. "Careful, Greatfather," cautioned the white-blond exorcist. "Even now, when you offer her mercy, she would steal your soul if she could." He slapped her again, this time with enough force to wrench her head to one side.

"That's enough, Nivane," Father Bellamy commanded. "Our goal is to drive the demons from her soul, not to brutalize her. There is a better way to silence her witch's voice." Bellamy gestured to the third, still-hooded man. "Gag her."

"Yes, Father." The third exorcist approached, a corked gag in his gloved hands. As he neared, Ellysetta's nose twitched in distaste. This exorcist reeked of onions and bacon, a smell she would forever associate with the despised Den Brodson. At that very moment, gloating satisfaction and hatred rolled over her in waves.

"Gods save me." She stared in horror at the third exorcist. He was close enough now that she could see beneath the shadow of his hood. Blue eyes surrounded by stubby black lashes stared back at her above a nose that had been broken more than once in childhood bully brawls. "He's no exorcist, Greatfather! He's De—"

The second exorcist, Nivane, grabbed her manacled wrists and pushed a small hidden button. Tiny spikes shot out all around the inside of the cuffs, piercing her skin. A scream strangled in her throat, cutting off her voice. "If you do not weave magic, the bracelets will not punish you," Nivane proclaimed loudly. "Cease your lies. Give up your unholy ways. Beg the Bright Lord to forgive your sins, and join him in the Light."

Ellysetta tried to force him back with a thrust of Earth and Air, but the instant she called magic, debilitating agony wreathed her wrists with fire and sent red-hot razors of pain vibrating up her arms.

Den grabbed her roughly and shoved the corked gag in her mouth. "You'll regret rejecting me," he hissed in her ear. "I would have honored you as my wife. Now I'll command you

as my whore." With his hands hidden from view by the folds
of his red robes, Den squeezed her breast so hard she could not
hold back a muffled cry. "Before I'm done with you, you'll
plead to lick my feet."

"Lay her on the altar," Father Bellamy ordered. "The
bracelets will contain her demons for the moment, but we
must hurry to begin the exorcism."

Hands grabbed her and lifted her off her feet. Her struggles
were no match for the four men as they carried her easily
across the short distance and laid her on the altar.

⸎

Gaelen skidded around a marble column. There, in the center of
the offering bowl on the altar of a lesser god, a dark *selkahr* crystal pulsed with forbidden power. A partially melted gold chain
surrounded the crystal. The *selkahr* must have been disguised as
some sort of pendant, the crystal itself lying dormant within its
camouflage until the activation spell had been triggered.

A smoky tendril darted between him and the altar. Gaelen
slammed to a halt, barely managing to keep himself from
plowing into the lethal shadow of the demon. Magic burst
bright around his hands. He threw a five-fold shield into the
creature's path. It wasn't as strong as the weave forged by Bel
and the other four masters of the Feyreisa's quintet, but it was
still powerful enough to make the *dahl'reisen* demon hiss and
shrink back.

Formless blackness shifted and coalesced into the familiar
dark form of a *dahl'reisen* warrior. Smoky, translucent shadow
blades were draped across the creature's chest and strapped to
its back, exactly where Fey steel would have been, and in its
dark, undulating face, two glowing red embers tracked Gaelen's every move. The shifting shadows of the creature's face
sharpened into focus, forming a clear, dark image of mouth,
nose, cheeks.

A Fey face. A familiar face. A warrior who'd been a long-
trusted Fey friend, dear to Gaelen even when they'd both been
outcast from the Fading Lands. Esan vel Morian, one of the
Brotherhood of Shadows who had traveled into Eld on Gae-

len's orders, never to return again. Gaelen's heart—so recently restored by Ellysetta's touch—felt as though it would break in two.

"Greetingsss, General," the demon hissed.

Rain stood in silence as one by one the lords of Celieria were called to vote. One by one, they stood and called out aye or nay. Three-quarters of the way through, his shoulders slumped. The majority of all undecided votes had been cast and tallied. He had failed.

The Eld would be coming to Celieria.

CHAPTER TWENTY

Father Bellamy set a small red leather case on one of the benches surrounding the altar and thumbed open the latch. Long, sharp needles, each topped by a small dark crystal, gleamed against ruby silk.

"Hold her still," he ordered.

Den, Nivane, and Greatfather Tivrest clamped down on Ellysetta's legs and her right arm. Father Bellamy pressed a hand hard against her left shoulder. "Forgive me, daughter. This will hurt, but it is for your own good. Adelis, Bright One, Lord of Light, drive the darkness from this soul." Chanting the prayer of exorcism, Father Bellamy plunged the first needle into her flesh.

Ellysetta's back arched, and she screamed against the corked gag. The needle wasn't steel or silver. It was *sel'dor*. Her flesh went cold around the puncture, and insidious runners of ice infiltrated her body, radiating outward. The dark crystal atop the needle began to flicker with deep ruby lights. She felt a terrible pull, as if the needle and the crystal that topped it were trying to draw her very soul from her flesh.

A choked cry came from the side of the room. Mama stood there, clutching Selianne, tears pouring down her face, one fist stuffed against her mouth. "Please, Ellie, please don't fight them. Trust your soul to the Bright Lord. Please, kitling."

Anger burst into hot life. Mama had betrayed her. Selianne had betrayed her. Greatfather Tivrest had betrayed her. The people Ellysetta should have been able to trust, the two women she'd loved most, had betrayed her.

A second needle pierced her right shoulder. She screamed again against the muffling gag. Her fingers splayed, then convulsed, fingertips pressing hard against unmoving marble and adding the tiny agonies of fingernails cracking and splitting to a far greater pain. Her soul felt as if it were being ripped apart.

The glacial cold had invaded her entire chest now. She gasped for breath, and her body shook uncontrollably. A dark, gloating sentience brushed across the edges of her mind, and she could have sworn she felt skeletal fingers dragging across the skin over her heart.

At the far end of the altar, Nivane watched her with eyes that, for a brief instant, glowed like twin firepits. Fathomless black, flickering with frightening red lights. White teeth flashed in a triumphant smile, and the familiar sibilant voice from her worst nightmares sounded in her mind. *Hello, girl.*

Stark terror flooded every part of her being.

Her heels shoved hard against the altar slab. Her tortured body writhed as she tried to scramble away from the exorcist's unholy eyes and the Shadow Man's hissing voice. Hands clamped down, holding her fast. Gloating laughter danced across her skin, vibrating along the ice-cold needles stabbing her flesh.

There was no conscious thought in her reaction. No control. No magic weave. Only stripped-down, bare, primal instinct. Ellysetta's mental shields shredded, and absolute terror gave voice to a silent, preternatural scream.

«*Rain! Shei'tan! Help me!*»

⁂

Shock stole Rain's breath.

His heart stopped in mid-beat. Around him, it seemed as if time itself had stopped. Every person in the Council Chamber froze in place, utterly silent, utterly still. For one instant, nothing in the universe existed except a single, desperate, terrified cry.

A soul crying out directly to his.

Her soul.

«Rain! Shei'tan! Help me!»

For one brief instant, she was there, sharing his mind, his thoughts, his entire being.

And then she was gone.

"No." His hands trembled. His blood froze with fear. "No."

There was a great round skylight in the ceiling above Dorian's throne. Without conscious thought, deaf to the shocked cries of the mortals around him, Rain crossed the chamber in three Air-powered leaps and vaulted over the royals seated on the raised dais. A burst of strength and magic sent him exploding skyward. He smashed through the window as Fey and emerged on the other side of the shattered glass as tairen.

Fire scorched the sky as Rain Tairen Soul rocketed towards the Great Cathedral of Light.

Gaelen stared in dismay at the shifting, shadowy demon-visage of his comrade in arms.

"Esan, my blade brother, how did this happen?"

"Doesss it matter, General?" the demon hissed. "I ssserve and ssso you die." A lethal demon blade shot out, slicing hard and fast. Only reflexes honed by centuries of battle allowed Gaelen to dodge the deadly kiss of Esan's blade. Behind him, the sounds of battle filled the cathedral nave as Bel and the rest of the quintet engaged their two demons.

Gaelen drew the long, shimmering length of one *seyani* blade from its scabbard.

The demon laughed. "Ssssteel hasss no power over me."

"Perhaps not." The blades flashed with sudden brightness as Gaelen spun into the Cha'Baruk form called the Song of Death. "But the five-fold threads I've woven around it certainly do." Steel whistled through the air and sliced through the demon's midsection. The creature cried out, and his insubstantial form wavered.

Gaelen took advantage of Esan's shock and distraction to slam a five-fold weave into the *selkahr* crystal. The dark stone exploded in a shower of dust, and the demon portal collapsed. There! At least no other old friends or enemies would come to join the fight.

A hissing screech and a rush of cold air were the only warning he received as the demon swooped towards him. Gaelen spun round and fell back upon one knee, sword and five-fold shields raised to meet the *dahl'reisen* demon's attack. Sparks exploded around them as magic and demon swords clashed.

Esan was a Fey from the powerful vel Morian line, and for nearly fifteen hundred years he'd also been a close friend and sparring partner. He'd been one of the few Fey capable of laying the sharp edge of his blade on Gaelen's skin. Alive, that posed little problem. A little torn flesh and a bit of blood never robbed Gaelen of victory in the end. But now, the sharp edge of Esan's demon blades held the promise of death more swift and sure than even red Fey'cha. Gaelen couldn't afford the luxury of a single mistake.

He met Esan's split-second lunge with a lightning-fast parry and attack. With his steel serving as an anchor for his five-fold weaves, Gaelen didn't have to divide his concentration or expend vast amounts of energy to maintain his weaves. He could instead concentrate on the swordplay at hand, and at the moment, that was a very good thing.

Esan had never accepted defeat easily. Even as a demon, that much had not changed. Each clash of blades shivered down Gaelen's arms and rattled his back teeth. Esan was not holding back his blows. This was no friendly sparring match; it was a fight to the death.

Gaelen had to work hard simply to survive each passing chime. He ducked and danced, leaping lightly from altar to floor to pew, spinning from one fluid form of Cha'Baruk to another. His swords flashed in ever-moving arcs of beauty and death. Esan countered every blow.

"We must end this, my friend." Each moment that passed put Ellysetta's life in greater danger. "I can free you from this dark service, Esan." Negotiating with a demon was futile, Gaelen knew. Yet some stubborn, unrelenting remnant of Fey loyalty made him try. This corrupt soul that now attacked him had once been a beloved friend and blade brother with a soul as bright as it now was dark. "Come, my brother; if any hint of Fey still remains in your soul, cease this battle and let me grant you peace."

The demon snarled and advanced, blades flashing.

Gaelen countered with the whirling strokes of the Ring of Fire, but Esan's attack was too fierce, too punishing. It drove him back, and he stumbled over an uneven tile in the floor. For a split second, Gaelen's perfect form faltered. He held his blades too far apart—barely a handspan too much, but that was all the opening the demon needed.

The shadow blade sliced down with lethal accuracy.

And clashed in a shower of sparks against a shining, magic-girded *seyani* sword.

"Your bladework's good, but your footwork could use a little practice." Kieran smirked.

"Cheeky git." Gaelen drove his five-fold-powered swords deep into the *dahl'reisen* demon's heart. The demon wailed and writhed as beams of magic pierced its darkness, sundering the grip of evil that held Esan's soul in thrall. Gaelen poured power into his weaves. The shadowy figure shimmered, its dark, smoky form growing ever more translucent, like mist burning off in the Great Sun's light.

"Go with peace, my brother. May the gods illuminate a path to guide you back into the Light." When the last shadowy remnant of the demon faded, Gaelen leaned against a wall, resting his head on the back of his hands, and sucked in several deep, restorative breaths.

"No time for napping, Uncle!" Kieran chided. "We've got work to do!"

Gaelen forced himself back to his feet and sprinted after Kieran to join the others, who were once again weaving a five-fold assault on the Solarus door. "When this is done, puppy, and the Feyreisa is safe behind the Mists, I'm going to teach you respect for your elders." He gave his sister's son a smile dark with promise.

Kieran grinned. "You can try."

"I never just try." Tossing back the long strands of his hair, Gaelen frowned at the quintet's five-fold weave. "That's not going to work, vel Jelani. Five-fold isn't enough." His eyes met and held the Fey general's. "Six-fold is her only chance. Will you stay your blades?"

Bel's mouth went grim. "Weaving Azrahn is a banishing offense."

"Save her first. Banish me later. Just don't stab red in my belly until after we break through. Agreed?"

Bel searched the former *dahl'reisen's* eyes for any hint of treachery but found only honest, stoic intent. "Agreed," he said.

The next instant, an icy chill emanated from Gaelen, and Bel's back teeth ached from the sudden cold and sickly sweet smell as a sixth rope of power formed.

Azrahn.

Bel couldn't stop the instinctive clutch of horror that made him recoil a step from Gaelen. The former *dahl'reisen's* ice-blue eyes had turned pure black, sparkling with red lights like deep, smoldering fire pits. Those nightmare eyes met his gaze for an instant, then turned to concentrate on the spiraling weave of forbidden magic gathering in Gaelen's hands.

Bel had never been this close to a Fey weaving Azrahn.

Fey law demanded Gaelen's banishment or his death.

Instead, Bel opened his weave and let the *dahl'reisen* add the ominously pulsing rope of dark power into the weave.

"Hold steady, Fey. Tighten the weave." Shining threads condensed, magic concentrating into lines of blazing light. "Aim for the hinges. Now!"

The six-fold weave, a thick line of pure power, shot out. The door frame screeched and sparks flew as weave met enchanted metal. For several seconds, the first hinge resisted the Fey assault, spitting defiant sparks and radiating scattered destructive slivers of the weave in all directions. But strong as the magic-resistant construction of the Solarus door was, the concentrated assault of their weave, strengthened even further by that deadly sixth thread, was stronger. Slowly—far too slowly for Bel's liking—the metal of the first hinge began to bubble, and then to melt.

We're coming, Ellysetta. Hang on. Bel didn't dare spare even a flicker of Spirit from his weave to send the thought.

❦

Ellysetta floated in a cool, dark void, enveloped in utter silence, free from all pain. Was this death? Or had the agony of the exorcists' torture merely driven her mad?

A chuckle sounded in the darkness, the gloating sound sliding over her like a snake.

She spun in blind panic, seeking the source of the laughter, her frantic gaze finding only darkness all around her. She tried to flee, but the laughter pursued her. Mocking. Triumphant.

"We meet again, Ellysetta."

Her heart clutched with familiar terror as the Shadow Man's voice hissed across her senses.

"Show yourself, coward!" she challenged.

The darkness surrounding her lightened. Utter blackness became depths of gray. In it, she could make out a shadowy figure, tall and robed. A sash covered with dark, glittering jewels was tied about his waist, and beneath the hood shone a gleam of pallid, cadaverous flesh. Red flashes of light sparked from the darkness of the hood above bloodless lips. Fresh panic nearly overwhelmed her.

"Rain was right, Shadow Man. You are a Mage."

More laughter. "Not 'a' Mage, child. 'The' Mage. I am Vadim Maur, the High Mage of Eld, the greatest Mage who has ever lived."

Ellysetta turned and ran.

❦

«*Ellysetta! Shei'tani!*» In the few seemingly interminable chimes it took to fly from palace to cathedral, Rain continu-

ously called to Ellysetta on the Spirit path and tried to dupli-
cate the call on the same, deeper, soul-to-soul path she had
used. She didn't respond.

Massive twenty-five-fold weaves still enveloped the Isle of
Grace in a dome of impermeable magic. He circled the dome,
looking for a weak spot. His tairen vision saw the flows of
magic easily, every strand a vibrant, pulsing rope of power.

There.

He found a spot where the weave was thinner, and a tiny
square where the threads themselves were only four-ply. Someone had started to unravel the weaves here.

Rain filled his tairen lungs with air. A strong twenty-five-
fold weave could resist tairen flame for quite a while. A four-
fold weave could not.

Wings pumping, he reared back, hovering over the weak
spot in the weave, and exhaled. A fine spray of venom from his
fangs mixed with tairen breath and tairen magic ignited just
inches from his muzzle. An enormous jet of flame roared forth.

More like Fey Fire than simple match-to-tinder, tairen flame
could burn anything in its path: wood, rock, metal, flesh, even
magic.

The small, four-fold patch burned quickly, leaving a hole too
small for a tairen to fit through but just wide enough for a lean
Fey king.

Rain's tairen form dissolved. His Fey form plunged neatly
through the opening, falling freely, rapidly. He waited until the
last possible moment to summon a slide of Air to break his fall
and landed running.

<hr/>

Weeping, Lauriana watched her daughter's tortured form and
prayed for forgiveness. She'd witnessed at least part of the first
exorcism when Ellie was a child, but this was a hundred times
worse. The way Ellie screamed, as if her very soul was being
ripped from her body . . .

She was quieter now. Her screams had tapered off to a
moaning, delirious ramble after Father Bellamy inserted the
eighth of the required twelve needles. Her body was shivering

violently, making the needles at her knees, thighs, hips, and shoulders tremble, and she was breathing in shallow, shuddering gasps.

Lauriana pressed her hands to her lips. *Oh, Ellie, dearling, forgive me. I never wanted to hurt you. I only wanted you safe.*

A muffled roar filled the Solarus, quiet at first, then growing louder. Greatfather Tivrest cast a frightened glance over his shoulder. "The Fey! They're breaching the Solarus door! Flaming hells, Bellamy! I thought you said they couldn't break through."

Father Bellamy stared at the melting metal. "That's impossible! I saw the ancient designs myself. This Solarus was built to withstand a direct assault by a five-fold weave."

"But not a six-fold weave," Nivane said. "Someone out there is weaving Azrahn."

Lauriana's lungs stalled. The Fey were breaking in? Dread shivered down her spine. The archbishop had promised her the Fey would not be able to detect the exorcism, and he'd been wrong. He'd promised her the Fey could not break in, and now it seemed he'd been wrong about that too. She had witnessed the Fey's fierce defense of Ellie. They would not treat kindly anyone who brought her harm. Gaelen vel Serranis had once murdered an entire family line for the actions of only one member. Oh, gods, what had she done?

"There's not much time, then. We must exorcise what demons we can." Father Bellamy reached for the ninth needle.

"You're right, Father," Nivane agreed. "There's not much time. Not enough to continue with this charade in any event."

Before Father Bellamy could do more than look up in surprise, Nivane plunged a black dagger in his back. On the other side of the altar, the third exorcist drew another blade from within his robes and drove it between the archbishop's ribs.

Lauriana screamed. "Dear gods! You've murdered them!"

"I do love a keen sense of the obvious," Nivane sneered.

"No one ever claimed she was the brightest candle in the lamp. But at least she came in useful." The third exorcist threw back the hood on his robe, revealing an all-too-familiar face.

Lauriana clutched her throat. "Den? Den Brodson? What's the meaning of this?"

Den gave a dark smile. "I'm fulfilling my vow, madam. I'm claiming what's mine. Thank you, by the way, for all your help in making it so convenient for me."

For the first time, Lauriana saw Den for what he truly was— not the brutishly handsome son of a friend or a potential suitor for her daughter's hand, but as a sneering, cold-eyed manipulator who'd stop at nothing—not even murdering the Archbishop of Celieria—to get what he wanted. "Ellie was right about you all along. You *are* a filthy little toad."

Den's face darkened with a scowl. He turned to Nivane. "Let me kill her," he urged.

"Not unless she gives us no other choice. The master wants her alive. He thinks she may yet come in handy."

Lauriana clutched Selianne's arm. "Selianne," she whispered urgently, "we've got to stop them. We've got to save Ellie."

Her spine went rigid at the feel of a cold, sharp blade pressed against her ribs. She turned a shocked, disbelieving gaze on the girl she'd all but helped raise. "Selianne?"

"I'm sorry, Madame Baristani. I can't let you interfere."

"No." Lauriana's lips trembled as she whispered the denial. "Not you, too. Ellie loves you like a sister. How could you betray her?"

"How could *I* betray her? Oh, Madame Baristani, what is it you think *you've* done?" Selianne's face twisted in anguish. "They have my babies. They vowed to kill them if I didn't help them. You, of all people, know there's nothing a mother wouldn't do to save her child."

"They who? Who's behind this?"

"The Mages of Eld."

At last, too late, Lauriana realized how completely she'd been duped. They'd discovered her greatest fear and played expertly on it, convincing her that Ellysetta's soul was in danger. All Selianne's visits, her whispered worries, had been designed to feed Lauriana's fears so she would lead her daughter into this trap.

Everything Rain vel'En Daris had said was true. The Mages were at work, and they would do anything to capture Ellie. They would turn Ellie's friends—and even her own mother—against her.

Instead of saving Ellie, Lauriana had betrayed her in the worst possible way.

Darkness whirled past Ellysetta, but if there was ground beneath her racing feet, she did not feel it. When she stopped running, the High Mage was still there, a malevolent shadow among shadows, a chilling breath of ice down her back.

"Any hope of escape is futile," he whispered. "No one will come to your rescue. Everyone has betrayed you. Your mother, your friend, the Tairen Soul. You are all alone."

"Not everyone has betrayed me," she retorted. "Gaelen and Bel haven't. They're out there fighting for me even now. They will save me."

"Will they? Do you think they did not sense the exorcist hiding in the Solarus? Or read your mother's and the archbishop's intentions in their unguarded thoughts? They knew what was in store for you, and they wove a cage of magic around you to ensure you could not escape."

For one instant, her certainty faltered. Was it possible? Her heart fluttered in her breast, and doubt stabbed her like an icy dart.

"Why would they do that?" she challenged weakly. She was ice cold and shivering. Some dark, invisible force was pulling at her, tugging her towards the Mage like steel to a lodestone. She resisted the pull, but her efforts were sluggish and exhausting.

"Because they know what you are. *My child*, Ellysetta. My daughter. My greatest achievement. The child I created to destroy the Fey."

"Liar." She tried to laugh, but the chattering of her teeth ruined the effect. She felt so cold, as if all the warmth of the world had been siphoned away. "You outwitted yourself, Mage. *Sel'dor* doesn't burn Eld flesh, but it burns mine. I'm no daughter of yours, and the Fey know it, despite your trying to convince them otherwise."

She'd hoped to rattle him, but it didn't work. "You think in such common, limited terms," he sneered. "Any mongrel dog can breed a whelp. Where's the genius in that? I'm talking about siring something far greater than flesh."

Cold winds swirled around her. Icy, invisible fingers tugged and poked and prodded, seeking every weakness in her defenses, leeching away her resistance, her hope.

"Your soul, girl. I'm the father of your soul. I created it, and now I've come to claim it."

On the lawn surrounding the cathedral, Fey warriors battled what appeared to be an army of demons. Many—too many—warriors lay dead or dying on the ground, and the others fought a grim battle for their lives.

As Rain ran, he saw yet another demon rising out of the ground and tasted the cold sweetness of Azrahn. He slammed a concentrated five-fold weave at the spot, and the *selkahr* crystal buried there exploded.

«*Fey, follow the scent of Azrahn. Selkahr crystals are buried in the ground. Destroy them to close the demon gates. Miora Felah ti'Feyreisa!*»

"*Miora Felah ti'Feyreisa!*" The shout echoed from all corners of the embattled isle.

Rain took the cathedral steps four at a time and burst through the carved double doors leading to the nave.

In one glance, he took in the shattered altar to the left of the door, the unmistakable signs of battle, and the group of six Fey weaving powerful magic at the back of the nave. Frost was forming on the pews near Gaelen, and the entire cathedral was filled with a sweet smell so thick Rain's stomach churned. The former *dahl'reisen* was weaving deliberate, powerful Azrahn.

Rage rose up inside Rain. A billowing gray mist surrounded him, sparking with the powerful magic of the Change.

A tremendous roar shook the cathedral, filtering through the small breach in the Solarus shields and making the crystal sconces rattle. Lauriana flinched and cried out.

"The Tairen Soul has arrived," Nivane said. He raised a

brow. "I wonder if he'll scorch the Fey wielding Azrahn, as Fey law dictates."

The second hinge melted, and now scorching tongues of tairen flame licked voraciously at the door frame. A sardonic smile twisted Nivane's mouth. "Apparently not. So much for Fey law. Grab the girl and let's go."

Den bent down to grab Ellie, then hesitated when she moaned and her eyelids fluttered. "She's waking up."

"She's got enough *sel'dor* in her now to be no trouble to us. Pick her up. I'll open the portal." Nivane yanked the long, wavy-edged Mage blade from Father Bellamy's back and dragged the exorcist's crumpled form to the far side of the room.

He gave a short laugh and glanced back at Den. "The Guardians are so used to pocket-sized bits of flesh, Bellamy will be quite a banquet for them." He jabbed the Mage blade deep into the dead man's chest. The large, dark crystal in the pommel of the knife flickered with ominous red lights.

Nivane backed several paces away from the body, and Lauriana heard him murmur something in a foreign tongue. The dead priest's body began to smolder. A small black pinprick formed in the air above. Dark shadows swept out of the small opening, hissing and circling around the body.

━━━━∽≈⊱⋅⊰≈∽━━━━

Ellysetta cried out at the sudden familiar sensation of ice spiders crawling over her flesh. The feeling was much stronger than ever before.

"You see?" the Mage whispered. "You can feel it, can't you? The darkness in your soul. The great gift I gave you when you were still a child in your mother's womb. Open yourself to it, girl. Embrace it."

«Do not heed him.» A strong voice, familiar yet not, penetrated her consciousness. A man's voice. *«Don't grant him access to your soul. He uses your fears to hold you here when those you love most need you. Look at the truth he hides from you.»*

Faint light penetrated the shadows enveloping her. The Solarus stretched out below her, as if she were perched above the chamber looking down through a tinted glass.

"You!" the Shadow Mage hissed. "You will regret your interference."

Ellysetta cried out at the sight of Selianne holding Mama at knifepoint. Greatfather Tivrest lay sprawled on the marble floor, a knife protruding from his back. Den was hefting Ellysetta's own limp body over his shoulder.

And Father Bellamy . . .

The exorcist was obviously dead, his mouth open in a soundless scream. Above him, a dark shadow widened like a gaping maw.

In the swirling shadows, Ellysetta caught frightening glimpses of wild eyes, gnashing teeth, and wide, bloody mouths. She watched in horror as the priest's body was torn to shreds before her eyes. Flesh peeled back from bones. Blood sprayed up in unnatural red fountains. Bones splintered and turned to swirling white powder. Clicking, hissing, slurping, the demons consumed every last scrap of Father Bellamy's body and soul. In seconds, all that remained was a shredded red silk tunic, sucked dry even of bloodstains.

Above the remains, the dark hole widened rapidly and formed what appeared to be a doorway leading into utter blackness. The demons pulled back to frame the doorway, hissing, their formless shapes undulating like deadly shadow snakes.

The second exorcist, Nivane, motioned, and after a brief hesitation, Den walked towards the drowning blackness of the portal. Weeping, Mama stumbled towards it as well, prodded forward by the knife in Selianne's hand.

Ellysetta heard what sounded like a muffled groan, and a sudden sharp pain in her chest made her cry out.

"Listen to me, girl." The High Mage's voice was back, but where there had been crooning seduction, now there was cold command. "Everyone you love has betrayed you. No one is coming to help. They've all abandoned and reviled you. You are alone. Your struggles only postpone the inevitable. You cannot hope to stand against me."

The oppressive weight of his will pressed hard against her own, urging her to give up and let the inevitable happen. She wavered on the knife's edge of surrender; despair washed over her in steady, unrelenting waves. She was no warrior, the despair whispered. She had neither the skills nor the strength to defeat him.

«*No, child,*» a second voice urged. This time, it was a woman's voice, throbbing with encouragement. «*Do not heed him. The ones you love are near. Your mate is with them. They fight for you. You must not surrender. If you let the Evil One claim you, your mate will die, and without him, nothing can prevent the Evil One from destroying your soul. Fight him, child. For your mate. For your soul. Fight him for all the lives he has destroyed.*»

«*Ellysetta! Shei'tani!*» Rain's call flared across her senses, a bright, warm light blooming in the icy darkness.

The pain of the exorcism and betrayal had driven her here, to this shadowy realm. The High Mage had kept her distracted, filling her mind with doubts, playing on her fears. But now, revitalizing energy filled her, a wellspring of renewed hope.

Rain. He'd come back.

"Do not listen to those foolish creatures!" the Mage cried. "You cannot stop what is happening. Do not fight it. Let yourself go."

"No!" she shouted defiantly. The shadow world fell away in a dizzying rush. Her senses flooded back to her, nerves howling, *sel'dor* burning like live coals embedded in her flesh.

She woke screaming.

CHAPTER TWENTY-ONE

Shrouded by the long, wild mass of her hair hanging in her face and blinded by pain, Ellysetta struggled to find her bearings. Den had slung her over one beefy shoulder, with no regard for the way his every motion drove the *sel'dor* needles deeper into her flesh, scraping metal against bone. Eight searing needles, each one topped by a voracious, evil crystal, fought to consume her blood and soul.

She hung on to consciousness by will alone. If she let them take her into the Well, she—the person who was Ellysetta—would never return.

«Ellysetta! Shei'tani!» Rain's call pierced the fractured shields surrounding the Solarus, and she almost wept with relief. Never had a sound been so welcome.

"We're out of time. Get her into the Well, now!" Nivane cried.

Den sped up, rounding the corner of the altar table. Ellysetta's hair dragged across one of the velvet-topped marble benches. And there, still open, its evil implements winking in the bright light of the Solarus, sat the exorcist's leather case.

Her hand shot out. Her fingertips snagged the corner of the case lid, and she yanked it towards her. Half a dozen needles spilled to the floor, but she managed to snatch up a handful of the torturous implements before she lost her grip on the case.

With every ounce of strength she possessed, she drove the razor-sharp points into the back of Den's leg.

The butcher's son howled and dropped to his knees, spilling Ellysetta onto the floor. She landed hard. Her head cracked against the marble floor with enough force to leave her dizzy.

"Scorching thrice-damned slut!"

Ellysetta forced her eyes open. Den Brodson was sprawled on the floor nearby, his torso twisted around as he tried to pull a handful of needles out of his leg.

"Don't pull those out, you fool." The pale-haired exorcist snapped the order. "You can't enter the Well bloody. You'll drive the demons into a frenzy. *Sel'dor* wounds don't bleed as long as the metal stays in the flesh." Muttering a curse, Nivane started towards Ellysetta. "I'll get the girl," he barked. "Selianne, get the mother into the Well."

Mama. Ellysetta caught a glimpse of her mother's tear-stained face and the knife at her ribs. Ellysetta yanked the gag out of her mouth. "Selianne, no!" She scrambled back as Nivane approached. "Don't listen to them! Fight them! Don't let them use you for evil!"

"Don't waste your breath," Nivane sneered. "She traded her soul to the High Mage's apprentice, and through him to the High Mage himself. And now, my dear, it's time for you to renew your own acquaintance with the great Master Maur."

Her fingers ripped at the *sel'dor* needles at her hips and thighs. The needles fought extraction, causing excruciating pain as she pulled them free. One . . . two . . . by the third, she was screaming. She flung the needles away and reached for another.

"Foolish girl. Do you really think that will help you?"

"You can't take me into the Well bloody, can you?" she countered raggedly. "And without *sel'dor*, my wounds will bleed."

Nivane reached for her leg. She kicked out, but he grabbed her ankle and yanked her towards him. "True. But that just means I get the pleasure of piercing you myself."

She kicked again, catching Nivane's jaw with the edge of

her foot. His head snapped back, and blood dribbled from the corner of his mouth.

"*Petchka!*" His fist shot out. Pain exploded across the left side of her face, and the force of the blow sent her skidding backwards across the slick marble floor and halfway under the altar table. Her hands tangled in the bloody folds of Greatfather Tivrest's robes, and her fingers brushed against something hard and cold.

The scepter.

Tivrest's crystal-topped scepter, which he'd used to generate the five-fold weave around the chamber.

She was a long way from understanding the intricacies of magic, but she'd spent a lifetime reading Fey tales and Fey poetry. Crystals were objects of power. If Rain could close a demon portal by smashing the crystal that summoned it, it only stood to reason that smashing the scepter's crystal would destroy the five-fold weave it had created.

She tried to grab the scepter, but Nivane pulled her out from under the altar before she could get a good grip. She screamed as he plunged an exorcist's needle back into the bleeding wound at her hip.

«*Mama!*» Her body arched in torment as *sel'dor* punished her use of Spirit. «*The archbishop's scepter! Smash it! Hurry!*»

"Brodson, you sniveling porgil," Nivane snapped, "grab those needles and get over here. Help me plug her wounds."

From the corner of her eye, Ellysetta saw her mother break free of Selianne's grip and lunge towards the archbishop's body. Lauriana grabbed the scepter and lifted it high.

As she brought it smashing down towards the unforgiving marble of the altar, Selianne snatched the scepter from her grasp and gave a brutal shove that sent Lauriana sprawling. Her head cracked hard against the edge of the altar table, and her body crumpled to the floor, where she lay motionless.

"Mama!" Ellysetta tried to crawl to her aid, but Nivane still held her ankle and Den was limping towards them, gathering the needles she'd pulled out of her body as he approached.

A cold smile curved Selianne's lips. "A worthy effort," she said, but the voice that issued from her lips was not her own. "What strength you possess, to weave such powerful Spirit despite the amount of *sel'dor* in your flesh. I daresay twenty rings will not be enough to hold you. My master has done well indeed."

A loud thud boomed through the Solarus as something rammed hard against the door. The door shuddered and began to give way. Selianne—or rather, the creature controlling Selianne—cast a backwards glance.

"Nivane, Brodson, have done with your fumbling. Bind her remaining wounds tight. Even with the scepter's weave intact, it won't be long before the Fey break through. I am coming to you now. Bring the girl to me in the Well!"

Ellysetta glimpsed what looked like glittering stars moving in the darkness of the Well of Souls. As the lights drew closer, she realized the stars were actually reflections off the collection of jewels fastened to the sash of an Elden Mage. He was approaching the Solarus.

There was no time left. She turned back to Selianne. The awful, mocking black eyes stared back at her from her friend's face.

Ellysetta's teeth clenched, and her muscles drew instinctively tight. Waves of torment shuddered through her as she reached for her magic. *Please, gods, help me.*

"Smash the scepter, Selianne!"

Every needle in her flesh shivered, and each tiniest tremble sent bolts of discordant energy stabbing through her body. The threads of her magic, never cooperative to begin with, bucked and fought her will only to unravel helplessly as *sel'dor* worked its evil. Screaming in torment, Ellysetta redoubled her efforts. She could feel the barriers in her mind rebelling against the call, restricting the flow of her power even as *sel'dor* punished her for the attempt.

Writhing, she shrieked aloud, "Gods help me!"

She felt a tiny snap, like a soap bubble popping on the skin. An ephemeral wisp of cool, sweet, tingling magic breathed through her. An unfamiliar thread, untouched by the bane of *sel'dor*, throbbing with power.

She seized it, formed it, and thrust it into Selianne's mind with a dagger-sharp command.

Selianne's head reared back. Black eyes flickered, darkness fading to bright, familiar blue. Horror and confusion were etched upon Selianne's face. "Ellie?"

"Smash the scepter's crystal, Selianne!"

"Ellie . . . I . . ." Selianne put a hand to her head. Already her eyes were darkening again.

"For the gods' sake, do it! Quickly!" Ellysetta pushed the compulsion deeper, only to reel back in sudden terror and comprehension as she brushed against Vadim Maur's familiar evil, gloating consciousness.

Excellent, wonderful girl, he hissed.

She had a split-second image of a pale, triumphant face and glowing silver eyes. A voice murmured words in a tongue she did not know. A phantom blade plunged deep into her chest, piercing her heart with ice. She shrieked in denial as the terrible dark descended upon her.

<hr />

Lauriana stirred. Dazed consciousness returned, girded with nauseating pain. Dear, sweet Lord of Light.

She heard Ellie's voice cry out, "Smash the scepter, Selianne! For the gods' sake, do it! Quickly!" And then she heard a terrible scream. Ellie's scream.

Lauriana's eyes snapped open.

Her daughter lay on the Solarus floor, weeping brokenly. Blood smeared her gown where she had yanked out half a dozen of the exorcists' needles in defiance of her attackers, but her fierce resistance was over.

Sel'dor manacles clanked against stone as Nivane and Den grabbed Ellie's arms and hauled her to her feet. She dangled limply between them, her head lolling forward on her neck.

"Time to take you home, girl." A man Lauriana didn't recognize stepped out of the gaping black portal into the light of the Solarus. He was dressed in long, flowing scarlet robes, a sash studded with sparkling jewels tied round his waist. Memories of childhood lessons and picture books filled with illustrations of evil magic wielders gave her a name to put to the stranger.

Elden Mage.

"You've led my master on a long chase all these years," the Mage said, stepping closer to Ellie. "But your days of hiding are over." He nodded his head at the men holding Ellie. "Get her into the Well," he commanded. "Primages Severn and Gobel are leading the Black Guard not far behind me. They'll keep the Fey off our heels. Selianne, bring me that scepter."

"No, Sel." Ellie groaned and lifted her head with obvious effort. "Don't do it."

"Obey me now, girl! Remember your sweet Cerlissa."

Selianne began to tremble. Darkness swirled in the young woman's eyes as awful blackness battled to consume her.

"Don't listen to him, Sel!" Ellie urged. "Remember Father Celinor's teachings. For children of the Light, there is always a choice. Fight him! Don't let him use you for evil."

"Selianne, obey me!"

Lauriana gazed through the tangled veil of her hair, gauging the distance between herself and the scepter. If she were quick—and if the gods were kind—she might just be able to reach the scepter and smash it before the Mage managed to kill her.

She accepted the prospect of her death without flinching. Ellysetta was her daughter, her beloved first child. Everything she'd done, she'd done out of love, to save Ellie's soul. Lauriana would willingly lay down her own life to keep her daughter safe.

She closed her eyes and gave a small, fanning wave. "Adelis," she murmured softly, "help me right this wrong. I'll pay whatever price you demand, but please, Bright One, grant me the strength to save my child." She took a breath, gathering courage and drawing her legs up beneath her. She would have only one chance at this.

A powerful boom rocked the Solarus door on its few remaining hinges, and the Mage glanced towards it. Taking advantage of his brief distraction, Lauriana scrambled to her feet and lunged. Her fingers closed around the round head of the scepter.

"Mama, watch out!" Ellie cried.

Lauriana glanced up just in time to see the Mage fling a globe of blue-white magic at her. It came fast. Too fast to dodge.

Selianne lunged towards Lauriana, but instead of attacking her, Selianne pushed her out of the way. "Madame Bari—" Her voice was cut off abruptly as the blue-white light consumed her.

Lauriana cried out in horror as Selianne literally dissolved before her very eyes.

"Fool!" the Mage spat. "Idiot!" A second globe of magic gathered in his palm.

"Mama!" Using her captor's grip as anchor, Ellie screamed and kicked out with both feet. She caught the Mage behind one knee just as he released his magic. The deadly Mage Fire went high, scorching the air over Lauriana's head and explod-ing harmlessly against the magic-fortified wall behind her.

With desperate haste, Lauriana smashed the scepter against the marble floor.

The crystal shattered.

The Solarus door burst inwards with a thunderous crash. Rain Tairen Soul and Ellysetta's quintet leapt through the So-larus doorway, swords bared, magic blazing.

Never had Lauriana seen a more welcome sight.

"They're coming, Ellie! The Fey are—" Her cry broke off as a sudden sting set fire to her chest and a wave of weakness swept over her. She looked down, half expecting to find a smoldering hole in her chest. Instead, a dark, jeweled dagger hilt quivered inches from her heart.

"Stupid woman." The Mage swept out one arm, and Lauri-ana went flying. Her body smacked hard against a column to the right of the altar and crumpled in a broken heap.

"Mama!" Ellie cried out, lunging against her captors' grips.

"Nivane, damn you!" the Mage shouted as he flung a roil-ing, blue-white ball of Mage Fire across the room to halt the Fey's advance. "Get the girl into the Well now!"

⟶⟶⟶⟶

Gaelen and Rain reacted with identical speed, spinning five-fold weaves in almost perfect unison and flinging them out with equal force to meet the deadly onslaught of Mage Fire. A third weave from Ellysetta's quintet followed a scant heartbeat later.

Mage Fire and five-fold weaves met with a concussive blast. The room shook from the deafening boom, and in the dome overhead, mirrored tiles shattered into dust.

As the blinding flash of exploding magics faded, Rain saw Ellysetta struggling against two scarlet-robed men, screaming for her mother, whose fallen, motionless form lay crumpled against the base of one of the room's six columns.

His eyes flamed with fury at the sight of Ellysetta's bruised face and the *sel'dor* manacles clapped around her slender wrists. Worse yet were the filthy, torturous needles plunged deep into her flesh. Without interference of the five-fold weave protecting the Solarus, he could feel every burning pain as if it were his own, and a mix of shame and rage consumed him.

The cowls of her captors' robes were flung back, revealing their faces. The pale-haired one Rain didn't recognize, but the other . . .

The Tairen Soul smiled with predatory fierceness. The butcher's son would pay for every wound he and his soul-cursed companions had visited upon the Tairen Soul's mate.

«Keep the Mage occupied.» Rain ordered. *«I'll see to the rult-sharts holding my shei'tani.»*

«Aiyah, Rain,» Bel answered. Beside him, Gaelen and the other four warriors of Ellysetta's quintet wove powerful ropes of magic to batter the Mage's shields. Blades were useless until they succeeded in breaking those shields, but then . . . then the Mage would regret laying his accursed hands on the Feyreisa.

Rain shimmered into invisibility and raced around the perimeter of the room towards the gaping Well of Souls, reappearing beside the two men holding Ellysetta.

The pale-haired exorcist grabbed a fistful of her flame-red curls and thrust the sharp edge of a Mage blade against her throat. "Come another step closer, Tairen Soul, and I'll slit her throat," he warned.

"*Nei,* I don't think you will." Rain's eyes flamed. Air and Earth shot from his fingertips.

The pale-haired man's eyes bulged and his mouth opened on a desperate, soundless gasp as Rain wove every breath of air from his lungs. The fingers of the man's knife hand straightened one by one until the blade at Ellysetta's throat clattered to the floor. Fire flamed in Rain's eyes, and the man's skin turned bright red and hot to the touch.

Convulsing, the man released Ellysetta and staggered back, beating fruitlessly at the unseen flames consuming his body from the inside out. Rain sent a red Fey'cha flying. His aim was straight and true, and the razor-sharp blade sank to the hilt in the man's right eye socket. Deadly tairen venom worked fast. The man barely twitched before he fell dead to the floor and his body burst into flame.

No death so swift and neat for the butcher's son, though. Rain smiled and pulled black. *Nei*, he vowed with grim pleasure, not swift, not neat, and definitely not painless.

The butcher's son took one look at the menace in Rain's eyes and leapt into the Well.

Free, Ellysetta raced to her mother's side.

Rain spun to face the Sulimage battling the quintet behind him.

"Rain, watch out!" Bel shouted. A hail of arrows came flying out of the Well.

Rain grunted as arrows sank into his shoulder, thigh, and back. *Sel'dor* set his flesh aflame. Snarling, he spun to the left and sent an incinerating blast of Fire into the Well. The pain nearly drove him to his knees. He roared a furious challenge over the echoes of the screams from within. "*Fey, ti'Feyreisa!*" he cried. "We've got company!"

Black-armored Eld soldiers poured out of the Well like bees from a disturbed hive. With them came two men wearing the deep blue robes and heavily jeweled sashes of experienced and very dangerous Primages.

<hr/>

"Mama." Desperate with fear, Ellysetta fell to her knees beside her mother. "Mama, hold on. I'm here." She started to pull the knife blade out of her mother's chest, but stopped before she touched it. Unless she could prevent the wound from bleeding, pulling that knife free would guarantee her mother's death.

Ellysetta attempted to summon healing magic, only to bite back a cry as the Eld's poisonous metal burned her flesh. Sobbing, she yanked out the remaining exorcists' needles and fumbled with the manacles. The metal scorched her fingertips. She found the button that retracted the spikes digging into her wrists, but she couldn't find the release catch. Where was the release catch?

She could feel her mother slipping away as the cold dark of death crept ever closer.

Rain spun a rapid series of five-fold weaves, trying to block the Eld from escaping the Well into the room, but there were too many. The Primages peppered his weaves with Mage Fire, ripping holes in his defenses. Eld soldiers raced through, black swords raised.

A shadow flew at Rain from his right. He spun on his heel and brought the Fey'cha in his hand slashing up to greet it. His eyes widened with surprise.

Gaelen grunted and plowed into him, knocking Rain off his feet just as Mage Fire struck the exact spot where he'd been standing.

"Thank me later," the former *dahl'reisen* quipped, patting Rain's cheek before jumping to his feet.

"Fool. I could have killed you."

"With black?" Gaelen snorted. "Not likely." He pressed one hand to his side and wove green Earth to stem the flow of blood from the wound made by Rain's Fey'cha. With the other hand, he fired red Fey'cha in rapid succession at the enemy, bringing down the ones who'd gotten past Rain's defenses, then firing more lethal blades into the Well. Demons howled and swirled in a frenzy of hunger as blood poured from Eld wounds. Chilling screams filled the Solarus as demons consumed the dying. "Not that it was a bad strike," Gaelen added. "If you hadn't pulled back, you'd have pierced both liver and kidney. But black? In a fight? Your *chatok* should be ashamed."

"It was red until I saw it was you." Rain thrust him aside and spun a wide five-fold weave to block a sizzling globe of Mage Fire. He grunted as the painful concussion vibrated up his arms. "Put your Fey'cha where your mouth is, vel Serranis. There are several hundred soldiers in there, and much as I'd enjoy a good forty-to-one fight, it's too risky with Ellysetta here. Time to end this dance." He intercepted a fresh volley of Eld arrows with a billowing cloud of Fire and shot three red Fey'cha at a small knot of Eld who'd broken through the left barrier. "Can you close that portal?"

Gaelen ducked a ball of Mage Fire and dug the curved end of a *meicha* into a soldier's belly, gutting him with one swift, brutal slice. "The Mages aren't powering anything, so there's got to be a *selkahr* crystal around here. A big one. Somewhere near the portal."

"Try looking behind those two Primages and the sixty or so armed Eld beside them."

Gaelen grinned. "I knew there had to be a sense of humor in you somewhere, Tairen Soul." He arched a brow. "Keep the Mages off me?"

Rain met his gaze, humor replaced by somber promise. "I will."

The former *dahl'reisen's* grin faded. He gave a short nod. "*Beylah vo, kem'Feyreisen.*" *Meicha* in one hand, red Fey'cha in the other, he dove to the right and came up fighting.

The Mages had punched another hole in Rain's barriers. Soldiers were pouring through, scrambling over the bodies of their fallen comrades. Rain spun a whirling vortex of Air in their path. They screamed as it lifted them off their feet and flung them with shattering force to all corners of the room.

Behind him, a loud explosion shook the Solarus, and he heard Bel and the others cry out in surprise. He glanced over his shoulder. The Sulimage had knocked the quintet off their feet. A globe of Mage Fire grew bright in his hand. He flung it at Cyr, and the Fey died without a sound.

Rain threw red at the Eld's back, distracting him just long enough for the rest of the quintet to scramble to their feet. Bel lashed out with a four-fold weave. Kieran, Teris, and Kiel combined their weaves into thick ropes of magic and pummeled the Mage's shields.

Another arrow caught Rain in the back, just below his shoulder, piercing his lung. Excruciating pain dropped him to one knee and set his chest on fire as he wove Air to keep the lung from collapsing. A dozen Eld slipped past his shattered weaves and advanced on him, arrows and blades flying.

❦

"Hold on, Mama," Ellysetta pleaded. With every second, she could feel her mother growing feebler, her life seeping away. She couldn't wait for the Fey to help her. She would have to find a way to weave healing herself, in spite of the *sel'dor* shackles.

Gathering her strength, she stretched out her hands over her mother's wound. "Bright Lord, aid me," she whispered, and drew the magic up from the shining well within her. *Sel'dor* burned like fire at her wrists, but she set her jaw and persevered. She would summon magic. She would weave it. She would save her mother. The burn became agony shooting up her arms. A low, guttural, moaning cry of defiance rattled in her throat. *I will do this! I will! Please, Bright One, help me!*

A weak trickle of Earth flowed into Lauriana's body. Not enough, not nearly enough to save her, but enough so Ellysetta dared pull the Mage blade free. She flung the evil thing as far across the room as she could while keeping one hand pressed to her mother's chest.

Her mother stirred, eyes fluttering. Ellysetta choked back a sob. "Hold on, Mama."

❦

Lauriana heard her daughter's voice calling to her, muffled as if it were very far away, but growing louder. When the Mage had stabbed his blade into her heart, her world had plunged into darkness, and her consciousness had been cast on a cold, black sea where relentless, currents tried to drag her towards a terrible abyss. She'd fought against the currents, afraid of what lay waiting in the abyss. The fight had sapped her strength. She was tired now. So tired.

But the currents had stopped, and her daughter was calling.

With effort, Lauriana opened her eyes, and her laboring heart skipped a beat.

For a moment, she thought she was dead and a winged Lightmaiden of Adelis had come to fly her to the Haven of Light, but then she realized the Lightmaiden's face was familiar. Different—so bright and beautiful—but familiar. A face Lauriana had loved since the moment she'd first laid eyes on it twenty-four years ago.

"Ellie?" she whispered.

A halo of light surrounded Ellysetta. A glorious beacon, fierce and untainted, blazing like the Great Sun. The light swirled and spun, reaching out to Lauriana as if Ellysetta were trying to weave the brightness to chase away the dark of Lauriana's approaching death.

"Oh, Ellie," Lauriana breathed. Awe, love, and regret bloomed in concert. Whether by the Bright Lord's will or the proximity of her own approaching death, Lauriana knew she was seeing, for the first time, the shining glory of her daughter's true soul. A tear trickled from her eye. All these years she'd been so blind. All these years she'd worried that the power trapped in Ellie was evil, yet now she could see how very wrong she'd been. "You're so beautiful . . ." She tried to lift a hand to her daughter's face, but her limbs felt heavy as stones.

Ellysetta caught her mother's faltering hand as it started to fall and clasped it to her cheek. Tears spilled freely down her cheeks. She could feel the cold invading her mother's flesh as death crept inexorably closer. "Stay with me, Mama. Don't leave me."

"I promised the Bright Lord, my life for yours." Her mother's lips curved in a faint smile. "It was a good bargain." Her voice grew thin and her words slurred as breath and strength faded from her. "I love you . . . kitling . . ."

A sudden flash of darkness crowded the edge of Ellysetta's vision, and rough hands grabbed her shoulders, hauling her to her feet. Two Eld soldiers had broken past Gaelen and Rain's defenses.

"Let me go!" Ellysetta fought their hold. "Mama!"

"Mama!" one of the men echoed in a mocking, falsetto voice. "Mama! Mama!" His face went hard. His black sword slashed down. Ellysetta screamed, and Lauriana's eyes opened wide on a silent gasp as the blade sliced through her neck.

Ellysetta screamed again as her mother's head rolled grotesquely free of her body. "No!" she cried out in horror and disbelief. *"No!"*

"Mama's dead, girl," the man sneered. "Gone to meet her maker, and now you're coming with us to meet yours."

A red Fey'cha thunked home in his throat. He gave a choked sound and dropped stone dead to the floor. Beside him, his partner met a similar end.

Ellysetta barely registered their deaths. Numb and frozen with shock, she stared at her mother's body. A memory played in her mind, of Rain speaking of Sariel's death. *They cut off her head so she could not be healed.* Not even Marissya could heal Mama now. She was gone. Irrevocably dead.

A strange, frighteningly empty place opened in Ellie's soul, a cold, barren, aching place where always until this moment there had been a glow of warmth that corresponded with the presence of her adoptive mother. Anguish burned like concentrated acid, searing into the deepest, most guarded part of her soul. Rage and something else rose up to greet it. Strong and wild and violent, that dreadful something swelled within her, straining against the confines of the barrier within her mind.

Her head, her body, her entire being felt as if it were on fire. Pain gripped her with stabbing, thorny hands. White agony crowded her vision, and violent tremors shook the ground beneath her feet. Tremendous pressure strained her senses, relentless and intensifying beyond her capacity to bear. She screamed again, a ripping shriek of anguish, denial, and fury that reverberated with wild force through consciousness and soul.

The lifelong, unseen barrier within her snapped. Power, hot and violent and immense, poured through the breach. *Sel'dor* shrieked at her wrists, then shattered, its acid evil no match for the blazing strength of her magic. She threw back her head as the magic rushed to fill her. It didn't feel as she had expected it to. It wasn't black and evil and twisted as her mother had always raised her to believe magic would be. It wasn't sickly sweet and corruptive like what the Mages wove. It was electric and exquisite, glorious and frightening all at once. She reached out for more, drawing it to her effortlessly until she felt as if her body was gone and she was living flame.

She was an infant goddess who had just discovered that she could do more than merely rail against those who had wounded her. She was a young tairen who had just discovered the purpose for the venom in its fangs. She was magic, pure and hot, endless and deadly.

Her mother was gone. And the Eld were to blame.

She would destroy them.

With a roar of fury, Rain swung the heavy, deadly swords in his hand, gutting his two opponents, then whirled to fling searing Fire at a knot of ten more trying to get to Ellysetta. From the corner of his eye, he saw one of the Primages turn towards Gaelen, blue-white Mage Fire gathering in his palms. The snarled and plowed a rumble of Earth beneath the Solarus floor. Floor tiles buckled and shifted. The Primage staggered. The globe of Mage Fire veered sharply left, scything through half a dozen Eld. Blackened, half-consumed corpses dropped to the ground.

Without warning, a blast of power slammed through Rain, so fierce and so raw it made him stagger. From half a continent away, he heard the savage, triumphant roar of the tairen in his mind, and an instinctive echoing cry tore from his own throat.

Ellysetta. He spun to face her and froze in his tracks.

Power crackled around her like a nimbus. Her long, fire-kissed hair blew back away from her face on an unnatural wind and her eyes blazed like twin suns as she faced the Elden warriors.

"*Shei'tani,*" he whispered. He lifted a hand to shield his eyes as her incandescent form rose up into the air.

"YOU WILL DIE FOR WHAT YOU'VE DONE!"

Her voice was a crack of thunder. The Solarus's crystal chandeliers shivered a delicate cry of warning a bare instant before the ground shifted violently. Glowing with angry green Earth, soil erupted into the room and a giant fissure opened up in the marbled Solarus floor. Shrieking, several Elden warriors tumbled to their deaths. Massive chunks of plaster, glass, and stone rained down from the dome and ceiling, crushing indiscriminately.

Lightning seared the air. Through the shattered roof, Rain glimpsed roiling black clouds, marbled with blue, white, and red lines of power. In mere seconds, Ellysetta had summoned a raging tempest in the sky. Violent fists of wind tossed grown men like matchsticks, flinging bodies through the air. Torrential rain poured down, vaporizing into mist as it touched the fiery aura surrounding Ellysetta.

A barrage of barbed *sel'dor* arrows darkened the sky. The Eld soldiers had recovered from the shock that momentarily gripped them all.

"Don't harm her, you fools! The master wants her alive!" The shout came from the Mage battling Bel and the remaining members of Ellysetta's quintet. He sent a blast of blue-white Mage Fire to intercept the arrows. The Mage Fire consumed over half the arrows, but the rest continued on their deadly course.

Rain flung a shield around Ellysetta, but the protective bubble collapsed inward as soon as it formed, absorbed into Ellysetta's glowing aura.

She swept one arm forward, and a fiery five-fold weave of magic shot from her fingertips. The arrows disintegrated instantly. Another five-fold weave seared the air, this one aimed directly at the Mage standing beside the Well of Souls.

"Ellysetta! *Nei!*" Rain flung out his own weave to weaken and misdirect hers, but his magic fell away from hers like tinder curling back from the heat of a blaze. He could only watch in horror as Ellysetta's weave sliced through the air with lethal accuracy.

The blazing shaft incinerated the Primage's shields as if they were paper. In slow motion, Rain saw the large, charred black hole appear in the Mage's chest as the five-fold weave burned through him, saw the look of disbelief on the Mage's face as he realized his prey had slain him, then saw the man's flesh bulge outward as Ellysetta's magic ignited the concentration of power held within the Mage's body. Rain barely managed to shield his eyes before the Mage exploded in a violent blast of light, heat, and vaporized flesh.

Rain waited for the agony, waited for Ellysetta to shriek in horror and pain as the death she had just caused claimed her own life and then his.

The pain never came, nor did its corresponding deadly price.

The Mage's final scream still echoed amid the din of battle as more tendrils of Fire shot out from Ellysetta's fingertips and scorched through Elden warriors. Bodies flamed like kindling. The Elden warriors who had rushed in with such triumph scattered in fear and confusion, screaming as tongues of Fire and a hail of red Fey'cha rained down on them, decimating their numbers in seconds.

Dozens fell before Rain heard the remaining Primage cry, "Retreat!" The Eld invaders fled back into the black chasm that had spawned them, leaving half their number dead and dying in the ruins of the Great Cathedral's Solarus.

Ellysetta's hand shot out. The red-robed Sulimage leapt for the Well just as a sizzling bolt of power incinerated the spot where he'd been standing. The remaining Primage wasn't so lucky. Rain shattered his shields and cleaved him in two with one savage blow. Demons howled and swept out of the Well, circling and consuming the Mage in seconds. Shredded blue Mage robes and the jeweled sash that had circled his waist fell in a small heap to the floor.

Gaelen smashed a fist of five-fold power into the *selkahr* crystal holding the Well open. The crystal shattered, and the doorway to the Well of Souls collapsed.

«*Ellysetta, shei'tani.*» Rain turned back to her and reached out with all his senses, crooning her name on every pathway, including that fragile thread of communion she'd forged between their souls and the even more astonishing thread over which he'd not shared fellowship with another Fey since the Mage Wars. *«Kem'reisa.»*

Primitive, driving Rage still throbbed within her, hissing, hungry for blood and death. At his call, her head turned. Her eyes seared him, and an answering fury rose hot in his veins. His own eyes went fire-bright and a low growl rumbled deep in his throat as the tairen strained for dominance within him. He held her gaze, a match of power to power, will to will, mate to mate.

«They hurt us. They slew our mother-kin» Her voice was a vibrant, multi-ply thread, the voice of Ellysetta . . . and something more. Those whirling sunburst eyes turned to regard the brutalized remains of Lauriana Baristani, and her Rage flared higher. *«They must die.»*

«Aiyah,» he vowed. *«And they will. They will flee from us like prey on the Plains of Corunn. This I promise you. But not yet, kem'reisa. First we must save the tairen and the Fey.»* Her attention shifted back to him, and he forced his own anger to calm. He held out his arms. *«Come back to me, Ellysetta. The pride needs you, and so do I.»* He spun compulsion and need on every path they now shared.

At first, he wasn't sure his call had pierced the veil of bloodlust, but then he felt her Rage shift. The furious, whirling radiance of her eyes dimmed slightly, and he felt the gentle part of her soul swim slowly back to the surface.

"Rain." This time her voice was all Ellysetta, shocked and shattered. "Oh, Rain." The blaze of light surrounding her winked out, and her body plummeted from its great airborne height towards the torn, jagged tumble of marble, earth, and stone below.

He leapt forward, magic flying instinctively from his fingers in a rapid weave of Air that slowed her descent and cushioned her fall. She hovered above the ground, embraced by Air until he reached her and snatched her to his chest. Her skin was warm to the touch, the pulse at her neck rapid but slowing, and even now she glowed with a visible brightness.

Ellysetta's vast magic had at last been unleashed and in that moment the facade of mortality that had hidden her all her life was ripped away, revealing the stately Fey queen she was born to be. The familiar lines of her face were still there, but they seemed purer now, breathtaking. Even the endearing freckles that had sprinkled her skin were burned away, leaving silky, pale Fey perfection.

She was still Ellysetta, but the shy mortal girl was gone. In her place stood a dazzling Fey *shei'dalin* with eyes that blazed with astonishing power.

The remaining warriors of her quintet gathered round, mouths gaping, Fey stoicism lost in stunned amazement and breathless wonder. Nowhere in the Fading Lands was there a woman who shone so bright. Nor ever had been . . . except possibly the legendary Fellana.

For beneath Ellysetta's long auburn lashes, in a face that now gleamed with the luminescent beauty of the Fey, a tairen's eyes looked out where once mortal eyes had been. Shining prisms of opalescent green with no hint of white, they glowed with latent magic.

"Rain," Bel breathed. "Gods' blessings, Rain, is she . . . ?"

"Tairen Soul," Rain confirmed. "The first born since I came into the world twelve hundred years ago. The first female Tairen Soul ever recorded."

In Eld, locked away in the dark stone confines of his cell, bloody and weakened from the punishing wounds he'd earned for aiding his daughter, Shannisorran v'En Celay gave a weary smile of triumph. His mind reached out across a familiar path, instinctively sharing the vision. *«Can you see her, Elfeya?»*

Alone in her silken prison, Elfeya wept with love and joy and tried to hide her fear. *«Aiyah, beloved, I do see her. She is glorious.»*

CHAPTER TWENTY-TWO

Farewell, dear brave and valiant soul,
    take flight on gilded wing,
Soar high and laugh upon the wind,
    while songs of honor sing
'Til once again the Gold Horn sounds,
    your soul to battle calls,
Resplendent blaze of hallowed flame,
    to triumph over all.
    —*Farewell, Brave Soul*, a Fey Warrior's Lament

Outside the cathedral, the battle with the demons was over, and the remaining Fey warriors gathered the dead. Two dozen warriors lay side by side in the scorched grass, their luminescent glow of Fey life extinguished. The grim proof of their desperate struggle left Rain hollow inside, scooped out like a gourd drum so the loss could echo freely inside him. He'd seen too much death in his lifetime, lost too many dear to him. It hurt. No amount of battle fatigue had ever made it stop hurting.

«*Oh, Rain . . . so many lost.*» Ellysetta's fingers twined with his, squeezing tight.

He'd faced battles far worse than this, where the dead carpeted entire valleys and blood turned mighty rivers red, but this battle left a particular wound on his heart, a sorrow that would never be forgotten. Because this was *her* first battle, *her* first bitter draught of loss. Friend, mother, so many of the Fey she'd begun to call by name—all lost in less than a bell. Rain would have given his own life to have spared her that.

"Come away, *shei'tani*. There are none here in need of healing. Demons do not leave wounded." Gaelen had dug the *sel'dor* shrapnel from Rain's shoulder, chest, and leg, while Kieran had helped a weeping Ellysetta guide healing weaves of Earth and Spirit to close Rain's wounds and steal away his pain.

The whirling tairen radiance in Ellysetta's eyes had subsided, leaving Fey eyes, bright as spring grass, with a slightly elongated pupil. The raw, wild power of the tairen had also quieted. Already her inner shields were instinctively rebuilding, as they'd been doing all her life.

When the warriors stepped forward, intending to send their fallen brothers' bodies back to the elements, she stopped them. "*Nei*," she said. "My countrymen have been blind too long. Let these brave Fey serve the Fading Lands one last time, as proof of the evil of the Eld." She met Rain's gaze, and he nodded.

The Fey tore down the weave surrounding the Isle of Grace, and King Dorian's armored guardsmen rushed across the bridges, followed by what appeared to be the entire Council of Lords.

"What have you done? The holiest cathedral in Celieria— wantonly destroyed!" Lord Sebourne charged onto the scene, his florid face filled with righteous indignation. "Blessed gods!" he cried, catching sight of Greatfather Tivrest's body being carried from the cathedral. "Is that the archbishop?" He turned to face Rain, eyes wild, spittle flying. "Murderers! Demons! Servants of the Dark!"

"Be silent!" Ellysetta's voice cut across Lord Sebourne's, curt and commanding.

The border lord gaped. "You dare? You impertinent peasant! I'll have you—" His voice broke off in sudden confusion as he realized the fiery-haired woman at Rain's side was not the same shy Celierian girl he'd sneered at before. "Who are you? What demonry is this?"

Rain smiled grimly. "Careful, Lord Sebourne. My mate is peasant no longer. She is Ellysetta Feyreisa, a Tairen Soul now in more than title, and you threaten her at your peril."

"My word," King Dorian muttered, staring in stunned amazement at Ellysetta's changed appearance. "How is this possible?" It was obvious Dorian could not completely shield his senses from her unveiled *shei'dalin* power, the dazzling beauty, the glow of love that made him ache to protect and serve her.

"A glamour," Rain answered. "A powerful weave placed upon her when she was but an infant to bind her magic and hide her true heritage so the Eld would not find her." He turned a hard gaze on Annoura, who stood gaping at her husband's side, staring at the Drab who'd been transformed so unexpectedly into a beauty who overshadowed Celieria's most celebrated Brilliant. "So the Elden Mages would not find her."

Turning back to Dorian, he added, "The Mages attacked her in the Great Cathedral during the Bride's Blessing." He gave a quick, terse summary of what had happened, then eyed King Dorian grimly. "The Eld have learned to travel through the Well of Souls. They can deliver armies right to your doorstep, and you will have no warning until they appear."

Murmurs of fear rippled through the courtiers, punctuated by the mutterings of several nobles who remained blindly determined to doubt.

Lifting his head, Rain addressed the entire crowd of nobles. "More than two dozen Fey slaughtered. The archbishop and head of the Order of Adelis murdered. Ellysetta's own mother slain before her eyes. This was not the work of the Fey or the *dahl'reisen*." He held Annoura's gaze until haughty surety faltered and she looked away. "This was not the work of kind, peaceful neighbors offering the hand of friendship." He eyed Sebourne coldly. "This was no Fey tale or bogey story." A last hard glance at Morvel had the priggish Great Lord sputtering helplessly. "This was a coordinated Mage attack, engineered by the High Mage of Eld himself. The Mages are alive and well, and ruling Eld once more. The Mage-claimed are already among you. Take a good look, my lords." He gestured to the destruction behind him. "This is but a taste of what the Eld can do—what they *will* do if you allow them within your borders."

Some of the fierceness faded from his expression. "What inspection you wish to make of the fallen, make it now. We burn the Eld dead within the bell and the others before dusk. It is not safe to let night fall on the bodies of the Mage-slain."

For once, not even Annoura gainsaid him.

Ellysetta stood beside the curtained windows of Rain's palace bedroom. Outside in the distance, beyond the city's western gate, twin columns of smoke rose up against the backdrop of a brilliant orange and pink sky. By Rain's command, the bodies of Greatfather Tivrest and Father Bellamy had also been burned that afternoon in funeral pyres just outside the city walls.

Now only her mother's pyre yet waited.

The bedroom door opened behind her. Even without turning, she knew it was Rain. She could feel every part of him reaching out to her, his scent, his mind, his soul, all calling to her senses. Her Fey heritage and the newly awakened power of the tairen stirred forcefully in reply. Stripped of the powerful barriers that had concealed and protected her all her life, every inch of her body felt fragile and overly sensitized—like tender new skin barely formed over a deep, painful wound.

Her fingers tightened briefly on the drapery. "Is it time?"

"Your father is still in the chapel with your mother. I told him we'd give him another quarter bell, but that is as much as we dare. The sun will set soon, and your mother's soul will be in danger if we wait any longer."

She nodded. "I heard Lady Marissya come in not long ago. Did the Council reconsider?"

"They did. The borders will remain closed." After witnessing the destruction at the cathedral, King Dorian had summoned his lords back to Council to reconsider their vote. "Lord Sebourne and a handful of lackwits still voted to welcome the Eld, believing they would 'keep the Fey in check,' but most, thank the gods, had more sense."

"What of Selianne's family?" Ellie kept her back firmly to him as she asked the question. "I know you dispatched a quintet to look for them." She'd confessed the truth about Selianne's heritage and why she'd kept it a secret from him.

She heard Rain sigh. "Her husband is dead, has been for days. Her mother hanged herself." She closed her eyes. "We found her children sleeping in the apartment above her mother's shop. Gaelen checked them. They've both been Marked."

Oh, gods. Ellie pressed a hand to the cold, aching spot above her heart. She wanted to weep. "How many times?"

"Once, but that is enough. They do not have your Fey blood to help them fight further claiming." He hesitated, then added, "They cannot stay in mortal care, and I cannot allow them into the Fading Lands. Gaelen has left to take them someplace where they will be safe."

"Where?"

"He would not say. He merely said it was their best chance for survival, and their souls' only chance to remain free."

She bit her lip and nodded. "Selianne would want that. She loved them so much." The distant pillars of smoke grew hazy as tears welled in her eyes. "Ten days ago I was a mortal girl with a head full of Fey tales. Now I'm a *shei'dalin* and apparently a Tairen Soul, but the Fey tale hasn't ended nearly as happily as I always dreamed it would."

His fingers threaded through hers and gently tugged her around to face him. Sadness and understanding darkened the lavender of his eyes to violet-blue. "They never do, *shei'tani*. For the Fey, there is always bitter with the sweet."

"For every great gift, the gods demand a great price," she murmured.

"*Aiyah*. And it is only through our willingness to bear the price that we prove ourselves worthy of the gift."

"What if the price is too high?"

"Sometimes it can be. It was, once, for me. I bore it only because I had no choice. Sometimes that's all you can do."

"Is that why you came back?" she asked. "Because you had no choice?" She saw him wince, felt the surge of remorse and shame. A day ago, she would have rushed to apologize and soothe him. Now, she pulled away and put several steps between them. "Gaelen and the others told me the soul hunger would drive you back to me. That you would not be able to deny it. Is that why you returned?"

"I was a coward to leave you as I did," Rain admitted. "I wasn't thinking. All my life, I've hated nothing so much as the Eld. And when Gaelen said you were Eld. . . . when he revealed the Mark . . . it was more than I could bear. I didn't know what I might do if I stayed, so I fled." Sorrow darkened his eyes. "I know I hurt you. I know I've made you doubt me, and I regret it deeply, but the decision to return was my own, made freely."

"Because without me, the tairen and the Fey will die?"

He shook his head. He spread his hands, searching for the words to explain. "The further away from you I flew, the louder grew the voices of the souls I bear, reminding me of my own unworthiness and how bravely you accepted me despite the blackness of my soul. The tairen reminded me how much they and the Fey sacrificed to save me, when I was more unworthy of salvation than Gaelen when you restored his soul. And I realized if I failed you, I would fail in everything. My life would have no purpose. No honor. No hope. I would have no soul worthy of redemption." He reached for her hands, gripped them tightly, forcing her to feel the emotion, the truth, pouring from him into her. "When Sariel died, I longed for the day another Tairen Soul would be born, so I could at last join her in death. And here you are, a Tairen Soul, but death is my dream no longer. You've made me want to live again, Ellysetta."

As declarations of devotion went, it was beautiful, stirring. Ellie, the girl who'd drunk Fey-tale dreams like water, would have near swooned. Ellysetta, the woman who'd learned better, gently extracted her hands from his.

"You think because I am a Tairen Soul that everything Gaelen said is untrue, but it isn't, Rain. The High Mage confirmed he was my father. At the cathedral, during the exorcism, he gained access to my mind and he told me."

"He is a father of lies," Rain answered without hesitation. He cupped her face, thumbs feathering across her cheeks.

"You're a Tairen Soul. No Eld halfling could bear that power."

She covered his hands with hers, stopping the caress. "He isn't the father of my flesh—even he admitted that—but neither is he entirely a liar. Something of him *does* live inside me, not in my body, but in my soul. Something more than a Mage Mark. I can feel it even now." That bit of the High Mage was still there, cold and dark, lying like a stalking demon in her mind, waiting to pounce. "I wield Azrahn, Rain. I used it today, trying to save Selianne."

She sensed the fear that immediately consumed his thoughts. He, too, remembered Gaelen's warning about the dangers of weaving Azrahn on the Mage-claimed. She clenched her jaw and met his gaze. "The High Mage put another Mark on me. When I wove Azrahn." She said it almost defiantly . . . and waited for his revulsion.

The expected recoil didn't come. He drew her into his arms instead, and would not let her pull away. "You should never have known such horror," he whispered. "I should have protected you better. I *will* protect you better." He laid his hand over her heart, and the warmth of his palm penetrated the chill of the Marks. "We will find a way to unmake the Marks, just as Marissya unmade the mark that worthless *rultshart* Brodson forced upon you."

When she looked up at him in disbelief, he smiled sadly. "I deserve your doubt. I rejected you when you needed me most, and I will live with that shame forever. But I will not make the same mistake again, Ellysetta. I will not turn from you. I am yours, no matter what magic you wield, no matter how many Marks you bear."

"The High Mage will try to use me to destroy the Fey. To destroy you."

"He will try, but we will not let him succeed." When she didn't respond, he gave a small sigh. "Wait here. I have something for you in the other room." He slipped through the bedroom door and came back a moment later, carrying a bulky, silk-draped object. "I asked your father to make this for me, that first night. I meant it to be a wedding gift, but I think it's more fitting now as a courtship gift." He drew the silk cover away, revealing an exquisitely carved statue.

Ellysetta's breath caught in her throat, and she reached for the gleaming treasure in Rain's hands. Fingertips touched grainless ebonwood and satiny fireoak. The carving seemed so real, she could almost feel the warmth of life in the wood. "Papa did this? It's the most beautiful piece he ever made."

"It is a masterful work of art," Rain agreed. "No Fey could have done better."

Beneath Sol Baristani's skillful hands, a tairen matepair had come to life in fireoak and ebonwood. The female was a lithe and lustrous creature with emerald eyes and gold-veined wings folded against her back. She sat on her haunches, a feline queen. At her side, a larger male Tairen carved of almost grainless ebonwood had extended one wing, curling it protectively over his mate, the underside of his shadowy wing sparkling with diamond dust. Ebonwood and fireoak tails were entwined in an utterly tairen gesture of devotion, but the twining was so intricate that Ellie could scarcely believe her father had managed it without magic. Both tairen wore a look of tender pride as they gazed down on a pair of round little kitlings playing at their feet, one black, one a rosy auburn, both slightly mottled.

"The matepair look exactly as I imagined them," Rain said. "From that very first night, *shei'tani*, I saw you more clearly than I knew. I saw your true soul—and my true place at your side, protecting and defending you from harm. The kitlings were your father's touch," he added. "He called them a father's wish for his daughter. When I went to see him in the chapel just now, he gave me the statue and told me I should tell you that."

Outside, the sun hung low on the western horizon. Night was approaching. Rain held out a hand. "Come, *shei'tani*. Let us see your mother's soul safe to rest. When it is done, I ask that you consent to be my wife. Not because your father pledged to me your troth, and not because the gods declared it should be so, but because *you* wish to bind your life to mine."

Ellysetta looked up from the exquisite tairen family in her

hands. Rain's eyes were filled with open longing and shining with promise. Perhaps the girl who loved Fey tales wasn't completely gone, after all.

She slid her fingers into his. "*Aiyah*, Rain, I will marry you."

⌒⊶⦿⊷⌒

Lauriana's body was placed on a gilded litter and borne by Ellysetta's quintet down the cobbled roads to her funeral bier outside the city walls. Sol walked behind the litter, holding the twins by the hand. Rain and Ellysetta followed them, then Marissya and Dax. Bringing up the rear marched all the Fey in Celieria, clad in full ceremonial dress, steel gleaming in the waning light, silken banners of red, violet, and gold waving in the breeze. It was a funeral procession worthy of a queen.

"I never thought you would so honor her," Ellysetta whispered, brought to tears by the unexpected tribute. "I thought you would despise her for arranging my exorcism."

"If honor were reserved only for those who never err, none of us would be worthy," Rain answered. "When she saw how she'd been used against you, she gave her life to set you free. There is much to honor in that."

As they walked through the city, Fey voices rose in crystalline waves to sing an ancient Fey lament for valiant, fallen heroes. The song was one Ellysetta recognized, usually reserved for warriors who died performing great deeds, and she wept with a mix of love and sorrow and pride. She could not have held back her emotions even if she'd tried. They poured forth like a river overflowing its banks, weaving into the notes of the song.

Ellysetta wore no *shei'dalin's* veil. She'd refused when Marissya made the suggestion, saying she'd already spent too much of her life hiding who and what she truly was. Her unveiled brightness shone like a beacon. Now unleashed, her innate magic, the compassion and healing peace of a *shei'dalin*, spread out in waves of light all around her.

In the wake of the procession, the Celierians who had spent their last week in growing turmoil and groundless anger found themselves sobbing as if their hearts would break. The Shining

Folk, who'd seemed so threatening of late, now appeared like heroes of old, noble and gracious and good. In their midst walked a woman of incomparable beauty, bright as the Great Sun, her hair like coils of sacred flame. Just the sight of her banished the shadows from their minds, and those who caught her verdant gaze felt seeds of love and hope bloom in their breasts.

The procession wound through the streets and through the western gates to the last unlit pyre. Ellysetta's quintet bore Lauriana forward and laid her body gently on the oiled wood, then stepped back as Father Celinor began the Celierian service for the dead. When he was done, Sol stepped forward with a lighted brand to ignite his wife's pyre.

Lillis and Lorelle clutched Ellysetta's hands, not at all frightened by her changed appearance but seemingly comforted by it instead.

"Does it hurt her, Ellie?" Lillis asked in a small voice as the flames engulfed her mother's body.

Fresh tears spilled from Ellysetta's eyes. She knelt quickly and caught her sister up in a fierce hug. "Oh, kitling, no. Not at all. She's with the Bright Lord now."

"In the Haven of Light?" Lorelle asked.

"Yes, Lorelle, in the Haven of Light, singing glorias with the Lightmaidens." She caught Lorelle in her arms as well, holding both girls tight and sending up a heartfelt prayer for the gods to grant them both peace and help them past the loss of their mother. The twins sighed and snuggled closer, their small arms twining tightly about her neck.

Lauriana's pyre burned quickly through sunset and the ensuing twilight, extinguishing itself just as night fell over the city. When the last flame subsided, Fey Fire-masters dispersed the remaining heat and gathered the ashes. Ellysetta and her sisters returned to the palace while Rain took Sol aloft to throw the ashes to the winds so they might settle in the soil of the land Lauriana Baristani had loved.

Afterward, in King Dorian's private chapel, with the Fey, Ellysetta's family, Lords Barrial and Teleos, and the king and queen in attendance, Rain Tairen Soul wed Ellysetta Baristani in a quiet ceremony officiated by Father Celinor. The grand pomp of the royal wedding Lauriana had envisioned gave way to simple elegance, consisting of a few exquisite flowers and a priest, which was all Ellysetta had ever really wanted to begin with.

She wore the gown Maestra Binchi had created and the wreath of the Gentle Dawn roses her mother had selected, but there the Celierian bride ended and the Fey *shei'dalin* began. Around her neck and waist, dripping in loops of golden links, gleamed the *sorreisu kiyr* of all the Fey who'd died on her behalf. Bel and Gaelen's bloodsworn daggers hung in jeweled sheaths at her hips, and Rajahl vel'En Daris's crystal glittered at her wrist.

Marissya stood as Ellysetta's Beacon, and with impeccable, unflinching grace, Master Fellows served as her Honoria—because no matter how scandalous it might be to have a man stand as Honoria, he said it simply wouldn't do for a queen to wed without one. When Father Celinor invoked the final blessing and pronounced them man and wife, a sense of peace and rightness settled over Ellysetta, almost as if Mama were standing there beside her, watching with love and approval while Ellysetta joined her life with the man the gods had chosen for her.

Following a brief bridal supper, Rain escorted Ellysetta to their suite for a few bells of privacy while the Fey prepared for departure. Once there, however, Rain found himself at a loss.

He was freed at last from the restrictive Celierian customs and oaths of honor that had bound him since the day of their betrothal, and need for his mate beat at him.

The call of her soul was so strong, the echoing desire in his body just as powerful, and the tairen clamored for its mate, but she had just lost her mother. He could feel her grief, her sorrow, battering at her, and through her, him. To pounce on her now, demanding mating, seemed the vilest sort of selfishness. She needed time to grieve.

Determined to do the honorable thing, he escorted her to his bedchamber, spun a swift Earth weave that changed her wedding gown into a fine linen nightrail, and kissed her once, gently, on the lips before turning to leave.

"Rain?" she called when he reached the door. "You're leaving me?"

"*Nei*, of course not," he vowed. "I'll be right next door. You get some rest. We leave in the small bells, before the city wakes, and our journey will be long."

Ellysetta frowned at him, perplexed by the way he was clinging to the bedchamber door. He looked ready to bolt. "But this is our wedding night."

His gaze dropped. The knuckles on the door frame clenched harder. "*Aiyah*, and I know it is not the happy day you wanted. You are grieving. My needs can wait."

Relief filled her. His hesitation wasn't because of her Marks or the forbidden magic she wielded. "But my need cannot," she told him softly. "Yes, I'm grieving, but there's been too much sorrow, too many tears. I would end this day in hope—with joy between us. Is that so strange a request?"

He peeled his fingers away from the door frame. He crossed the room and approached the bed. "*Nei*, not so strange. There is nothing I want more." Slowly, giving her ample time to change her mind, he took her in his arms. Her long hair spilled over the crook of his arm, silken soft and so fragrant every breath was a scented bliss. He bent as if to kiss her, then paused again just before his mouth met hers. "Be sure, *shei'tani*, that this is what you want. If you have the slightest doubt, say so now, and I will go."

"I don't want you to go." She reached up to touch his face and pull him down to her. "I want this, Rain. I want you."

He took her mouth in a long, slow kiss, his lips parting hers gently to share the moist heat of a breath as the kiss deepened. *«You are so beautiful, shei'tani.»* His voice whispered in her mind, husky, low, intimate. *«You always were, but now, with your brightness unveiled, even more so.»*

«You make me feel beautiful.» He always had. Even when

she'd still been plain, mortal Ellysetta Baristani, he'd made her feel like the loveliest woman in the world.

He kissed her slowly, leisurely, taking his time. Nibbling her lower lip, teasing the upper one, feathering kisses across her face until she shifted and nipped at his mouth in impatience. His brows rose. "Impatient, *shei'tani*? What would you prefer? This?"

His hand trailed down the front of her nightgown. The fabric parted without a whisper of protest, falling away in silken swaths to bare the soft fullness of her breasts. The delicate torment of the sliding fabric and the subsequent small breath of air drew her nipples tight, twin buds of soft pink. His thumb brushed across them, sending a tiny quake of sensation shooting through her that echoed across his own senses.

"Or perhaps this?" Slowly he bent his head and took her in his mouth.

"Rain . . . yesssss. That." Her breath hissed out on a heated sigh, and she clasped him to her breast. Her head tilted back and her eyes closed as his tongue teased the sensitive peak.

She tasted of sunlight and springtime, of blossoming flowers and crystal waters. Each stroke of his tongue on her flesh was a tiny sensory illustration of what life would be like in the Haven of Light. Beauty, pleasure, peace, completion. Belonging. Everything he'd always wanted, and the promise of much more than he'd ever imagined.

His body answered with an ardent surge, hungry for more than teasing glimpses of fulfillment, ravenous for the gift every Fey warrior dreamed of.

He pulled back just enough to drink in the sight of her, pale and shining in his arms, the silvery glow tinted with deep, warm tones as her own passion rose in response. Her bright Fey eyes glowed a verdant green so rich and deep he could lose himself in them.

Ducking his head again, he scattered soft kisses across her skin. "When I was a boy, before I found my wings, I tried to dream of what my *shei'tani* would be like. I could never picture her, because in my heart I knew I was destined to fly, and I knew the sacrifice that would require. But there's not a Fey warrior born who does not dream of finding his truemate, so at night, after my parents went to bed, I would sneak out of the *shellaba* and lie beneath the stars and ask the gods if they could somehow find a way to give a tairen a truemate."

"You never told me that before."

Color rose in his cheeks, making him look far younger than his years, and more vulnerable. "It was such a foolish, selfish dream," he said. "Being a tairen is a rare and great gift of its own, and as I grew older, remembering how I begged for more made me ashamed."

Her hands reached up to frame his face. The sweet kiss of her fingertips and the warm glow of her eyes bathed him in acceptance, soothing the sting of ancient childhood embarrassment. "Wanting love is not selfish, Rain. We're all born missing the connections that make us complete." Her thumb smoothed across his lips, and she smiled when he answered the caress with nibbles and kisses. "I dreamed of finding a place where I truly belonged, even though I had a family who loved me. And even though I knew I was neither as good nor as beautiful as the princesses I read about in Fey tales, I still dreamed of finding my one true love."

He caught her thumb between his teeth, the flare of jealousy small but instinctive. Tairen did not share. Just as quickly, he realized what he'd done. He unlocked his jaw to release her and feathered a quick kiss of apology. "Did your true love have a face?"

She laughed softly, not missing the jealousy, nor misunderstanding its cause. "He did."

"Well? What did he look like?"

Her smile faded until only a wistful hint of it clung to her lips. "You."

His eyes blazed, and his head swooped down to claim her mouth. His arms slid around her, steely bands that clutched her tight and pulled her hard against him. He kissed her until she was breathless and melting against him, then pressed his face into her hair and nuzzled the soft skin behind her ear.

"Perhaps I should not be so pleased that there has never been another in your heart but me, but in truth I cannot find the humility to be sad for it." A low, growling purr of satisfaction rumbled in his voice.

"Can you not?" She laughed, a bewitching sound that sent his pulse skyrocketing. Her hands roamed over his chest, cupping the swell of pectoral muscle. Her nails scraped lightly across his flat nipples, teasing them into small, tight points. She paused to rub a testing fingertip across the pebbled flesh, then met his eyes and smiled. Her power flared. Magic leapt from her flesh to his in a breathtaking flow of energy.

Blood rushed to his groin in a hot, almost painful swell. He groaned and gave a rueful laugh. "Careful, Ellysetta, or you'll finish me before I can even begin."

"Then begin," she insisted. Her hands trailed down his sides and tugged at the closure of his leather breeches. "You've shown me what to expect, and I find I am impatient."

He didn't need a second invitation. Earth sprang from his fingers, dissolving boots and leathers and the remains of her nightshift, leaving both of them bare to each other. She gave a small gasp at her sudden nakedness, but despite the brief flood of color that darkened her cheeks, she did not flinch or pull away.

She was the same to his eyes, yet so astonishingly new. Her beauty radiated on so many levels, a banquet to his senses, and her emotions caressed him in waves, urging him on, singing to his soul a new song of her own . . . not Spirit, not tairen, but woman. Captivating and compelling. *Come to me, Rain. Make me your wife.*

He moved without thought, his hands reaching for hers, breath exhaling in a soft groan as his fingertips rediscovered the exquisite satin of her skin. At last, he had the freedom to claim what was his. By the laws of her culture and in the eyes of her family, the mating he'd hungered for was no longer forbidden—it was their right, his and hers.

He stroked the gentle, slender curve of her body, from the roundness of her breast, to the narrow tuck of her waist, and on to the soft flare of trim hip and thigh. A tingle of magic followed in the wake of his hand, the sparkling lights of his own essence dancing across her skin and setting her senses afire.

"It has been a thousand years since last I knew a woman's body," he murmured. "I pray I do not disappoint."

Though he said it with a small smile, she heard a greater sincerity than he would have wanted to reveal. He feared the truth of this joining wouldn't be as stirring to her as the illusions he'd woven with such mastery.

"The only possible way you could disappoint me, Rain, would be to leave me now." She arched against him and slid a leg over his. Her foot traveled up the rock-hard muscles of his calves to tease the backs of his thighs. His sex gave a hungry, surging pulse as her gesture opened the nest of curls between her legs.

"You do play with fire."

She laughed, a throaty purr that rolled over his skin and made every cell leap in reaction. "It must be the tairen in me."

His own tairen flexed its claws and gave an answering growl of approval. "Then take my flame, *shei'tani*, and burn for me."

He bent his head and devoted himself to setting her afire, body and soul. Flows of magic swirled around her like a thousand stroking hands. His mouth claimed first one breast and then the other, teasing the soft nipples into tight, aching peaks. Alternating breezes of tingling cold warred with sultry heat, the combination an intoxicating, erotic play that roused every inch of her skin to aching sensitivity.

Her hands dove into the silky thickness of his hair, clutching tight. Her hips bucked against him in restless invitation, but he only laughed against her skin and left his weaves to tease and provoke her while he pressed a burning trail of kisses down the smooth, sweet softness of her belly, tasting each tender fingerspan of skin, drinking in her scent, rubbing it on his face and lips, breathing it in until her essence filled him so completely he could not take a breath that did not taste of her. Lower still his lips traveled. Hands found the soft swell of her rounded buttocks and gently lifted her hips.

Elysetta gave a thin, breathless cry as he bent his head to feast on her. She tried to close her legs against him in a last, instinctive rush of Celierian modesty, but he would not allow it. *«As you reminded me, our vows have been spoken, shei'tani. By your customs as well as mine, there can be no shame between us. All that you are is mine to discover and adore.»*

She felt the slow, lingering lap of a tongue and nearly leapt off the bed.

«You taste of honeyed cream, shei'tani.» He took another leisurely taste of her, followed by an insistent, probing dart that was wholly wicked. All the while, his weaves cupped and teased her breasts until she thought she would fly apart. *«Open for me.»*

Gods save her. Inner muscles clenched tight in rippling spasms. She squirmed against the hands that held her fast and groaned as he laughed softly against her most intimate skin. Helplessly her legs fell open, and her eyes closed on wave after wave of indescribable sensation as teasing tastes became long, savoring strokes that turned her veins to rivers of smoldering fire. Pressure built up inside her as her hips assumed an instinctive rhythm, rising and falling to meet each sinful stroke of his tongue.

At this moment, all he wanted in life was the taste of Ellysetta on his tongue, the scent of her filling his nostrils, the feel of her soft skin filling his hands. Through touch, skin to skin, he shared every fevered emotion speeding across her shattering senses. The sound of her sobbing pleas and the restless leap of her hips drove him wild. Within his soul, the tairen roared.

Ellysetta closed her eyes as a torment of sensation rolled over her. The roar of the tairen resonated along the thread of their bond like a bolt of lightning, setting every fiber of her being blazing to sudden, incandescent, throbbing life. Her back arched. She flung her head back.

"Rain!" Oh, dear gods. *"Rain!"* The climax burst over her in a thousand shuddering explosions, each stealing her breath and shaking her to the core.

He rose up above her, eyes blazing, his mouth parted in a triumphant, near-savage smile. The hard, thick length of his sex entered her body on a single breathtaking thrust. If there was pain, he stole it from her, leaving only the feel of his body inside hers, stretching her, filling an emptiness she'd never known existed.

His hips drew back, and she almost wept in protest, clutching at his hips with an instinctive plea. He surged forward again, and she cried out in wild pleasure.

Within her mind she saw the tairen, roaring in triumph as it leapt to claim and dominate. For the first time, her own wildness rose up in savage answer. Within her soul, she felt the sweep of wings and claws, the thunder of tairen bodies meeting in an ancient, untamed mating, while together, on their silken bed, Rain and Ellysetta's Fey bodies surged in an equally fierce union. Her hand curled, and she raked her nails down his back, matching his unrestrained passion with her own.

Rain threw back his head and roared. He rose up on his knees and drew her hips up with him as his body pounded in a relentless beat. As she sprawled on the silken sheets of their bed, Ellysetta's hair spilled across the pillow in coils of flame. Her breasts bobbed with each powerful thrust of his hips, and as he watched, the Fey glow of her eyes grew brighter and brighter until they were whirling opalescent pools, blazing with an inner fire. Tairen eyes.

Again and again he drove her to the edge and pushed her beyond it, loving the sound of her cries ringing in his ears, loving the shocked, dazed look on her face as pleasure shook and shattered her. Her inner muscles convulsed around him, silken, tight, rippling in a series of fierce spasms that stole the breath from his lungs. Every muscle in his body clenched tight in response, straining as her climax detonated his own.

It swept over him like a wild wind, ripping away all thought, all doubt, leaving only a bedrock of unshakable certainty in its wake. This was the primal, elemental beauty of life, the passionate exchange of flesh and breath and essence, two halves made whole. This moment with her was the reason he'd been born. She was the reason for his life.

He fell back beside her against the softness of the mattress and regarded her from dazzled eyes as his ragged breathing slowly grew even. She was such a wonder to him in every way. A salvation he had never expected. A joy he had never deserved. And here, now, lying beside him, her soul so bright she shone like a star, she was the most beautiful woman he'd ever known. Strength blazed beside her *shei'dalin's* compassion; her will was threaded with the purest steel and the tairen's fierce wildness. When she finally embraced the entirety of her abilities, she would be a force of nature, a Feyreisa of such power as the world had never known. It humbled him to realize that he, Rainier vel'En Daris, was the warrior chosen by the gods to stand beside her, to protect and aid her, to . . . love her.

Unexpected tears gathered with surprising swiftness, filling his eyes and spilling over.

"Rain?" She reached for him in concern.

He gave a small, embarrassed laugh and lifted a knuckle to wipe away the betraying moisture. "This Fey learns humility after all."

She did not return his smile. "What is it? What's wrong?"

"*Las, kem'san.* Nothing is wrong. I only just realized something I should have known all along." He carried her hands to his chest, then cupped her face with one hand while wrapping the other around her waist. He held her close, skin to skin, so that with her *shei'dalin* senses she would feel for herself the wonder that bloomed within him.

"From this day forward, no matter what happens between us—even if we never complete our bond, even if we cannot save the tairen or the Fey—I want you to know this one thing, Ellysetta Baristani." He smiled into her eyes and gave her the words.

"My heart has followed where my soul has led. *Ke vo san,* Ellysetta. I love you."

He felt the faint tremors that rippled through her when the truth of his emotions washed over her senses. Her brows drew together and her forehead creased in a confused frown. She wanted to believe, longed to believe, but her fear of opening herself up to another betrayal made her doubt him.

He pressed a kiss first at one corner of her mouth and then the other. "Your soul calls out, *shei'tani*. Mine answers." He drew back to meet her gaze, and held it with a steadiness she could not doubt. "And I would have it no other way." He lowered his head and claimed her lips with aching gentleness and dazzling intensity, pouring into his kiss every hope, every dream, every ardent wish, all coupled with a steadfast vow. He repeated the words in Feyan, then sang them to her in the rich tones of tairen song, his song, the song she had been born to hear, carrying in its wordless symphony the essence of all that was Rain.

Tears shimmered in Ellysetta's eyes. She could taste his emotions like a rich, many-layered spice, a truth she could not disbelieve, a promise she knew he would die before betraying again. He was offering her, at last, the love she'd always dreamed of, the acceptance she'd always longed for.

Closing her eyes, she returned his kiss and drank in his shining promise of devotion. Her arms wrapped around his neck, holding him close. «*I love you, too, Rain. I always have.*»

Against her hip, his body stirred as love became passion and passion became need. She took him into her body, smiled with breathless wonder as once more he filled and completed her.

And afterward, as they lay together in spent silence, the first fragile thread of communion that had fallen silent last night began softly to sing once more. A second, shimmering new thread joined the first, adding its own melody, tender and bittersweet, tempered by loss, deepened with forgiveness, and stronger than the song sung between them before.

In the small silver bells of the night, with no fanfare to mark their passing, the Fey departed Celieria City.

Sol and the twins were packed up as well, traveling west with Lord Teleos and the Fey. They would stay on Lord Teleos's lands near the Grarreval, guarded by ten quintets who would help Lord Teleos fortify his defenses and train his men in the Fey arts of war.

Outside the western city gates, Rain stepped away to summon

the Change. Ellysetta closed her eyes as the swell of his magic swept over her, calling to her own, long-buried gifts. And when he crouched before her in tairen form, magnificent and fierce, his black fur gleaming like the richest ebonwood in the silver-bright light of the moons, she was glad she'd been born to stand at his side.

She would choose him. She would always choose him. She would leave her family and everything familiar to her. She would embrace her magic. She would defy laws and kings and Mages and demons and even the Church of Light to be with him. She would tear down the barriers that still lived in her mind, confront whatever darkness lurked behind them, and defeat the Mage who thought to claim her soul. That soul—and every part of her—belonged to Rainier vel'En Daris. There could never be happiness for her that did not include him.

At Rain's word, Ellysetta ran forward and vaulted into place with a boost of Air. When she was seated, Rain drew back on his haunches and sprang into the sky. His wings unfurled, snapping taut as they caught the wind, pumping to gain height and speed.

The night air was warm and sweet, and the Mother's light gleamed like a beacon, calling the Fey home. Rain Tairen Soul's shadow raced over the moonlit ground, heading west towards the Fading Lands.

Key Celierian Terms

Bell: hour

Chime: minute

Dorn: Furry, round, somnolent rodent. Eaten in stews. "Soggy dorn" is an idiom for someone who is spoiling someone else's fun. A party pooper.

Keflee: A warm beverage that can act as a stimulant or aphrodisiac.

Lord Adelis: God of light. While Celierians worship a pantheon of gods and goddesses (thirteen in all), the Church of Light worships Adelis, Lord of Light, above all others. He is considered the supreme god, with dominion over the other twelve.

Rultshart: A vile, smelly, boar like animal.

Key Elden Terms

Azrahn: The soul magic forbidden by the Fey for its corrupting influence but used and mastered by the mages.

Primage: master mage

Sulimage: journeyman mage

Umagi: a mage-claimed individual, subordinate to the will of his/her master

Key Fey Terms

Beylah vo: thank you (literally, thanks to you)

Cha Baruk: Dance of Knives

Chadin: student in the Dance of Knives

Cha'kor: Literal translation is "five knives." Fey word for "quintet."

Chatok: mentor in the Dance of Knives

Chatokkai: First General. Leader of all Fey armies, second in command to the Tairen Soul. Belliard vel Jelani is the cha-tokkai of the Fading Lands.

Chervil: Fey expletive similar to bastard, as in "you smug chervil."

Dahl'reisen: Literally, "lost soul". Dahl'reisen are unmated Fey warriors who have been banished from the Fading Lands either for breaking Fey taboos or for choosing to walk the Shadowed Path rather than committing sheisan'dahlein, the honor death, when the weight of all the lives they have taken in defense of the Fey becomes too great for thier own souls to bear. Dahl'reisen recieve a physical scar when they make the kill that tips thier souls into darkness.

E'tan: beloved/husband/mate (of the heart, not the truemate of the soul)

E'tani: beloved/wife/mate (of the heart, not the truemate of the soul)

E'tanitsa: a chosen bond of the heart, not a truemate bond

Felah Baruk: Dance of Joy

Fey'cha: Fey throwing dagger. Fey'cha have either black handles or red handles. Red Fey'cha are deadly poison. Fey warriors carry dozens of each kind of Fey'cha in leather straps crisscrossed across their chest.

Feyreisa: Tairen Soul's mate; Queen

Feyreisen: Tairen Soul; King

Ke vo san: I love you.

Kem'falla: my lady

Kem'san: My love/My heart

Krekk: Fey expletive

Ku'shalah aiyah to nei: Bid me yes or no.

Las: peace, hush, calm

Maresk, mareska, mareskia: friend (masculine, feminine, plural)

Mei felani. Bei santi. Nehtah, bas desrali: Live well, love deep. Tomorrow, we (will) die.

Meicha: A curving, scimitar-like blade. Each fey warrior carries two meicha, one at each hip.

Miora felah ti'Feyreisa: Joy to the Feyreisa

Pacheeta: A silly bird; not very smart.

Sel'dor: Literally "black pain." A rare black metal found only in Eld that disrupts Fey magic.

Selkahr: Black crystals used by Mages. Made from Azrahn-corrupted Tairen's Eye crystal.

Seyani: Fey longsword. Fey warriors wear two seyani blades strapped to their back.

Sheisan'dahlein: Fey honor death. Ceremonial suicide for the good of the Fey. All Fey warriors who do not truemate will either commit sheisan'dahlein or become dahl'reisen.

Shei'tan: beloved/husband/truemate

Shei'tani: beloved/wife/truemate

Shei'tanitsa: the truemate bond, a mating of souls

Sieks'ta: I have shame. (I'm sorry; I beg your pardon)

Tairen: Flying catlike creatures that live in the Fading Lands. The Fey are the Tairenfolk, magical because of their close kinship with the Tairen.

Tairen Soul: Rare Fey who can transform into tairen. Masters of all five Fey magics, they are feared and revered for their power. The oldest Tairen Soul becomes the Feyreisen, the Fey King.

Teska: Please

Ver reisa ku'chae. Kem surah, shei'tani: Your soul calls out. Mine answers, beloved.

For My Readers,

Thank you so much for picking up this book. I hope you've enjoyed meeting Rain and Ellie as much as I've enjoyed writing about them—and I hope you'll keep an eye out for the conclusion of their story, *King of Sword and Sky* and *Queen of Song and Souls,* coming in October & November 2008 from Leisure Books.

Please be sure to visit my Web site, **www.clwilson.com** to sign up for my private book announcement list, enter my online contests, and scour the site for hidden treasures and magical surprises. I hope you linger a while to learn more about the Fey and the Fading Lands—as well as other Fey tales and C. L. Wilson novels coming soon.

I'd love to hear from you. Please, send me a Spirit weave, or, if you prefer, you can take the nonmagical route and just e-mail me at **cheryl@clwilson.com**.

Sincerely,

C. L. Wilson